SAHARA DIAMONDS

BY

Christopher Coxhead

1

For Paddy

Sahara Diamonds

Page

Prologue

Conflict Diamonds

In January 2002, the Sierra Leone Civil War ended after nearly eleven years of savage conflict which devastated the small West African country. It was concluded by the intervention of British troops and the illegal mining of diamonds in that country was finally ended.

These Conflict or Blood diamonds, as they are known, were mined during the civil wars in Central or West Africa. They account for about four percent of the sale of diamonds in the world today.

To help prevent this fraudulent trading, the Kimberley Certification Process came into being in 2003. One of the first results of this was to stop the sale of diamonds from the Congo, a country through which a disproportionate number of these Conflict diamonds were passing.

People who now had diamonds in Sierra Leone because of the war found them difficult to move in the aftermath. Many were, and still are, hidden in holes in the ground until their nefarious owners could find a method of moving them on.

In May 2014, the deadly Ebola virus struck Liberia, Guinea and Sierra Leone itself. It took a full year and international help to contain the virus, with Sierra Leone only recently being declared free of the deadly disease.

Naturally there were major concerns in neighbouring countries and panic ensued throughout West Africa. Nigeria was at first partly affected by the Ebola outbreak but with some luck and government intervention there were few known cases of the disease in that country. Part of the International response to Ebola came from the International Red Cross and Red Crescent Movement, they used some of their supplies stored in Nigeria to help attack the Sierra Leone outbreak.

Just north of Freetown the capital and across the Sierra Leone River, reached by local ferries is Lungi, Sierra Leone's international airport. Branching off and crossing the south west end of the main runway heading north and east is the Port Loko road, a main artery which returns to the river in the hinterland at the conurbation.

In a small village set back into the encroaching jungle just off to the north of this major road an ex-fighter of the rebel forces had been hiding ever since the peace, he had blended back into village life, just as if he had never left.

You would never see this ex-rebel, Yamba Wilson partially clothed because of the Revolutionary United Front tattoos on his back and front, an absolute giveaway to the national Police Force who were still hunting for these mercenaries.

In June 2014, the Ebola outbreak reached Yamba's village and decimated the already small population. The relative poverty and poor sanitation helped to lay waste to all but three small children who were sent off with many other orphans to separate compounds throughout the West African country.

Realising he was dying and while he was still able Yamba dug up and retrieved the small canvas bag containing a dozen conflict diamonds, his civil war spoils. He handed them over to his eight-year-old nephew Samuel who was to be one of the three survivors. As he hung the bag around the boys neck he told Samuel the bag contained lucky omens which would protect him from the disease and evil spirits and he must always wear the bag.

The boy and the other two newly made orphans, were amongst a multitude of children who all ended up in an overrun orphanage alongside the International Airport at Lungi.

It was quite pleasant and relatively safe there, being close to Mahera Beach and the Atlantic Ocean.

The children learnt to fend for themselves and their fishing exploits supplemented their diet which was helped by the mounting numbers of aid workers.

To Samuel the dirty canvas bag was unimportant, it was hidden in clear view being just one of the few possessions of a small boy. He knew only it was something that had belonged to a distant dead Uncle.

Chapter 1

Diamonds Present

Damilola asleep in her U N C H R tent on the edge of the Lungi Airport woke at seven with the roar of an incoming jet. With the morning light, she could just see the other bed in the small tent. It was unoccupied, her fellow aid worker having returned home to Morocco the previous day.

Damilola was due to go home shortly and had told some of her young charges of her impending departure. She was the lesser cousin of a Chief of the Ikwerre tribe from south east Nigeria. A nurse, she had volunteered to deliver aid to the stricken children of Sierra Leone. She was a kind woman in her early twenties and easily befriended many of the boys in her care. A lot came to trust her during this year looking after the children.

 She rose quickly from under the mosquito netting, rinsed her face in some bottled water, brushed her teeth and rapidly dressed before making the way to her duty post.

Today she was looking after the first aid tent to which any of the orphan boys in the compound could see her about small ailments or injuries. When she got there even though it was hardly light there was a long queue of the young lads waiting outside the temporary hut with its Red Cross and Red Crescent Insignias.

She was surprised and worried in case the whole camp had all been attacked by some sort of virus in the one night. At the head of the queue was a tall emaciated boy, who must be about sixteen. The tattoos on his arms and scars on his face marked him out as having previously been a boy soldier and he looked quite serious.

Damilola unlocked the door, opened the medicine cabinets and shouted.

'Right who's first?'

The ex-boy soldier was first through the door followed by a host of smiling faces as the rest of the queue tried to crowd into the small space.

The young man reached across the counter and opened his right clenched fist, sitting on the palm was a brightly polished fishing hook shining in the light of electric bulb which lit the hut.

'Madam this is for you, to say thank you.'

At that he dropped the hook onto the counter and left the hut abruptly, after he left all the boys filed up to the counter and left something as a present of thanks. There was nothing extravagant, a piece of whittled wood, a polished stone, a cleaned sea shell and other little objects.

Damilola resolved to return them in some way, she was highly embarrassed, these boys had so little and she had no idea how to reciprocate their wonderful gesture.

The previous evening the ex-boy soldier who the other boys looked up to called them all together and insisted everyone should find something they could give to Damilola as a thank you.

Samuel one of the youngest in the camp felt he had nothing, then he remembered the dirty canvas bag containing the bag with the lucky little stones Uncle Yampa had given him. When it came to his turn at the end of the queue he took the bag from round his neck and dropped it unnoticed onto the pile of objects on the counter.

Relieved he had found something satisfactory to pass onto the Nigerian nurse he no longer gave it a thought as he rushed to join the boy's football game outside.

Later that day Damilola piled all the objects into a plastic bag resolved to leave them for the boys when she left the following week

At first Damilola didn't bother to look in the dirty canvas bag, it was only because it was so dirty amongst all the other clean objects, she decided to give it a clean and undid the rotten drawstring holding it together.

The small stones inside didn't exactly shine out at her, but she was sure she knew what they were. It was with a racing heartbeat that she rapidly cleaned them up to reveal the uncut stones. At first not knowing what to do she checked to make sure no one could see her and stuffed the bag of diamonds into her pocket.

For the next twenty-four hours she was in a panic, it was alright being in possession of such a hoard, but she had no idea what to do with them or how to realise their potential value.

Chapter 2

Return Home and Valuation

It was only when she spoke by telephone to her mother that a solution occurred to her.

'Damilola now you're coming home safe from that dangerous place you need to settle down, find a nice boy, get married and start producing my grandchildren.'

It was a permanent joke between them, her mother had only managed to conceive the one child and she was desperate to dote on some grandchildren.

Damilola was in a quandary she only had feelings for one person. Damilola was gay and she was in love with a young lady called Chisaru, but she was nearly unobtainable being the daughter of a Chief.

When Damilola finished speaking to her mother the thoughts about the Chief's daughter made her realise the girl's father might possibly offer her a solution and make him look favourably on a possible liaison between Damilola and Chisaru. Without wasting a moment, Damilola decided to telephone the Chief immediately.

The Chief's mobile was answered after only two rings, the Chief was surprised to get the call from his younger sister's only child.
'Damilola, isn't it?'
'Yes sir.'

'How's your mother?'
'I haven't seen her for a while, what can I do for you?'
Damilola paused unsure for a moment, she hadn't properly thought this through. How could she explain about the diamonds without giving the game away to any possible eavesdroppers?'
Eventually she settled for a large hint.
'Sir I'm due home next week and I have some really marketable goods to bring back with me.'
The Chief quickly grasped the situation, obviously the girl had something hot and lucrative to bring back but couldn't say outright what the goods were, after a moment's thought he answered.
'That sounds good, e mail me at this address and I'll find a way of helping you.'
The Chief gave Damilola the address and made her repeat it back so there could be no mistake.
Within moments Damilola had e mailed the Chief about the 'shiny objects.'
He replied that Damilola should be patient while he, the Chief gave it some thought.

It was only twenty-four hours before the Chief had made some decisive moves. With some astute manoeuvring on the Chief's part, Damilola was not to be sent home by the normal commercial flights where there was a danger of the diamonds being discovered.

She was to return to Port Harcourt as super cargo on a returning aid flight.

The Chief as always on the lookout for new ways of increasing his fortune had now done some work for himself. He knew how he could, with the right manoeuvring double his money or better.

The Chief concocted a tale which made out he had bought the diamonds from a warlord in the Sierra Leone hinterland and needed money up front to pay the supposed seller.

He knew another Ikwerre Chief, a night club owner in Port Harcourt who was always amenable to this sort of investment, mind you the man was very dangerous if crossed. The Chief would also have to make sure Damilola was properly compensated to keep her fully onside.

Negotiations were done quickly over the phone, it was arranged an agreeable sum would be paid over to the Chief's Swiss bank account once the diamonds reached Port Harcourt and were properly valued.

The following week, on the Friday, the Chief was waiting for his niece to land at Port Harcourt Airport. Being an aid flight and considering Port Harcourt had no scheduled International flights to and from the airport there was only a small Custom's presence. The Customs Officers were members of his own Ikwerre tribe and weren't about to interrupt one of their Chief's, welcoming home a local heroine of the Ebola crisis.

The Chief sat back in his white Jaguar outside the Port Harcourt air terminal on the east side of the runway about five that Friday evening. He watched as the chartered Boeing 737 appeared out of the grey, low cloud base and come in over the thick jungle from the north to land safely on the main runway.

The Chief waited in the air-conditioned comfort of his Jaguar, out of the oppressive heat and humidity of the early evening. He had at first, been waiting in the terminal, their air conditioning having failed once again, he had returned to the car.

Earlier an officious uniformed Official had been about to ask him to move the Jaguar but when he realised whose car it was, he had made a half bow before going on to cause problems for family trying to unload their purple Corolla outside the terminal. Damilola departed the white fronted building and looked both ways before identifying her uncle's car. The Chief exited his vehicle and opened the boot for Damilola's one large battered suitcase. They greeted each other with a hug, Damilola took the opportunity to whisper in her uncle's ear.

'I've got the bag with the diamonds, nobody even looked at me.'

The Chief smiled.

'I should hope not.'

The Chief looked around no-one was taking much interest, but he didn't want to advertise this meeting more than was necessary.

'Just get in the car, we've no need to publicise our presence here.'

Safely ensconced in the Jaguar, the Chief drove them south towards the city. Damilola was keen to get home after a year away but from their route it was obvious her Uncle had other plans.

'Where are we going?'

'We've someone to see Damilola, have the merchandise ready.'

'After that we can drop you at your parents, my young sister will be pleased you're home safe and well, I'm sure.'

Throughout the rest of the short journey, through the evening rush hour traffic, Damilola was encouraged to and regaled her Uncle with the good and bad experiences of her previous twelve months.

The trip of thirty miles took almost an hour because of the traffic as they pushed their way through to the other side of the city and into Port Harcourt Town. Here the Chief drove the Jaguar into a partly-paved dingy side street.

He parked with his inside wheels on the mud-soaked verge trying to leave enough space for other vehicles to pass on the narrow thoroughfare. The equatorial night was fast approaching, the shadow thrown by the three-story wooden shacks on either side of the road, were exacerbating the loss of light. There was no street-lighting and the rough looking dingy thoroughfare was totally unlit. A small number of lights could be seen illuminating a few windows and open doorways, these did little to lighten the darkening passage.

Damilola uncertainty, concern and tension in her voice asked.

'What's this sir?'

'It's alright we have to get the diamonds checked and my contact may know someone in Europe who can legalise them.'

'Come on Damilola, don't worry.'

Damilola shuddered but she didn't want to embarrass herself in front of her Uncle, still scared and not reassured by the Chiefs words she stuttered out a whispered reply.

'I'm, I'm, fine honestly.'

The Chief impatiently shook his head in disbelief, leant across Damilola and grabbed a black rubber torch from the glove compartment on the passenger side of the car.

'Let's get this done.'

They exited the vehicle into the dingy street, Damilola looked around anxiously expecting muggers or other demons to leap out of the shadows.

The brief dusk had now turned into night and the only useful illumination once they had shut the car doors was the Chiefs torch.

An animal, probably a rat was heard to scurry under one of the wooden shacks, there were still only a few dim lights from the buildings to help them realise they were close to human habitation. The Chief took them into a narrow-boarded alleyway between two of the buildings.

He strode purposefully forward, counting out his paces under his breath, their feet rattling the wooden planking that acted as a walkway. Damilola was now really frightened, she hung onto the Chief's shirt as she followed her uncle into the torch-lit blackness.

Abruptly the Chief stopped and Damilola not realising this bumped into her Uncles back.

'Sorry!'

The Chief ignoring the minor collision grunted and concentrated on illuminating the wooden wall on their left, looking for something.

'Got it.'

Whispered the Chief as he lit up a tight-fitting door, there was no visible lock or door handle visible.

The Chief handed the torch to Damilola and told her to wait. Pulling his mobile from his right trouser pocket, the Chief powered it up and dialled up a land line he had previously memorised. A few moments later they both could hear a phone ringing faintly behind the door.

After four rings, it was answered, it appeared to Damilola no-one spoke on the other end of the line because as soon as the line was connected the Chief spoke into the receiver

'We're outside.'

'Just the two of us like I promised.'

There was no answer, neither was one expected because the Chief immediately switched the mobile off and powered it down.

Damilola guessed it was to prevent them being tracked.

There was a momentary pause, then they could hear the sliding of bolts on the other side of the door.

Damilola shook with fright, with the torch switched off it was pitch black in the alleyway with no light source, she gripped the Chief's shirt more tightly.

Finally, the last bolt was drawn, the door opened silently and outwardly onto the alleyway. The pair of them were illuminated by the internal lighting. A large man in jungle fatigues carrying an Uzi sub machine gun gestured them inside by waving the gun at them to indicate they should enter.

'Come on move it, get your asses in here.'

Damilola who was shocked and frozen to the spot, didn't move immediately but was harangued by the gunman.

'Bloody hell, shift will you.'

Even though the Chief knew what was going to happen, the sudden bright lighting caused even him to pause for a moment before he, now closely followed by his niece dashed into the interior.

They arrived in a well-lit corridor which looked modern and was painted a light yellow on fairly new plastering. The air was suddenly cool, Damilola realised the place was air conditioned. She surmised the workmanship on the entry door must have been special and expensive. While they had been stood in the darkness there had been no hint of this well-lit interior.

An unseen large, well-muscled man stepped up behind them and spoke.

'Apologies people but I have to search you.'
The Chief knew the score and had already emptied his pockets and outstretched his arms in compliance. Damilola followed suit grasping the precious canvas bag and her Nigerian passport in her right hand. The search of their bodies was comprehensive and thorough. The searcher ignored the fact she was a female and groped her small, breasts while bringing a gasp of surprise from Damilola when his fingers passed briefly across her crotch. Finally satisfied the searcher turned and indicated they should follow him.
He led them to a door at the top of a short, rising, carpeted corridor, the walls decorated with dark wooden sculptures which Damilola recognised as from local artists. Opening the white interior door ahead of them inwards they were taken into an enclosed room.
It was very well lit and was occupied by one, old, half-caste gentleman sitting at a stainless-steel table facing them in the centre of the room. The windowless air-conditioned laboratory type space was at odds with the alleyway they had just left.
On the far two walls were rows of modern metal lockable office cabinets and in the far corner was a large modern white safe with electronic locking.
The old man looked up from where he was inspecting some jewellery which he returned to a plastic bag.

'Good evening , you have the merchandise?'

The half-caste who asked the question was elderly, thin, with a shrunken grey-bearded face. His physical presence may not have been up to much, but he commanded the room from his black-leather, swivel chair.

'I'll not get up or introduce myself, the less we know about each other the better, I'm sure.'

Damilola looked at the Chief in query, the latter nodded in answer before telling his niece.

'Right show the man.'

Damilola still clutching the bag of diamonds tightly, stepped forward and reluctantly handed the bag over to the man behind the table. Her heart which she realised had been pounding relaxed. From being frightened about the responsibility it was such a relief to be relieved of the cause of so much heartache and worry of the last couple of weeks.

The expert didn't reach out for the oilskin bag immediately, firstly he laid out a piece of green baize cloth before grasping the bag from where Damilola had deposited it. Carefully he opened the bag before tentatively shaking out its small occupants onto the cloth.

The uncut stones didn't look worth all the trouble people had gone to get them this far. Very quickly the jeweller who was inspecting the merchandise with loupe and tweezers sighed, nodded and grinned.

'Good, good.'

Damilola standing alongside her Uncle went to say something but seeing this the other nudged her and put his right forefinger to his lips indicating silence.

After a few ums and aha's the old man put his loupe down and looked up, the Chief and his niece waited expectantly, the tension in the room was almost palatable.

The jeweller cleared his throat.

'What you have here, is a nice set of conflict diamonds, it is possible that my cousin in Antwerp will be able to regularise them for say thirty percent of their eventual sale price.'

'In my humble opinion, they will certainly be worth in the region of a million pounds sterling or more when cut.'

He waved both his hands palms down over the jewels.

'I will warn my cousin of their impending arrival, but you will have to work out how to get them to Antwerp.'

Damilola took an intake of breath at the estimated value and whistled quietly, the Chief pulled out a thick wad of mixed currency from the back pocket of his trousers and handed it over to the jeweller.

'Thanks, pass on my appreciation to your cousin and tell him I hope to have the diamonds in his hands early in the New Year.'

Damilola took back the oilskin bag which the jeweller handed over after carefully counting the stones into it.

They were escorted back down the hallway to the alleyway door. It was only when Damilola saw the three closed circuit televisions she realised how tight was the security. The CCTV showed the road where the Chief's car was parked, the alleyway and the secure outer door. The infra-red showed everything as clear as day, it was obvious the old man in his windowless room had some serious security.

'It's all quiet.'

The guard with the Uzi hanging from his chest reassured them as he unbolted the outer door.

The pair quickly returned to the Jaguar and made their way out of the town, Damilola was highly excited to think that she had been looking after things that were worth all that money.

'A million pounds was that right?'

'That's right but we must get them to Europe first and that will be somewhat awkward and may be a little expensive, but it isn't anything for you to worry about though.'

The Chief handed Damilola another brown envelope containing a large cash sum of Naira.

'That's to compensate you for the trouble you've gone to but remember from now on what occurred is never to be spoken about, don't forget I have ears everywhere.'

Damilola was aware of her Uncle's reputation for dealing fiercely with recalcitrant members of the tribe and others.

'Of course, I know nothing, have seen even less and my lips are sealed.'

'Good I would expect nothing less of a niece of mine.'

'To help with your silence, if you go to Elizade the Toyota franchise in the morning, there's a nice new Rav 4 with your name on it.'

Damilola couldn't believe her luck a nice nest egg and a new piece of transport as well.

'Oh, that's brilliant thanks so much.'

They arrived at her parents' house, as the Chief opened the boot of his car he leaned over to Damilola and reminded him.

'Remember you are to forget everything.'

'Don't mention the diamonds ever.'

'Don't even think about the diamonds.'

The Chief put his right forefinger to his own lips to indicate silence.

'Any loose talk now could be very dangerous for both of us.'

'Something of such value means there are people out there who would like to cause us considerable grief.'

He emphasised the point fiercely by making a slashing the throat gesture across the front of Damilola.

Damilola stuttered.

'Yes sir.'

She grabbed her battered suitcase and gratefully staggered off into her parent's residence. Part of her wishing she had never met the jewels and another excited by her sudden windfall.

Chapter 3
Car Find

Oscar, in his Company car stopped at the open double gates of the Chief's compound and sighed in exasperation.

Tacked to the wooden gate post on the right side of the drive, a hand-painted metal sign proclaimed.

'Our apologies road to house closed for repairs.'

He peered out through the windscreen of the company's four by four, it was no good the monsoon's torrential downpour wasn't about to let up. He was going to have to leg it up to the Chiefs bungalow.

The surrounding jungle was prevented from invading the Chief's compound by a corrugated-metal, green-painted, fence at least six feet high.

Oscar pulled his blue company umbrella out, it was lying on the floor in the passenger car well drying out. Grabbing his blue company hold-all he exited the vehicle into the hot and humid downpour. Bracing himself he set out to walk the couple of hundred yards along the curved stone and mud driveway to the Chiefs bungalow at the far side of the compound.

At the moment of leaving the car a particularly loud thunderclap presaged a sudden squall. Instead of the normal vertical downpour the wind drove the rain horizontally across the compound and within a fraction of a second destroyed his umbrella.

Steeling himself against the storm's onslaught Oscar cursed and threw the now useless brolly down in the muddy earth. It was picked up by a severe gust of wind and launched into the surrounding forest.

Swearing again under his breath in disgust, Oscar broke into a run along the driveway, he quickly became soaked to the skin in the storm. The only part of him to stay dry were his feet encased in the sensible tan boots he had the foresight to wear that morning.

If it hadn't been for the closed driveway, the useless cheap company logoed umbrella and the monsoon, he wouldn't have had reason to stop at the Chief's Barn, roughly halfway to the residence.

Oscar was twenty-eight, he had full head of damp dark brown hair, was six feet tall, naturally fit which with his Grenadian heritage made him look younger than his years. He was a graduate of the University of Central Lancashire's Business School, a keen cricketer and learning his way through the vagaries of doing business in West Africa.

He did well to stay upright as he splashed and slipped his way along the muddy driveway. The noise of the storm was loud, he could hardly hear the squelching of his running feet.

A flash of lightning followed almost immediately by a massive thunderclap was enough for the moment and he sought the immediate shelter under the overhanging roof of the Chief's large barn. A hefty, modern, silver, corrugated-metal, structure part way up the drive. Its shiny exterior like a shining beacon through the monsoon rains.

Both of the floor-to-ceiling doors were fully open, hooked back onto the front of the structure. They presented Oscar with a temporary haven away from the elements, he jogged into the shelter of the building and turned in the dry to look out at the raging elements. A mixture of oil and damp mustiness gave off a mixed aroma in the dank atmosphere inside the barn.

Oscar couldn't claim the rain was unexpected, it was mid-morning in June 2015, about 3 kilometres south west of Port Harcourt in the Niger delta. Heavy downpours with little wind and the occasional vicious squalls were to be expected, less than five degrees north of the Equator in West Africa at this time of year.

With the heavy rains, the River Niger filled its mangrove strewn waterways all over this part of the West African country. The major part of its confluence ending here in the appropriately named Rivers State.

The silvery, regulation, welded, metal, supports of the barn bolstered the corrugated sheeting which made up the vertical walls and leaning roof, keeping dry the interior's contents. The heavy rain pounded loudly onto and cascaded off the lower end of the un-guttered sloping gable. Standing just inside the wide-open doors the noise of the rain on the metal roof was deafening, almost cutting out the clamour of the external tempest.

With his bare hands Oscar brushed the rainwater of his face and with the fingers of his right hand slicked back his hair. He couldn't however do much about the water that had already seeped between his neck and shirt collar and which was now running uncomfortably down his back.

It took a moment for his eyes to adjust to the gloom when he turned and peered into the interior of the barn.

Just as his eyes adjusted, the wind outside dropped as the squall passed through, the sky lightened slightly but still the rain fell. It now lashed down vertically with no winds to blow it off course.

Oscar prepared to make a dash for the Chiefs bungalow, he paused taking a moment to glance around again.

A partial realisation, perhaps an unconscious thought, some sort of sixth sense, made him recognise he was missing something. Oscar looked behind him again back into the barn's interior. A hint of brightness, a brief burst of colour which stood out from the rest of the gloomy interior.

He concentrated hard, his eyes searching amongst the two vehicles and the other equipment stored in the capacious outbuilding. Just beyond the Chiefs pristinely polished, new, white Jaguar XF and the more practical, well muddied black Mitsubishi Pajero family runabout was the hint of something, colours that were out of place. It hinted at something totally unexpected.

There was a suggestion of bright blue and the shape of a vehicle underneath a dirty green tarpaulin hidden at the rear of the barn. The mildewed cover had slipped, Oscar could see the bright colour which suggested something distinctive, he thought couldn't possibly be found in a barn in the depths of south eastern Nigeria.

Now facing inwards, he sneaked a look back into the compound, the rainfall was still heavy, and he could only just see the shape of the bungalow. There was no one in sight and he felt sure if he took a moment to investigate he would be uninterrupted.

He had a desperate need to know, the suspense was palatable. In the end, his curiosity got the better of him. He strolled rapidly into the interior of the outbuilding, his heartbeat racing in anticipation.

On reaching the mildewed covering, he dragged it off the vehicle. Underneath was what due to the colour, he half-suspected but which still shocked him it being so astonishing. The blue which had first caught Oscar's attention turned out to be a huge advert for Red Bull covering most of the near side of a left-hand drive Volkswagen Touareg Rally 2 decked out in Dakar Rally colours. The only interruption to the Red Bull advertising were the white painted names of the Chief and his wife on the near side door and the large VW decal to the rear of the vehicle.

The bright blue paint on the vehicle was what had attracted him, he was a keen car freak and the colour had been difficult to miss. Without realising what he was doing he fist pumped and shouted out aloud.

'Wow, it is.'

Oscar racked his brains.

'How did an Ikwerre Chief in the Niger Delta get hold of one of these, they're only built for the Dakar rally?'

For a moment, he was fully engrossed in his discovery, it was only when the noise of the pounding rain on the corrugated roof eased he remembered he was trespassing. It wouldn't help his relationship with the Chief and his family if he was caught snooping in their barn.

Carefully he did his best to restore the tarpaulin to its original position over the vehicle before returning to the wide-open doors of the building. He had a cold sweat on now, felt chilled because of his damp shirt and the relative coolness of the barn's interior.

He looked down at himself, his light blue shirt was soaked with a mixture of rainwater and his own sweat, his tan trousers had streaks of damp running nearly to the crotch and he knew he didn't look very presentable for his meeting with the Chief.

Oscar hoped he would have the opportunity to tidy himself up for the appointment when he arrived at the bungalow. He wasn't too concerned about his present apparel knowing he had fresh shirt and trousers in his hold all. Locals tended to wander around in flip flops or at best open toed sandals, Oscar though was cautious and preferred the relative safety of the protective boots he was wearing in this bug and snake infested part of Africa.

The rain having petered out into a light steady drizzle, Oscar looked across and could now quite clearly see the bungalow with its open, covered, wide porch. Its two glass domed ceiling lights lit, a welcoming beacon through the rain-soaked, morning, gloom.

In no time, he completed the fifty-metre dash to the welcoming building, although lighter, there was still enough rain to ensure his shirt was like a wet rag and he felt extremely uncomfortable Tugging the bell-pull, he heard it chime inside the double-fronted, white PVC, front door. A dog barked in the rear of the house, Oscar didn't remember a dog on his last recent visit, but one of his many informants had told him about a white fluffy thing now proudly owned by the younger of the Chief's two teenage daughters.

After what seemed an age, the left door opened slowly, a small, black, female face peeked out through the widening gap. The person inside recognised the visitor and threw the front door wide open. An elderly, female, body followed the heavily wrinkled face.

She was dressed in a grubby white dress, tinged grey from over washing in poor quality water, with the inevitable thin, black, flip-flops on her tiny feet.

The face on top of the body beamed out a smile as Oscar greeted her.

'Hello Marcia.'

The little elderly lady was a maid of all work in the Chief's house, her mouth full of white teeth between her red lips, grabbed hold of Oscar's hands and spoke rapidly in brief, short statements.

'Welcome Mr Oscar, you are a naughty boy, you're late.'

'He's expecting you in his study.'

'You're all wet.'

'Where's your umbrella?'

'You can't see him like that.'

'You have brought a change of clothes?'

'I know, I know, it's raining, it never stops at this time of year as we know only too well.'

She paused for a moment to catch her breath giving Oscar a chance to intervene.

'Yes, I do have a change of gear, can I use the bathroom, a nice big fluffy towel would be good as well.'

'Of course, Mr. Oscar.'

Marcia grabbed hold of his right hand with her left, led him down the short hallway to the entrance of a visitor's bathroom. There were framed photographs on both walls of the hallway. These were of the present-day family and the Chief meeting famous personalities. Pride of place went to a picture of him with the present President of the Federal Republic of Nigeria.

Oscar also noted a picture of the Chief and his wife alongside a Dakar Rally car. It was like the one in the barn and either side of the couple were two rally drivers in their blue decal covered overalls, carrying Red Bull sponsored helmets.

Once safely installed in the small bathroom, Oscar got changed and thought about his meeting with the Chief.

Oscar worked for a service company which fixed things for many of the International Conglomerates who were reaping the benefits of this oil enriched region. One of his many tasks were to make things happen and keep the locals happy. This meant amongst many things keeping the states leaders onside, which was why he was visiting the Chief today.

The Chief was a Paramount leader of one of the clans of the Ikwerre tribe they were the main inhabitants of the Rivers state of Nigeria. This area was crucial, it was from here much of the crude oil, upon which Nigeria's debt ruined economy depended, was found and exported.

The Ikwerre are different from most of the Nigerian tribes, the clan Chiefs' were generally treated as equals, with normally no overall leader, whereas other Nigerian tribes generally had only one Paramount Chief as their elected principal.

Oscar was here today to discuss the annual licence fee which the oil companies paid the local leaders. This helped to facilitate the safe transport of oil through the pipelines which traversed this south-east corner of the country. Most of these pipelines because of the boggy nature of the delta were above ground and carried some of the crude oil to either the Okrika refinery or the majority to the huge oil storage tanks on the estuary of the Bonny River, where it emptied its muddy polluted fresh water out into the Bight of Bonny just over two hundred miles north of the equator.

There had been some problems in previous years with local people breaking into the pipelines to siphon off the crude oil and use it to light their stoves. A Government tax on cooking oil and the poverty endemic in that part of Nigeria had made the possibility of free fuel seem particularly enticing.

The light crude of the Delta burnt easily and was a temptation but in a confined space the gases were very combustible, some families had lost their relations to these small but deadly explosions. Even worse several breaches of the crude oil pipelines had caused even larger disastrous catastrophes, killing and maiming dozens of locals.

When a breach was made everyone wanted a piece of the action, they would crowd round the ruptured pipeline like bees to a honeypot. Any available container that could be found was used to filch the light crude oil which could be used unrefined to power practically any sort of engine.

It was one of Oscar's tasks to persuade the Chief's and hopefully their people not to interrupt the flow of oil.

Chapter 4

The Meeting

Now all spruced up in his freshly ironed, short-sleeved, light-blue checked shirt, matching light blue shorts, new white socks and well-polished black loafers. His previously worn boots and damp clothing bundled into his company hold-all. Oscar returned to the hall and presented himself to Marcia. She reached up from her diminutive height of 1.6 metres and straightened an errant collar.

There was a sudden fit of giggling, Oscar looked towards the partially open door at the end of the short hallway, two heads appeared out of the shadow followed by the Chief's two nubile daughters, one of them cuddling and stroking the head of the source of the previous yapping.
'Hallo Oscar.'

They chorused, giggling as only teenage girls can, a mixture of shyness, inexperience and a quest for knowledge.

'Hi Chisaru, Hi Oroma.'

'Just here to see your Dad,'

Chisaru the elder, nearly eighteen and about to take a trip to see family in London, flashed her dark eyes at their visitor and asked?

'Have you met Aldi?'

'You mean Oroma's new dog.'

'No, he wasn't here the last time I visited.'

Oscar walked over to the younger Oroma, she was holding the source of the yapping, a Bichon Frisse. He gained kudos with the girls by tickling the little dog's chin whose barking was soon stopped by this intervention, instead the small creature looked back at Oscar with a look of contentment.

Oscar was aware the newest arrival in the Chief's household was meant to compensate the younger daughter. She wasn't felt to be old enough to accompany her elder sister on a London adventure, an eighteenth birthday present for the elder daughter.

Oscar employed a team of local informants throughout the Delta to keep him abreast of all gossip and situations which might occur. This was done so he could hopefully anticipate and solve any possible problems before they were likely to occur. The expenditure this took to keep him ahead of the game came out of a large pot of ready use money in a local bank account.

The company accountants for want of a better term, referred to the money as Oscar's Petty Cash.

Many of these informants, his moles, had been inherited from his predecessor. Oscar by now had cultivated some of his own very useful sources which had already enabled him to nip many a local crisis in the bud before it happened.

Oroma herself shrunk back a little in teenage embarrassment, when Oscar reached out to the puppy. He smiled nicely at the girl's embarrassment.

'Hope you look after little Aldi, remember a dog can be better than a friend.'

'Well after diamonds that is.'

Marcia already worried because Oscar was late for his meeting interrupted the pleasantries

'Mr Oscar.'

'Sorry girls got to go, your Dad awaits.'

'See you soon, have a good trip Chisaru.'

With a last adjustment to his shorts and a glance in the hallway mirror to make sure he looked right for the meeting with the Chief, he followed a rapidly departing Marcia.

She escorted him to the far end of the hallway, then left through an open door. They entered a large dining area furnished with dark African mahogany chairs surrounding a highly polished dining table. This had placings for up to sixteen people. On the inside wall of this long room was a pair of crossed Assegai over a straw shield. Opposite these the outer wall of the dining room opened out onto a patio, through a pair of large sliding glass doors.

The maid led Oscar towards a heavy black wooden hardwood door, almost hidden in the dark mahogany panelled wall in the opposite corner of the room. It was slightly ajar. The house was very quiet, just the faint sound of modern rap music from where they had entered, presumably from one of the daughter's rooms.

As they reached the entry, Marcia knocked on the panelling alongside the partly open door.

The deep voice of the Chief answered from the other side.

'That'll be okay thanks very much Marcia.'

Marcia gave a toothy grin and returned to the hallway from whence they had come.

'Come in Oscar don't wait out there.'

Oscar pushed open the door to the Chief's study, it was a large room about half the size of that from which he had just entered. The door was again in the corner of this room. On his left side, the wall was almost completely covered by another set of glass sliding doors looking out onto the previously seen patio. The other three sides of the room were covered in dark wooden bookshelves from floor to ceiling, these appeared to be almost groaning under the weight of their books.

With their front facing the sliding doors were a pair of large cowhide leather armchairs which could extend so the person using them would have a footrest. Facing outward towards the glass and on a leather, revolving desk chair behind a large, ornate rosewood desk, which was at least a hundred years old sat the Chief.

This was definitely a male environment, there was the smell of recent cigars and sitting in front of one of the bookcases was the latest Sony 65-inch Smart Television, it could have overwhelmed the room if it hadn't been for the extensive library. The Nigerian gentleman Oscar had come to see was in his early sixties, with a very dark West African complexion, black hair peppered with grey, cut very short so it almost appeared as stubble. The Chief gave an impression of seniority and of someone who was in charge at all times. He looked prosperous, well-fed and although slightly rotund he carried it well. He was wearing a crisp short sleeved white shirt, freshly pressed and a smartly creased pair of black trousers.

Oscar thought he must have dressed appropriately for their meeting because instead of the expected sandals or flip flops the Chief wore a pair highly shined black patent shoes on bare feet.

The Chief waved to the upright wooden chairs the other side of his desk.

'Take a seat and welcome to my humble residence.'

The Chief asked after Oscar and joked jovially.

'Trust you didn't get too wet making your way in, but it is the time of year when our Nigerian climate intends we should always be a little damp.'

He laughed deeply the noise emanating from deep within his lungs came out in a deep throated sound.

'Sorry you couldn't park by the house, we're worried about the state of the drive in the Monsoon.'

'I've promised to get the contractors in after the rainy season is over.'

Then Oscar having only just sat down the Chief suggested which he knew was meant to put Oscar on the back-foot straightaway.

'Let's make ourselves more comfortable, shall we?'

The Chief got up and came around the desk indicating Oscar should move to one of the armchairs.

'Thanks, it's always a pleasure to see you sir.'

Oscar reached into his blue hold all and retrieved a prettily wrapped jewellery box containing a brooch.'

He reached forward and passed the sweetener to the Chief.

'I have a little present for your good lady,'

'Thank you Oscar I'm sure it will be appreciated.'

'Can I offer you some refreshment?'

'Thanks, I would appreciate something cool.'

The Chief shouted for Marcia and almost immediately she entered the study with a tray of cold drinks, it was clear she had been ready and waiting just outside the office door.

Oscar accepted a freshly squeezed lemon cordial sipped from the glass and looked out of the glass doors at the teeming rainfall.

He felt relaxed he was after all only here to pay his respects, to keep in touch with the Chief and make sure his area of influence within River State was causing few problems. There also had to be agreement about what would be sponsored by the Companies, Oscar's Service Company was representing. The whole thing was a balancing act, they both knew some of this sponsorship was to be looked after by the Chief and his acolytes so that peace and cooperation would continue within their area of influence. It was only for Oscar and the Chief to agree the division of the sponsorship monies to keep everyone happy.

Oscar's service company were working as agents for most of the international companies working in the Delta, the sponsorship payments Oscar arranged were seen by the National Government of Nigeria as bribes but there would have been an insurrection if these fees were terminated.

There was pressure on from the Federal Government to at least ensure these fees were paid in the local currency Naira and then they could be subject to Federal taxes. The previous payments of foreign currency were helping to depress the Naira as these monies were often secreted away in European bank accounts or used for investment in foreign property.

To the Paramount Chiefs the payments were Facilitation fees and respectably earned. There were problems because there had been a major reduction in the value of the Naira against the British Pound and American Dollar. Oscar was having to renegotiate all the Facilitation fees to take this into account now he was paying out only in the local currency.

He did however have some flexibility to pay about ten percent of the sponsorships/facilitation fees in foreign currency from his petty cash, this wasn't well advertised around his Chiefs and gave Oscar a little flexibility when there were problems.

The Chief was a pragmatist and understood the problem, he wasn't too concerned now, and a facilitation fee was agreed with few difficulties. The Chief was more interested in talking about Premier League football and his favourite team Arsenal. He was very critical of Arsene Wengers recent failure to convert good starts into a league title and was more hopeful of the season that had just started. Oscar who never advertised his dislike of all things Premier League was clued up enough to make decent points in the discussion. He knew full well the Chief was keen and had access to a box at the Emirates, on his frequent visits to the United Kingdom.

After about an hour discussing the local conditions and agreeing the Chief's facilitation fees, Oscar subtly brought the discussion round to cars and rallying. The Chief aware of what was happening diverted the discussion onto the Dakar Rally by commenting.

'I think it's an embarrassment to the African continent that the Rally is no longer held here and goes to South America instead.'

Oscar nodded his head in agreement.

The Chief ranted on.

'It's an absolute disgrace, a pure piece of sport can't be allowed to pass safely through North Africa because of some Muslim Brigands.'

'I was there you know?'

'What at the Dakar Rally?'

'We went to Dakar to see the finish.'

'Oh, when was that.'

'Back in 2007, the oil company was a major sponsor and flew a plane load of us Chiefs and wives to Senegal to watch the last two stages and the finish.'

'I won a prize in the raffle at the celebration dinner.'

Maybe this was the answer to the Rally car in the barn, but surely the Chief and his wife couldn't have won that, could they?

'What was that, hope it was something worthwhile?'

Oscar now thought he knew what was coming, not realising the Chief was leading the conversation into the place he wanted it to go.

'One of the rally cars a Volkswagen Touareg Race 2.'

'It's in the barn you passed on the way up the drive.'

'We've only ever had it out a couple of times because it's so uncomfortable with all the race harnesses and only two tiny seats in its full rally trim.'

Oscar couldn't hold back his admiration and enthusiasm.

'Wow, it must be quite something to own though.'

The Chief smiled to himself he was sure the agent sitting in the chair next to him was going to be his means to selling the rally car on. He had fully researched the man and knew Oscar was a real motor enthusiast.

'Unfortunately, it hasn't been properly maintained and I doubt it would be able to start now but you are welcome to have a go if you're interested.'

'The wife was quite unhappy when we won the Rally Car she was rather hoping to win one of the other prizes, such as the week in Paris at the Ritz.'

'I must say I now quite agree with her, I was very pleased at first to be the centre of attention. Especially when we were interviewed by the BBC after the celebration banquet and of course there was all the hullabaloo when the car arrived in a container at Port Harcourt docks. The N.T.A, (Nigerian Television Authority,) Channel One was there, we made the National News and then of course there were all the newspapers, we were quite the celebrities for a few days.'

'There's a photograph out in the hallway from the Nigerian Tribune, they were quite kind and sent it to me already framed.'

'Would you like to see the car?'

The Chief not waiting for an answer rose from his lounge chair with some alacrity.

'Follow me.'

He continued as he strode through the office door shouting.

'Marcia, we need an umbrella.'

Not wishing to be impolite and upset his host's enthusiasm, having already noted the photograph on his way in' Oscar had to move rapidly to keep up with the older gentleman.

As they made their way through the property the Chief continued to enthuse about the trip to Dakar back in 2007. Reaching the hallway, he proudly stood alongside the framed press photograph.

'Not aged too much have I, just put on a few kilogrammes.'

He grinned patting his portly belly proudly.

'No sir, you hardly look a day older than the photograph.'

Replied Oscar hoping to ingratiate himself with his client.

Surreptitiously glancing at his watch, he realised he was going to be late for his next meeting with one of the Chief's cousins who was also rated as a Paramount Chief of the same tribe.

He cursed to himself and was wondering how to extricate himself from the bungalow when the Chief opened the front door, unfurling the umbrella and committed Oscar.

'Let's go'

This concentrated Oscar's mind and raised a quandary.

Should he now make his excuses and probably upset his host, or could he risk the wrath of and let his next client down.

Fortunately, the monsoon rains outside took on a heavier beat and they could both hear the pounding of the incessant water outside as the Chief went to step off the porch.

The raindrops could be seen bouncing off the red tiles on the floor of the entry and seeing this as a means of resolving his dilemma Oscar seized the opportunity.

'The monsoon is awful sir.'

'Better I see your raffle prize another day, when it's perhaps a lot drier and it will stop you getting soaked.

'I really am keen to have a look at such an icon.'

'Alright then but I will expect to see you soon.'

They made their way back through to the Office, so Oscar could retrieve his hold all. Then before he could leave, Marcia was called and told to fetch the daughters, so they could say their goodbyes.

Marcia let him out of the double fronted main door and Oscar dashed through the pelting rain back down the drive to his company car, taking a sidelong glance into the barn and towards the tarpaulin covered car as he sprinted past the opening.

***

While Oscar was getting drenched racing back down the driveway, the Chief returned to his office. Once there he placed a call to a local number.

'Kudo.'

Chief Kudo the night club owner was only interested in the Rally Car because the Chief had suggested it as a way of moving the diamonds into Europe.

'What's happening?'

'Just had the agent round.'

'Yeah, what happened?'

'I got us talking about the car after I saw him sheltering from the rains in the big barn.

'I'm not sure but I'm pretty certain he's seen it.

The Chief paused in thought for a moment and stroked his chin with his free left hand

'In fact, I'm sure he has.'

'Something he said when we were chatting about the machine, it just came across like he already knew it was there.'

'Anyway, he's promised to come back and have a look.'

Kudo intervened.

'Do you reckon he'll be up for it?'

'Don't know but as we thought, he's a keen motor head, we'll just have to wait and see if he took the bait.'

'Whatever happens we've lost nothing if he is interested it'll be a useful conduit when it's shipped back to Europe, otherwise we'll have to try something else.'

Chapter 5

Saturday Afternoon at the Golf Club

A month later, on a Saturday afternoon in the middle of July, Oscar was sitting on a tall rattan covered stool, elbows leaning on the glass top of the Port Harcourt Golf Club bar. He was nursing a cooling Gin and Tonic, his second of the afternoon. He was feeling miserable and fed up, the West African monsoon was still doing its best to wash Port Harcourt and its surrounds into the Bonny River and Oscar whose first monsoon this was, felt depressed with always having to change out of damp clothing due to the humidity and water bucketing down out of the continually leaden grey skies.

Except for Oscar and a family of four eating in the dining room area, the Golf Club was empty. There were no golfers, the course being closed now because of the permanent inclement weather.

Even the Nigerian barman, dressed in a natty red waist coat, was bored he was trying to make himself look busy by shoving some glasses from the dishwasher back onto the shelves.

Oscar had hoped he would be joined by others from the local ex-pat community as the Golf Club was their normal haunt on a weekend when they weren't working.

Above the mirror located on the wall behind the bar was a brass plaque with writing etched into the metal, it had always intrigued Oscar because from where the patrons sat on their stools at the bar it was quite impossible to quite make out what the lettering was alluding too.

Raising himself from his present apathy, Oscar took a sip of his freshly made g and t and signalled across to the barman by waving his right hand. The barman seeing Oscar required attention strode across.

'Yes sah.'

Oscar recognising the military tones in the barman's speech and seeing the way he presented himself smiled and asked.

'Albert it's driving me crazy.'

What's that sah?'

'Every time I sit this side of the bar I see that bloody plaque and can't see the wording clear enough to make the text out.'

Albert laughed and with a huge grin stretching from ear to ear said.

'Neither can anyone else sir.'

'What's the big secret then?'

'It's nothing really it only commemorates the building of this Thomas Collins designed course in 1928.'

'Thanks, thought it would be something more interesting.'

The bar man returned to his post at the other end of the bar and Oscar returned to his ruminations, elbows resting on the bar, his bronzed face supported by the open left hand under his chin.

It hadn't been a good week; the place was full of despondent rumours and some of his sources were telling him that certain Paramount Chiefs were threatening to kick off because of the new arrangements to pay their Facilitation Fees in Naira.

Mind you it was nearing the end of the rainy season and that didn't help. No matter how many times people went through the monsoon everyone still got fed up with the flooding and getting wet every time they stepped outdoors. Tempers always got a bit frayed at this time of year.

Oscar had cautiously been holding back on the ten percent foreign currency allowance and paying all the Facilitation fees in Nigerian Naira. There were some unhappy local leaders as a result. It was the wrong time of year to be doing this when everyone was a bit down, Oscar was determined to err on the cautious side and push the envelope with the surrounding Chiefs knowing what he saved now, gave him much more room for manoeuvre later in the financial year.

Even so he was taking a bit of a battering in his meetings with these gentlemen, their influence controlled everything that came to pass in the River State. Presents for their wives were no longer helping very much.

A typical meeting with two of them yesterday had resulted in some implied threats against the pipelines if he didn't find a more amenable solution shortly.

At first Oscar had got away with blaming the Federal Nigerian Government up in Abuja but that excuse was beginning to wear thin nowadays. He needed to create an equitable solution as soon as possible. The companies his agency serviced would not be happy if there were further disruptions because the local hierarchy were annoyed, Oscar might be looking for a new job. The large, white, three-bladed, propeller fans hanging down from the ceiling moved the turgid air around the poorly air-conditioned room. The fans were a relic of the original colonial furnishings of the clubhouse and their simple design did still help to provide some relief from the heat and humidity of the Niger delta. Oscar who always perspired freely, noted with relief the fans and the air conditioning had done enough to finally dry the sweat from his back and his short-sleeved light blue checked shirt was no longer sticking to his body.

He was so immersed in his morose thoughts, he never noticed or heard the newcomers to the bar until he was pummelled on the back and a voice from the Western Isles of Scotland rasped in his ears.

'I do believe sonny it's got to be your round.'

Oscar grinned and swivelled round on his stool.

'Hiya Mac how's the dredging?'

'Brought up any dead bodies recently?'

Although they both laughed at the question it wouldn't have been the first time one of Mac's company dredgers had scooped up human remains in one of the mangrove lined canals the machines kept clear.

Mac himself was from a long line of expat Scottish Engineers, although he had been born somewhere in the Far East, Oscar wasn't sure where. Mac's father, who had started as a tanker engineer, had been fulfilling a contract for a rig build when his son had made his way into the world. Mac had spent most of his life abroad with his parents, plus the three years of a University degree at Kings College London. This still hadn't prevented him gaining the rich Gaelic tones of a man from the Outer Hebrides from his parents.

He was a large man both in size and character and was the Chief Engineer for an international dredging company. Mac topped two metres and was sturdily built, his ginger and unruly mass of hair topped a huge ruddy face partially covered in a bushy full beard and moustache.

Oscar finally realised Mac was accompanied by a small pasty-faced man in his early thirties.

'Who's your new mate?'

'Meet Jim, he's come out for a look see, with a view to taking over from me when my contract ends at the end of October.'

'Interesting.'

'Usual please, one for Jim as well.'

Oscar signalled to Adam the barman at the other end of the bar with three outstretched fingers indicating he wanted three more long gin and tonics.

Mac grabbed two of the drinks from the barman and led his companions to a low rattan glass topped square coffee table surrounded on its four sides by a mixture of well-worn lounge chairs. He slumped down into a large black leather armchair which squeaked in protest at this abuse.

The other two followed, Mac took a big slug of his ice-cold drink.

'There's nothing like a tall gin and tonic in the tropics Jim,'

'The quinine in the tonic helps keep the malaria away.'

'Well that's my excuse anyway.'

He laughed and his whole body rumbled along with him.

'As I said, this is Jim or James as he was christened, he arrived yesterday.'

'The poor bastard signed up to do my job.'

Mac laughed again and thumped Jim on the shoulder with a heavy right hand.

Jim winced and rolled his eyes at Oscar and for the first time since they arrived got a chance to contribute to the conversation

'Only got in yesterday they sent me round the houses, flight from Manchester down to Heathrow, KLM to Schiphol then the same to Lagos before the local flight out here.

I was exhausted when I got in, Mac picked me up at the hotel a couple of hours ago, so I feel like I'm totally lost, I shouldn't be jet lagged, there's only an hour difference with the UK.'

'The heat and humidity are something aren't they?'

'Does it ever stop raining?'

Mac chortled.

'This is nothing son.'

'Last month was the real wet, it's dying down now, you'll soon get used to it but you need to remember my advice and keep yourself properly lubricated.'

Mac drained his glass and waved his left hand with three fingers at the willing Albert who acknowledged the order with a brisk wave of his right hand.

They settled in for the afternoon and their conversation wandered all over the shop once Jim passed on his history, where he graduated and his recent experience at a large refinery in southern England. The conversation continued onto sport and wandered all over until Jim a keen fan brought the conversation round to Formula 1 and Lewis Hamilton.

That was the point when Oscar remembered the Touareg and he decided to regale his companions about the discovery in the Paramount Chief's barn.

'You really won't believe what I've found?'

He paused for effect.

This niggled Mac who tended to become impatient quickly and he retorted loudly.

'Come on ye Sassenach bastard out with it, you're holding back just to wind us up.'

'Of course.'

Oscar laughed having achieved his aim of annoying the Scotsman.

'Alright, alright, I've found an old Dakar Rally Volkswagen Touareg in one of the Ikwerre Chief's barns, I think it's from the last rally that went into Dakar in 2007.'

'What the hell is he doing with something like that?'

Jim interrupted.

'More importantly where did it come from and are you sure it's the genuine article?'

'He's one of my Paramount Chiefs in River State who I have to keep sweet.'

'He has it under a mildewing tarpaulin in his barn where he garages his other cars.'

Oscar continued, explaining about the Chiefs jolly to Dakar and the raffle at the celebration dinner.

'I don't know if he even bought a ticket or they were just part of the whole package, you know like a ticket at each table place at the end of rally banquet.'

Jim thought about the situation and suggested.

'It's probably not one of the three which took part but a spare, still a nice prize though.'

'If it's the 2007 model and it could be made to run you would have an eight-year-old rally classic that either finished or went to the last African Dakar Rally.'

Jim thought about it for a moment then went on.

'It could be worth quite a bit of money back home.'

Mac interrupted his relief's musings.

'What do you mean by quite a bit of money?'

'In tens of thousands I would have thought, as long as you return her in a pristine state.'

'At a classic car sale or auction people would be sure to pay top dollar if you have the paperwork to prove its authenticity, even if it's the spare.'

Mac stroked his bristly ginger beard and took another swig of his drink.

'Alright let's think about this,'

'According to our newly arrived expert.'

'We have something here that could be worth a small fortune back home.'

He paused for thought and then raising his hand to stop the other two interrupting.
'It will be nine years old in the New Year, has probably been rotting in that barn most of the time, and would take some work to get it right.'
Then he beamed through his facial hair.
'Just the sort of challenge I like.'
'Right Oscar what will the Chief want to get rid of it?'
There were a few moments of silence as Oscar put his mind to the idea of purchasing the Dakar Volkswagen Touareg from the Chief.

'I'm not sure how much he'll want.'

'He's had the glory out of it and I reckon he just wants rid of it now.'

Mac interrupted and got to the point

'We should between the two of us be able to raise enough Naira's to pay the Chief's price.'
Oscar shook his head.
'No, no, I reckon he won't be happy with that, he'll want Sterling, US Dollars or at a push Euros.'
Mac had nearly two years in Nigeria heading up the engineering side of the dredging company. He got paid in sterling into his UK bank account but received generous living expenses while in the Delta, he had plenty of loose Naira lying around as he rarely dipped into his expenses.
Oscar was in a slightly different position but would be able to access some foreign currency funds if the Chief was insistent. Like Mac he had a wad of Naira lying around.
Oscar looked over the other side of the table at Mac who was grinning with a twinkle in his eye. Oscar knew that look, the Scotsman was planning something outrageous.
He nudged Jim.

'That Jock bastard is scheming in that head of his and I'm not sure I'm going to like it.'

Mac spoke while grinning at his two compatriots.

'It'll be no good if you can't get the car, we'll not decide anything until you see if it can be done.'

'Either way there's nothing to lose and if my idea comes to fruition there'll be some fun and maybe even a bob or two in it for you and me.'

Oscar couldn't let his compatriot get away with not telling them and argued his case.

'Christ, you can't leave it at that, I need to know what you are planning if I'm going to buy the bloody thing.'

Jim pleaded with the Scotsman.

'Yes come on tell us what your idea is.'

'Can I get involved?'

'You can use your expertise and check out what a piece of machinery like that might be worth in good condition back in Europe. When you get home next week e-mail me some figures, we can decide if my idea is going to be worthwhile and has any chance of coming to fruition.'

The other two tried to argue with Mac but he stubbornly refused to tell any more, insisting that he didn't want to put Oscar's negotiations under any pressure, it would lessen the disappointment if these failed and they couldn't get hold of the Rally car.

Chapter 6

The Lunch

It had been mid-July when Mac suggested Oscar have a go at acquiring the Dakar Touareg Rally 2. It wasn't until nearly a month later in the first week of August he finally got a chance to approach the Paramount Chief at a local conference of big wigs at the Elkan Terrace Hotel.

It's rated the best hotel in Port Harcourt and Oscar's service company always invited all the important locals for a luncheon in the annual two-week break.

The two-week break is a rare phenomenon only seen in the south east of Nigeria. For a period of two to three weeks at the end of July, beginning of August every year, the monsoon rains recede before returning with a vengeance later in the month. The locals treat it as a bit of a holiday and hence the Agent's luncheon had over the years become a fixed function on the social calendar.

Oscar hadn't seen anything of Mac since their Saturday afternoon libations at the Port Harcourt Golf Club. There had just been a couple of e mails, one passed on from Jim about the possible sale values of a pristine Dakar Touareg Rally 2 in London or Paris and the other enquiring about any progress with buying the Rally Car.

Oscar liked the idea of trying to acquire the Rally car but was cautious about Mac's big idea, he suspected it could be fun but probably bloody risky as well. He had been busy since the afternoon in the Bar of the Port Harcourt Golf Club and had little time to think of a solution to how he was going to tempt the car's owner to relinquish possession of his Rally prize.

It wasn't until the buffet lunch that Oscar had time to approach the Chief in the hubbub of important guests and company executives. There was a mixture of dress, many of the Nigerians were dressed in their loose-fitting, colourful, cooler, local attire, while others were in good quality summer weight suits, most of which had been made by European tailors.

Oscar, the money man was busy answering questions and making promises of further individual meetings when the smiling Chief walked up to him with an invitation.

'Hi Oscar, can see you are busy.'

'Have you got a moment?'

'Of course, sir.'

The Chief grabbed Oscar's left shoulder lightly and leaned over to speak quietly into his left ear.'

'I'm in trouble with my ladies, it appears you've been forgotten when Chisaru's eighteenth birthday invitations were sent out.'

'That's all right s...'

Oscar was interrupted by the smiling Chief.

'Of course, it's not, we all want you to be there.'

'Tomorrow afternoon, about two.'

'She's off to London forty-eight hours later.'

'Off course sir, I'll be there, wouldn't miss it for the world.'

'That's fine then.'

The Chief released his grip on Oscars shoulder and made his way to another part of the room, while Oscar suddenly realised he was going to have to produce an appropriate present for an eighteen-year-old in less than twenty-four hours.

The following afternoon Oscar smartly attired in a newly pressed shirt, trousers and highly polished shoes drove up to the Chief and his family's compound. He had solved the present problem by scurrying round to a local jeweller earlier in the day. He didn't stint on the birthday girls' present and bought something smaller for her younger sister. The presents could all be written off against expenses and were worth their cost because they gave him a further chance to mix with the major players locally and nearly as importantly their spouses. Besides he might get the chance to broach the subject of the possible Touareg purchase.

There were few problems with parking in the Chief's compound thanks to recent resurfacing of the driveway and as if to help the celebrations the sun poked its head through the gradually receding, grey, monsoon clouds. In deference to all the important local dignitaries he parked his company car on the verge of the approach road outside the compound and made his way up to the bungalow, past the inviting open entrance to the barn.

He glanced in and was surprised to see the Rally Car uncovered and sat in the middle of the building. It was surrounded by several young men and girls, mainly dressed in fashionable European clothing, the young men favouring low cut jeans with their underwear poking above the waistband.

The front door to the house was open when he arrived, mature local people mainly dressed like yesterday in colourful local costume were milling in and out of the double doors. Oscar realised he might be the only non-local present and although well-known and greeted by many of the guests he felt a little uncomfortable. He was saved by the Chief's younger daughter Oroma, her little dog Aldi racing alongside her, who dashed out of the front door and grabbed him by his right arm.

'It might be Chisaru's day, but Daddy told me I have to look after you.'

Oroma dragged Oscar into her home tucking her left arm through his right in a proprietary manner.

She skipped alongside her bewildered guest, Aldi bouncing along beside her.

'You're to be my guest of honour.'

Oscar was baffled by the attention but pleased the Chief had thoughtfully appointed someone to look after him. It was easy to follow the young girls lead, she pulled him into the dining area and pointed out the buffet which was not only making the main dining table sag under the weight of the food but also covering every other available space in the large room. The Chief's wife was overseeing the catering company which was supplying the repast in honour of their elder daughter.

The Chief's spouse gave Oscar an effusive hug and apologised.

'I'm sorry I missed you last time, it's really nice you could come.'

'I hope you don't mind but my husband's appointed Oroma to look after you.'

She tousled her younger daughter's hair who protested.

'Mum please don't it's embarrassing.'

Oscar was surprised but pleased with the enthusiastic welcome, he was determined to ride his luck and persuade Oroma to take them out to see the Touareg.

He needn't have worried once he had received her mother's effusive greeting, Oroma led him briskly outside through the dining room's patio doors, her arm still proprietarily linked through his while Aldi raced ahead of them yapping furiously.

A lot of people were saying hallo as they passed but the teenager didn't stop leading him determinedly to the barn and through the young crowd surrounding the Rally car.

Letting go of his arm and spreading open her own arms Oroma said loudly.

'Well Oscar what do you think of this?'

At Oroma's exclamation, the youngsters surrounding their object of interest moved aside to allow the newly arrived couple a proper view.

There it was the mainly blue Touareg Rally 2 car in all its glory its Red Bull sponsorship clear to see, the VW decals on each side of the rear were almost in pristine condition.

Since his previous visit someone had been given the task of cleaning the car within an inch of its life. The bonnet had been lifted off to show the 2.5 litre, five-cylinder diesel engine. It looked immaculate, almost like new as if it had only just left the factory. The Carbon Compound bodywork meant there could be no rust, someone had replaced the rally tires, the normal road rubber looked a little out of place on such a beast.

Oscar admiring the rally car had done his research, he knew this machine had come out of research by Volkswagen, Audi and Porsche. All three had produced SUV's from the results of the combined work done by their teams.

There was movement behind him and Oroma, and all the youngsters who had been admiring the spotless car, moved back to make room for the smiling Chief and some of the other Ikwerre leaders who were accompanying him.

'Well Oscar what do you think of my raffle prize?'

'I've had her cleaned up and am thinking of putting her on the market.'

'Maybe I could even find a driver and sponsorship to run her in some of the African Rallies next year.'

'Well sir she's scrubbed up really well.'

'Does she go?'

'No Oscar, unfortunately not, I am sure she'll drive alright but I need a good specialist mechanic.'

'You don't want to take a special machine like this down the local garage, do you?'
He said temptingly, aware Oscar would have all the right contacts if he wanted to get the machine running.
'It's not the sort of car I would trust to a local establishment either sir.'
'I might be prepared to make you an offer.'
'That's only if you're really interested in selling.'
'I tell you what Oscar, you have a good look at the car and I'll think about your idea.'
'Would you mind if I took a couple of photographs,'
Oscar asked reaching into his pocket for his mobile phone.
'No of course not, please help yourself.'
'Oroma will look after you, please enjoy the party.'
He left with his accompanying band of Paramount Chiefs and they, in a group, chatting amiably, strolled back towards the house.
Oroma tugged at his arm as Oscar took his photographs.

'I can be a model like at the car shows,'
She said draping herself across the side of the machine.
She blushed, embarrassed at the giggling from some of the older girls surrounding them. Then to cover her confusion she asked.

'Oscar do you want to get inside the car?'

'The seats are tiny and moulded, they're not very comfortable, it's difficult you have to climb over a metal bar and there are all sorts of extra gauges, I don't know what they're all for.'
Oscar aware of Oroma's embarrassment and anyway wanting to look at the interior answered in the affirmative. He opened the nearside passenger door.
'Let's have a look and see.'
'You get in the driver's side.'
Once both were seated inside the Touareg, Oscar began to explain the interior to Oroma who was wriggling uncomfortably in the driver's seat. Meanwhile Aldi yapped at them no longer the centre of attention.
'All the extra gauges are to give the driver and co-driver extra information about how the car is performing.'
'The seats are moulded for the individuals I expect, it's due to the lengthy periods they spend in them when they're competing in a rally.'
Oscar climbed over the side roll bar and into the co-driver's seat, it was quite a snug fit, but he wasn't too uncomfortable. Except for the two seats and the extra instrumentation attached to the dashboard the cab of the Touareg was quite bare, there were many coloured electric wires taped with electrical tape disappearing into the rear of the machine but not much else. Everything looked trimmed down.

After explaining to Oroma what everything was used for, Oscar was persuaded to leave the intriguing machine and return to the bungalow.

His presents were greeted with lots of Oohs, Aahs and hugs from the two happy girls, Oroma was particularly pleased at being remembered and given the responsibility of looking after Oscar, she and Aldi never let him escape all evening. It was good for his male ego but didn't allow him much leeway to circulate and keep in touch with those of his contacts who were present.

Even so he considered the visit a success as he left the party, he felt he had planted the idea of buying the Chief's car, now it only remained for him to wait for the result and to inform Mac.

Chapter 7

Conflict Diamonds

Near the end of the party the host and Chief Kudo met at a pre-arranged meeting in the study of the bungalow. The blinds were drawn by the Chief who made sure he locked the door on the inside leaving the key in the lock in the unlikely possibility that someone else tried to gain entry either accidentally or deliberately.

He invited Chief Kudo to sit, opened a cabinet whose doors appeared to be a volume of books and offered the other Chief a drink. When he was served the Chief sat down behind his desk and spoke.

'Well I've set the bait with the agent, we'll see if he comes back with an offer, if he does I'll squeeze him hard for a good price.'

'The Scottish Engineer's contract is up in October, he's done his two years and a replacement has already been sorted, plus he's got a load of Naira he can't use elsewhere so he needs to lose that before he leaves.'

'But how does them buying the rally car help us get our diamonds into Europe?' asked Chief Kudo.

'If they acquire the car they're going to want to ship it in a container to Europe.'

'Shortly before it leaves we'll plant the diamonds in the framework of the Touareg.'

'When it gets to Europe it will be easy for one of our contacts to separate the car from our friend and then recover its precious cargo with negligible risk for us.'

'When will we get hold of the diamonds?'

'They came back on a Nigerian Red Cross Flight last Friday.'

'It was bringing back staff and unused resources from the Ebola outbreak in Freetown.'

Chief Kudo was of course excited by this news and voiced the obvious question.

'Where are they?'

'Can I see them?'

'Hold on let's get the business side of the deal out of the way first.'

The diamonds were locked up in their grubby bag in a safe behind one of the bookcases. The Chief intended gaining as much out of this gift as he could which is why he was pretending they had to buy the stones off a non-existent seller.

'We agreed to split the cost, I'll need your share of the money drafted into my account by Monday. I can put it into a holding account for payment next Friday when the diamonds will be released by the supplier's agent.'

'It's an awful lot of money,' complained Chief Kudo.

'We've been through all this before, we are investing in diamonds that are worth a small fortune as long as we deliver them to our cutter in Antwerp. We'll both be making at least ten times what we are paying the source in Freetown if we make a safe delivery and by using the Rally car we are mitigating the risk to us.

'Okay I know all that but how can we be re-assured.'

This annoyed the Chief how thick was this nincompoop, still if he was going to con the idiot, he the Chief better play along.

'That's the point you can't.'

'Fine that's settled, now I think we had better return to my daughter's party otherwise we'll both be unpopular with our wives.'

Chapter 8

The Decision

Arriving home just after midnight, Oscar e-mailed Mac about the party and the Chief's offer to sell the Rally 2 Touareg. Now the purchase was feasible Oscar added a note reminding the Dredging Chief Engineer of any suggestions on how to proceed before the negotiations took place.

Mac must have been having a late night as well because there was an almost instant reply suggesting a meeting later that day.

Oscar picked up the telephone in his rented apartment near the centre of Port Harcourt and rang the Scotsman.

After a number of rings, he was about to put the phone down when there was a change in tone and it automatically transferred to a mobile contact.

For a while as it continued to intermittently buzz at the other end of the line Oscar thought there was going to be no answer but just as he was about to return the portable phone to its cradle it was answered.

It was very noisy at the other end of the phone and sounded like a very loud engine was roaring in the background. There was another scratching noise as if someone was trying to adjust the phone when finally, Mac shouted down the line above the background noise.

'Who is it?'

'What do you want, decent people are in bed this late at night.'

'Well neither of us are, so what's your excuse?'

'Bloody generator on one of the dredging barges been playing up and they rang me just as I was about ready to go and meet a nice young lady in town.'

Knowing his friends' reputation with the ladies, Oscar couldn't bear to think of what nice young lady Mac might be referring to but replied.

'You said to meet today, when and where?'

'Golf Club say two thirty this afternoon.'

'Alright see you then, cheers.'

He put the telephone down and made his way to bed.

***

Later that day, just before the appointed time, Oscar arrived in a taxi at the Port Harcourt Golf Club. Mac was already there, Oscar didn't see him until when ordering a drink, the smiling Nigerian bartender Albert pointed to the grinning engineer in the far corner of the large room.

Oscar strolled past some late lunch diners and over to where Mac was holding up a large fresh, cool gin and tonic. Mac bowed and joked.

'Greetings o bearer of glad tidings.'

'Thanks, the car looked really good, it's been cleaned up ready for inspection.'

'Never mind that what's it like, will it go, is it any good?'

'Better than that the Chief allowed me to take some photographs.'

'It looks smashing, but the engine doesn't turn over.'

Oscar handed over his mobile, so Mac could look at the pictures. Mac studied them all closely before concluding.

'The battery's probably dead sitting there in the barn like that.'

'Well what's your plan?'

'Give us a moment.'

'Your photographs are good enough, they tell me most of it.'

'They've cleaned it up pretty good especially the engine, depends what damage has been caused inside though, it's sat for years in this hot and humid climate, not the best way to treat a piece of machinery.'

He scratched at his beard.

'Give us a minute while I think this through, then I'll tell you and you can let me know what thoughts you have.'

They both sipped at their gin and tonics, Mac passed the mobile back to Oscar and a glazed look came into his eyes as he mused over the problem.

After a minute or two he straightened his back and launched into his ideas.

'Bear with me, let me get the whole thing out first and then you can pick holes in my argument.'

'My two-year contract finishes in October when Jim takes over, I know the company are talking about January before they'll need me again something about eighteen months dredging the Mersey approaches.'

'You go back home for at least a month on leave about the same time I finish and you're always saying November's a crap time to go back to the UK so how about a bit of an adventure?'

'My Nigerian visa isn't out of time until mid-November.'

'After Jim arrives I've got time if necessary to finish off getting the job ready.'

'What job?'

'Patience, I propose we make his lordship an offer for the Dakar Rally Touareg Race 2, isn't it called?'

'Something like that.'

'If we get the chance we'll pay him with all those spare Naira we can't use, otherwise I'm prepared to sweeten the deal with some of my sterling savings back in the UK.'

'No doubt he'll have a bank account in some tax haven somewhere.'

'Then I want us to drive it back to Europe.'

Oscar was astounded at the idea, he hadn't expected this and looked across the table open-mouthed at the idea.

'Besides Jim's input, I've made some enquiries.'

'I think we can make a killing if we get it back to Paris or London.'

'It'll go down a bomb at one of them classic car rallies or something, I've even asked one of them big London auction houses and they're really interested.'

Only proviso is, we arrive with it in working order and done up neat.'

'What do you think?'

A thousand questions raced through Oscar's brain, the distance, visas, terrorists and the sheer weight of things to organise, he confided these misgivings to Mac.

Mac eschewing confidence laughed off Oscar's worries.

'You're the organiser you can fix the visas and everything, I've already sorted a route out, up north to Niger, keeping to the west to miss Boko Haram.'

Then when we're through Niger, there's the Algerian bit to the Med. If that isn't right, we'll go out west into Morocco. Then there's loads of ferries across to Spain or France.

'Should only take four days but we had best plan for a week.'

'Once we get the car I'll take it apart, get some new and spare wheels and it will be ready, I'll have it better than new.

'Oh, I do love a challenge.'

Mac's enthusiasm was infectious, Oscar laughed in response.

'But why can't you do it up and then we ship it home in a container.'

'Where's your sense of adventure?'

'What else would you be doing in dank bleak November back home?'

The more he thought about it the more Oscar liked the idea and like Mac said his enforced leave in the UK at the end of October didn't look to be much fun.

There was no longer any partner to go home to she hadn't wanted to follow him when Oscar was offered the contract in Nigeria and they had parted amiably. Everything he owned in the UK was at his parents in Ascot and after a year in the heat of West Africa he wasn't looking forward to the damp cold of Britain in October/ November.

After further thought and while replenishing their alcoholic refreshment Oscar returned from the bar drinks in hand and said to Mac.

'Alright I'll go for it, what have we got to do?'

'Smashing I knew you would see sense, I've already made a start.'

With that he fetched an old battered leather brown case from where it had been resting against the side of his chair and pulled out a red HP laptop.

'Give us a sec. while I power this up and I'll tell you what I've done.'

'First of all, we have to be able to buy the car.'

Oscar brightened at the mention of buying the car.

I can always pay more of his Facilitation fee in foreign currency, he'll like that. We've been told to hold back on foreign currency transactions, I've been giving nothing out. I've a fair amount I can apportion in the Chief's direction to sweeten the deal if necessary.

Oscar thought for a moment grimaced and continued.

'I hope we won't have to use any of our savings, mind you I suppose we can't lose, we'll either be making money on the sale of the Touareg or maybe we'll be bones in the desert for the vultures.'

For a while using Mac's laptop they investigated the possible routes north to the Mediterranean. There were a variety of choices, they both agreed they would have to keep an eye on the Boko Haram situation around Northern Nigeria and crossing the desolate border between Niger and Algeria.

Once they got to Abuja, Nigeria's capital, they had the choice of ploughing on straight north through Kano or if there were reports of Boko Haram playing up they would have to divert on the more westerly route through Sokoto.

It was decided that with his expertise Oscar as Mac had previously suggested would be responsible for their Algerian and Niger visas. The visas would entail a visit to Abuja to go to the Algerian and Niger consulates but as Oscar had to visit the Capital frequently because of his liaison work he should be able to achieve the visa requirements on one of those trips. They would need to decide on their travel dates before he could make their applications.

Mac was going to take responsibility for re-engineering the car, loading it with extra temporary fuel tanks, supplies and particularly water.

The only thing left to do was to persuade the Chief to let the Touareg go for an acceptable price.

They both agreed that Oscar would arrange a meeting if possible at the Chief's compound with Mac present. He wanted to ensure it was going to be possible to put the Rally car back on the road. It would be no good acquiring the vehicle if Mac couldn't get it fit for the journey they intended.

Finally, happy with their plans, Oscar made a final request of Mac.

'Let's buy the car sure, though I think we should keep our plans as secret as possible.'

'Why's that?'

I just think it would be good security, there's no point letting West Africa know there's a pair of thick Britishers driving through some of the roughest regions in the world.

Mac laughed.

'You could be right.'

'Agreed.'

They toasted each other and downed their drinks

Chapter 9

The Negotiation

Before leaving the bar, they looked for the first available date they could both get together and arrange an appointment with the Chief. It turned out they couldn't get together until the following Friday afternoon. Oscar agreed he would try and arrange the meeting with the Chief for them both at that time. He rang the Chief at his business office in Port Harcourt first thing on the Monday morning to try and arrange a convenient time. His suspicions weren't aroused, he was though mildly surprised when the Chief showed an eagerness to fit in with their plans. Oscar just thought the Chief must be keen to move the Touareg. A meeting time of two thirty was agreed and Oscar contacted Mac to tell him of the plan.

'I'll pick you up and we'll go together.'

'No it's alright I'll make my own way.'

Friday of that week Oscar arrived first at Chief's compound, he drove in ten minutes before the scheduled meeting in the middle of a heavy thunderstorm. The interior of his company car was lit up by huge flashes of lightning creating ghostly passages through the heavy rainfall. This was severely curtailing visibility and turning day into night, at times the car's headlights hardly penetrated the murk. Large claps of thunder rolled across the cloud base and the windscreen wipers struggled to cope, racing from side to side across the windscreen.

He parked in front of the barn, his headlights lit up the interior. In the forefront of the building sheltered from the rain was the Dakar Rally 2 Touareg in the same position as nearly a week ago. It still appeared clean and smart but for the seized engine it looked ready to go.

Ten minutes later the thunderstorm had eased, there was only light rain pouring from the very low, dark-grey clouds above his vehicle. Oscar left his car and walked into the barn, glancing at his watch. There was no sign of the Chief or his Scottish partner even though it was already five minutes after the appointed time of the meeting.

He was a bit surprised minutes later when he heard the roar of a heavy diesel from the lane outside. The cause of the loud engine pulled up in front of the compound entrance and Mac jumped down from the passenger side of the dirty white cab of a Scania truck. It had a hoist at the front of the vehicles loading bay. There was the dredger company decal on the door of the cab and the rear of the vehicle was empty.

Mac grinned as he walked into the compound.

'Hi sorry I'm late this thing is a beast to drive up this lane and if we are going to buy this car I needed someone who knew to work the crane on this bloody truck.' With a wave of his right hand he introduced the Nigerian truck driver sitting in his overalls in the driver's seat of the truck cab.

'Looks alright doesn't it.'

He continued making his way towards the Touareg in the front of the barn.

Oscar was fearful of Mac's confident approach and thought this might upset the Chief he cautioned his partner,

'Hang on, hang on, I haven't been up to the house yet, we had better see the Chief first.'

'Alright we'll see the old man first.'

They both made their way through the light rainfall towards the bungalow, by the time they reached the double fronted entrance doors Marcia already had the door open on one side and a pair of multi-coloured white fluffy towels to dry them off.

'Sir's in the study, I'm to take you through once you are ready.'

They both dried themselves and Mac combed his hands through his unruly mop while Oscar combed his damp hair back into order. Marcia led them through the house to the Office and once again knocked before opening the door and allowing the two ex-pats entry.

The Chief was on his feet to greet them and Oscar introduced his partner. The Chief hadn't met Mac before but knew of him. He started talking to Mac about the necessity of the dredging company in keeping the local waterways navigable

While they were getting to know each other, there was another knock on the door and Marcia re-entered with tea and coffee on a tray.

Mac was impatient to make a proper inspection of the Touareg but knew it was necessary to stay calm and observe the formalities. After nearly two years in the Delta he understood hospitality always came first. No business could be undertaken and any break with this tradition would be frowned upon.

Still this took a while and his impatience must have shown when the Chief commented on Macs concerns.

'Eager to start I see.'

'No sir, well that is if we're going to buy the car I've got only a limited time to put it onto the truck.'

'It has to be back at the depot by five thirty otherwise I'm paying the driver's overtime out of my own pocket.'

'That's fair enough let's go and have a look, shall we?'

The Chief led the way out of the bungalow and down to the barn.

The Chief was a bit disappointed he hadn't expected them to take the vehicle immediately, he had really wanted to arrange the sale and have time to secrete the conflict diamonds before they arranged to take the Touareg away.

On reaching the car Oscar wanted to look at one thing only and after a few minutes inspecting the engine he was satisfied.

The two of them had previously agreed that Oscar would do the negotiating so when he got up from inspecting the vehicle Mac grabbed his partner's arm and shocked both him and the Chief.

'One million Naira, here now cash today.'

He reached into his back pocket and pulled out a wad of Nigerian currency.

'No arguing no quibbling, 1 million right now and we'll load it up and be gone within the next thirty minutes.'

Oscar mouth agape stared at his Scottish partner while the Chief looked wildly about him.

Then Mac threw in another shocker by threatening the Chief while waving his one million Naira wad in front of them.

'If you want to haggle over it we'll start at half that tomorrow, that's only five hundred thousand and we'll give you the money by banker's draft, you'll have to declare it to the Nigerian tax man.'

'Five minutes to think about it and then we'll be gone and start again tomorrow at half as I said, take it or leave it.'

'Come on Oscar we'll wait outside the barn and give the Chief his five minutes.'

Mac pulled at Oscar's arm dragging him away from the barn leaving the shocked Chief to his own thoughts.

Oscar whispered to his companion who was pointedly looking at his wristwatch.

'Bloody hell what are you doing mate?'

'How much is a million Naira anyway?'

'My brain is addled after that.'

Mac grinned.

'Not as much as you think, £3330 at this morning's exchange rate but I can't take it home, it's just burning a hole in my pocket.'

'Anyway, what do you reckon?'

'Do you think it's a goer?'

Oscar had got over his initial surprise.

'Don't know if it'll work but it shocked the old bastard, it was really funny, he never closed his mouth, he looked like a fish out of water.'

Back in the barn the Chief was truly shocked at the Scotsman's brashness and trying to gather his wits. He had different thoughts some quite positive.

One million Naira was a bit less than he hoped for, it was cash and all under the table.

Perhaps though it would be better idea not to plant the Diamonds too early there were enough tribesmen in the shipping offices down in Port Harcourt to keep him informed when the two Brits intended to ship the car.

Mind made up he went to find the two men to close the deal.

'Alright it's a deal.'

Mac pulled two sheets of paper out of his shirt pocket.

'Thanks Chief just sign these for us.'

'It says we've bought and own the car, it doesn't say the price.'

The Chief tried to keep a smile on his face but seethed inwardly the blasted Scotsman had thought of everything and in the Chief's own back yard as well.

Money and receipt exchanged they parted at the barn the Chief returning to the bungalow. He said he had work to do in his office, he didn't really want to watch the departure of his raffle prize.

Like a pair of children Mac and Oscar both grinned from ear to ear careful not to celebrate in sight of the Chief. Even so Oscar couldn't help himself and punched Mac lightly on the arm.

Mac shouted to the truck driver to reverse his machine up to the barn. In less than thirty minutes the Rally Car was loaded up onto the back of the truck and on its way to the engineering shop at the Dredging Company's base.

Oscar took his pal back there while they discussed the future and congratulated him on such an audacious move. There was a lot of laughter when Mac commented on the Chiefs expression when he presented the already printed receipts.

Oscar resolved to get up to Abuja as soon as possible and requested Mac's passport not unsurprisingly the Scotsman had it already to hand fully expecting the day's result.

'I haven't checked yet, I'll see what other things we need and then I'll give you a bell.'

Chapter 10

The Preparation

After much research Oscar concluded the only way to obtain visas for the passage through Niger and Algeria was to use an agency. The nearest Embassy and Consulate for Niger was in Accra, the capital Of Ghana, five hundred miles and two flights away. There was no way he could get the time off to make his way over there, nor could he afford the waiting around time either. On top of this was deciding when they were likely to travel as it was an entry requirement with both countries that they supply copies of confirmed hotel bookings.

After a brief meeting with Mac to complete his application electronically, supply bank statements, copies of vaccination certificates and passport photographs, Oscar was in position to arrange their visas.

They agreed their travel dates expecting to leave Port Harcourt on Monday 2nd November and tentatively anticipating arrival in Niger on Thursday the 5th. They were going to allow three days to reach the top end of Nigeria in case there were any teething problems with the car, also to give enough time to divert if Boko

Haram was causing trouble. Oscar allowed another four days for travelling through Niger before crossing into Algeria. They expected they could traverse Niger in three.

With both submissions complete, Oscar couriered everything to a visa service company who would be able to sort out the necessary documentation.

Except for this brief meeting they didn't get another chance to meet up until a rowdy birthday party a couple of weeks later at the Golf Club.

Mac looked like he had started the celebrations early, he was well inebriated, and Oscar had to drag him out of the noisy main room to give him the latest information. Oscar couldn't wait to find out how far Mac had got on with the repair and renovation of the Touareg.

'I've got all the paperwork back it was returned last week and everything is good to go.'

'That's alright then you've done your bit and I've nearly done my part.'

He paused for a moment, as if for effect.

Mac staggered a bit and leaned against the panelled wall of the corridor in which they stood. He raised his right finger to his lips peering around as if he had something confidential to tell and slurred.

'Shhh.'

'Alright, alright, what?'

'The Touareg's ready.'

Oscar laughed, pleased.

'Great what's the secret?'

'Don't want to make the Chief envious, he might be jealous and sabotage it.'

He emphasised the point again by putting his right forefinger to his lips.

'Shhh.'

Oscar laughed jovially at his partners antics.

'When can I try the car?'

'I'll need to try it out before we depart, won't I?'

'Yeah alright, I'll fix something, now let's get another drink I'm thirsty.'

It had been a fraught few days for Oscar not everything he was meant to keep under control had been going well. There was a threatened refinery strike over Christmas and some of the Chiefs were in near revolt over the lack of foreign currency.

'What the hell.'

He thought draining his glass and following Mac.

'We'll be out of here in just over a month, everything else can wait.'

The Chief had been making his own plans and was holding an impromptu meeting. He had calmed the protest of Chief Kudo who wanted to see some action towards getting a return on his investment.

The Chief had by offering a decent financial incentive, plus implied threats cultivated a contact with one of the local engineers in the dredging company's engineering workshop. This enabled him to be kept in touch with the progress of the Touaregs restoration.

The Chief did wonder why they were making it so roadworthy when he expected the pair to ship the machine back to Europe in a container. He put it down to the vehicle being made more saleable.

His informant had surprised him even more a couple of days ago when he told the Chief about added fuel and water tanks. The uncomfortable rally seats had been torn out and replaced with more comfortable furniture from a scrapped Volkswagen. This didn't make sense and the Chief began to wonder what he had been missing.

***

Although Mac had boasted at the golf club party about the Touareg being ready to go it wasn't for another ten days on the 14th October that Mac rang Oscar and arranged for them to meet at the airport.

Oscar was impatient to see the re-constituted rally vehicle and it was a relief finally to reach the airport relief road and at its end the airport car park.

The car park was practically empty, at the far end a smiling Mac was standing in front of the renovated Rally 2 Volkswagen Touareg, accompanied by a four by four and trailer.

As Oscar approached the Touareg, his heart thumped with excitement and in expectation. It looked immaculate almost as if it had just been released by the factory in Germany. Their planning and division of labour was about to come to fruition.

He pulled up close but not too close he wanted to get the full effect and his company car would only spoil the view.

Mac walked over to Oscar as he exited his car and slapped him on the back.

'What do you think?'

'Wow.'

Together they walked over to the Rally Car, the first impression hadn't failed him. It did look like it had just come out of the factory ready for the 2007 Dakar Rally. Oscar walked round the car slowly, he could smell the fresh paint and that of a newly renovated engine. Oscar admired the work, somehow Mac had resourced the correct Decals and it looked just like the photographs from that era.

Mac smiled and asked again, knowing the answer from the enthusiastic grin spread across Oscar's face.

'What do you think then?'

Oscar answered with a question of his own.

'How did you get all the stuff to make it look so right?'

'You can buy anything on the net nowadays, if you know where to look.'

'That's why it took so long I've been waiting for all sorts of bits and pieces to be flown in.'

Mac talked through where he had acquired all the kit, he thought the car wouldn't have been numbered being the spare, he had re-numbered it 301 anyway.

All the advertising was on the blue car, the two side, top and bonnet Red Bull decals, the silver VW in its requisite circle, the high Castrol, the yellow Luk and the BT were all there. Mac pointed to the driver's names in white on the doors and caused Oscar to laugh and thump Mac playfully in his chest.

'You've got to be joking?'

'No.'

Instead of the Chief and his wife's names, Mac had arranged for their names to be stencilled one above the other on the two doors in white lettering.

'Get in and have a look around.'

Like a child in playground Oscar clambered over the roll bar onto the driver's seat and peered into the rear of the car. Mac was describing to Oscar what he could see in the interior of the Touareg.

'I've replaced the front seats with something more comfortable. I haven't chucked them just arranged for them to be shipped home. I've kept the rally style seat belts for safety reasons.'

'I've boarded out the rear but only after I added an extra fuel tank which fits the contours of the car.'

'The plastic white tank is for water there's baffles in it to stop the water surging and upsetting the stability of the car.'

'There's not much space for baggage, because I'm at the end of contract all my kit is being shipped home anyway'

'As well as the seats, I've arranged to ship everything I've taken out of the car back home, we can put it back into its rally sate before auctioning it then.'

'I've taken every bit of the engine apart and rebuilt it, there was hardly a need for any parts, the stuff it had already was pretty good because it had hardly been used.'

'What do you reckon then Oscar?'

'Do you want to give it a go?'

'Bloody right.'

Mac gave Oscar the key, by this time a small crowd of onlookers had been attracted to the colourful car at the far end of Port Harcourt Airport. Mac had to wave them back as Oscar started the Touareg's engine, it emitted a hearty roar, when he revved the engine. Mac leapt into the passenger seat alongside and instructed his partner to take it out along the main road but gently at first because the accelerator, clutch and brake pedals were highly sensitive.

The crowd parted quickly when Oscar trying out the brakes shuddered to a halt as he stalled the engine.

'Bloody hell you weren't kidding about sensitivity, were you?'

Mac tightening his seat belt laughed at Oscar's outburst.

'We'll soon get used to it, after a few miles in the local traffic we'll be like veterans.'

Oscar concentrated as the onlookers disappeared in his rear-view mirror, he found the driving seat quite comfortable and very secure. The double strapped orange rally seat belts making him feel extremely safe, they were noticeable but didn't appear to discomfort him in any way.

Taking advantage of the near empty airport road, he effortlessly accelerated up to sixty miles per hour, the Touareg responded quickly and with hardly a murmur from its 2.5 litre TDI engine. By the time they returned to the car park and parked the small crowd had dispersed. Mac could check on Oscar's progress. Oscar could reassure the other on the progress of their visas and other permissions. The agency in London had couriered the Algerian paperwork back to him the previous week and he had been promised the Niger documentation within the next few days.

They loaded the vehicle back onto Mac's trailer and he returned the Touareg to the safety of the dredging company's workshop.

***

That night the Chief travelled into Port Harcourt and to a dingy bar down one of the darkened side streets to the west of the Aba Expressway. He parked the family runabout close by a working lamp post casting a yellow glow in the evening twilight. To secure his vehicle he paid off a grubby local urchin boy to keep an eye on the car. The boy sat down cross-legged on an old truck tire to the side of a lamp post to look after the vehicle. The Chief made his way through a grubby dark red curtain into the bar, local Bayelsa dance music greeted him, a few couples were dancing on the small wooden dance floor to his left while to his right the main part of the bar's lighting came from surrounds of the wooden bar top which went the length of the bar.

He made his way around the dance floor and to an almost enclosed booth with four seats on the rear wall. Taking a seat, he was soon approached by a thin emaciated girl carrying a tray. She was clothed in little more than a thigh high red, mini dress and four-inch heels.

She leaned closely across him while lighting a nightlight waxed into a porcelain white ashtray. He tried not to wince as he got the whiff of her cheap perfume and stale sweat.

The candle lit she remained in position and he could just see down the plunging neckline to her braless chest, before she could say anything he spoke.

'Two beers and no I'm not interested in what you have to offer before you ask.'

'Yes sa-ah.'

She straightened, she wasn't offended and at least she didn't have to ask, mind you she wouldn't have minded, he looked a better class of gentleman than normally frequented the establishment.

The two beers arrived quickly and when the girl left, a shadow separated itself from the far end of the bar and sidled across before sliding into the booth opposite the Chief.

'Beer there.'

Uttered the Chief quietly leaning across the table separating them.

'What have you got for me?'

The heavily built guy had a thin cotton jacket over his dark blue boiler suit which hid the badge on its chest pocket, he spoke to the Chief.

'The car is ready, but I haven't heard when they're shipping it.'

'He took it out on a trailer this afternoon.'

'Yes, I'm aware, he showed it to his agent chum out at the airport.'

'They're going to do something shortly; my bosses are changing; the Scottish Engineer finishes in about a fortnight.'

The Chief was pleased they finally appeared to be closing in on the end game.

'Good now have you thought any more about where you can secrete my package?'

'That's easy, there's a plastic tank in the rear of the car, it's been added, I can hide something of the size you described in there.'

'Are you sure it will be invisible?'

'Yeah it's opaque, dark green plastic and fixed in position.'

'What's it for?'

'Don't know and like I told you, they've got rid of the rally seats and put more comfortable ones in.'

The Chief reached into his back pocket and pulled out the oilskin bag containing its precious haul which was now about to undertake another International journey.

He pushed the bag across the table with his left hand and from his trouser right trouser pocket hauled out a brown envelope containing a decent wad of Naira, this followed the diamonds as both were quickly disposed of and hidden in two voluminous pockets of the boiler suit.

The Chief spoke quietly.

'There's a bonus if the parcel reaches its destination.'

'But!'

The Chief reached across and grabbed his compatriot's left wrist fiercely before snarling.

'Your life is not worth mucking me about.'

'No tricks.'

'No looking in the bag.'

'Just do what I've paid you for.'

'Understand!'

The man was really scared now the Chief had a reputation for dealing severely with those that let him down.

'Yes sir.'

At this and aware his reputation was enough to ensure his wishes were carried out, the Chief rose threw some money on the table.

'That's to pay for the beers, you can have both.'

The Chief departed and returned to his vehicle satisfied with the result of his evening, he was concerned about the changes his contact had informed him about but didn't think they could be especially important.

Chapter 11

The Leaving Do

Two weeks later, on the Saturday evening the thirty first of October, Mac held a leaving do for all and sundry at the Port Harcourt Golf Club. He splashed out most of his remaining Naira on refreshments for at least a hundred people and as it was open house, a lot of the local tribal head men turned up with their entourages. Most of them knew Mac from his company's dredging of canals through the mangroves of the Delta and River State, which had impinged on everyone's lives at one time or the other.

The Chief, his wife and two daughters, Chisaru having recently returned from her birthday trip to London had been invited to the celebrations. It was Mac's way of saying thanks for the Touareg.

He also wanted the Chief particularly, to find out in person about their proposed expedition with the Touareg.

Meanwhile unknown to the two ex-pats the Chief's acolyte had easily placed the diamonds at the bottom of the water tank while working on nights the week before. There was plenty of security outside the dredging company's compound but none once you were past the security guard at the gated entrance. The Chief on his way to the Golf Club driving the family in the pristine Jaguar was concerned. He still had no idea how Oscar and Mac were going to dispose of the Touareg. Even now there were no reports from any of the local agents about the Rally Car being booked onto a ship, nor had either Oscar or Mac ordered a container to transport the vehicle.

He couldn't understand what was going on, this was a rarity, he never normally allowed himself to end up in the sort of position, where he had lost control of a situation.

It was also getting difficult to keep Chief Kudo happy, wh could see little progress was being made towards a return on the investment. Even worse he made a caustic comment about the lack of progress and loss of control of the situation. Chief Kudo used his night club in Port Harcourt to run nefarious activities all over the Delta and wasn't likely to forgive the Chief if something went wrong. The latter was having misgivings about involving the night club owner and was beginning to wish he hadn't been so greedy.

Early in the evening, an Ikwerre Chief whose tribal area included the Dredging compound made a small speech and thanked Mac for his contribution over the previous two years. Too much ribald comment from some of the workers Mac stood up and made himself visible to all by standing on a chair. He offered up his thanks for the help and cooperation of everyone locally during his time in the Delta and acknowledged the hard work of the other workers at the Dredging Company.

When he never mentioned the rally car, a chant went up from some of the more rowdy and inebriated members of the crowd.

'The car, the car, what's happening to the car?'

The Chief who was standing next to his wife watching the presentation, was also very interested and waited fraught with concern.

Mac held up his hand and hushed the audience, he paused for a moment as if for greater effect. He was trying to think how he was going to explain their plans. Then he thought, 'sod it,' and gave his audience their answer.

'Oscar and I are driving it home and we're leaving on Monday.'

He grinned at his audience and promptly stepped down from the chair.

There was a moment of stunned silence before the room erupted into an avalanche of noise as everyone started to speak at once.

When people realised what Oscar and Mick were proposing there was a lot of debate for and against the idea. There were a few who thought it sounded like a great adventure and good for them. The consensus was what with the Muslim army of Boko Haram to the north, the possible Al Quaeda outpost in the south of Algeria, never mind the bloody Sahara itself, the pair of them must be crazy, stupid or both.

Mac went over to Oscar put his right arm over his partners shoulder and squeezed playfully.

'That's got them talking, hasn't it?'

'I wish you hadn't, some of them look really upset, observe the Chief for instance, he looks like you told him you were screwing one of his daughters.'

'I only wish.'

They couldn't talk together any more as they were being crowded by people who wanted to ask about their proposed expedition.

The Chief was fuming, all his plans were thrown awry by the latest news. There wasn't going to be time, or any chance of recovering the diamonds. The Touareg was in its secure position in the Dredging Company's compound and there was no way of getting close to it before Monday morning. Desperately thinking as to how he could recover the situation, he listened to those asking the questions about the Saharan expedition and gained a lot of the answers he was going to need.

Having got all, he could from the question and answer session that was taking place he moved outside to the Golf Club veranda and sat down away from the noise of the party to work things through in his mind.

He wasn't one to panic but needed to look at the pros and cons of the situation. In allowing the diamonds to make their way to Europe overland this might turn to his advantage after all, there might be less of a risk than the original chances of the thieving dockworkers stripping the Touareg before it even left Nigeria.

After about half an hour of uninterrupted thought he came to a decision it would mean choosing the right people and making the preparations rapidly, but it was possible and would have to be done.

Powering up his mobile from alongside his now empty glass on the table in front of him he called Damilola his niece.

'Damilola I know you've been sitting on your arse spending my hard-earned cash since you returned, I've an urgent job for you.'

'But sir, I've…'

The Chief interrupted.

'No buts, I know about your hidden proclivities. I know you're practising your odious ideas with the wife of the Detective Chief Inspector from the Central Police Station.

There was a loud noise of complaint from the other end of the phone which the Chief answered.

'You wouldn't want him to find out, would you?'

Damilola pleaded with her Uncle.

'Please you can't tell him, he would kill us.'

The Chief listened and let his niece's pleadings subside.

'I'm pleased you've got that out of your system.'

'Now say your goodbyes, get a good night's sleep you're going to need it because you'll be busy for the next couple of weeks or so.'

'Oh, by the way, her husband.'

'I suppose she's told you he's working really late questioning that supposed murderer from Ogbogoro, well the poor sod has coughed to it a couple of hours ago.'

'I reckon he'll be getting charged about now, I suspect your girlfriend's other half will be on his way home shortly.'

There was more upset from the other end of the phone and sounds of a hurried explanation to the lady concerned.

'Oh, and Damilola I need you fully fit and healthy, so please don't get caught.'

'That would mean you upsetting me, I would be even angrier, you don't want to know the consequences of annoying me.'

The Chief concluded with that thought and ended the call.

He wasn't happy having to use a woman but at the last minute like this he didn't feel he had much choice, having to keep those with a knowledge of the diamonds to a minimum. He also was one of the few to know about Damilola's lesbian tendencies and therefore had the perfect hold over her.

Going back inside to the party he went and said goodbye to the two British ex-pats before arranging for his wife and daughters to make their way home in a taxi. His daughters were upset at him for leaving but his wife was used to this, she believed her husband was going off to amuse himself with a young lady somewhere.

Having fulfilled his responsibilities to the family and his hosts, he made his way outside to the white Jaguar.

Chapter 12

The Chief's Watching Brief

The Chief wouldn't have cared if he knew about his wife's thoughts but those and a visit to a young female were the last thing on his mind.

He drove the Jaguar into the heart of Port Harcourt City's red-light district and parked across the road from a night club advertising loud music, pole dancing and other delights. The clubs name was lit up in different coloured lights above a pair of black swing doors.

Either side of these were posted two very large bouncers dressed in black trousers and black short-sleeved, collared shirts. Each man must have weighed in at around one hundred and eighty kilogrammes, the one on the right side of the doors was the older and taller but had a pronounced beer belly that spoke of too much consumption of the local Grand Lager.

The other bouncer was slightly smaller but even more imposing his shirt buttons strained by the heavy muscled upper torso within.

There was a queue of customers awaiting entry, the club being popular and extremely busy. The Chief walked to the head of the column and the elder bouncer half bowed and held one of the doors open for the august personage.

'Sir.'

The Chief nodded his head in acknowledgement and made his way inside. He could hear the stifled protests of the intended customers in the queue outside. He didn't think anything of it, just accepted the privileges of someone with his status.

Inside the door there a scantily dressed young girl sitting behind a desk waiting to take the entry payments.

'Are you a member sir?'

'No young lady but I'm not here to enjoy myself, I'm here to see the owner.'

He smiled at the girl.

'We have some business to discuss, he isn't expecting a visit, he'll want to see me though.'

'Who shall I say is here?'

Asked the receptionist picking up the phone on her desk.

He told her and waited patiently, he could hear and feel the heavy throbbing beat of the music the other side of a heavy black curtain. It separated the foyer from the night club and did little to hold the smoke back from cigarettes and other less legal substances.

A young couple hanging onto each other in a passionate embrace caused an increase in the loudness of the beat as they passed through the heavy curtain intent on exiting the club. She squealed loudly as her partner squeezed her bottom, just below the short skirt which only covered half her buttocks.

The cashier/receptionist put down her phone after having described the Chief to someone at the other end of the line.

'Sir he's upstairs in his office and someone is being sent down to show you the way.'

The noise increased again when the entry curtain was pushed back again and the owner of the club, Chief Kudo, his arms outstretched stepped through and hugged his associate.

'Welcome to the business.'

'Come on through, let's go to my office, what can I do for you, nothing wrong I hope?'

He turned and led the way into the club without giving the Chief a chance to answer this effusive greeting.

The Chief followed the owner across his premises, the club was hot and noisy. It was packed to the rafters and visibility was poor due to the apparent lack of ventilation. Smoke hung heavily under the low, black-painted ceiling.

They skirted the dancers, passing between drink laden tables and couples in, kissing and fondling each other. A Disc Jockey stood behind a bunch of strobe-lit speakers, urging the crowds of dancers to a greater frenzy.

At the far end of the room the Chief could just make out the lengthy bar crowded with queuing would-be customers. The other side of the bar in another room, there were almost naked dancers clinging to their poles while sweating men ogled their nubile bodies.

They were soon in the owner's office and the noise died abruptly once the insulated door was closed. The room was imposing, at one end was a large desk surrounded by chairs. On the nearside wall were four closed circuit televisions one covering the entrance, the others viewing the bar, the pole dancing area and the part of the club encompassing the Disc Jockey. A security guard sat at a small table watching the screens while occasionally making notes in a notebook in front of him. The room was clean, dimly lit, windowless and cool from two heavy duty air conditioners.

The Chief expressed his surprise.

'Didn't realise you had everything as organised as this.'

Chief Kudo answered with a chuckle.

'All bases covered, it's sometimes useful to know who is interested in whom, you might say.'

'Take a seat.'

He indicated a comfortable black armchair to the front of the large dark hardwood desk behind which was a chunky dark brown leather covered swivel desk chair into which the owner settled himself.

'Now first things first, what do you want to drink?'

The Chief opted for a cola and at that the owner picked up a telephone hand set and placed the order.

'Now to what do I owe the pleasure, I hope our investment is safe?'

The Chief looked behind him at the man watching the CCTV.

'Is your guard safe?'

'Yeah, he's deaf, sees a lot and hears nothing, just what I need in my office.'

The Chief explained the problem he needed someone immediately to accompany Damilola and keep an eye on the Scotsman and his partner through the African part of the journey.

He explained that the person they used would share the workload with his representative Damilola. They must be Nigerian and therefore wouldn't require visas for Algeria or Niger. They must be trustworthy, clever and know how to handle a firearm because the Chief didn't intend to send their representatives into that cauldron without some sort of security.

'If it's not going to be safe can't we get the parcel back?'

'It's too much of a risk, it's too late to break into the Dredger Company's compound and the chances of successfully robbing them on the road are worse.'

Chief Kudo's friendly mood changed, he rose from his chair and started waving his arms in agitation, his anger caused the muscles on his face to tighten and he raised his voice in fury and screamed at the Chief.

'What the hell have you got us into?'

'That's a hell of a lot of money I've got invested in this,'

The Chief concerned about his partner's not unexpected reaction tried to return to his idea for resolving the situation.

'I fully understand your concern but whatever way we try to get the diamonds to Belgium, you knew it would still be a risk.'

My idea is, we have our own team to help the Brits on their way if necessary and I'll supply Damilola if you'll find someone else who's really able to handle himself.'

Chief Kudo sat back down although leaning forward in his seat, his anger simmering and only partly abated.

'Alright I get it.'

'I'm not happy though.'

'I've got the ideal man, just out of University, did his degree through the Nigerian Army, he's had one or two problems with some senior staff in the Officer's mess and they don't want him anymore.'

'Who is he?'

'You've just seen the lad, Kinikanwo the younger one on the door outside.'

'Well let's get him in and have a word.'

'I'll have the word,'

'He'll work with your niece no problem.'

The club owner put down his marker in insisting he briefed his man thus enforcing his right to be treated as an equal.

'I can supply him with some sort of firepower, what sort of transport are you going to give them?'

The Chief had thought of this on the way over.

I can get hold of a recently serviced Land Rover Discovery, the 2012, three-litre, V6 edition.'

'It has all the power, four-wheel drive, and it's like new.'

'It belongs to my father who is struggling with Alzheimer's it's hardly been used.'

'At least it will put some mileage on it, I think it's done less than two thousand.'

They agreed they would meet with their two representatives at the Chief's around ten o'clock the following day when they would finalise their arrangements.

At that moment a scantily clad waitress knocked and entered the office bearing the Chief's coke on a round metal tray.

Chief Kudo existed out on the edges of society where he was involved in many dodgy and violent dealings. The Chief didn't want to upset the man further or give him the opportunity to take control, he waved his arm and got up out of his seat.

'Thanks, but I'll pass on the drink, get home and get some sleep.'

'It's going to be a busy day tomorrow.'

Chapter 13

The Matriarch

The Chief's wife was surprised to find him at home when she arrived back from the Golf Club with their daughters. He was not in a good temper and after snapping at a minor infringement by Oroma everyone quickly retired to bed with few goodnights. His wife tried to placate him in the bedroom, at first, he rebuffed her advances still fuming at his best laid plans going awry. He felt embarrassed and was sure he looked like a fool to Chief Kudo and was worried about the others reaction.

He was finally placated, his mind taken elsewhere by the obvious attractions and amorous efforts of his wife, in the end he slept soundly and was brightly awake at eight on the Sunday morning.

After a brief breakfast and a fresh cup of black coffee he was on the road across town to his parents. Although they were still alive his father's Alzheimer's meant he had to relinquish his title to his son on the onset of his horrible illness, about five years previously.

It only took about twenty minutes, to make it across town to the north of the city, that early on a Sunday morning. The Chief turned into a compound which housed a colonial style two storey house in white. It had an upper balcony all around the upper storey. The Chief could see his mother sitting on a garden seat outside. It was relatively cool; the sky was almost cloudless; the sun had only just cleared the tops of the tropical trees surrounding the grassy compound.

By the time he reached the front door of the house, his mother was waiting there to greet him, he hugged her.

'How's father?'

She replied with a shrug of her shoulders, a noticeable sign of defeat in the frown in the contours of her aging facial features 'Not too good.'

The Chief first acted dutifully and climbed the dark wooden stairs to the first-floor landing. He walked across to enter his father's bedroom. A small nurse in a light blue uniform stood back politely as the Chief entered the bedroom. He indicated she should return to her seat and went over to his father lying under a white sheet on the king size bed.

He was ignored and disappointingly the Chief realised his wizened parent didn't recognise him anymore. He could now understand his mother's shrug.

One thing he wouldn't feel so guilty about was removing his father's Land Rover Discovery, it was obvious the Old Man didn't have long for this world and would never be able to use it again.

Returning to the Ground Floor and on entering the kitchen he found his mother brewing fresh coffee for the pair of them and sat down on a high stainless-steel stool with white melamine seat at the similarly white breakfast bar.

His mother was astute and didn't give him a moment to settle, before demanding an answer.

'Right what's going on?'

Her husband might have given up his rights to the son as a Chief in the Ikwerre tribe but this diminutive woman with her greying afro still considered herself to be the matriarch of the family. For all she only stood around one point five metres and weighed in at fifty kilogrammes the whole clan including the Chief were frightened to death of this woman, his mother.

'I need the Discovery immediately and can't promise when you'll get it back.'

'You can have the Discovery but something's gone wrong with the movement of the diamonds, hasn't it?'

The Chief answered uncertainly, wondering how she could possibly know about the contraband.

'Well yes.'

He went on to explain to his mother the present crisis and the way he was going to try and resolve the situation. After reprimanding him for the Chief's and his colleague's ineptitude his mother sat herself on another bar stool on the opposite side of the breakfast bar from her son head in hands and thought through the situation.

Her son sipped at his thick black brew and waited, he daren't interrupt the thoughts of this woman who had not only bore him and his siblings but commanded the family since the day as a sixteen-year-old newlywed, she had become the wife of the thirty-year-old Chief of the Ikwerre tribe.

After a few moments she lifted her head and looked her son straight in the eyes.

'Are you sure you cannot recover the diamonds from this Rally Car before it leaves and without anyone knowing?'

'It's possible.'

'It would almost certainly result in some mishap and because of our close connection some of the mud would be sure to stick.'

'Alright you can't recover them now, when and how were you going to get them back eventually, assuming the car makes it to Europe unscathed?'

'We're not bothered about robbing them over there, they'll have to stop and sleep sometime, so we'll just retrieve the stones then.'

'Besides they're taking all the risk, unbeknownst to them.'

There'll be no suspicion that the family had anything to do with it either.'

'How will you do that?'

'I will, I'll be in Spain at Almeria or Marseilles in France when their ferry docks in Europe.'

The Chief explained how he would deliver the diamonds personally to the jewellers contact in Antwerp. It would be safe because of the open borders thanks to the Schengen agreement. He intended flying into Paris or London once he knew the Touareg had crossed into Algeria then he could be ready to go wherever they were going to land on the Continent.

His mother all business now, not liking the situation but prepared to go along with the idea asked.

'Have you thought about what equipment your two followers are going to need?'

'Not really, not yet, haven't had much of a chance.'

'Well one thing you are going to need is a satellite phone because there's going to be no mobile phone masts crossing the desert where they're going.'

The Chief smacked his head with the palm of his right hand.

'Why didn't I think of that?'

'Where the hell am I going to get one of those on a Sunday of all days?'

'That's not difficult I'll get hold of the chair of Central Dynamics, he'll get me one, he has always fancied me, and I can wrap him round my little finger.'

The Chief didn't say but thought,

'I bet she can.'

'If it weren't for my father there would be a bunch of man friends queued up outside her front door.'

He smiled at his mother.

'Thanks, when do you think I can collect it?'

The lady preened herself sitting up on the barstool and pushing her fingers through her hair smiled and coyly whispered.

'Oh once I get on the phone I think I can safely say it will be here for you to collect by mid-afternoon.'

The Chief glanced at his watch and realised he was going to be late for the meeting back at his office in the bungalow.

'Got to go mother, where's the Discovery keys.'

'Oh no you don't I want to check out your personnel and make sure they're up to the job.'

'You get back, I'll bring it, I'll only be five minutes behind you.'

The Chief dashed out of the parental home and raced to his Jaguar while setting his mobile to ring his wife.

Gasping down the phone as he roared away from his parents.

'Darling, Damilola and two others are due at the house any moment.'

I know was the reply, 'I've given them coffee on the patio, where are you?'

'Just left the parents and here's the bad news, mother's coming over, she will be five minutes behind me.'

The Chief held the mobile away from his ear as some choice unladylike language boomed through the ether. There was a pause in the diatribe and the Chief got a chance to interject.

'You know what she's like, it's impossible to stop her once she has decided to do something.'

Unfortunately, we're going to have to bear with the cyclone when she arrives.'

'You know she loves the girls, get them to fuss over their grandmother when she arrives.

He suspected that wouldn't be enough, there was going to be a lot of interference before he could get approval for the plans he was trying to implement.

Chapter 14

The Followers Preparation

The Chief left his parents and returned to his compound.
Everyone had already arrived for the meeting. The new Rav 4
of Damilola's was left outside the barn and a black BMW 6
series was parked outside the front door of the bungalow.
When he opened the front door, his wife was waiting for him,
she had given Damilola, Chief Kudo and his ex-military bouncer
refreshments on the patio and they were being looked after by
the Chief's two daughters.

She launched straight into her husband.

'You know I need notice when your mother's visiting!'

'It's bad enough she picks faults in everything, you could have
at least given me chance to get ready for her.'

'She's a demon.'

At that the Chief's wife stalked off into the house.

The Chief followed her through the bungalow, trying to placate
his other half.

'I know, I know, I'm sorry, I need the Discovery and she
insisted.'

'I don't care even the thought of her being here is giving me a headache.'

'Alright I'll try and keep her with me all the time she's visiting.'

'You have no idea, you just don't understand.'

She stormed off towards the kitchen shouting for Marcia and the Chief went in search of his guests.

They were all on the patio where he found both of his daughters keenly looking after Damilola, Chief Kudo and what must have been the ex-army Officer turned temporary bouncer. He scrubbed up rather well, was smartly turned out in black blazer, open necked white shirt, and black trousers and matching highly polished brogues.

He was the sort of person who would stand out in any crowd of people, he had that sort of aura. He was the epitome of humility, politeness and had a winning smile.

He had already captured the hearts of the Chiefs two girls, they were totally in his thrall, ignoring the other two visitors. Chisaru the elder, even had a hand proprietarily resting on the young man's arm, her younger sister was green with envy.

The Chief very quickly aware of the effect soon put a stop to the doe like eyes of adoration from his daughters.

'Gentlemen, Damilola my office please.'

He said indicating the way back through the dining room.

'Oh and girls, Grandma is on her way over.'

'I suggest you make yourself a little bit more presentable.'

He pointed to his eldest daughter's tiny red skirt.

I don't think she'll like your belt, will she Chisaru?'

Panic struck, the girls dashed inside and through the house to their rooms followed by the raucous laughter of the men.

Damilola grinned at their discomfort.

On reaching Chief's office he invited them to sit.

'First my mother is on her way over with the car you will be using, a nearly new Land Rover Discovery.'

Damilola and Chief Kudo swore, the Chief's mother's reputation was well known. They respected her and knew she ruled with a rod of iron as far as the Chief's family was concerned, it was difficult taking orders from this little woman.

Before any of them had further chance to take over the conversation the office door opened, and the lady concerned, accompanied by a strong aroma of expensive perfume sauntered into the Office. Everyone automatically stood but it was the temporary bouncer who took control of the situation.

'I'm Kinikanwo.'

'Please take my seat,' he said indicating the office chair he had just vacated.

'I'm sure we can find you some refreshment before we start.'

The Matriarch was immediately and completely captivated by the dapper young man and his attention. The Grandmother of nearly sixty cooed like a teenager.

'Oh, thank you sir, yes please, I'll have a coffee.'

The Chief picking up on the new vibe vacated the office rapidly to make sure the matriarch's coffee was quickly on its way. The only conversation until the refreshment arrived was between the Grandmother and the attentive young man. He praised her complexion and complimented her on her two lovely Granddaughters. She for her part hung on his every word like a dumbstruck teenager.

Once her coffee had arrived, the five of them got down to business. The Chief's mother made a point of handing the Discovery keys to Kinikanwo and explained that the satellite phone would arrive at the bungalow around three.

They were then surprised when she coyly explained.

'Everything is now your business I'll go now and see my granddaughters.'

I'm sure if you listen to Kinikanwo you won't go far wrong. Kinikanwo smiled back at the departing lady, he knew he always had the ability to charm the knickers off any woman he wanted. Now he was lusting after the Chief's daughter Chisaru. He wondered if he would have time that evening to seduce the unsuspecting eighteen-year-old, she was so demure and innocent he suspected she hadn't been bedded previously.

His mind was taken off the possible pleasures of the flesh by the Chief explaining to Kinikanwo and Damilola what was required of them. After he had finished the clarification he made a request.

'Okay think what else you're going to need and let's make a list.' Kinikanwo led the discussion here, with his army training he knew what was needed and he rattled off a list of important supplies which the Chief noted.

The Chief was pleased with his colleague's choice, the young man appeared knowledgeable as well as versatile, that combined with his army experiences, meant it looked like Kinikanwo would be a very useful asset.

Damilola was not enthused about her intended partner on the expedition, she also loved Chisaru from afar but being shy and somewhat withdrawn, she was not pleased with the way Chisaru was so attracted by Kinikanwo.

Even so she spoke up.

'I'll need a Hijab head scarf or two, particularly for Niger and Algeria where I'm sure to encounter problems otherwise.'

'The other thing at hotels after Kano we better book in together as if we are married.'

Kinikanwo pointed out the obvious

'We'll likely lose the Rally car at times on the way up to the Niger border with Algeria but will easily find them again because of the limited routes through the country.'

'But the biggest problem will be staying in touch with the Touareg in the early stages until we reach the northern Nigerian border.'

'Also, I agree about sharing a hotel room, it makes sense in the Muslim areas of which there are a lot.'

He leered at Damilola.

Who catching the look spread out her arms and looked at Chief Kudo who had caught the look.

'Kinikanwo, you'll keep it in your pants, you're to work together and that's it.'

He raised his voice to push the point home.

'Got it!'

Kinikanwo sullenly nodded his head in agreement knowing his life was worth little if he disobeyed Chief Kudo's instructions. That point rammed home Damilola and Kinikanwo set off to find their supplies and took the Discovery with them. They were liberally supplied with cash from the roll of Naira the Chief still had in his back pocket. They spent the rest of the day equipping themselves and the Discovery with the gear they thought they would need.

Returning just as it got dark all four met in the Chief's office, Kinikanwo asked if they knew any of the plans of the Europeans in the Touareg.

The Chief exasperated had no answer, they didn't even know the departure time of the Touareg on the following day.

It was Kinikanwo who provided the answer.

'They have to go through, or at least past Abuja, right.'

The other three nodded agreeing with him.

'There's three ways up to the Capital, all have to cross the Niger.'

'Onitsha is the normal route, it's one hundred and eighty kilometres north of here and about three hours away on the fastest road.'

Kinikanwo thought for a moment without interruption.

'I reckon they'll not leave before eight tomorrow morning, Damilola and I will leave at six and make for the bridge and we'll be up there about nine.'

'If you get someone to follow them up to the airport road they'll know by then which route the Touareg is going to take and you can contact us.'

The Chiefs nodded their heads in agreement before Kinikanwo continued.

'If it is one of the other easterly routes we'll be able to cut across from Onitsha and pick them up that way.'

'Right I'll take the Discovery and pick Damilola up at six in the morning, alright.'

Chief Kudo jumped in before anyone else had time to speak.

'I'll fix for someone to follow the Touareg in the morning.'

Damilola nodded agreement, pleased she would have time to return her new car to her parents' compound.

Arrangements made, Kinikanwo picked up the satellite mobile and each went their separate ways.

Chapter 15

Discovery delay

Everyone made their way to their cars; the Chief accompanied them and shook hands with all three. He wished Damilola and Kinikanwo luck and encouraged them to keep in touch daily if possible.

Kinikanwo's boss left first in his immaculate BMW, followed by Damilola but only after she had confirmed where she needed picking up in the morning with Kinikanwo. The latter settled into the Land Rover Discovery's comfortable driver's seat and adjusted it to suit his body, he watched the Rav 4 depart with Damilola and put the car into gear.

There was a female giggle from behind his seat, he looked in the mirror and saw the Chief waving and hurrying across the compound towards the rear of the car. The girl giggled again and Kinikanwo not believing his luck spoke quickly.

'You had better be quiet and keep your head down, your father is on his way over, looks like I forgot something.'

'Oh crap don't tell him please?'

'It had better be worth something,'

He could see the girl's father coming level with the rear offside corner of the Discovery, Kinikanwo couldn't believe his luck, adventure and a young woman in debt to him all on the same day.

In panic a distraught, female voice whispered from the rear of the vehicle.

'Yes alright,'

'Shhh he's here.'

Kinikanwo lowered the driver's side window.

'You've forgotten the satellite phone.'

The Chief breathing heavily, gasped, due to the extra exertion of running out after the Discovery

'It was on the desk in the Study.'

'And when you come back you'll be very welcome to visit, I've never seen anyone turn my mother to jelly like that.'

The risk taker in Kinikanwo wanted to keep the conversation going, he hoped the threat of discovery would scare the girl in the back and make her even more grateful when he didn't give her away.

'That's alright sir my mother taught me to be polite and look after all the ladies.'

The Chief lightly thumped the car door.

'Well done again, safe trip and don't forget to keep in touch.'

There was another whisper from the rear.

'Is he gone?'

'Not quite yet, I thinking he's coming back.'

He deliberately didn't move off and took a moment to place the satellite phone in the glove compartment, adjusted his seat and rear-view mirror again. Kinikanwo took his time keeping the girl on tenterhooks for a while longer.

The Chief waited patiently a couple of metres away, pleased to see Kinikanwo was taking his time and making sure everything was in order. Seeing the driver appeared to be ready to move he remarked aloud.

'Don't forget, keep us informed.'

'Good luck.'

Chisaru hearing her father's voice so close tried to shrink further into the floor space between the seats.

'Thanks sir.'

Kinikanwo finally set the Discovery in motion and wound up the driver's window and salivated at the thought of the young lady just behind him

'You're safe now.'

There was movement behind him and a pair of female hands reached over his shoulders and covered his eyes.

'Guess who?'

He deliberately swerved the car.

'Chisaru let go I can't see.'

'We'll end up in the ditch.'

Chisaru screamed joyously a mixture of delight and fear.

'You were fantastic, thanks for not telling, father would have killed me.'

'Alright now join me in the front and fulfil your promise.'

'What promise?'

'To make it worth my while if I didn't tell your father you were in the car.'

'It depends on what you want me to do.'

She crawled between the front seats and into the passenger seat, she nearly fell into his lap at one point as the vehicle lurched into a pothole on the back road.

Kinikanwo looked across the dark cab at Chisaru as she fumbled with the seat belt. He could smell her light perfume, she appeared to have on the smallest of miniskirts, like the red one he had seen earlier. This tiny white skirt was complemented by a narrow white tank top, which only just covered her erect young breasts. He couldn't be sure but there appeared to be no bra. He started to get aroused at the thought. He barely noticed the white four-inch heeled, peep-toed shoes. Having set her seat belt Chisaru glanced back at the young man whom she had crushed on immediately she saw him that afternoon.

'Where are we going?'

'I don't know, we can't really go into town in case your father finds out you're missing.'

'That's alright, mother thinks I've gone to a friend's, she'll cover for me, I've done it before.'

'Can't we just stop somewhere, I want to find out all about you, where a gorgeous hunk like you has been hiding and everything?'

Kinikanwo was flushed with arousal, his trousers were having difficulty containing him, he realised Chisaru had no intention of going home that evening.

All thoughts of an early start and the expedition disappeared from his mind. For a moment he couldn't think straight then he realised he could take her back to his pad. It wasn't up too much just a single room, the army had taught him to look after his kit, the bed was made, and the place was clean and tidy.

'What about my place,' he suggested running a hand up her near thigh to the lower edge of the mini skirt.

Chisaru wasn't so sure now, it had seemed like a great adventure hiding in the Discovery. Now she was having some doubts although her mind was being confused by Kinikanwo's sure touch.

Breathing rapidly, she whimpered huskily.

'Can't we just park up somewhere first.'

'That's alright, we'll do that then, whatever you want but don't forget you owe me.'

She tensed momentarily and then relaxed as he continued to stroke her inner thighs.

He thought quickly, then had his mind made up after seeing an empty shopping precinct car park. He pulled in and drove into the furthest, darkest, corner.

He undid his seatbelt and reached across for her, reluctantly at first, she tentatively released her own. His long arms enabled one hand to brush her inner thigh and the other to cup her near

131

breast. Chisaru shivered and groaned at his touch, then turned and leaned across towards him.

Seizing the opportunity, he picked her up and lifted her from the passenger seat and onto his lap. At first, she was shocked at his strength and then accepting she leaned her head into his chest. She could feel his manhood threatening to impale her. He pressed his mouth onto hers and she opened her lips willingly as his tongue sought entrance. His busy hands were up under her skimpy tank top and releasing her young breasts to his voracious touch.

After the fumbled ministrations of young men, she had previously gone out with, this was different. He quickly removed the rest of her clothing and she allowed him to take her there in the car straddled across him. The first time was quick, fulfilling and exciting causing her to scream with the intensity of her orgasm.

She didn't object afterwards when he drove too and carried her into his small apartment. Rapidly they took each other's clothes off and tumbled onto his bed, their love making was more leisurely this time, Chisaru felt fulfilled and lucky to be seduced by someone who knew how to grant a woman's every need. She couldn't get enough of him, they made love late into the night, even Kinikanwo was beginning to find her insatiable when they finally fell into an exhausted sleep.

The next thing they both knew was when Chisaru woke to a strange sound coming from somewhere on the floor besides the bed. Ignoring the sound, she looked across at the naked

Kinikanwo, stretched and moved across the bed reaching for him.

Kinikanwo's body reacted slowly, he stretched lazily, tingling and becoming aroused from the touch of Chisaru's hand. It felt good, he slowly opened his eyes when he heard the noise from the floor start up again.

Then he remembered, it was light, he shouldn't be here, and he was already extremely late.

'Bloody hell I'm in trouble.'

He yelled as he leapt off the bed and hunted the source of the noise. It was his phone and Damilola was on the other end when he finally retrieved it from his trouser pocket.

'Where the bloody hell are you?'

'It's alright I just overslept.'

'What's the time?'

'Just after seven we're in the crap if either of the Chiefs' find out.'

'Don't panic I'm on my way, I'll be with you shortly.'

He gasped loudly as Chisaru grabbed hold of his hardening member.

Damilola heard this and recognised the signs of a sexual encounter before Kinikanwo had chance to switch off his mobile.

Chisaru wouldn't let him go immediately and rolled on top of him.

'Damn, Damilola is just going to have to wait.'

He said, grabbing and twisting both Chisaru's nipples between the thumb and forefingers of both his hands.

Everything was rushed from there on, he threw his passport, clothes and hunting knife into a holdall. He realised he had to make arrangements to get Chisaru back to her parents.

She was more prepared than he realised, with a scrunched up green dress and underwear in her handbag to replace the night before's sexy but inappropriate day wear. She gave him a long lingering kiss and squeezed his tight buttocks in front of the bus queue when he dropped her off shortly after leaving his apartment.

It was nearly nine before a tired but pleasantly sated Kinikanwo roared to a halt outside the house of Damilola's parents.

Damilola didn't greet Kinikanwo, she just slung her rucksack on the back seat of the Discovery and prepared to get into the passenger side of the vehicle but Kinikanwo got out and handed her the keys yawning tiredly.

'You drive, I'm shattered.'

Damilola was not pleased, she took the keys and made her way to the driver's side, she wasn't happy that her now erstwhile colleague was late because of a woman. As she eased out into the traffic she let her colleague know of her displeasure.

'You're a bloody idiot, we're right in the crap now, over three hours late because you have to spend the night with some slag and can't get out of bed in the morning.'

'If the bloody Chief and your boss find out about this, we'll be right up the creek.'

'For Christ's sake stop panicking, it's alright, we've got miles to go, anyway we must be in front of them, our contact hasn't phoned in, we have to be ahead of the Touareg.'

Kinikanwo envisioned Chisaru's naked body and smiled, then spoke hoping to mollify Damilola's anger

'Sorry about this morning though, I'm normally a lot more professional than that.'

'It was though an extremely unexpected diversion last night.'

Kinikanwo grinned at Damilola who turned briefly towards him.

'You mean a woman?'

'No better than that.'

Then Damilola remembered the Chiefs daughters had been all over Kinikanwo the younger one like a little puppy but Chisaru had looked like she was undressing him every time her eyes lingered on the ex-soldier's body.

'Not Chisaru the Chief's daughter?'

Kinikanwo just smiled.

'Well the other one's a bit young yet.'

'You dirty bastard, now I understand why you were so late.'

Damilola seethed at her partner, she was so angry, not only were they late but the girl she had hoped to court, had been sullied by this gigolo.

This made her more determined to help Chisaru see the error of her ways.

Kinikanwo tucked a folded-up shirt between himself and the passenger side window and slept as they made their way out of Port Harcourt.

Damilola edged the Discovery slowly through the monstrous morning traffic, briefly onto the Aba Expressway, then after only thirty metres slowly taking the next exit two hundred and seventy degrees until they were northbound on the East/West road. They continued to crawl along as they were held up by the end of the morning rush. Damilola was worried about the possible wrath of the Chief, with them getting later and later. The morning wore on but fortunately once they bore right towards Elimbu the traffic northbound began to thin. Their main problem being mopeds and motor cyclists on their small bikes. They would insist on coming from the opposite direction on the wrong side of the road to beat the city bound crush.

Now reasonably clear, they soon cleared the city suburbs and were out onto the main highway. They passed east of the lake at Igwuruta and made progress to the north, over on the left-hand side they could see aeroplanes landing and taking off from Port Harcourt Airport. It was just ten o'clock and had taken them nearly an hour to clear the City because of the traffic, Damilola thought they were about three hours behind the original plan. Kinikanwo woke he wasn't worried, there was a long way to go although Damilola looked scared to death.

'Don't be so bloody concerned.'

'After all, until we get a phone call from the Chief we know the Touareg hasn't left.'

'We must already be miles ahead of the game.'

Kinikanwo hadn't recognised the some of the cold atmosphere coming from Damilola wasn't just panic but also anger at

Kinikanwo's sexual antics. If he had known he wouldn't have cared, his own attitude was that all was fair in love and war. After all he had been there before, he lost his job as a Nigerian Army Officer because of the sex-addicted teenage daughter of an Army General.

At the time she had been well worth the risk of losing his position.

Chapter 16

Monday 2nd November 2015 - Leaving

There had been some delay leaving the Van Oord Dredging Company's compound. The two adventurers had wanted to creep away in the early hours but since Mac's announcement about driving all the way back to Europe, the news had spread like wildfire and they hadn't been allowed to depart unscathed. Mac had informed Oscar they couldn't leave until after eight because the carrier picking up the rally seats and other gear from the car that they were shipping back to the UK wasn't due until that time.

Mac hadn't been ready to court any publicity; the higher ups had spoken to his boss back in the UK over the weekend. A last-minute phone call on the previous day had meant Oscar, himself and the Touareg were on show at the entrance to the refinery for the local press.

The Port Harcourt Telegraph had outdone themselves with a social and business reporter as well as the requisite camera man. There was even a camera crew there from the National Television Service with a young lady, dressed in a smart brown check suit waving a microphone at anyone who would speak to her.

Mac was popular, he may have only been working there for two years but because of the way he treated everyone, his popularity with the ladies and his friendly manner, both the Management and staff had come to regard him as one of their own.

The pair of them posed for the press and answered their questions. Besides members of the Dredging Company staff, quite a local crowd was building up. They were no doubt, in part, attracted by the logo of the Nigerian Television Service on the green transit van which was parked alongside the entrance. Stood by the Touareg, they were filmed and photographed, Mac apologised to his compatriot.

'Sorry about this but the hierarchy insisted anything for some good local publicity.'

'That's alright, all part of the adventure and it won't hurt my profile.'

'Besides we are in no hurry, we haven't got to be in Niger until Thursday, plenty of time.'

Behind them the gates of the compound opened, an overloaded forty tonne truck tried to exit. The driver sounded the truck's deep throated horn as he tried to make his way through the crowds surrounding the Touareg.

This helped to disperse the crowd of sightseers. The television news team had interviewed everyone that could speak and rushed off to another venue and the powers that be seemed to be satisfied with their positive publicity stunt.

The two could now mount the immaculate rally car and start their journey north. First through Port Harcourt and then out into the country but always north or thereabouts towards Abuja, the Sahara and hopefully Europe.

Mac was driving, they were dressed in matching, pristine, drivers-rally suits which Oscar had purchased. He had acquired three each and had a logo made to celebrate their expedition. The logo showed the car crossed by a north pointing vertical arrow. Mac was quite impressed with the idea and thought it made them look like professional drivers. Oscar was more practical he rather hoped their outfits would make the customs procedures easier and smooth their way.

By nine that morning Mac was driving carefully away from the compound and they both waved cheerfully at the dispersing crowds who were shouting their good wishes as the Touareg passed through them.

Neither of them was looking for, or noticed a small grubby Nigerian man in a heavily stained once white boiler suit. He drove and an even dirtier, rust-streaked, old white Toyota which pulled out behind the Touareg. The car wasn't in the best of condition and as the driver accelerated off the hard-packed sandy kerb, across the crumbling edge of the tarmac and onto the road, the Corolla back-fired loudly. This was accompanied by a cloud of black oily smoke emitting from the exhaust. A flock of black crows rose screeching in protest from the mangroves lining the ditches on either side of the road. The trail of smoke followed the sickly vehicle.

The two in the Touareg heard the bang of the exhaust, took no notice and didn't connect it to their progress round the eastern side of Port Harcourt.

The Corolla continued to follow, its emissions becoming thicker, its occupant unaware of the engine's rapid decline towards termination.

When they edged out onto the north south expressway it was just after ten in the morning. The early traffic rush had eased, the road was quite clear, Mac decided to give the Touareg its head and speeded up. The sight of the car in its Dakar Rally colours made them very visible, it turned excited heads in traffic from both directions and on the pathways alongside the highway.

***

Behind them the Toyota Corolla was struggling to keep up, the engine was starting to cough, it was obvious to those following the now continuous oily black smoke that the Toyota Corolla's problems were terminal. The Driver knew his car was struggling, it was ready for the scrap-heap, it was his only means of earnings and transport though.

His nephew was an employee at the night club, the owner Chief Kudo had insisted the nephew be the one to follow the Touareg that morning and inform his boss which route north was taken by the Touareg and its team.

The nephew hadn't wanted to get up after a late night, working at the night club, he had sub-contracted the job and responsibility to his Uncle who was now losing the chase.

The Touareg purred as it cruised along at nearly one hundred kilometres per hour. The pursuer's vehicle vibrated and rattled as its driver tried to push the accelerator to the floor in his attempt to keep up.

The speedo showed the terminal velocity of the dying car reaching eighty kilometres per hour, its driver suddenly became aware of a smell of burning, smoke started pouring out of the engine bonnet ahead of him and the machinery died suddenly, bringing the car to a shuddering halt, blocking the inside lane of the Expressway.

The demise of the Corolla was unnoticed by the occupants of the Touareg who were happily progressing around the east side of the town.

Quickly evacuating his terminally deceased car, the sub-contractor kicked the offside front tire in exasperation and screamed some Igbo expletives at the thinly grey clouded sky above. The car itself as if objecting to the foul treatment by its owner, burst into flame, its driver ran and quickly vaulted over the barrier rail to safety.

Moving further along to a safer part of the road verge he sat on the barrier and contemplated what he was going to do now. He didn't seem aware of the havoc his burning Corolla was causing, the following traffic was quickly backing up, a few brave souls tried to manoeuvre their way past in the outside lane until the moment when the petrol tank blew up, throwing debris from the Corolla in all directions.

The Uncle desperately needed the money his nephew was paying him for following the Rally Car. Even more so now his clunker of a car was dead. He came to a decision and decided he was going to have to lie, pretend he had done what was asked and hope he guessed right.

Pulling his mobile from his rear pocket he dialled his nephew and told the unsuspecting young man.

'The Touareg has just passed the airport road and looks like it is bound for Onitsha.'

'Thanks very much, see me on the club door this evening and I'll pay you.'

The failed pursuer, seeing approaching sirens, not wishing to answer any awkward questions about un-roadworthy cars, departed the scene hastily, leaving the backed-up traffic and dead Corolla for someone else to deal with.

Unfortunately for the Uncle, his nephew and their pursuers the occupants of the Touareg had decided to take the more easterly route to Abuja. Believing although it was slightly longer in distance, it had less hold ups and certainly no bottlenecks like the bridge at Onitsha.

Meanwhile Chief Kudo had been appraised of the supposed westerly route of the Touareg and was in the process of contacting Damilola and Kinikanwo in the Land Rover Discovery who should have been in Onitsha by now.

Kinikanwo picked up the satellite mobile when it rang, fortunately he had his wits about him and he shouted at Damilola.

'Quickly stop on the side of the road.'

Damilola pulled over she guessed why they why they needed to be stationary so quickly. They should have been stopped at Onitsha an hour ago and needed to make whoever was ringing think that was the situation now. She pulled over off the crumbling tarmac onto the hard-packed dirt edge of the road. As soon as Damilola switched off the Discovery's engine Kinikanwo answered the phone.

'Hi Boss, how's things, any news?'

'How's it going, where are you?'

'Fine thanks sir we're waiting up by the bridge.'

He wasn't lying, they were parked where the road crossed a small concrete culvert which was full of water, it just wasn't where Chief Kudo assumed Kinikanwo was alluding to.

'Good my source tells me they went past the airport road towards Onitsha about ten.'

Kinikanwo and Damilola were quite relieved it put them about an hour in front.

'Thanks.'

Chief Kudo closed the conversation.

'Keep in touch.'

Kinikanwo disconnected the call, Damilola started up the engine and edged them back into the northbound traffic queue. They were only about halfway to Onitsha and struggling with traffic congestion already.

They were passing through Owerri, capital of the state of Imo. A large truck with a brown, rusty, unmarked container had tried to turn left too sharply and caught the overhanging first floor of the white building on the street corner.

Local police were trying to direct the quickly building traffic jam down some very narrow side streets and out onto the A6.

It put two hours onto their journey before they were finally joining the A6 where it became the Onitsha Expressway. They made more rapid progress up this thoroughfare towards the lowest downriver bridge over the River Niger.

Ninety minutes later they approached the sixties, French-built crossing and ran into an almighty traffic jam, about three miles south west of the town of Onitsha. It was just after two in the afternoon when they came to a grinding halt.

***

Meanwhile further south and east the Touareg and its occupants had joined the A3 at the same roundabout as the Discovery. However just past Igwuruta they had stayed to the east hoping the A3 would take them more directly to Abuja and avoiding the known traffic jam at the Onitsha Bridge.

Mac had learnt from the truck drivers bringing spare parts to the Dredging compound of the unpublicised, new, strengthening works which although not meant to, often reduced the bridge to one way for most of the daylight hours.

The Scotsman was also certain the A3 Chad/Nigeria Highway would be quieter. It was normally used by heavy trucks carrying goods through Cameroon but at the moment it couldn't be used by that traffic. The border bridge at Gambaro had been destroyed in an explosion planted by the Boko Haram rebels. The pair were using the run to Abuja to get used to the Touareg, they were hoping to stay in Abuja for two nights and rest up before making their way to the Niger border via Kano. The plan today was to test out themselves and the Touareg by covering the six hundred and fifty-kilometre, ten hours plus drive in one go. They intended to take turns to drive in two-hour stints and had the extra day in hand in case of incidents.

It was unfortunate they had left the compound so late because it would mean some night driving something which they had not intended to do unless absolutely necessary. They knew by experience and statistics. Nigeria's roads were fearsome and at their most dangerous around nightfall.

Chapter 17

Monday Night

It was nearly ten that night before the two weary travellers made their way to the front entrance of Abuja's Transcorp Hilton Hotel. The Touareg, though dusty from the journey, like everywhere they had passed or stopped that day attracted attention. Even at the Hilton word soon got around and there was a swarm of people inspecting and prodding the unexpected rally vehicle.

Fortunately, there was a Hotel Doorman to direct Oscar to a secure parking area, while a tired Mac took their minimal luggage into the Reception desk to get them checked-in.

Choosing the luxury of the Hilton had been Mac's idea, he still had plenty of Naira to use up and as he had told Oscar.

'Life's going to be hard for a few nights, might as well live it up while we are in the big city.'

'If we need something, extra supplies, or we've forgotten something the Hotel's Concierge will know what to do or how to acquire it.'

They were also worried about the car being taken hostage or stolen. They wanted it somewhere safe and secure while they were in the Capital City. There were enough warnings about car-jacking's and hostage taking, they were determined they would always be on the alert and try and be as safe as possible.

***

While the two ex-pats were settling in and ordering haute cuisine from the twenty-four-hour room service menu. Damilola and Kinikanwo were slumming it over two hundred kilometres to the south in the small city of Lokoja.

With the crush of traffic due to the Onitsha bridge renovation, they had to wait three hours to cross the Niger's most southerly span. Damilola parked the Discovery by the roadside on the western side of the bridge just after four in the afternoon and they sat back to wait for the Touareg.

By six thirty the brief dusk announced the oncoming nightfall and Kinikanwo decided they should head north. It became obvious the Touareg was either severely delayed or had taken one of the two more easterly routes. This meant their informant had been mistaken or downright lied.

A telephone call back to his boss made Kinikanwo unpopular, he felt it was fortunate they were out of reach and couldn't feel the ire and blasphemy pouring out of the satellite phones speaker. In the end the Chief who was sat alongside Chief Kudo urged them to get north as soon as possible.

Kinikanwo was pissed off with the two Chiefs attitude, he felt they were being blamed unfairly. Damilola was more scared of her two superiors and was just glad they were making some progress.

Meanwhile she directed the Discovery firstly west along the Benin/Lagos expressway, a pothole, pitted, two lane highway that tested the suspension of the Discovery to its limits. She turned north on a side road to cut the corner to join the northbound A2, this road was even worse. When they reached the A2 they were delayed again with long hold-ups due to roadworks at Ewu Esan.

In the end they went through nearly six more hours of road hell. The Highway was mainly unlit, except when they passed through occasional villages. The tarmac on the edge of the road was crumbling into the sometimes hard-packed earth or otherwise glutinous mud. It was difficult to stick onto the road when the huge trucks coming the other way, ablaze with undipped lights and tired drivers, threatened to run onto the wrong side of the highway and shove them off the road. It was also impossible to slow down, if they did, inevitably a giant of a truck astern, would move up close behind and blind them through the windscreen mirror, while giving a deafening blast on his exhaust horn.

By the time they reached Lokoja, even the unflappable Kinikanwo, who was now driving had enough. He turned off onto a residential side street of the small city and parked up.

'What are you doing?'

'I've had enough I'm shattered.'

'That's because you didn't get any sleep last night.'

'I know, I know but this is crazy, we could easily get killed by one of those crazy maniacs driving those trucks.'

'I'm sure they are all keeping awake by chewing on Ganga as they drive.'

Damilola agreed but didn't want Kinikanwo to dictate their moves all the time.

'Alright but why have we stopped on this street?'

Kinikanwo yawned out a reply.

'It's midnight and too late to find a hotel this late on, we're going to have to sleep in the car and make the best of it.'

'It'll not be the last time on this trip, we might as well get used to the idea.'

Damilola still fuming with her colleague over Chisaru grudgingly saw the sense of this and before her partner could argue she had nipped into the more comfortable rear seats of the car.

With the car stopped, the interior was getting hot and humid, Kinikanwo lit up the ignition enough to lower all four windows a fraction before switching off again. This was just enough to let in a tiny breeze to circulate the already stifling air inside. The opening of the window introduced them to the smell of the two great rivers which were meeting a few metres from where they were parked.

The Benue joined with the mighty Niger at Lokoja, the strong aroma of the mangrove swamps bordering the City seemed to overwhelm any other smells it was so strong.

Kinikanwo tried to find a way to lie across the two front seats but in the end put the passenger seat as far down as it would go and spent a restless night. He dreamed pleasantly though, the future delights promised by Chisaru on his return, permeated his sub-conscious.

Damilola also lay thinking of Chisaru before she dropped off to sleep, she was normally a cautious, shy, young woman of twenty-four not given to impetuosity, The Chief Inspectors wife had been an unexpected aberration caused by a dominant female who had introduced Damilola to the pleasures of a same-sex relationship. It was because of her undying love for Chisaru and the need to impress the girl and her father that she had volunteered for Sierra Leone.

She was sick at the thought of the Chief's eldest daughter lying with Kinikanwo. The guy could have any woman or girl he wanted, and it seemed took advantage of every opportunity to satisfy his lust. Eventually Damilola slept, exhausted and didn't wake until the morning.

Kinikanwo didn't think he had slept at all, he thought he had been trying to get comfortable all night. In fact, he was fast asleep when they were woken by a thumping on the near side of the Land Rover Discovery. Damilola turned over and peered out of the rear, nearside, window, it was light, and she could see the pathway alongside had lots of children in blue and white uniforms making their way towards a school. He could see the Academy behind the fencing alongside their vehicle. There was a river mist covering the upper floor of the two-storey school building.

Kinikanwo sat up and moved the passenger seat upright before stepping out onto the pathway. The kids walked round him as he stretched and yawned, it was obvious one of the little sods had banged on the side of the car and woken them up. Ignoring the staring children, he moved round the vehicle and jumped into the driver's seat, scratching the two days of stubble on his chin with his right hand.

'What do you reckon Damilola, I need a piss, coffee and something to eat all in that order?

Damilola who was clambering over the console into the front passenger seat grunted her agreement.

An hour later they had managed to find somewhere to complete all three assignments. Lokoja's newly opened Mr Biggs fast food restaurant, one of over one hundred and seventy in Nigeria solved all three problems and allowed them to prepare for the day's journey.

Damilola driving, pointed the car north, the banks of the River Niger close on their nearside. Its murky, muddy, grey waters headed south towards the Delta and finally the Gulf of Guinea. They passed the grey ferry of the Nigerian Inland Waterways Authority on the near bank of the two rivers. It was loading up ready to carry its cargo of vehicles and passengers to the eastern bank.

Once they passed the Kogi Polytechnic they joined the A2 again, here it turned north. All around them was low-lying jungle, the roadside appeared bare of habitation. In the daylight the oncoming trucks still appeared to want to hog both sides of the road but at least they weren't battling the headlights as well.

Thirty kilometres north of Lokoja they crossed from the west to the east bank of the river in slow moving traffic over the long bridge. They could see a dredger churning up mud from the river's bottom and were slowed to a halt just after the crossing. A green sign told them they had one hundred and eighty kilometres to go before reaching Abuja.

Damilola and Kinikanwo had discussed some of their problems especially not knowing the location of the Touareg and its occupants while eating breakfast at the Lokoja outlet of Mr Biggs. They couldn't resolve anything but decided to keep making their way towards Abuja, it was after all to the north and on the route to the border with Niger.

When leaving Lokoja, Kinikanwo received a call from Chisaru on his mobile and started to chat to her, he couldn't really say what he wanted because of Damilola next to him. She however was suggesting things she would like to do with him if they hadn't been apart. He was enjoying the one-sided conversation, not realising the anger and embarrassment Damilola was feeling as the phone call continued.

Fortunately, the communication was cut short by the loss of the signal as they exited the town. Damilola was livid and felt she had to say something, braving herself and putting on her fiercest voice she said.

'I bloody well hope you aren't going to just love her and leave, I care for her a lot, she's like a sister and I would be really annoyed if you let her down.'

Kinikanwo stayed silent for a moment or two, he realised he might have a problem. It was obvious Damilola was in love with the girl and didn't know how to manage the situation

Although Kinikanwo wouldn't normally have worried about the girl, after all there were lot more apples on the tree. He didn't particularly want to make the situation any more antagonistic. The next week or more was going to be difficult. They would have to work together in some of the world's harshest environment and he couldn't afford a rift with his erstwhile partner.

'You might not believe this love, even though I've only just met the girl and have only been away from her for just over a day I really miss her.'

'You have to trust me, I'm never going to intentionally hurt Chisaru.'

'Okay,'

Damilola grudgingly answered, not believing Kinikanwo for a moment, it was obvious the man would pursue any woman he could persuade into his bed.

'We can't afford to let our feelings for Chisaru get in the way of the job we have to do.'

'We need to concentrate on the task in hand, yes I took advantage of a situation, but it has to be over for now,'

Kinikanwo continued trying to use what he remembered from his army command psychology training. It was all about making the other person feel needed which was why he had given Damilola the option of suggesting a solution.

They were still stopped just over the other side of the bridge making scant progress. The large, mustard-yellow, road tanker ahead of them would start to crawl slowly forward for about its own length and then suddenly lurch to a stop. The traffic going to the west bank was flowing easily so it meant there must be something slow moving, or an obstruction on their side of the road. Still it gave them further time to discuss their next move. Damilola thought about their situation and answered her partner.

'We have to assume they're ahead of us now, they must have gone up the A3 and we've been given spurious information.'

'It would have helped, if we had been told more by those back at home.'

'They left late we know that, I reckon the furthest they would have gone is Abuja.'

'I think you're right Damilola.'

'I'll get the map out.'

They continued their conversation while slowly crawling forward, there wasn't much room on their side of the road, close to the hard-packed earth pathway alongside the broken edge of the tarmac was a drop into marshy low-lying mangrove jungle. Kinikanwo pulled the small-scale map from the glove compartment and opened it up so he could look at the possible routings and distances north out of Abuja.

'We've got another three plus hours or bloody longer if this traffic doesn't move before we'll be up to the Capital.'

Damilola changed the subject.

'We said we wouldn't drive at night and after yesterday evening I think we should keep to that idea.'

'I nearly shit myself last night, facing those crazy Ganga hopheads driving their trucks at us in the middle of the road.'

'What made it worse they either had no lights or if they did they were always on full beam blinding us all the time.'

'I just don't fancy our chances of not getting crushed or forced into one of the ditches alongside the road.'

As if to emphasise his point they crawled past a burnt-out Articulated lorry in the swampy ground alongside them, Kinikanwo seeing this was only too willing to agree with his partner.

'You're right, let's just aim to drive from dawn to dusk every day and try and get ahead of the Touareg.'

'I think if we are to be sure we catch them, we need to make Kano tonight though.'

Damilola agreed.

'Kano and a decent hotel tonight, hopefully?'

Kinikanwo the map opened on her lap agreed.

'We can but try, it's about another five hundred and fifty kilometres from here.'

'You realise we are just going to have to keep up this rapid progress until we get to Agadez in central Niger?'

'Why is that?'

Kinikanwo who had been studying the map noted.

'It's the first place that we both have to pass through.'

'Right.'

Damilola nodded and at that moment as if by magic, the road tanker ahead of them started to gradually accelerate. She followed, matching the speed of the vehicle in front, the road didn't widen but instead of swamp and jungle the highway was bordered by hard packed earth.

The reason for all the stop-start became clear when they passed a cart full of yams being pulled by a single donkey. It was moving in the same direction but now on the hard standing to the right of the road. The man escorting the donkey and cart was following his cargo, dressed in a dirty-white, full-length thobe.

Kinikanwo laughed and pointed towards the cart while shouting out an intelligible string of oaths at the reason for their delay.

'Bet that's the reason for the hold-up, not a care in the world.'

He looked at his watch

'It's eleven thirty already.'

'Pull over when you get an opportunity and I'll take over.'

Chapter 18

The Discovery makes progress

The Discovery and its occupants found they didn't have to go through Abuja and were able to skirt the city by staying on the A2. This time Kinikanwo had been able to think ahead, by mid-afternoon while Damilola was driving, he managed to acquire them a hotel room in Kano. It was difficult to find one that could offer them a modicum of security for the car but as there was little else available he made the booking using his credit card. Even so they only made it by eight that evening, even on a main highway like the A2 it was difficult to pass the trucks. Every time the highway made its way through any sort of habitation, there was some sharp braking for the frequent jaywalkers, these had ill-judged ideas of how quickly they could cross the busy road. Once they passed Abuja they went through their last bout of rain. A mighty thunderstorm with jagged forks of lightning threatened to overwhelm them, the darkened sky nearly obscured all the light. At times when the rain poured down, the windscreen wipers could hardly cope. Kinikanwo who was driving could feel the slipperiness of the road surface where the rainwater had mixed with petrol, diesel and oil spillages from the frequent and not always well-serviced, passing vehicles.

As they neared Kano the forest started to disappear and the scenery to become more arid. They were approaching the part of Northern Nigeria affected by the southerly edge of the gradually encroaching Sahara Desert.

Much relieved by reaching Kano safely the pair made their way into the Prince Hotel near the centre of the city. They both felt filthy as if they hadn't showered for a week and were desperate to get to their room and a fresh shower. Their plans were put on hold when Kinikanwo signing the register found they would have to eat immediately if they wanted food at the hotel. The dining room was about to close. After consulting with Damilola, they decided to eat straightaway as neither wanted to try and find somewhere else with food so late in a strange city.

***

Four hundred and thirty kilometres to the south the drivers of the Touareg were settling in for their second night in Abuja. They had spent the day making final checks on their equipment and buying a couple of extra items for the proposed trip. One item they had been unable to purchase in Port Harcourt was a couple of pieces of steel diamond deck to put under the wheels if the Touareg got stuck in sand. The hotel concierge easily found a shop where they could be bought.

***

Kinikanwo had to report in to the Chief Kudo, who was pleased with their progress. He thought their idea of making Niger the following day and sitting at Agadez on the only road north was sound.

Kinikanwo's boss hadn't been so kind back in Port Harcourt when on questioning the acolyte selected to initially follow the Touareg had soon admitted to sub-contracting the work to his poor Uncle.

The sub-contractor had been picked up and brought in to the night club. At first when questioned the poor unfortunate had pleaded that he had done what he was paid for. A tweak of his wrist by one of the bouncers caused the man to admit to the problem with his Uncle's car and his relations made up story about the route of the Touareg.

The Uncle had been located and with the employee had been taken into the yard at the back of the club, tied up and beaten senseless with baseball bats by two of the bouncers'

On completion of the phone call to chief Kudo, Kinikanwo relayed the tale to Damilola.

'He likes our idea of getting to Agadez as fast as possible.'

'He doesn't like the fact we haven't seen the Touareg, I'm glad we're a thousand miles north of the bastard.'

'He's a hell of a temper.'

Damilola's report to the Chief was greeted with some relief, her Uncle was convinced they must be well ahead and Agadez sounded like a good bet.

Chapter 19

Wednesday 4th - The Touareg arrives in Kano

The Touareg was the first to leave Wednesday morning, the two Brits were fully refreshed after their two nights in Abuja and keen to continue their journey. Oscar had arranged a six o'clock call, they filled themselves on the buffet breakfast before retrieving the Touareg from the secure compound and re-packing the car. It attracted the usual interest from the hotel staff and the few other residents who were around at that time of the morning.

This meant another round of selfies and answering the eager questions of those outside the Hotel.

They managed to extricate themselves, buckled up and Oscar who was taking the first turn drove them out of the hotel. There was a bit of a cheer and they both looked back and waved as they drove away.

They fought their way North West through the morning rush, until finally they reached the A2 and cleared the city northbound. Once clear of the Capital that early in the morning, most of the traffic was going in the opposite direction. They could make steady progress towards their intended night's stopover in Kano four hundred and fifty kilometres away.

Joining the A2 they passed to the south and west of Zuma Rock a distinctly protruding monolith towering above the surrounding landscape. This igneous protrusion of around seven-hundred and twenty-five metres in height was well recognised by Nigerians who know it well because its picture is engraved on the 100 Naira note.

Having left Zuma Rock, the 'Gateway' to Abuja, in their wake the two settled into their routine of each driving for two hours at a time. They had prepared and during the previous day planned for the journey. They were hoping to make Kano that night, cross into Niger the following day and overnight at Agadez before the long run up to Algeria. Everything depended on the advice they received from the powers that in Kano about Boko Haram and similarly in Niger about Al Quaeda.

Neither of them spoke much there wasn't a lot to say. What had seemed to be a bit of fun and adventure back at the Port Harcourt Golf Club was beginning to get a bit more serious and while both were excited, they were beginning to have serious misgivings about the possible dangers.

The four hundred and thirty kilometres on the busy highway was completed in an easy six hours with few problems and they were soon parking up at the front of the Bristol Palace Hotel in Kano.

The hotel was going to be their last hint of luxury for a few days and both were determined to make full use of its creature comforts while they had the chance. By five they were both luxuriating in the Hotel pool while taking advantage of the warm afternoon sunlight.

Mac who was sat in the shallow end supping a long cool drink shouted to his partner who was swimming gentle laps of the pool.

Don't get too used to this mate its goanna be sand, sand and even more sand from now on.

Chapter 20

Armed Encounters

Things were a bit more disorganised up ahead in Kano. After a late night in the hotel bar both had slept in, not an auspicious way to continue their journey especially when they intended crossing an international border that day.

Kinikanwo was the first to wake the cry of a nearby muezzin calling the faithful to prayers.

He cursed aloud when he realised it was already nine in the morning and they had done nothing. Kinikanwo sat up on the side of the bed with his feet on the floor, yawned, stretched and picked up a shoe which he threw across the room at the sleeping Damilola.

This assault was greeted by a yell from the unfortunate recipient who jumped up out of bed.

'What's that for?'

'We're bloody late that's what.'

'Come on let's get some breakfast and get out of here.'

'Alright but I need the toilet and a shower first.'

The pair completed their ablutions and within twenty minutes were eating a large breakfast in the dining room. By ten o'clock they were heading north.

They agreed the only way to guarantee finding the Touareg was to drive fast and hard, so they must be ahead and waiting when the vehicle and its occupants made it to Agadez in central Niger.

It might get uncomfortable if they had to wait a while. However, neither of them could think of any other way of guaranteeing a rendezvous with the Touareg.

They made their way out of the city past the Railway Station and onto the Market roundabout where they joined the A2 again and Damilola turned the Discovery north along the highway.

It took a while to clear the city, and its north-western marker the Mallam Amini International Airport. It was on their right as they passed the western end of the runway, a Turkish Airlines A320 Airbus swept over them, its shiny underbelly glinting in the morning sunlight as it took off to the west. There were still a few sprawling suburbs of Kano stretching for some kilometres north of airport. They were however soon out onto the arid plains where farmers were doing their best to defeat the encroaching sands of the Sahara.

Damilola couldn't understand why every walled in rectangle of land contained a couple of trees, sure there was obviously some sort of grain crop growing there but how did it manage here she wondered out loud. Kinikanwo had served in the Nigerian Army in the north and knew a bit about the agriculture of this sub Saharan region took his time remembering, before answering.

'They reckon the use of these trees to grow stuff has been going on for years.'

'They're are called Faidherbia Albida, they're some sort of Acacia tree and their shade and roots aid other crops.'

'What sort of things?'

'Mung beans and stuff.'

'You wait until we get further towards the desert they use the trees as windbreaks, they're planted in lines, North West to South East to give protection from the South-West and North-East monsoons.'

Damilola was impressed with her partner's knowledge and she continued to drive, looking out for lines of tall trees in the middle of the dusty landscape.

In Kano there had been little news of Boko Haram. the border had supposedly been quiet for about a month. Knowing this they decided to take the shorter, riskier route to the border. It would take them on a more easterly route but get them to a crossing and into Niger and Agadez more rapidly.

An hour after leaving Kano near the small town of Kunya they turned off the busy A2 and out of the dust clouds of the main-highway traffic. The Mutum road led in a North Easterly direction towards the small village of that name, the last habitation before the border with Niger.

Finally, Damilola got to see her lines of Acacia trees, with lots of them lining the fields on either side.

The road was covered in a layer of fine sand, and they were leaving a large plume of dust astern. They only came up on one other vehicle and at that point Damilola accelerated hard to pass the slower truck, taking them out of the enveloping dust trail as quickly as possible.

They saw another large truck approaching from the opposite direction going like a bat out of hell. It was driving down the centre of the highway and Damilola had to react quickly to avoid a collision. The vehicles passed each another in a cacophony of noise and dust, both sounding their horns loudly

Suspiciously, that was the last south bound vehicle and the truck they had recently overtaken turned off into a field shortly after they had passed.

At this point two hours after leaving Kano they changed drivers and Kinikanwo replaced Damilola behind the wheel of the Discovery. An hour later, having seen little but lines of trees in the fields and the occasional tethered donkey, they passed through the village of Jigawa.

Most of the buildings were to the left and north of the highway. Kinikanwo looked both sides of the road as they slowed in case of pedestrians but incredibly except for a pair of tethered camels and a few loose chickens scraping at the loose gravel there was nothing in sight.

Damilola said.

'Did you see that?'

'Yeah it was like a ghost town.'

Kinikanwo answered and then added.

'Weird wasn't it.'

Damilola turned casually to look back at the deserted village. She yelled at her compatriot.

'Shit go for it.'

'There's a truck load of armed men come out of that village behind us.'

Kinikanwo glanced in his rear-view mirror and accelerated hard pushing them both back in their seats as the V6 engine reacted powerfully to his urging.

Damilola who was now staring intently out of the rear window of the Discovery, could see a white pick-up with three men standing in the rear, a long black flag with Arabic writing trailing from the whip aerial in the middle of the cab roof. The three men were dressed all in black robes as were the driver and his passenger. He was leaning out of the passenger window pointing an AK47 in their direction. The trio in the rear had similar weapons and as Damilola watched all four of the armed men started shooting in their direction.

Fortunately for those in the Discovery, the AK 47 may be a superb assault weapon, but it's not very accurate.

With his army experience Kinikanwo knew that firing such a weapon from the unstable platform of a pick-up doing a hundred kilometres per hour, they were unlikely to hit anything never mind the speeding Discovery. Even more helpfully the Discovery was creating its own dust screen, quickly hiding them from their pursuers.

He wasn't going to hang about though and had the accelerator of the Discovery pressed to the floor. Its superior acceleration meant they were rapidly moving away from the danger. Quite quickly the armed men gave up their pursuit and in minutes the pursuers disappeared from their rear-view mirror.

Kinikanwo was worried they were in a bad situation, no doubt there were further rebels ahead of them. He pulled over to the side of the highway, all the traffic coming the other way had stopped altogether and obviously with the Boko Haram rebels astern of them there was going to be little help from that direction.

Damilola lurched out of the passenger seat and in reaction to the recent events, she was violently sick into a ditch lining the roadway.

Kinikanwo's army training took over and he took charge of the situation, Damilola was of little use, she was all churned up inside and starting to shake in reaction to the threat of the armed men, she had never been shot at before and it was bloody scary.

Kinikanwo decided they would keep going and soon had the Discovery bowling along, suddenly they saw some billowing dust ahead of them and out of this appeared another pickup similarly armed to the previous one.

Kinikanwo had little time to react as they moved towards each other with a combined approach speed of over two hundred kilometres an hour. He swung the Discovery across the highway and out into the dusty fields.

He had to turn across the front of the armed rebel's pick-up and to gain the fields to the north surmising that was the safer side of the road. They lurched and bounced as they crossed a narrow drainage ditch and there was a brief pause in their progress when they hit the wire fencing surrounding the field. The Discovery soon forced its way through with an almighty clatter before they were out onto the dusty, rutted countryside. This time the assaulting members of Boko Haram were more astute and had stopped their vehicle to give their shooters a more stable platform to work from. Fortunately they were as unsuccessful as their compatriots earlier.

Kinikanwo kept going due north leaving the sun, which had to be past its zenith, just over his left shoulder. The field was fairly flat, and they could make good progress away from their pursuers.

 Too late he saw the culvert in front of them.

'Oh shit.'

Damilola swore trying to curl herself up into a ball in the front passenger seat.

Her partner glanced in the rear-view mirror briefly and could see the pursuers had turned onto the field behind them.

He knew they couldn't afford to stop or turn away which would mean instant surrender and capture. Decisively he pressed the accelerator all the way to the floor, he could see where there was a bit of a bank before the culvert and aimed for this. Damilola was pressed back in her seat and being thrown against the seat belt, she screamed.

'Bloody hell, what are you doing?'

Kinikanwo concentrating hard, took a moment to reply.

'It's up and over, or into the clutches of those bastards behind us.'

He steered the Discovery at the fast-approaching gap, even over the rutted field they were nearly at one hundred kilometres per hour, when steering precisely he hit the bank and then they were across. The left rear wheel caught the lip but the four-wheel drive from the rest of the wheels and their momentum managed to keep the Discovery going ensuring their safe arrival on the opposite bank.

It wasn't without issue though, the pair of them were jarred quite badly when the car crashed down and all the air bags were set off obscuring visibility and making it difficult to steer the vehicle. Kinikanwo crushed the steering wheel airbag with his left hand as best he could and steered with the other, it was only a case of keeping the Discovery straight and steering it away from the pursuers.

After a few minutes of travel, glancing in the offside wing mirror he could see their pursuers dismounting from the pickup and waving their guns at the rapidly disappearing duo. Judging they were clear of the threat of the AK 47's he stopped and the pair of them disembarked the Discovery.

'How do we get rid of these?'

Asked Damilola forcing her way out from under the airbags.

'Easy.'

Laughed her colleague pulling a vicious looking Damascus knife from his holdall in the rear seat of the car.

He pulled it from its sheath and burst all six of the airbags before cutting most of them away from their holders.

Before we go any further, pass me my holdall again, there's something else we may need. On receiving the bag, he pulled out a pistol, Damilola was astonished.

'What's that?'

'It's a Steyr M-A1 semi-automatic, double-actioned pistol with a full load and it's what my boss got me for our protection.'

'What happens at the border?'

'Nothing, if I'm asked, I'll declare it.'

He said hefting the pistol and checking its actions.

'Right let's get on.'

Chapter 21

Friendly Fire

'We'll just have to keep going north until we reach the next main drag.'

Kinikanwo said.

At that they set off using the suns direction to keep them moving north. They came to an almost impassable barrier, a wind break of the albida trees. These were too close together to allow them to pass through and their direction forced the Discovery and its passengers to move to the north east. They were slowly making progress bumping along over the recently ploughed arid field. Coming out of the shadow thrown by the trees, they were confronted by a totally, unexpected problem. They had been spotted because of the dust trail they had been leaving behind them. A fighter pilot of the Nigerian Air Force was looking for strange vehicles in this area thanks to reports of another Boko Haram intrusion that morning. The Range Rover below him was too good to miss, he surmised it could only belong to the rebels out here. Gaining permission from his controller to attack he dove his fighter down to a low level.

The Chengdu F7 (Fishbed) fighter of the Nigerian Air Force with its green and sand coloured livery shot low over the roof of the Discovery. Kinikanwo stopped, they both got out of the car and watched it racing away to the east. What they didn't know was the pilot had dived too early, but he was determined not to miss this glaring opportunity.

 Meanwhile Damilola waved at the disappearing aircraft frantically, seeing the plane as some sort of saviour.

The Fighter shot up into the sky turning and then dived towards the earth as it began its return run. Suddenly Kinikanwo realised the reality of the situation, they were in serious trouble. He screamed urgently at Damilola.

'Quick, back in the bloody car!'

'But!'

Kinikanwo didn't bother answering, using all his energy to race for the driver's seat of the Touareg.

It was at that point Damilola got the message, even as she was clambering into the vehicle, her partner was accelerating and swinging the Discovery round, back towards the line of wind breaking trees. They were just in time, the shells from the fighter's 30mm cannon crashed into the ground in big spurts not far from where they had just been parked.

The Nigerian Air Force fighter rushed overhead but by the time it had swung round to come back for another strafing run, the Discovery and its passengers, were relatively safely ensconced on the west side of the tree line.

Damilola whimpered fearfully, a tear running down her left
cheek.

'What are we going to do?'

Kinikanwo was angry rather than scared and said out aloud.

'I'm stuck with a bloody crying woman, shot at by my own
bloody side, I'm going to get on the bloody phone.'

Grabbing the satellite phone, he thought for a moment, dialled a
number from memory, waited and when it was answered said.

'General, its Kinikanwo I have a problem.'

There was a pause.

Damilola looked across at Kinikanwo, wiped her damp eyes,
looked astonished at her partner and started to comment.

'What ....'

She stopped when Kinikanwo put a finger to his lips to indicate
he needed silence. He waved an arm all around and upwards to
indicate Damilola should keep a good lookout on the land and in
the sky in case any more armed men should approach, or
fighters return.

After some moments listening he replied.

'Sir I'm up north of Jigawa, there appears to be a strong force of
the rebels to the East of us. I believe they control the village,
plus we've just been strafed by one of our fly boys in a
Chengdu.'

Damilola heeded Kinikanwo's advice and was now
concentrating on looking everywhere. She left the vehicle and
scurried up to the end of the treeline to check there was nothing
going to surprise them from the east.

'Okay, we're on our own and the best you reckon is to head west before going for the border.'

He listened again to the General, he was getting irritated with the Officer at the other end of the phone. He thumped the steering wheel with his free hand in frustration.

'Thanks a bunch for nothing.'

Kinikanwo cut off the call and shouted to Damilola.

'Let's get out of here.'

Damilola was still at the north end of the treeline keeping a lookout for any further trouble. She came jogging back to the Discovery, her footsteps raising small sand trails on the dusty ground, Kinikanwo updated her.

'The General was of little help except for one thing, the Chengdu Fighter that had a go at us has gone back home.'

'Apparently it has engine trouble and the other six are unable to fly now either.'

'It's the usual, maintenance issues.'

Damilola was curious.

'How the hell do you know a General?'

'Oh him, it's just my Grandfather, he's nothing special, they just gave him the rank because he's been in the Nigerian Army for ever.'

'He's not far away in fact, at One Division Headquarters to the south west of us in Kaduna.'

'They'll tell the Head of Armed Forces of our experiences and there might be some action in the next day or so.'

'You mean you can just ring up the army.'

'Well yes, he is my Grandad after all.'

Damilola shook her head in disbelief.

'What are we supposed to do now?'

'The old General said to wait for nightfall, well I reckon he's wrong, I think we need to go west slowly to keep the trailing dust cloud down and find a decent track to follow.'

'Apparently there's lots of small villages around here and if we find one, we'll find a rough road to get away to the northwest.'

Damilola hadn't much choice but agreed in principle, they remounted the Discovery and Kinikanwo bumped it slowly across the next field. Damilola standing on the front passenger seat had her head out of the open sunroof to give them a fractionally higher and all-round lookout.

Reaching the other side of the field, they found a track and could head in a near westerly direction towards signs of habitation.

Damilola stuck her head back into the car.

'Can't see anything.'

'Okay, keep your eyes open.'

Damilola stood up on the passenger seat with her head out of the sunroof again, scanning the horizon and sky, trying to keep a three-hundred-and-sixty-degree lookout.

The track went through a farmyard, three alarmed white chickens scooted around the far corner of the single-story yellow building with black sloping roof. It had few windows and what there were had black bars over them. There was a similarly built barn in yellow also but half a storey higher at right angles to the farmhouse.

At first except for the chickens nothing else stirred in the compact, dusty earthen yard. Suddenly the stillness was broken by furious barking and an emaciated black dog with white markings came careering out of the barn. The hound tried to leap onto the bonnet of the Discovery to get at those inside. Damilola flinched at the perceived attack by the mangy hound. Unhappy at the failed assault the dog reluctantly resorted to nipping at the rear offside tyre.

The other side of the farmyard was a dirt track which looked like the only thoroughfare of any kind. It passed in front of the Barn in a north/south direction. With the farm dog alternately barking and attempting to puncture the rear tyre, Kinikanwo accelerated onto the track and took the road north.

The farmyard protector emitted a furious bark at the rear of the departing vehicle, chased them for a few steps, before settling onto its haunches in the middle of the track convinced it had scared the invaders away, job done.

Although they were now creating their own dust cloud, Kinikanwo concluded that once they hit any sort of thoroughfare it was better to take the risk of being spotted and making progress at forty kilometres per hour away from the perceived threat.

A couple of kilometres on Kinikanwo unavoidably drove the Discovery through a large pothole. There was a wail from above him, Damilola dropped down and thumped her bottom into the passenger seat rubbing her chin.

'Bastard roads that bloody well hurt.'

'When you hit that crevasse, the car roof came up and smacked me on the chin.'

Kinikanwo laughed.

'Better stay down here, put your seat belt on, hold on tight, we're going to try and out-run anything else that comes our way.'

He accelerated harder, the Discovery took it all in its stride, its excellent suspension ironing out some of the punishment being meted out by the rough road surface. Occasionally a larger bump in the road would cause two wheels to briefly lift off the track's surface and they would land with a bit of a thump, which both felt right up their spines.

Within half an hour they reached a junction and found a proper road surface, crossing in front of them. There was no crossing traffic, Kinikanwo swept them around to the west away from the assumed danger and pressed the accelerator to the floor. The Discovery as if sensing its freedom from the previous dangerous environment raced along the tarmacked highway. They raced across another crossroads and shortly after slower down for their return to the A2 which now crossed their path. There was a black Nigerian police truck, with its green and white stripe representing the Nigerian flag along its body, parked across the approach to the major road.

Seeing the approaching vehicle, two policemen in their green fatigues and protective black waistcoats peered across the roof of the cab of their transport, guns at the ready. Kinikanwo braked hard and brought the Discovery to a stop.

Tension in his voice he ordered.

'Out of the car Damilola.'

Damilola annoyed at the tone of her colleague's voice slammed the passenger door open.

Realising Damilola was unaware of their precarious situation and knowing how they acted in the next few seconds was vital, Kinikanwo whispered urgently.

'Slowly they're pointing guns at us, no sudden moves.'

Realisation hit, Damilola was suddenly very frightened and shaking again as Kinikanwo issued other instructions

'Hands in the air and walk towards them.'

'I'll be right alongside you, be careful, they'll be trigger happy and have itchy fingers.'

'They'll be scared to death out here on their own.'

'The rebels have taken out a lot of police patrols over the years.'

Damilola did as Kinikanwo told her carefully backing out of the car. She walked slowly along the road her partner matching her pace with his hands also raised high.

Damilola could feel he heart racing, she couldn't stop her teeth chattering, sweat ran into and stung her eyes but she didn't dare lower her raised arms. she tried to look at the two policemen in an unconcerned and unthreatening manner though in reality she was extremely frightened.

Kinikanwo smiled at the two officers and spoke quietly to his colleague as they slowly covered the twenty metres between them and the police vehicle.

'If they start shooting drop to the floor, make yourself as small as you can, they probably can't hit a barn door.'

Kinikanwo wasn't confident, he was surprised they hadn't been sprayed with bullets from the two automatic weapons held by the officers already. If they hadn't been shot at yet, there was a chance they might yet come through unscathed.

He knew it was important to act slowly, not give any excuse for a violent reaction. He hoped Damilola would continue to follow his lead as they slowly, one foot at a time, made their way towards the danger.

Suddenly one of the policemen, seeing they were no threat, laughed heartily and left his automatic weapon on the roof of his truck before walking over to Kinikanwo and Damilola smiling.

'Hi Kini, put your arms down, we're not in the army anymore.'

Kinikanwo lowered his arms gratefully as he recognised the ex-army colleague from their Officer training days. The pair of them hugged each other.

'It's alright Damilola we're old mates.'

Damilola gasped out a huge gasp, realising she had been holding her breath as they had approached the two police officers.

The other policeman was now taking little notice of them, he was concentrating on trying to light a cigarette in the strong, desert wind.

The two ex-army Officers passed on all the information they had. His old army buddy said he was supposed to stop all the traffic from the east, while Kinikanwo explained they were trying to make their way into Niger.

After more backslapping Damilola and Kinikanwo returned to the Discovery and turned north feeling a lot safer. The latter told Damilola he had joined and left the army together, his pal, who getting a better offer from the National Police Force, had moved on.

Time was getting on; thanks to the diversions they hadn't progressed as far as they planned that morning. Neither of them wanted another experience of night driving. The huge desert truck trains pounding their way behind or towards them were frightening enough in daylight, they decided to find somewhere to stop for the night.

They slowed to pass through Daura, Damilola suggested it might have a motel, Kinikanwo was dismissive of such an idea in the small town. They passed the local college and then the Unity Bank and Damilola began to be hopeful. Just as they were about to exit the small town, on their left-hand side appeared the Daura Motel, its neon sign, glowing like a welcoming beacon in the disappearing light.

Chapter 22

Thursday 5th November - Crossing into Niger

The following day Thursday, at the Daura Motel, Kinikanwo managed to obtain them some breakfast before they set out north towards the border posts. They decided not to take the shorter northerly route to the border after the previous day's escapades but too make the safer run to the bigger crossing point at Jibiya nearly two hours to the west of them.

The Touareg had left Kano just after seven in the morning and was only about thirty minutes ahead of the Nigerians when the Discovery pulled out of the motel and started its journey west. The Touareg was also making for the border post at Jibiya.

Oscar knew he could guarantee getting their exit visas stamped there, otherwise he would have problems with his re-entry when he tried to return to Nigeria in December.

The two vehicles rattled along with the border traffic, thirty minutes apart, both pairs of travellers were concerned about their safety on the Nigerian side of the border. Recent newspaper reports had suggested the long border with Niger was porous and run by smuggling gangs.

The highway was very busy, probably due to the rebel threat to the east of them. It was just over two hours later, after their trip westwards through the arid countryside alongside the A9 that Mac and Oscar arrived at the crossing east of Jibiya. There was a long queue of overloaded trucks, vans, cars and even motorbikes piled high with goods intended for their northern neighbour and beyond.

They arrived at the rear of the border traffic queue, behind a car and trailer stacked to the gunwales with what appeared to be mainly rolls of white cloth. The Dakar Rally 2 Touareg in its rally colours caused quite a stir as all the locals stopped what they were doing and crowded around the exciting new arrival.

They waited patiently in the queue. Outside it was very hot and the dry north-east wind was blowing layers of dust over everything. Every part of the dirt verge was occupied by locals taking advantage of the queue for the border. They were trying to sell tacky tourist items, fresh fruit and vegetables. Some enterprising souls had gas fuelled stoves offering hot food and drinks. Most had soft hand brushes with which they kept brushing the dust off their wares. There was even a Moroccan gentleman in a grubby tweed suit and red fez selling carpets off the back of a small lorry.

The queue to the Border Post stopped moving as the driver of a massive red and yellow tanker, two vehicles ahead of them dumped his vehicle and trotted back to get himself a selfie alongside the Touareg. He was a burly, black-man clad in a red and yellow boiler suit to match the colouring of his road tanker.

Oscar and Mac had realised on the trip north through Nigeria, they were going to be a major attraction wherever they stopped. They realised they needed to do something to appease the sightseers every time they halted. Mac had the idea of getting photographs of the car copied up to hand out and if necessary sign for the crowds. Consequently, while they were stopped in the queue Oscar got out of the Touareg smiling and distributed lots of these pictures. The crowd's inquisitiveness was pleasantly assuaged by the free present.

The tanker driver was a great help using his size like a bodyguard. Even so it took a while for the crowd to be satisfied and by that time the traffic queue, ahead of the stationary tanker disappeared leaving an empty road to the border post.

The tanker driver realising his task was now complete urged them back into the Touareg. He took his life in his hands, acting like a traffic policeman and stepped out in front of the southbound oncoming traffic to halt it and create space so they could overtake the truck ahead and his tanker.

The tanker driver seemed unconcerned as he stood there, right arm outstretched in front of him with palm raised. Until a black Land Rover Discovery came blasting up the wrong side of the road nearly knocking him over as it rushed through the narrow gap between the tanker, its driver and the drainage ditch on the side of the road. This wasn't the end of it for the tanker driver, having picked himself up from the roadway, where he had thrown himself to avoid the onrushing vehicle he tried again. He took up his policeman like stance once more and confronted an onrushing southbound truck. Fortunately, the little driver from Niger wearing a well-greased white T shirt in his overloaded Articulated lorry managed to use his exhaust brakes and stop just before he mangled the tanker driver all over his radiator. The acting policeman smilingly unconcerned, waved the Touareg through to the Nigerian Border Post, there was no queue now thanks to the hold-up.

Mac laughed.

'See mate, well worth the price of a few photographs,'

Oscar nodded his head in agreement.

'More seriously did you see that Discovery.'

'Yeah, impatient bastard.'

'No, it's not that, I know the vehicle.'

'What do you mean?'

'The Chief uses it sometimes, it's his fathers.'

'Not only that the I think the Chief's niece was in the front passenger seat.'

***

Oscar was right it was the Nigerians who with Kinikanwo driving and with the threats from his sponsor ringing in his ears had got impatient when they arrived at the rear of the border queue. Seeing the traffic coming the other way was infrequent, Kinikanwo had accelerated the Discovery up the outside of the stationary traffic having only twice needing to squeeze back into line to avoid oncoming southbound trucks. A cacophony of noise followed them as other more patient drivers gave voice by mouth and vehicle horns to their annoyance at this queue jumping.

They quickly cleared the stationary queue of traffic and it was Damilola who easily spotted the Touareg in its colourful livery surrounded as it was by curious onlookers. He excitedly shouted to his partner who was concentrating on the narrow gap between the tanker driver ahead and the verge of the road. 'There it is.'

'I know.'

With the tanker driver left gesticulating happily in the dust astern of them and the road ahead empty of traffic they soon arrived at the Nigerian Border Post. A whitewashed, rectangular, single-storey building.

On their right side they were by greeted by an Official in white trousers and green uniform jacket. He was taking one hundred Naira notes off every vehicle which were then waved on through the uplifted border post.

When they reached the Nigerian official, Kinikanwo who was driving, handed over two one hundred Naira notes and like the others was allowed onwards.

There didn't seem to be any identifiable change in the town as they made their way across the neutral zone. They could see due to fallen green sign propped up against a wooden post, the road was now designated the N9 by the Niger authorities.

There was no sign of a Niger Border Post and they had to pull into a building marked Douane in the village beyond the border. There was a barrier of colourfully painted oil barrels lining the car park, Kinikanwo steered the Discovery between two of them and parked alongside the single-storey, low-slung, white building with its sloping red-tiled roof.

When they entered the two clerks at their desks inside the hot, dry, non-air-conditioned building were dealing with a brisk trade. The clerk wanted to see the pair's passports, they were asked if they wanted to pay the tolls at the Douane. They agreed and were charged thirty Euros, (3,000 CFA [Central African Francs]) for three days unlimited toll charge. Damilola took the three-day pass which would allow them through the toll booths. Their Nigerian Passports meant they didn't need visas and the official indicated they were welcome to get on their way.

Not needing another hint Damilola and Kinikanwo made their way back to the Discovery and still having a Nigerian signal on their mobile phones they reported into their respective mentors. The Chief was unhappy with their progress until Damilola explained about their near misses with Boko Haram and the Nigerian Air Force. The conversation became more positive once the Chief realised they were ahead of their target. Kinikanwo's boss was happy they had encountered the Touareg, 'however he couldn't accept any further 'excuses,' as he called them and trusted they would now stay in control of the situation.

***

The Brits tried to think of the reasons for the Discovery's presence as they quickly drove the last few hundred metres to the Nigerian Border Post. It was the same Nigerian Border

Guard who had relieved the Discovery's two occupants of their 200 Naira. He glanced up because of the sudden lack of traffic then realised there was a bit of a celebrity coming through when he saw the dusty rally car.

Putting on a serious face he indicated that both the driver and his passenger should leave the car and present themselves in front of him.

Oscar whispered across the car to Mac.

'Crap an awkward sod.'

Grabbing their paperwork as the guard shouted to others inside the Border post the two adventurers left the vehicle and approached the official whose face suddenly lit up into a huge smile.

'Can we have a photograph with you and the car?'

He pointed to the other three guards hurrying out of the building all in the process of putting on and buttoning up their green tunic blouses.

Oscar sighed with relief and looked across at his Scottish counterpart who was shaking the first guards' hand and muttering.

'Unbelievable.'

It took about fifteen minutes of pictures and selfies with the guard's mobile phones and getting their permits stamped before they could leave the Border Post and cross over into Niger. The queue with the red and yellow tanker, with its smiling driver had built up again and was made to wait. Even then the officials didn't return to work immediately, the queue had to wait while the men compared photographs.

By this time the Touareg had reached the Douane Offices, there were three armed Niger Gendarmes waiting for them. There had been some sort of notification of their arrival. One of the metal barrels had been rolled away, there was space for them to drive through to the front of the building where armed Gendarmes marshalled them through.

They stepped from the car and two of the armed policemen waved them into the building. The other stayed outside alongside their vehicle.

A clerk checked their visas and passports, he stamped them before offering the three-day highway toll pass which Mac paid for in American dollars.

After the formalities were complete, the senior guard politely asked in English with a nasally French accent if it would be possible to take a picture of the famous rally drivers and their car. Would they mind if he could even have his picture taken sitting in the driver's seat?

They agreed willingly, after a series of pictures, while Oscar handed out free photographs to the crowd which had mysteriously appeared. This done to everyone's satisfaction they could set off northwards on the N9.

***

These delays put the Discovery and its occupants about twenty kilometres ahead of the Touareg. The road was still metalled but quite narrow, whichever was the driver had to keep an eye

190

on the side of the road to make sure it was alright to put a wheel off the tarmac when a wide truck came barrelling past from the other direction.

Kinikanwo stopped and handed the driving over to Damilola, he needed to work out a routing that would be safe but also get them to Agadez as fast as possible.

After a while he deduced the best and safest routing was through the southern city of Zinder thee hundred kilometres away. There they could turn north for Agadez. It would at times mean flirting with the northern Nigerian border but better that than lesser little-known routings through central Niger. There were no reports of Boko Haram making any recent incursions across to the Niger side of the border. He reckoned the faster more used highway was worth the risk.

'Damilola, I've worked out a routing, but it means we've got a straight seven hundred klicks to go.'

'What about stopping somewhere en route and doing it over two days?'

We can't, we don't know which route they're going to take in the Rally Car.'

'Why's that?'

Kinikanwo fumed he was used to making decisions and not having to answer to a bloody woman, especially one with her sexual preferences, he grudgingly gave his reasons.'

'We're now ahead of them right!'

'Yes'

'The only place I know they have to go through is Agadez, it's the pinch point everyone has to pass through to get to the Algerian border.'

'To keep on top of the situation, now we know where they are, we have to be in Agadez first.'

Damilola glanced over from the driver's seat at Kinikanwo and frowned, unconvinced by the latter's logic.

Kinikanwo sighed deeply before deciding to try and simplify the situation.

'Right, think of a square.'

'Yes.'

'Both of us are at the bottom left hand corner of the square and Agadez is at the top right-hand corner, now we can go up the left side and along the top of the square or along the bottom and up the right side.'

Damilola gripped the steering wheel tightly as she realised what Kinikanwo was trying to explain to her.

'I get it because we don't know which way they're going we can't risk them beating us to Agadez that's fine, let's go for it.'

Kinikanwo pointed out one unfortunate fact of this plan

'I know we'll not make Agadez until midnight, though it almost guarantees we're ahead and they would have to pass us then.'

Damilola cursed their luck.

'Blast, night driving again.'

'Yeah, I know, the roads shouldn't be so full of trucks though, the local authorities frown upon commercial vehicles driving these routes at night.'

'You sure the roads will be empty?'

'Bound to be, now can I book us a hotel in Agadez?'

'Suppose so.'

Kinikanwo had used his time overnight in Kano to do some forward planning. He already knew the best hotel in Agadez and had the telephone number programmed into the satellite phone. He dialled up the number and booked them a room, warning the Receptionist they were likely to be late.

Kinikanwo was in his element organising everything, this upset Damilola who was feeling undervalued again and having bitter thoughts about her colleague.

The first major town in Niger was Maradi, they used the opportunity before they turned east to refuel, topped up their spare drum and bought a large pack of bottled water.

Twenty minutes after they left the petrol station the Touareg pulled in to do the same thing.

Chapter 23

East and North

Oscar and Mac had tried to think of a reason other than themselves for the Discovery and the Chief's niece being at the border at the same time as them, any possible answer eluded them until Oscar came up with an idea as they pulled into the petrol station at Maradi.

'Mac, we need to search the car from top to bottom.'

'Oscar, you can't be serious.'

'I am.'

Oscar explained his reasoning to Mac.

'Either that Range Rover is the biggest and most unbelievable coincidence or they're following us.'

'Why would they do that?'

Mac continued.

'The Touareg isn't that valuable, they can't want to steal it back surely.'

'No, it's not that, I think we might be carrying something.'

Mac looked across at Oscar in the driving seat of the Touareg and thought for a moment while pulling at his chin with his left hand.

'You know you could be onto something, they were extremely interested in our plans, weren't they?'

Oscar pleased his partner had come around to his way of thinking explained.

'That's why we need to check over the car, we could have drugs, or anything planted in the vehicle.'

Mac had another idea, he nodded his head vigorously, put his right finger to his lips to indicate they shouldn't talk and indicated by waving the same hand to suggest they should leave the car. Oscar followed his partner out into the heat of the day and the pair walked about ten metres away from the Touareg, onto the dusty, concrete forecourt.

Mac spoke first.

'The more I think about it, what you said makes sense.'

Oscar was puzzled as to why Mac had dragged them away from the vehicle.

'Why can't we talk in the car?'

'Someone might be listening, if they've hidden something, drugs or the like we don't want them knowing we've found it.'

'Alright then, what do we do?'

Mac laughed, wiped his sweating brow with a grubby handkerchief before answering.

'We put the car in the shade next to the pumps and clear out the car to see if we can find anything.'

For the next two hours they silently emptied and repacked the vehicle and found precisely nothing. Neither thought to look inside the water tank although they would have seen very little because of its opaque panel construction.

The search finished, the now shattered British ex-pats completed their top-up of fuel and water. While in the shade of the petrol station canopy they laid their map of Niger on the Touareg's bonnet. It was hot, there was little cloud and a light dry breeze blew bits of discarded litter across the forecourt After discussing the possibilities, they decided to make their way north to Dakoro on the N1 first before making their way east to pick up the northbound N11 to Agadez. This would mean a campsite somewhere and they wouldn't make the Hotel Tidene in Agadez for another day. While they had mobile phone contact in Maradi Mac changed the original booking and Oscar looked through their information to find a secure campsite within reasonable distance from where they were presently parked.

All through their search a teenage lad of about sixteen clad in patched denim shorts and a Manchester United football shirt had sat watching them and said nothing until he heard them talking about their route. He got up from his cross-legged perch on an old tyre, shaded by the fuel station building, moved closer and interrupted their conversation.

'I am Ali.'

'I am sorry to bother you sirs, you must not go that way.'

'Why's that?'

Mac was amused with the idea of this scruffy kid advising them but willing to listen to the local child's thoughts.

'There are bandits and kidnappers that way, it isn't safe.'

'How do you know?'

'I have seen the bodies when they are found, it isn't pretty, you must go through Zinder.'

Oscar interrupted the kid.

'How come you speak such good English?'

'I learn it from the Premier League, Manchester good.'

He said tapping the Manchester United badge on his shirt.

'How do we know you're telling us the truth?'

'You don't, you must ask the cashier if I am correct.'

He pointed back to garage attendant and smiled.

Mac looked at Oscar who nodded.

'Alright kid thanks.'

Mac handed over one of their photographs and a twenty-dollar bill.

'Zinder, it is Oscar.'

Oscar had another look at the map before folding it and putting it back into the car.

'Right that's about two hundred and fifty kilometres, let's say four hours that will put us there around five.'

'There's no campsite advertised in the book, we'll see what we can find when we get there.'

'Great let's get on with it.'

'Agreed, let's get out of here.'

They accelerated away from the refuelling stop in a cloud of dust waving to the onlooking teenager through the open windows of the vehicle.

***

Up ahead in the Discovery Kinikanwo wasn't hanging about, they were making excellent progress along the N1, through their first proper experience of the Saharan desert. The section to Aguie the next major point of civilisation, eighty kilometres out of Maradi was completed in less than an hour.

What traffic there was, were the mainly large, generally overloaded Articulated lorries. They varied from the new with their pristine paintwork only soiled by dust from the desert sands, to older rust buckets which were still as enthusiastically driven but looked to be only held together with bits of chewing gum and string.

Ten minutes after passing through Aguie they left the N1 at Gazaoua a small village out in the desert. The only moving object some large crows and the listless wagging tail of a mangy dog resting on a sandstone doorstep.

The N1 headed north at this point, while the Discovery turned eastwards along the N10 towards Zinder. After ninety minutes close to the village of Korgom the road rose over an escarpment before zig zagging down into some arid farmland. The highway became the N1 again at Takieta, another small village, only there because the two roads met at that point. Here they changed drivers, both rushing urgently around the Discovery determined not to waste any time.

The traffic on this major east-west highway was thin except for the monster international haulage trucks they passed. Damilola and Kinikanwo put it down to the ravages of Boko Haram just across the border to the south of them.

Two and half hours later they were turning left and north onto the N11 by the Post Office in the middle of Zinder. It was now three thirty in the afternoon and people were starting to stroll around the boulevards and visit the shops which were just re-opening after the main heat of the day.

They were able to blast through Niger's second city in a few minutes, there being little traffic movement through the town. To the north of Niger's second largest metropolis, there was a massive truck park with what must have been around a hundred dusty, mainly white trucks parked up. There was an escarpment to the east towering over the N1 close to this massive vehicle refuge and it loomed over the highway as they travelled further north.

There was little conversation between the two of them and once clear and free of the city Damilola opened-up the Discovery. They were soon eating into the four hundred and fifty kilometres between them and Niger's most northerly major city, Agadez. Kinikanwo was convinced the Touareg and its occupants couldn't get ahead of them again. Damilola ever the pessimist wasn't so sure and was a lot more uncertain. She was positive that with the pace of the Rally car the Touareg could easily be in front.

Damilola was also still running scared, their encounter with the Boko Haram rebels and the Nigerian Air Force Fighter had really frightened her. Plus, she detested Kinikanwo, though she envied his confidence. Kinikanwo was always giving orders and making decisions without talking it through with her. She was also frightened of the Chief's reaction if they didn't manage to follow the Touareg successfully. Once they were clear of Zinder she built up enough courage to confront Kinikanwo with her concerns.

'You seem very certain they haven't rushed ahead of us by using the more westerly route.'

'If you're wrong we're in a right bloody mess.'

Kinikanwo tried to soothe Damilola's feelings.'

'Fair enough Damilola, you carry on driving and I'll re-check my calculations.'

Kinikanwo checked his calculations of distances and times and assumptions about what the Brits would do.

'If we get to Agadez tonight it will be impossible for them to be ahead and then they will have to pass us to get in front.'

'The only other route is longer and it's risky, there have been recent reports of abductions and drivers being held hostage.'

Damilola shook her head in frustration and inwardly disagreed with her partner's confidence.

***

Meanwhile at a more leisurely pace the Touareg was crossing the high point of the route to Zinder expecting to arrive before sunset at around five thirty. They were warned of the oncoming sunset when Oscar who was driving had to adjust the rear-view mirror to prevent the sun's rays blinding him.

Oscar slowed when he realised the desert on the left side of the road was busy with lots of horses and riders.

He eased off braked and they stopped to watch the fun from their side of the road. It was then they realised there was a dirt race track to their left. They had come upon some of the runners and riders awaiting their turn to race.

A magnificent grey Arab was doing his best to unseat a young black rider, clothed all in white with a red cap. An even younger groom who must have only been about ten years old was trying to hold onto the horse's head with a bridle. The poor kid was shaken off and the horse skittered onto the road in front of the Touareg. The frightened Groom jumped out in front of the horse and held both of his arms out, forward palms upraised in a warning to the Touareg to please not move.

Oscar switched off the idling engine hoping not to frighten the magnificent stallion further. He hoped it would help the rider and groom get the situation under control.

It was not to be, a large white oncoming Articulated lorry was less patient and sounded his deep throated horn. This caused mayhem amongst the half-wild equine thoroughbreds.

'Just hope one of those brutes doesn't get to close and damage the car.'

Mac commented as they sat on their side of the highway waiting for the melee to calm down.

After causing the initial commotion the driver of the offending vehicle realised his error and had the common sense to slow to a crawl as a crowd of mounted riders on their west African Barb stallions spread across the highway.

This bunch of riders surrounded the escaped stallion, calming the creature who was quickly returned to his jockey and the race track.

Having observed a race charge off around the sand track the white metal winning post sitting in front of a single Acacia tree. Oscar cautiously drove onwards into the city; all the side roads were of hardened earth and as they approached the junction with the N1 there a traffic jam. They were unable to see what was causing the problem at the T junction ahead and for thirty minutes they never moved. Mac decided he would have a look to see why they were being held up and walked off ahead to find out what was causing the problem.

Further up the road on the pavement corner of the junction and outside the main Post Office. Mac found a scrawny old Arab with a lined face of aging wrinkles sitting in a grubby white plastic chair. With the help of Mac's limited French and some sign language, he learnt the rush of traffic heading into Zinder from the south and east and clogging up the junction was because of the recent ravages of Boko Haram around the local border with Nigeria.

It appeared the local Governor had decided to open the border to the south of them a couple of hours before. This to allow people to flee the ravages of the Muslim rebels. The resulting hordes of refugees had started to reach the relative safety of Zinder in the previous hour.

Zinder was seen as a safe refuge because of the presence and protection of a contingent of the Niger army in the local barracks.

Mac also asked about accommodation but was told they would be better camping in the truck park to the north as the last time this happened every bed in the city was given over to the refugees from the border.

He worked out from the old man's gestures that there was chance of toilets and bathing facilities at the truck park.

Standing there watching he was in time to see the army take charge of the junction and stop the northbound traffic which allowed them and those ahead to turn left and north out onto the N11.

The second largest city in Niger was now crowded with the evacuees from the south. Overloaded cars and pick-ups thronged the sidewalks, every possible free space was taken up by these hordes. The highway itself was only kept clear by lines of The National Gendarmerie in their green paramilitary uniform. Gradually they made their way north through the crowds along the tree lined highway. They passed the modern looking football stadium where the traffic thinned, and they soon cleared the buildings at the north end of the city. The overwhelming escarpment to the east of the road was emphasised by the glow of the declining westerly sun lighting up its nearly sheer walls. At first it appeared to block the highway to the north of them but just at its nearest point to the road, they found the truck park.

The panoply of trucks was predominantly white coloured again, no doubt to reflect the strong desert sun. All were about to, or had already crossed the Sahara Desert, many had spare wheels, tow wires and extra drums of diesel fuel attached to the exterior of their cabs. They were all parked in a partially walled area on either side of the highway. Almost opposite the main park under the towering wall of the escarpment was a brick-built toilet-block of some antiquity.

Everywhere there were drivers from all over Africa, they were socialising in groups round open fires contained by old burnt and rusted fuel drums. Their mission of supplying Africa inviting the sort of camaraderie only otherwise found amongst the old Antarctic explorers

They parked up in the larger truck park to the west of the road, reckoning the security was greater hidden amongst the vaster number of vehicles. There must have been around a hundred of these, all with massive tractors for hauling their cargoes long distances.

Their logo's showed companies from all over Central, North and West Africa. There was even a modern Articulated lorry advertising its home base nearly seven thousand kilometres away in Harare, Zimbabwe.

Even though Oscar deliberately hid the Rally Car between two large trucks they were soon engulfed by curious truck driver onlookers. The endless supply of photographs made even more new friends and after explaining why they were there most of the curious departed.

Their two neighbours, friendly Palestine refugee brothers driving the two trucks between which they had parked, worked for a company in Algiers. They were on their way to Lagos with engineering parts for a new power plant. Dressed in grubby well-worn green boiler suits the pair were welcoming and offered up some of their mutton stew with rice.

This was bubbling in a blackened pot, over one of the fuel drum fires, to the front of the left-hand truck. Oscar and Mac were cautious about accepting, thinking about the risk of food poisoning. However they couldn't really refuse such generous hospitality without causing offence, both accepted and were surprised by the tasty if somewhat greasy offering.

Their companions advised them to sleep in their vehicle because when it was quiet, they said the place was infested with rats and the scorpions weren't very pleasant either.

They were prepared for this, part of Mac's renovations of the Touareg meant the front car seats could be laid back horizontally. They both said goodnight to their new Palestinian friends, retired early and were soon curled up in sleeping bags on each of the Touareg's now horizontal seats.

Chapter 24

Flat out to Agadez

While those in the Touareg were getting their heads down, the Discovery was labouring up a severe slope beyond the small town of Tanout less than halfway between Zinder and Agadez. Kinikanwo was driving, it was just after five in the evening and the sun was about to disappear behind the mountains on their left side. A lot of the road was partially covered in lightly blown sand, however they were making decent progress on the near empty highway.

Kinikanwo spotted something black on the road ahead but couldn't react in time to avoid the nearside wheels colliding with the obstruction. They both felt impact of the collision and then the car suddenly juddering which could only mean a flat tyre. Kinikanwo pulled them over to the hardened packed earth on the side of the highway, with them both cursing their luck. They prepared to change the nearside rear tyre which was shredded thanks to the collision with the road debris.

Working quickly together they unloaded one of the two spares and jacked up the car. At this point, they ran into a problem which Kinikanwo searching the glove compartment was the first to slowly realise. Fairly sure they weren't going to find what he was looking for and dreading the expected answer he yelled across to his partner.

'Have you seen it?'

'What?'

'The special box spanner, without it we can't remove the bloody wheel nuts.'

He slapped the top of the Discovery with his right palm in disgust.

'That bloody Chief of yours, couldn't organise a piss up in a brewery.'

He quickly stopped his diatribe, thought for a moment and quickly came to a decision.

'I'll watch the car.'

'You'll have to walk back to that last town and see what you can find.'

Damilola felt thoroughly miserable, she had more than enough of being ordered around, never mind this wild goose chase. She started to complain bitterly.

'Why the bloody hell should I have to go back?'

'Why can't you do it?'

'Because I must protect the car you stupid bitch, you reckon you can fend off a couple of bandits.'

'Well no.'

Damilola realised she had lost another argument and angrily grabbing a torch she marched back down the side of the road towards the lights of Tanout. These were getting brighter now in

207

the enclosing darkness; the sun had just set behind the engulfing mountains. For the first fifteen minutes the western sky was streaked red and gold which quickly turned into a darkening purple before suddenly the heavens were lit by millions of stars in the clear desert sky.

Damilola couldn't care about the desert sky above her. She knew she had to walk two rotten kilometres back to the town, to try and find a mechanic. There was little traffic and all northbound, only the odd heavy wagon risking the night run. Nothing going her way from which she might risk hitching a lift. Her Hijab which she had been wearing since their entry into Niger at least gave her face some protection from the cool, desert, night winds.

After forty minutes she trudged off the highway to make her way into Tanout. The streets were only dimly lit by the lights thrown from the single-story buildings. A carpet vendor in dirty white Thobe and brown sandals was loading his wares onto a long-suffering donkey. They were outside a small shop and the man was the first-person Damilola had met on the now deserted streets.

Having no French or Arabic it took a lot of hand signalling to communicate Damilola's need for a mechanic. Once the vendor understood he pointed eagerly to a light illuminating a green metal table with a couple of matching chairs twenty metres ahead. It displayed the international Coca Cola sign and proved to be the answer to Damilola's need.

Inside was a small café with only a single male sitting on a high stool leaning on a counter talking to a rotund Arabic gentleman in a white grease stained T shirt drinking coffee. Damilola approached them.

'Do either of you speak English please?'

The guy on the stool put down his coffee turned and looked out from his heavily grease stained features and answered.

'A little.'

Damilola explained her problem, the guy looked at her stood up in his filthy boiler suit picked up a rusty, blue tool box off the tiled floor.

'You pay?'

Damilola nodded her head vigorously and pulled some American dollars from her back pocket.

The greasy face in front of her lit up and an even greasier hand snatched away the proffered money.

'Follow me.'

Within moments they were making their way back to the Discovery in the mechanics battered grey Peugeot estate, which like its owner was covered in a grimy layer of dirt and grease.

They arrived back at the Discovery and in no time the mechanic somehow magically got the nuts off with something from his rusty blue toolbox. Once Damilola had put the spare wheel on the mechanic tightened up the nuts returned to his car and was gone the whole exercise completed in minutes.

It was now very late and meant it was going to be sometime in the early hours before they made Agadez. Both were shattered, dirty and hungry. On top of it all their morale was low because there was no sign of the Touareg and even Kinikanwo was worried he had made a mistake.

On top of everything else they were slowed as they encountered innumerable road works. Some of the diversions were slight while others took them up to a kilometre into the desert. Fortunately, the desert roadway diversions had been hardened and packed down tight by the passing of heavy trucks. There had been little rain recently, otherwise some of the detours would have been impassable.

Eventually at just after two in the morning they rolled into Agadez. Finding the Hotel Tidene was quite simple thanks to Kinikanwo's directions. There was nothing on the streets, the city was quite dead. Only the odd dim orange street light to help them locate the Hotel.

Both were too tired to worry about the security of the Discovery dumping it as near the Hotels entrance as possible. There were only half a dozen other travel stained vehicles in the parking lot, it looked like the Hotel Tidene wasn't particularly busy.

Looking through the hotel's glass locked front door, they could see a man in a uniform jacket stretched out in the Reception area. He was facing them, slumped mouth agape, fast asleep in an armchair. His tanned, bare-feet resting on an ornate wooden coffee table.

It took three rings of the door-bell and Kinikanwo banging his right fist angrily on the glass door to wake the slumbering Night Porter. Much to the chagrin of the two exhausted travellers, the gentleman took his time, sat up, stretched his arms, yawned and rubbed his eyes before rising slowly to his feet.

The short portly man looked at the front door as if in surprise, then stretched both arms wide, turned a half-circle and yawned with a gaping mouth. He looked at Kinikanwo and Damilola on the other side of the door, beamed out a huge grin and waved casually at them with his left hand.

Frustratingly for Damilola and Kinikanwo the Night Porter turned away and leisurely, strolled, further into the hotel lobby before disappearing around a corner.

Kinikanwo angrily banged on the door with both fists.

'What the hell is he doing?'

'Look.'

Damilola pointed back into the hotel lobby.

The Night Porter had gone to collect his keys, with his gold epaulets on his gaping open green uniform jacket and baggy stained grey trousers he was moving towards the front doors as rapidly as his unfit, rotund frame would allow.

He was trying to sort through the large bunch of keys and do up the jacket over his bare hairy chest at the same time. Finally, after achieving both objectives the front door was opened.

'Yes.'

Damilola answered lifting her right hand as a signal to Kinikanwo not to complain.

'We're late but we do have a booking.'

'We had a puncture.'

The Night Porter looked at them for a moment thinking while still preventing their access to the lobby of the Hotel. Then his face lit up as he remembered.

'The Nigerian party.'

'That's right.'

The uniformed porter retreated slightly bowed and with his outstretched arms welcomed them into the Hotel.

'Please come in.'

It still seemed like a long time before he could check them in and take a swipe of Damilola's credit card. Finding their room on the ground floor was easy and they were able to collapse onto their respective beds.

Neither of them cared much about their mission at that moment, at Kinikanwo's suggestion they switched off their mobiles and the satellite phone so as to remain undisturbed by their sponsors.

Chapter 25

Friday 6th Sandstorm

The following day, Friday, the two ex-pats in Zinder rose with the dawn, around six in the morning. Although they could lay down both had an uncomfortable night and neither had slept very well.

Mac got up first, deciding to try the shower and ablutions across the highway. Around him some of the truck drivers were moving in the same direction, while others with curtains or blinds drawn across their cab windows were sleeping on.

He joined the queue at the brick-built building, once inside the stench of urine and excreta was too awful even for his strong stomach. Out of necessity he urinated but left the building retching. The mainly African drivers laughed at his discomfiture and some ribald remarks in many languages followed his hasty retreat from the building.

On hearing of Mac's experience, Oscar forgot the idea of having a shower and found a piece of desert to relieve his bladder.

They breakfasted on biscuits and water, from their bottled supplies, before getting underway. There was plenty of movement in the truck park and they followed a white, Algerian, high-sided truck and trailer onto the northbound side of the N11. There were plenty of trucks already making their way north, it was easy to overtake them, except for the occasional local car or pick-up, there was little southbound traffic. Mac who was driving commented.

'No sign of the Discovery then!'

Oscar who was still convinced they were being watched grimaced and yawned before replying.

'No but we'll see, after all the only route north has to be through Agadez we'll know when we get there.'

Mac thought his colleague was worrying too much after all they had found nothing when they searched the Touareg.

They were soon clearing the northern outskirts of Zinder and after thirty minutes they were out on their own, having caught and overtaken the early starters. These were wending their way slowly uphill between the two massive rocky slopes. Now was no traffic ahead and little coming the other way, Mac soon had the Touareg cruising at one hundred and forty kilometres per hour. With the work put in on the engine, the car seemed to purr, taking everything including the rising highway in its stride. The diversions for the occasional roadworks which blocked the highway were taken without any problems. They made good progress, quickly eating into the four hundred and fifty kilometres between Zinder and Agadez.

Mac stretched whilst gripping the steering wheel tightly.

'Feels good doesn't it.'

'What's that?'

'The adventure, an empty road, great car and nice dry, warm weather.'

Oscar mused

'I know, the toilets might not be up too much, but this is fun.'

'Mind you the dry weather might be coming to an end, look at that ahead.'

Oscar said pointing at the dark and cloudy sky ahead of them, its red tinged covering started as a darkening of the northwest horizon but as they made rapid progress northwards, it quickly covered all the sky ahead of them like a portent of doom.

Another diversion took them off the road to the left, even with the storm rapidly approaching them. Mac negotiated their route, following the yellow arrows marking the diversion.

Up to then neither had commented any more on the approaching storm but Mac who was still driving decided.

'Soon as we get back to the highway, we're going to stop and see how bad this gets before we go on.'

'Sure thing.'

Oscar agreed, he feared the frightening darkness which was quickly turning day into a disturbing nightfall.

They sky became darker as the first of the dark clouds blotted out the sun behind them. The first warning of the storm's ferocity was when both felt the car lurch to the left as it was battered by an extreme windblast. Then the storm was upon them.

Without warning the view out of the windscreen was minimal, the winds picked up even further, the desert sand, turning the outside air into a rapidly, driven, brown-soup, like fog. The noise was horrendous they couldn't have heard each other even if they had tried to speak.

Mac slowed the Discovery to a crawl, an arrow pointing to the right loomed briefly out of the maelstrom, He eased them slowly in that direction not realising the wind had already blown the sign ninety degrees off course.

One moment they were crawling along, the next they were slowly tipping over onto the car's nearside. Mac engaged the four-wheel drive and tried to drive away from the edge of the slope. He was unsuccessful. Slowly and ponderously at first, the angle of incline increased, then as gravity took over they listed even more rapidly.

Mac yelled loudly, enough to be heard above the tumultuous roar of the storm

'Damn it, Oscar, hang on.'

Oscar had no chance to reply, his body's natural instinct was to lean away from the slope as the car tipped into the unknown abyss.

Mac reacting fast, quickly released his seat belt switched the engine off and tried to open the driver's door on what was now the upside of the car. He wanted to see if by using his weight he could stop the car's inexorable movement the other way. It was no good the car teetered for a second and then rolled over twice before ending upside down, slamming the now unharnessed Scotsman around the cab.

When the vehicle came to rest upside down, Oscar found himself hanging face down, his chest sore from where the seat belt had crushed him as they flipped over. He was lying horizontally held secure by the seat belt. He tried to release it, the crash seemed to have interfered with its mechanism and it wouldn't let him go.

The car was surrounded by the desert sand, the noise of the storm was still roaring around them although it was becoming quieter as the wind driven sand started to cover the Discovery. At first, he couldn't see his Scottish colleague then he realised Mac was caught between the driver's seat and the side roll bar, his head a mass of blood from a cut on his forehead.

Oscar had a moment of panic, banging at the broken mechanism of the harness, he stopped quite quickly when his hands started to hurt, and his brain told him how futile his actions were, instead he shouted above the banshee wailing of the wind.

'Mac, wake up you jock git.'

There was no answer, he realised his partner must be out cold. Furiously he tried to release his harness, again without success. There was nothing he could reach, nor anything useful to him, trapped like he was, hanging looking down into the front passenger well from his seat. He could only reach back with his head and touch the passenger seat.

Oscar found he couldn't work the seat mechanism either to get in a better position. He began to feel extremely uncomfortable very quickly, the seat belt was beginning to bite into his shoulders and already sore sternum

His first instinct of panicking hadn't helped with his breathing, he was already struggling for breath thanks to the constrictive cross bands across his chest.

The storm eased, and Oscar could hear better and he was given further reason to panic when he realised something was dripping behind him. Desperately he tried once again to release the locking mechanism of the seat belt, thinking there must be fuel escaping. He screamed at his partner to wake up and realising he was getting nowhere, resigned himself to their fate and slumped sobbing onto his imprisoning harness.

When nothing happened, he realised he couldn't smell the tell-tale odour of diesel fuel he stopped crying and made himself calm down and think rationally.

He stretched and turned his neck as far as he could until it hurt, it was then he realised they might be safe from the risk of a diesel fuelled fire. The spare water tank had a tiny gash in it and water was dripping onto the sand on the inside of the upside-down roof of the Touareg. He was hanging with his head slightly downwards, remembering the First Aid courses he had attended, he knew unless he could raise it blood would soon be flooding his skull.

He resolved to keep lifting his head above the horizontal to prevent this happening.

Oscar looked at his watch, it was midday and they had been like this for over two hours now. The roar of the wind had disappeared it was quite dark in the cab of the car and at first, he couldn't understand what had happened.

He tried to work out what was occurring, then realised, they were buried upside down and were now part of their own newly-formed sand dune. That's why it was nearly dark and why the sounds of the storm had disappeared. Unless Mac came around from his concussion they had a major problem constrained as Oscar was.

No one except the guys at the Douane on the border really knew of their existence in Niger, he doubted anyone would look for them in time to be rescued. After all they were north of Zinder, against British and Commonwealth Foreign Office advice and because of the risks, against the Niger Governments instructions. Mac had to wake up.

***

In Agadez Kinikanwo and Damilola were just coming around in their shared room in the Hotel Tidene. The former's stomach rumbled as he sat up, he remembered they'd hardly eaten the previous day and he was desperately hungry.

'You awake.'

'Am now.'

Damilola grunted at her colleague rubbing her eyes with both her fists and stretching leisurely.

'Right shower then grub.

'Alright.'

By one in the afternoon they were making short work of the hotel's lunch buffet.

Sitting back on their chairs in the dining room their hunger assuaged they switched on the three phones. There were several irate messages from the Chief and Chief Kudo and two of concern from Chisaru expressing her love for Kinikanwo. Damilola overhearing the messages from Chisaru, which Kinikanwo didn't bother to hide, was fuming. She couldn't believe the other man's lack of feelings and was convinced Kinikanwo was deliberately trying to upset her once again.

Firstly they both rang their bosses back in Port Harcourt to re-assure them about their progress north. Neither of the recipients of the phone calls were happy but they were less anxious because of the distance made up by the Discovery and the fact they had passed their target the previous day.

After the phone calls the pair of them considered what they should do about finding the Rally Car and its occupants. Kinikanwo led the discussion.

'One of us needs to take the car and watch the N11 at the south end of town that way we can't miss the Touareg when it finally arrives.'

'The other one needs to quiz the locals and see if it has already passed by.'

Damilola shook her head.

'That's highly unlikely.'

'I know but we have to check because we have been asleep.'

Once again Damilola resentful, felt like Kinikanwo was taking over and arranging everything without any consultation.

'Who's going to sit in the car?'

'You are.'

'Why?'

'That's unless you want to go around questioning all the locals who speak French which I can converse in and you can't.'

Damilola realised she didn't fancy trying to question the local Muslim men and opted for being the lookout.

'Alright I'll take the car and watch out for the Touareg.'

By two that afternoon Damilola was sat on the side of the road someway south of the city at the southerly junction of the N11 and the Agadez airport road. In her mind she illogically still felt unfairly treated and an all-consuming hatred for the Kinikanwo was gathering in her brain. At least the bastard had obeyed instructions and not made a pass at her.

Kinikanwo started at the hotel desk, at first, he couldn't find out from an officious Reception Clerk if the two Europeans had a booking. He got around this by slipping a backhander to the cleaning woman who was doing the rooms. After a brief call from the room phone she was able to find out the previous day's booking by Oscar had been moved to that evening. Gratefully he sauntered from the hotel and tried to ring Damilola. There was no answer and Kinikanwo assumed she must be out of range in the desert south of the city.

Satisfied they were now ahead, he wasn't tied down to anything, he went back to the hotel room and started to ring Chisaru on his own mobile.

His reverie and pleasant lecherous thoughts about her were rudely interrupted by his boss on the other end of the Satellite phone. There was little he could say to stem the outrage at them not having seen the Dakar Rally Car for over twenty-four hours. His boss wasn't even concerned about their travails but was single minded about the Touareg and that was all. After being reprimanded quite severely the man rang off and left Kinikanwo wondering what was upsetting his Chief' so much. Almost immediately the phone call finished it rang again, this time it was the Chief who was much more empathic he expressed his horror about them nearly being caught by the rebels and fired on by their own Air Force. He was pleased that they expected they would be alongside the Touareg that evening.

Kinikanwo felt a lot better, although if the Chief found out about his eldest daughter, the reaction would certainly be totally different.

South of the city Damilola was looking south through the Discovery's windscreen at a very dark cloud hanging over the far horizon. She had parked up just before the junction of the N1 and N11, her lookout duties were quite boring. For some reason there had been hardly any traffic on the two roads and nothing northbound along the N1 since she parked up.

She determined she would stay until sunset, about five thirty, there would be no point after that she reasoned. She wouldn't be able to see the markings of any car coming through, there being no street lighting.

***

Further south at the newly-created, Discovery-hiding, sand dune, Oscar was in a sea of pain. There was nothing he could do about it, he had tried again and again to reach anything that might help to break him free and everything that might assist them was inaccessible.

He was now extremely thirsty, cocooned like this in the dune which was being heated by the afternoon desert sun. The noise of the water dripping from the water tank only made things worse, it being so near yet so inaccessible. He was very concerned about Mac; the Scotsman was still out for the count at least Oscar knew he was still alive. Occasionally he would painfully manoeuvre himself to where he could see the Scotsman's chest moving up and down. Even worse if he allowed his head to drop for any length of time the pressure of the blood rushing to it gave him a splitting headache.

The light was fading now and there was nothing to do but hope and for the first time since his childhood pray for some sort of miracle escape from their sandy tomb.

Chapter 26

Agadez

It got to the point about six in the evening where because of nightfall and dust in the air Damilola couldn't distinguish the little traffic now coming from the south. She turned the Discovery around and returned to Agadez, taking the opportunity to refuel the vehicle at a petrol station near the airport.

On the returning journey through the dimly lit streets of the city, she was fortunate not to collide with a camel which came sidling down the road towards her. Damilola stopped to allow the stately creature to wander past

. Out of curiosity she looked closely at the cargo slung either side of the Dromedary's single hump. It appeared to consist of a pair of rectangular heavy looking blocks wrapped in cloth. Turning around to resume her journey back to the hotel she realised she wasn't going anywhere for a while as the single camel was now followed by a loaded train of dromedary's passing either side of the vehicle. A hint of dirty grey from a poorly wrapped block which nearly scraped the offside wing mirror made Damilola realise she was surrounded by a camel train of salt. It took about twenty minutes for the caravan to slowly plod past her stationary vehicle.

Kinikanwo was sitting in the hotel reception waiting Damilola's return. Damilola waved and went to get some refreshment from the bar before joining her companion.

Placing her drink on the coffee table Damilola recounted her boring afternoon at the crossroads south of the city.

'The only bloody thing of interest was the odd flight taking off over me from the airport.'

'It was really weird there was hardly any traffic until a whole bunch of trucks came up the N1 about five.'

'Don't worry about it Damilola, they're booked in here tonight.'

'They were booked in at the hotel last night but rang and changed it to tonight, so we're laughing.'

Kinikanwo grinned and continued.

'Funny thing is neither of us or those in the Touareg are supposed to be here anyway, that's why the hotel is so empty.'

'Why's that?'

'Apparently there's a local uprising of Touaregs and the Niger government has banned all tourists from the province of Air, this place is the capital.'

'The hotel staff reckon its killing the Tidene's tourist business, there's only us, the odd businessman coming through the airport, a couple of ex-pats updating the airport's infrastructure and some others with an aid team.'

They ate a dismal meal amongst a few of these African and Arab businessmen, who must have flown in on one of the only two daily flights from Niamey, Niger's capital.

The two of them spent the rest of the evening until midnight hanging around in the hotel's reception.

As the clock hanging on the wall behind reception struck midnight Damilola decided she had enough of hanging around. 'I'm off to bed.'

'They'll get here in their own good time and if they arrive overnight we'll see them in the morning.'

'Yeah fair enough, I'll join you.'

On the corridor on the way to their room, Kinikanwo felt he couldn't resist and stroked Damilola's bottom. Damilola knew this sex maniac would try it on sometime and was ready for him. Turning fast she pivoted on her left leg and with her boot shod right foot kicked Kinikanwo in the crotch.

He collapsed to the floor, eyes watering, gasping for breath and holding his injured pride and joy.

'You were bloody told.'

'You don't touch me ever.'

Satisfied she stormed off to bed.

***

Many kilometres to the south at the Touareg, nothing had changed. Mac was still unconscious; his cohort Oscar was still hanging from his seatbelt in various states of agony. Even though he kept lifting his head, so it touched the headrest, his neck muscles were now giving him agony. Unexpectedly he found if he reached behind him with his arms over his head and round the seat head rest he could grab hold of his Afro and hold his head at least level with the rest of his body. He found this change in position would for a while would give some slight relief, for a while anyway.

Oscar knew it was nightfall when everything quickly turned black, night in the near tropics comes quickly and so it was that previously there had been enough light through the dune for him to see what was happening but now to add to his agonies it was pitch black.

By now Oscar had almost given up on Mac and was beginning to feel like the Discovery was going to be their coffin and the dune their grave. His only consolation in amongst the pain, darkness and his desperate need for a drink of anything was that he knew his mate was still alive. Occasionally there would be a sharp intake of breath which would be followed by a rasping exhale.

Early on Oscar had been desperate to urinate but he had held onto it, his bladder had complained but it was a minor irritant compared to the other pains. Occasionally half in hope he would, with his hands fisted, bang away at the release mechanism without avail. Each attempt was becoming feebler because the hands were much bruised, and he was dehydrating rapidly.

Eventually sometime during the early hours his hair slipped through his hands, his head dropped, and he drifted into an

227

exhausted sleep. When he woke he found he could see again as daylight had dawned. Looking at his watch, he saw it was just after seven in the morning and he could see the rise and fall of Mac's chest as he breathed in and out.

Mac now had another problem sitting on his exposed chest, just above his waistband was a scorpion. It looked frightening to the trapped Oscar, it scuttled up the body and sat on Mac's nose. The arachnid sat their paused for a moment its sting at the end of its tail poised as if ready to strike

Oscar shut his eyes, at first not able to watch but then he just had to see what happened and re-opened his eyes.

Momentarily he forgot all about his pain and discomfort as the adrenaline kicked in due to the tense situation.

A drop of sweat ran into Oscar's right eye causing it to sting, he blinked and when he looked again the scorpion had vanished.

After that excitement the day dragged on, the only change being gradual, with him getting thirstier and hotter, his lips were cracking now, and his tongue felt swollen. The world turned, and the sun moved through the sky evidenced by the changing shadows in their tomb. Mac still somehow breathed but stayed unaware in his coma. Oscar was grateful Mac was still alive but desperately needed him to come out of his unconscious state. Occasionally he tried shouting at the comatose Scotsman and the world outside their cocoon but as the day wore on, Oscar's throat became so parched, he could hardly speak.

Day drifted into night again, Oscar's pain had become almost acceptable, he seemed to be drifting in and out of consciousness himself as suddenly another bite sized chunk of the day would seem to have disappeared each time he came around.

***

At the Hotel Tidene, Kinikanwo booked them in for another night shortly after lunch when they realised the Touareg hadn't arrived.

Just as they were finishing a light lunch in the hotel dining room they were approached by a member of the Niger Gendarmerie Nationale who dressed in his paramilitary uniform, was accompanied by a member of the National Police Force.

It was obvious the member of the Gendarmerie thought he was in charge, he started to question them closely in French. He demanded to know why and how they had managed to drive to Agadez from Zinder without permission.

Kinikanwo struggled to translate the rapid French for his partner which only upset the officer

'Vous n'avez pas l'autorisation pourrait ont été kidnappée par le banditisme local.'

'I think he says we have no authorisation to travel and we could have been captured by local bandits.'

Damilola smiled and tried to defuse the officer's anger

'Excusez me non parlez.'

This seemed to rile the member of the Gendarmerie even more and he threatened to arrest them until his colleague took him to one side and reminded him he didn't have the authority in the city as the it came under his jurisdiction.

The Police Officer in his Green uniform was very tall, Damilola reckoned about one point nine metres but exceedingly thin, standing barefooted in sandals made of dried leather, spoke fluent English and was polite but forceful.

'Are you intending to travel north to Algeria?'

Kinikanwo replied.

'Well yes, is there a problem?'

'Hadn't you realised before when you set out that due to some unfortunate banditry by the local Touaregs, it is unsafe to travel the N11 north of Zinder.'

'We had intended to travel up to Algeria in a couple of days and then up to the Mediterranean coast.'

There was a grunt from the Gendarmerie.

'Stupide idiote.'

'Why would you be travelling in such dangerous country?'

'For the adventure.'

The Local Police Officer was somewhat mollified by this reply.

'When you leave, whether south or north, even though you are Nigerians and don't need papers, you must still notify my colleague before you leave.'

Kinikanwo nodded his head in agreement.

'Okay that's fine we'll do that.'

Damilola spoke for the first time since the officers had accosted them, she was scared to death of the uniforms and all the hardware they were carrying and almost whispered.

'Yes of course we will.'

The pair of them were grateful to see the uniformed members of the Niger government depart the hotel and sat back to wait the arrival of the Touareg which they thought must surely come today.

***

Back at the sand dune tomb it was becoming dark again, nothing had changed, and Oscar had resigned himself into his body giving up at some stage. He felt they were doomed. After all this time he just couldn't see Mac coming out of his coma at any stage soon.

His throat was swollen through the lack of fluid and his lips were blistering, as night drew in he felt cold. Although the sand of the dune held the day's heat from the desert for a while, the desert was a lot cooler at night especially so late in the year. He shivered, clothed as he was, in only shorts and tee shirt.

About one in the morning he was woken from his comatose sleep by some rustling sounds. At first, he thought it must be a burrowing creature of some sort, the rustling sound increased, it appeared the noise was all round him.

Gradually the darkness became less distinct, the noise changed into a whistling sound, suddenly he could see the outline of the interior of the car as the whistling became a roar and the sand above the upturned car was blown away by the windy blasts of another storm.

Oscar slowly realised he could see outside when lightning flashed across the western sky. The wind cleared his nearside

231

window of sand. A horizon became visible as the storm thundered around them.

Suddenly both ears popped painfully as the pressure was released. There was a really close crack of thunder and then almost immediately another flash of lightning, so close it momentarily made the interior of the car distinctly visible. Abruptly as if it hadn't been there, the storm was gone, after the brief cacophony of noise everything was quiet again. The drip had stopped, Oscar could just hear the breathing of his unconscious partner.

There was still sand in the air but if he half turned and looked over one of his shoulders he could see twinkling lights of the stars in the heavens above. It was brilliant he thought at least they were no longer underground. Despondency returned when he realised nothing had changed, they were still part of a sand dune, they were still trapped, Mac was still comatose. In frustration even though his throat was dry and swollen he rasped out a scream at the heavens above him.

Oscar burst into tears only a couple trickled out of his dehydrated body, he sobbed and his whole torso vibrated with the anguish.

He stopped his outpouring of grief when he thought he felt an imperceptible movement of the Touareg. Oscar wasn't sure, momentarily he held his breath. It appeared as if the car had slid slightly towards the opposite side.

Desperately, using all his remaining reserves of strength, he threw himself from side to side in the seat harness.

He stopped after thirty seconds panting with exhaustion. This time he could see his near side window was imperceptibly raised further out of the sand.

Frantically he did everything he could to make it happen again, throwing himself against his bindings in a last desperate bid for freedom. Nothing happened, he slumped back onto the harness that was imprisoning him determined to try again once he had regained some of his strength.

Suddenly the car was moving without his help, slowly at first it started to slip down what was now a slope on the far side. The dune now eroded by the recent storm collapsed away. The car lurched and began to roll onto the other side and then it just went.

The car turned upright, dumping Oscar back into his seat temporarily and relieving the pressure from his sore chest. Before he had a chance to react the car rolled again, the far door opened and the unharnessed, comatose, Scotsman was flicked out of the car like a rag doll.

The seat harness did the job it was meant too and held Oscar securely as the Touareg rolled over and over rotating a further two and half times. It finished up on its side slightly unbalanced at the bottom of the dune.

Oscar threw himself towards the far side and helped it go over, thumping down onto its four wheels.

He tried the seat belt quick release button on the sports harness and with the pressure of his weight gone it let him go. He sobbed with relief as he scrabbled around for a now easily reachable bottle of lukewarm, fresh, drinking water.

Firstly, he thirstily drained the first bottle, before tipping the dregs over his head and then in relief he laughed uproariously. He was looking east through the unbelievably un-cracked windscreen, twenty metres away the shiny tarmacked N11 glinted in the light of the gloriously starlit night sky.

Taking another bottle of water, he opened the still working passenger door and made his way out of the Touareg to look for his compatriot. Looking up the slope of the remains of the dune which still must have been ten metres high, he could see the grey outline of Mac's body halfway down.

Rapidly as his bruised and sore body would allow, he forced himself up the dune. With every step his feet slipped back down the slope, he managed with difficulty, to force his way upwards. He was about two metres away when the previously supine figure moved and tried to sit up, causing a cascade of sand down the slope which almost caused Oscar to fall back down the incline.

The silence was broken by Mac roaring loudly.

'What the, what happened, where the bloody hell am I?'

'Hang on I'm coming.'

'No need I'm on my way.'

Mac slid on his backside down the slope past Oscar towards the now battered Touareg.

Oscar gratefully followed and joined his partner who was sitting with his head in his hands, his back resting against the front offside tyre of the car.

'What happened, I've got a really bad headache it's like I've spent the night drinking some rotgut whisky.

Oscar handed his pal a bottle of water which Mac drained thirstily, Oscar explained their situation.

He had worked out that the diversion for the roadworks had sent them over the top of a decaying dune, which with the sandstorm winds burying it had caused their accident.

At first Mac wouldn't believe it was now the early hours of Sunday morning and he had been unconscious for thirty-six hours. Oscar had to show the unbelieving Scotsman the date on his watch to prove what he was saying.

Lifting his sore body from his seat on the sand alongside his partner, the Englishman half in hope than expectation, sat down in the driver's seat of the Touareg and turned the ignition key.

'Here goes nothing.'

Much to his surprise the engine fired straightaway and burbled happily as if there wasn't a problem in all the world.

Mac started to laugh but stopped because it hurt his head.

'What did you expect?'

'I thought it would be damaged and to have leaked oil or fuel or something.'

Mac dragged himself up alongside the driver's door.

'It was always going to fire up, I took the bloody thing apart and put it back together again.'

He patted the bonnet affectionately.

'Now can we get to where we were meant to be going two days ago?'

Chapter 27

Sunday 8th Hotel Tidene

Oscar sat in the driver's seat of the Touareg while the concussed Scotsman found his way to the nearside before plonking himself down in the passenger seat. Oscar handed over another bottle of water while drinking one himself in a more controlled manner.

Neither said anything, both were wrapped up in their thoughts realising how lucky they were to escape alive out of the sandy tomb. Oscar who had survived the thirty-six hours hanging from the rally car seat belt, perhaps realised, more than his mate, how fortunate they were to be alive.

Looking up at the clear sky through the windscreen, there were more stars than the brain could contemplate, there was no light pollution to spoil the scene. Being only just north of the equator they could see a lot of the southern constellations, the faint pole star its position pointed out by Dubhe at one end of the Plough was low down on the northern horizon.

Mac was the first to speak while sipping at another fresh bottle of water.

'What do you reckon, what happens now?'

'I think we take one thing at a time and sit here and have something to eat from the emergency rations.'

'Good idea, I'll go and get something,'

Mac started to exit the car when Oscar stopped him by grabbing his inside arm.

'You stay there, we don't know yet how serious your concussion is.'

'I'll bring us some grub.'

They sat there in the car recovering from traumas of the past day and a half, gorging themselves on some of the emergency rations. At times Mac thought he was going to be sick, he was very nauseous but was determined to keep the food down. He, unsurprisingly had a blinding headache which was starting to ease thanks to a couple of Co-codamol which Oscar retrieved from their medicine box.

Oscar buried their waste and went to check out the car with a torch. Everything looked fine from the outside, the carbon fibre bodywork had held up well. He could see there were a few scratches but nothing to concern them. Reluctantly he got back into the car, at least it was the driver's seat and not the other from which he had been hanging for so long. He started the car up again and checked the gauges, there were no warning lights on the lit-up console. Oscar checked all the light functions and the wipers, even the windscreen washer still worked.

He next went to the passenger side of the vehicle and strapped the Scotsman into the car, he checked once he had connected the buckle to see if it would release properly and surprise, surprise it worked beautifully giving them no cause for concern. Mac was getting a bit irritated at his mates fussing although he understood why Oscar was concerned. He himself realised he was a bit of a mess and knew from previous experience of supervising others when accidents happened how dangerous concussion could be.

It was now four in the morning, Oscar drove cautiously down onto the N11 and turned northwards towards Agadez. He drove on sidelights, there was nothing else going either way on the highway and they had agreed for security reasons, it was best not to advertise their presence, more than they needed to.

It took Oscar nearly four hours to reach Agadez and find the Hotel Tidene, they had been able to speed up when it got light around six o'clock and had seen nothing until a convoy of large trucks escorted by a military personnel carrier passed them going the other way, south towards Zinder.

They found the Hotel Tidene easily, Oscar could park almost outside the front doors. His biggest concern besides Mac, who had dozed part of the journey, was the need to secure the Touareg.

Even at nine thirty in the morning the now slightly battered Touareg was attracting interest. He solved the problem by paying three Arab youths to dish out photographs and do security duty.

Grabbing their overnight bags, neither thinking or caring to look out for the Discovery, they made their way to the Reception where the uniformed clerk was welcoming but concerned about their bedraggled appearance.

Mac was holding a bloodied rag over the cut on his forehead and Oscar seeing himself in the mirror on the wall behind the receptionist realised how dirty, gaunt and scary they must look to the clerk.

After their booking was confirmed Oscar wanted to do something about Mac's injuries, the Scotsman steadfastly refused to attend the local hospital. Now in the relative safety of the hotel it didn't take much for Oscar to relent after all they were exhausted, and clean beds were the greater temptation. As they turned away from the Reception desk Oscar grabbed his partners arm.

'Alright Mac let's get to bed then but if you're sick or anything else we'll go straight to the Medics.'

Mac nodded his head in agreement, too tired to speak as they made their way to their hotel room.

***

Neither saw Damilola and Kinikanwo, who watched on interested from the seating in the Reception Area. To the Nigerians both Brits looked exhausted and the Scotsman looked ill, his tanned face was very pale, he staggered slightly a couple of times as the pair of them made their way out of Reception.

As soon as they were clear the two Nigerians rushed outside to have a look at the state of the Touareg. It was clear the car had been in the wars. It was covered in dust, they could even see sand on the inside of the vehicle and there were some long scratches spoiling the previously impeccable paint job.

After looking over the Touareg and walking back into the hotel away from the interested bystanders Kinikanwo was the first to comment.

'Not too bad but something has happened.'

'Yeah, they made it alright but what's the point we're knackered.'

'If we're to obey the Gendarmerie thug, we can't go north or south in the Discovery without his permission, we're stuck in this god forsaken hole unable to leave.'

'God you do whinge Damilola, you're so pessimistic.'

'Let's be positive put our brains together and think our way out of this, that Gendarmerie is less frightening than my boss.'

Kinikanwo pointed outside.

'We're here to do a job, wherever they go we follow.'

'But!'

'Shut it, when they go, we do as well.'

Sat back in Reception away from the crowd around the Rally Car, they sipped tea and put their mind to a solution, Damilola surprisingly was the first to speak.

'Yeah, you're right, I don't think it matters, I agree with you we just have to follow the Touareg.'

'Look at it this way they're going north, we have too as well, if we're stopped they will be as well, it'll be a trouble shared.'

Kinikanwo nodded his head in agreement.

Damilola said.

'I've been thinking about this, whatever happens we won't be able to return through Niger.'

'We'll have to flog the Discovery when we reach the Mediterranean and fly home.'

Kinikanwo liked her idea a lot and unthinkingly answered.

'I would be back with Chisaru a lot quicker as well.'

'It's Brilliant Damilola.'

He slapped the furious Damilola on her back.

Damilola was beyond angry now, she was biding her time but when this trip was over she would find a way to get back at the arrogant bastard. Somehow, she would change Chisaru's mind about Kinikanwo. Surely, she must be able to see the insecurity in hooking up with a womaniser like this arrogant bastard.

They booked another night in the hotel and sat around waiting for the Touareg's occupants to make their next move.

Unfortunately, they had another visit from the grinning member of the Niger National Gendarmerie. This time he was unaccompanied and was looking to cause Kinikanwo as much grief as possible.

Kinikanwo had to do his best to understand the Gendarme using his partial knowledge of the French language. What it boiled down to, was blackmail. The man smirking in his paramilitary uniform indicated that, if they left the city into his area of control, any part of Niger outside the major towns. He would arrest them for their own protection and deport them back to Nigeria. Of course, they would have to leave the Land Rover Discovery, so it wouldn't rust away he would buy it off them.

Kinikanwo explained to Damilola what the Gendarmerie was proposing.

'The bastard really wants to steal the Discovery.'

Damilola shook her head in annoyance.

Kinikanwo as best he could, told the Gendarme that he was a robbing bastard and they would burn the car before they would hand it over.

Damilola didn't understand what his colleague had said to the Gendarme. He realised Kinikanwo might have gone too far when the grinning Gendarme's face contorted in anger and his right hand slipped towards the pistol in the black leather holster hanging from the waistband of his uniform trousers.

The Gendarme angrily wagged a finger at the Nigerian and spoke in English.

'I haven't finished with you.'

'You will be really sorry by the time this is over.'

Damilola looked at Kinikanwo

'What have you said to him?'

'Why's he so pissed off?'

'I refused to let him have the car that's all.'

Damilola was fuming, not only was the idiot shagging the girl he loved but his tactless conversation was threatening to get them thrown into prison or worse.

Kinikanwo was cheesed off as well and was determined that he wasn't going to bow to the wishes of the uniformed, thieving, bastard in front of them. He raised his right arm, stepped forward and using his index finger jabbed the Gendarme in his large belly twice.

'Piss off back to your sewer otherwise I'll complain to your boss, General Mounkaila in Niamey.'

The Gendarmerie stormed out of the hotel muttering all sorts of repercussions.

Kinikanwo gave the back of the departing figure two fingers and told Oscar.

'That's him sorted, I'm off.'

'Where are you going?'

'For a swim.'

Damilola swore to herself, angry that her partner felt he could just swan off when he liked, without a care to what was happening with the Touareg and its passengers.

Kinikanwo didn't care, he was certain the British guys weren't going anywhere for a while. He wasn't going to sit around Reception all day when there was a nice tempting piece of French ass out by the pool.

He had learnt already that the lady he had espied earlier, was the wife of an NGO working at the local hospital. She had certainly sized him up yesterday when he walked past her sunbathing on the terrace by the pool.

He went back to the hotel room, stripped down to his shorts made his way outside to the swimming pool and grabbed a seat on the sunbed next to her.

She appeared to be about thirty-five, was something to admire, with just her thong and an undone string top. She was lying on her front and working on her suntan in the dry desert heat.

Kinikanwo didn't hang about making conversation.

'Couldn't help noticing but you seem to be burning up.'

'Would like me to rub some of that Factor 50 into your back.'

Without waiting to be asked he pick up the bottle of oil from the beside her sunbed.

The Frenchwoman pretended to be surprised at the interruption and holding her bikini top over her firm small breasts turned her head, looked up at the handsome Nigerian and nodded.

'Ouis Monsieur that would be lovely.'

She, Francoise was bored and had noticed this hunk of a man the previous day and wondered. Her husband had promised her travel and excitement, not being stuck in a three-star hotel in some flea-bitten town. It wasn't even safe for her to go to the shops. Not that there was anything worth looking at when she managed to find an escort to take her there. Besides she could feel the Muslim men disrobing her with their eyes every time she ventured out of the safety of the hotel.

She sighed with pleasure as Kinikanwo massaged her back while rubbing in the suntan oil, too late she realised she had made the noise aloud.

What the hell she thought and relaxed as he began to approach the erotic parts of her body.

He was kneeling on her towel on the tiled floor alongside her and massaging from the neck to her buttocks. He reached down to either side of her body and massaged the sides of her torso. She was taking the utmost pleasure from his strong hands and as he reached up to bring his hands down the length of her body again, she lifted her breasts off the sunbed, he reached under and squeezed them before continuing down the rest of her stomach.

Flushed and desperate to take this further, she wriggled out from under the Nigerian's enticing hands, stood up holding the bikini across her breasts, looked around to make sure no one was watching, grabbed Kinikanwo's right hand with her left and rushed away from the pool, dragging the only too willing man behind her, into her ground floor room which had patio doors out onto the pool area.

Back in Reception Damilola was getting bored and came to the same conclusion as her compatriot, the two men they were supposed to be following, were unlikely to be doing any travelling that day. She decided to join her fellow Nigerian by the pool for want of anything better to do. When she reached the pool, there was no sign of anyone, she asked a waiter who was passing if he had seen anything of the other Nigerian but got a negative response. Undecided Damilola checked their room but there was no sign of her missing co-driver just some newly discarded clothes on the others bed.

Now confused, Damilola picked up her I Pad and went back to Reception where she knew she could order some tea, get a Wi-Fi connection and do some work on her nursing studies.

Kinikanwo spent the rest of the day in Francoise's bed. About four in the afternoon when they were lying naked sated after making love for the third time Kinikanwo thought to look at his watch.

'It's four, what time does your husband return?'

She panicked and screamed.

'Oh no, he could be here at any moment.'

Kinikanwo grabbed his clothes and hopping frantically on one leg as he put his shorts back on, rushed out onto the pool terrace.

He returned to his room had a shower and got changed, he was exhausted he realised as he washed off the excesses of the day in the shower. Francoise had been insatiable, they had hardly stopped for hours and even his renowned sexual stamina had been tested.

Getting dressed Kinikanwo made his way to Reception to find some food and Damilola to see if anything was happening with the Touareg.

Damilola had spent the day in the hotel reception, she was watching out for any movement of the two men they were supposed to be following and working on her I Pad. She was fuming about her compatriots' disappearance and once again being left to hold the fort. When Kinikanwo appeared about five, freshly showered and changed Damilola blew her top and let her anger show by shouting at her fellow driver.

'Where the bloody hell have you been?'

'Relaxing.'

Kinikanwo laughed and went to sit down but Damilola jumped up and jabbed the other in the chest with her left index finger. You're bloody irresponsible and don't give a sod for anyone do you?'

Kinikanwo tensed and gave Damilola a piercing look while grabbing her offending wrist and squeezing it hard.

'You don't touch me.'

'EVER!'

'Understand.'

'I still owe you from last night.'

Damilola was beyond caring and tried to shake off Kinikanwo's hand which was squeezing her wrist painfully.

Instead she grabbed Kinikanwo's shirt with her right hand and pulled the taller man towards her looking up into his face. Her own creased with the anger she demanded to know where Kinikanwo had been.

'I'm not interested in your bloody feelings, I'll say it once more where the hell have you been?'

By this time the noise of their argument was attracting attention, a waiter who had been about to ask Kinikanwo if he wanted anything, stood back dumbfounded, mouth open about a metre away. Meanwhile the hotel manager hearing the argument raced across from his office behind the reception desk.

Kinikanwo fed up with his fellow compatriot and his continuous whinging pulled the hand off his shirt leaned down and spoke fiercely but quietly into Damilola's left ear.

'If you weren't so bloody thick, you would realise those two aren't going anywhere today, so I considered myself to be free to do what I want.'

Damilola stepped half a pace back, clenched hands on her hips.

'Alright so what have you been doing?'

'Not that it's any business of yours but I've been getting screwed by that French Madame.'

'You bastard Kinikanwo.'

'What about Chisaru?'

'Please , you are causing an unfortunate disturbance.'

The pair were in their own bubble now and totally ignored the hotel manager who was now standing close by wringing his hands and hoping to quiet the volatile situation.

Kinikanwo didn't give a toss for what Damilola thought and decided to ram home his advantage over the weaker sex.

'What about her, she's special I'll give you that but she's only one of my many willing shags.'

Kinikanwo emphasised the last word because he knew it would really upset Damilola.

Damilola feeling like she had lost to the arrogant bastard once again, stormed out of the front of the hotel trying not to let her emotions get the better of her. She couldn't stay and face that man any longer, she was so choked up with frustration. She was scared she might burst into tears and wasn't prepared to give Kinikanwo the satisfaction of doing so. She stumbled to the Discovery and sat inside trying to think of a way to vent her anger.

***

About this time Oscar woke in the room he was sharing with his Scottish partner. Unexpectedly he had slept like a log, he hadn't thought he would sleep that well, what with the bruising to his sore chest.

The first thing he thought about was Mac's concussion and injuries? He felt guilty for sleeping so long and shot across to the other bed to check on his companion

He needn't have worried Mac seemed alright, there was a slight noise from his nasal passages as he breathed out but nothing of great concern.

Oscar thought to himself.

'That bloody Jock must have the constitution of an ox.'

There wasn't much Oscar could do, he didn't want to make too much noise and wake the other man. He felt too dirty without a shower to want to leave the room and explore the hotel. In the end he settled for a bottle of water from the room fridge and to reading the latest 'Reacher,' on his Kindle.

Oscar sat on his bed reading the e-reader until it got so dark he couldn't see the screen anymore, he sat back relaxed and content to wait.

Eventually about an hour after dark with a grunt and a slight lifting of his head the Scotsman came around. Oscar who had dozed off, his back to the headboard, was immediately alert and switched on his bedside light.

'Take it easy mate, don't try and get up, let's have a look at you first.'

He shuffled off his own bed and went to have a look at his partner who looked up blearily from atop his bed.

'I feel great now.'

'What time is it Oscar?'

'We must have slept the clock round.'

'We did, it's just after seven in the evening.'

'How about we get cleaned up and I take you to see a medic.'

'Ah stuff that son, I feel good as new what I need is a shower, grub and a long cool beer.'

About eight, they both, freshly cleaned up and presentable, made their way to the dining room to top up their depleted food reserves. They didn't see the two Nigerians eating separately at the opposite end of the dining area.

Once they had ordered their meal Mac insisted they should look at getting on with the journey.

'Once we've got fed I reckon we should plan on getting out of here tomorrow.'

'Don't know about that, if you won't see a Doctor I reckon we should rest up for thirty-six hours to make sure you're okay.'

'Don't talk crap, I've got a head like granite I'll be alright.'

'Let's get up early and go for the border in one go.

Oscar knowing the figures shook his head.

'I don't think so, it's around five hundred kilometres and the final bit is on sand.'

'Alright let's compromise, we'll have a couple of drinks, get our heads down and start out at first light.'

'If we get close, we'll decide then alright.'

Oscar thought for a moment while glancing round the Dining Room, it was then he saw Damilola and Kinikanwo and realised the Nigerians must definitely be following them. It was too much of a coincidence they were here in Agadez as well.

This was enough to make him change his mind.

'Mac we'll go first thing because those Nigerians are still after us.'

'What do you mean?'

'Don't look behind you but they are sitting over the other side of the room.'

Mac started to turn his head, Oscar whispered severely.

'Don't.'

'Right finish the meal get our heads down and get up at five and out of here.'

Mac nodded his head.

'Alright.'

The pair quickly polished off their food and departed the Dining Room deliberately avoiding any contact with the Nigerians.

The Brits didn't realise the two Nigerians were in conflict and weren't speaking to each other as they ate their meal.

They also didn't know the representatives of the National Gendarmerie and Police, had visited the hotel to see them earlier in the day.

Hearing about the Touareg's travails and the request not to be disturbed the officials decided they would call on the esteemed rally car drivers when time allowed the following morning.

The Hotel manager was told to inform the Touareg's drivers, they weren't to leave the hotel until after the Officials visited the following morning.

Their intention was to tell the pair of them to return south to Zinder. Except for the International truck convoys nothing was to be allowed to visit the area around the border with Algeria because of the problems with the tribal rebels. The government of Niger were averse to offering up easy hostages for the insurgents.

The message wasn't passed onto the night porter or maybe he didn't read the Manager's instructions. In the end he only saw the two ex-pats the following morning when they, with their overnight bags in tow asked the porter to unlock the front doors.

***

It was obvious to the two Nigerians the ex-pats didn't intend to leave that day, Damilola went to bed early and pretended to be asleep when Kinikanwo returned to their room shortly after.

Chapter 28

Monday 9th An unfortunate Death

After sleeping the day through Mac and Oscar didn't sleep much that night. About five in the morning they were both up and ready to get underway while they waited for the safety of first light.

While they were waiting Oscar took the opportunity to check Mac over.

'How's your headache?'

'Haven't got one, last time was when we got here.'

'Open your eyes and let me have a look.'

Oscar stared at the pupils and unlike twenty-four hours before there was no dilation of either pupil.

'You must have a head of iron.'

'Good Scottish granite actually.'

Mac laughed as he tapped the side of his head.

They descended on the night porter, paid their bill and departed just as it was getting light at six on that Monday morning, a week since they left Port Harcourt.

One of their Arab security boys was curled up in his Bisht cloak, sitting alongside the nearside front wheel of the Touareg. Oscar had forgotten all about his little security team. He generously compensated the youngster for looking after their vehicle.

Oscar turned the car round and as he reversed he looked for and on seeing it pulled up alongside the Range Rover Discovery with its Nigerian number plates. He looked at the blue numbers on the green and white Rivers State registration plate.

'Mac, that confirms it, we're definitely being followed.'

'That car belongs to the Chief, well his father but he can't drive anymore he's senile.'

Mac thought for a moment before answering.

'Sod it they are not ahead of us now, Oscar open her up and we'll be miles away before anyone realises we've gone.

By six thirty they were back on the N11, as Mac suggested Oscar was accelerating hard on the empty highway and they soon cleared the northern outskirts of the small city.

Ten minutes after starting they came upon a line of northbound trucks. A convoy going in the same direction. The convoy must have left Agadez just before first light. Oscar who was driving didn't try to overtake but held back to stay out of the dust cloud trailing the procession. It seemed impossible to pass the cavalcade of trucks which extended for some distance and as the convoy was making a decent speed they settled for patience.

***

About half seven that morning Kinikanwo was woken by the noise of their shower, he could see the ruffled bedclothes on the other twin bed and assumed it must be Damilola.

The night before Kinikanwo had determined they would have to sort out their problems with each other. If they were going to have any chance of completing their mission, they needed to work together.

Damilola came out of the bathroom fully dressed and pointing Kinikanwo's own Steyr pistol at him. She fired the gun in the general direction of Kinikanwo who was still lying on top of his bed and had no time to react.

Damilola had never fired a pistol before and her shot went wide splintering a hole in the bed board.

Furious at missing with the first shot, she fired again but by this time Kinikanwo had responded, having rolled off the bed, the second shot gouged a hole in the wall above the bed board.

Damilola turning to follow the moving target got off another shot, it was too late Kinikanwo was already grabbing hold of her gun hand and the bullet shattered one blade of the ceiling fan which started rattling as it lost its synchronicity.

Damilola wasn't for letting go and the gun went off again the bullet embedding itself in a wooden desk opposite the beds.

The two strained against each other Kinikanwo's normally stronger body being almost overwhelmed by the anger and adrenaline of the woman who had a vice like grip on the gun.

Even as they struggled Damilola kept trying to depress the trigger of the gun but by now Kinikanwo had his left index finger through the trigger guard preventing this from happening.

Neither spoke, too breathless in their struggle for superiority. Gradually Kinikanwo's superior fitness and experience finally began to tell and he gradually started to twist the gun out of Damilola's hands.

In a last desperate attempt to regain superiority Damilola pulled the trigger again, unfortunately for her Kinikanwo had extracted his finger having turned the gun barrel away. That fifth, nine-millimetre bullet went straight through Damilola's right eye and impacted on her brain killing her instantly. The body, for that was what it was now, slumped. Kinikanwo in shock let it go and the dead Damilola dropped to the floor.

At first, Kinikanwo was numbed by the situation. Very quickly his survival instincts kicked in, still naked he rushed to the hotel room door. Carefully he opened it slightly to see if anyone was reacting to the noise of the five shots from the Steyr.

There was no movement in the corridor outside the room, fortunately it was early enough and there were no staff about yet. The hotel had few guests and he could only hope none of them had been disturbed by the fight. Relieved because it appeared no one heard, or if they did, no connection appeared to have been made with their room.

He eased shut the door and sat down on the end of his bed contemplating his dire situation.

The whole thing had been totally unexpected, he hadn't realised how much he must have upset Damilola to cause the attempt on his own life. Although he always managed to enjoy life and survive most difficult situations, this one was going to be hard to beat.

A series of dire thoughts raced through his mind.

There was no way he could call the local constabulary they were already upset with him.

That bastard from the Gendarmerie was going to be laughing his head off, he would no doubt take the Discovery and make sure his mates were not going to believe any self-defence plea. To Kinikanwo having the blackest of thoughts there was no doubt if caught he would have no chance.

He would be dumped in some rat-infested hellhole of a prison before being convicted of murder.

On top of that, if there was sharia law here in Niger, the executioner would use some sort of horrible sword, the thought of it made even Kinikanwo tremble.

He knew he had to get out of the hotel, Agadez and Niger as soon as possible, urgently he opened his road map on the bed and looked at his options.

He immediately realised he couldn't go back south, that would just take a phone call to Zinder. He would easily get picked up as there was no way to bypass that metropolis.

If he went north, he would have to find a way round Arlit. At first looking at the map he thought he could take the route past the salt mines at Teguidda n Tessount in the west. When he looked closer, parts of the road weren't even categorised. It also looked mountainous, he could see himself trapped for days up there.

Kinikanwo decided he would just have to go for it and clear Arlit the last major town before the Algerian border as soon as possible. It was after all only two hundred and forty kilometres to Arlit. If he could get through there before the alarm was

258

raised, he should be able to bypass the border post just over two hundred kilometres further on. The longer no one had any suspicions of Damilola's death the better chance he would have of making a clean getaway.

He re-packed his bag, switched off his mobile and the satellite phone so he wouldn't be interrupted.

Thinking about what might slow down the police's investigation he destroyed Damilola's passport, flushing the pieces down the toilet. He crushed her mobile and checked Damilola's gear to make sure there were no further means of identification. Kinikanwo re-loaded the Steyr, he had no intention of being arrested because he wasn't expecting any chance of being found innocent if he got picked up. Hiding the gun in his bag he went down to reception. It was quiet, there was no sign of any alarm, only Francoise going out of the front entrance on the arm of her husband. She looked back at her lover and licked her lips in a sexy manner. Even in his straitened circumstances he couldn't help but smile in return, remembering yesterday's fond memories.

To try and put off any suspicion from the hotel staff, he booked for another night and asked for the room not to be cleaned that day as his colleague was not feeling well and shouldn't be disturbed. The Receptionist made a note to inform the room cleaner and the other receptionists.

Chapter 29

To the Border

Leaving the hotel Kinikanwo returned to the Discovery and drove out onto the streets of Agadez. He had no thoughts about the Touareg not noticing its disappearance. Checking the Discovery's fuel gauge, he thanked goodness for Damilola's thoughtfulness, he had nearly full fuel tanks. Even so Kinikanwo stopped at the petrol station to fill up the empty half dozen green plastic petrol cans and buy plenty of bottles of fresh water.

Just north of the city the N11 became the N25 and the former route turned to the west. Kinikanwo could see the mountains and a sign in French warning of the precipitous dangers on that particular road. He sighed with relief at his decision to take the more direct route and pushed the Discovery hard on the near empty highway.

Shortly after crossing an empty desert wadi, there was some evidence of recent rainfall, the road began to climb, the sandy surrounds turned into mainly rocky environs. There were many tight bends as he rose and although he was a good driver he had to slow at times particularly when he came up behind a typical, local, overloaded, high-sided truck round which he daren't pass until they cleared the hairpins. With each hold up his anxiety rose, so sure was he that Damilola's body wouldn't stay unfound for too long.

He was only up in the mountainous area for thirty kilometres, the highway then dived through some further hairpins back down into the desert. Even with the hold-ups and the occasional diversions onto the sand, partially rutted by the heavy trucks during the recent rains. Kinikanwo was approaching the southern environs of Arlit by midday a journey of just over three hours.

For all his bravado he knew this could be it, he was sure he could hear the pounding of his heartbeat over the noise of the Discovery's engine.

The first hint of the town was some single-storey, white buildings on both sides of the tarmacked road. Then on his left a large, mud-brick, walled, compound. Through the open gates he could see some of the overloaded, massive, trucks which traversed the north/south road through the Sahara. They were being guarded by men in full Arabic clothing, armed with what looked Kalashnikovs.

Seeing this evidence of such security and aware he would have to act fast if confronted, Kinikanwo placed the Steyr atop the passenger seat in case he needed it rapidly.

The main route turned left at a roundabout and followed the northern wall of the compound, Kinikanwo eased slowly down the very straight East/West Avenue.

Not knowing where to go, he looked out carefully for the green notices to indicate any N25 signs. A right turn past a compound advertising the Nigerien National Transport, the white-walled enclosure must have contained a further hundred plus trucks and what looked like Transport Office. Parked outside the offices was the reason Kinikanwo was involved in this bloody catastrophe.

'It's that bloody Rally Car.'

He screamed out loudly in frustration at the windscreen of the Discovery as he drove by the wide entrance to the truck depot. He slowed to a crawl, the two Brits were standing alongside the Touareg talking to a dark-skinned man in tan shorts with similarly coloured boots on his feet and a short sleeved collared white shirt covering his upper torso.

'What were they doing there?'

With all the earlier panic he hadn't even realised that the Touareg was no longer out the front of the hotel, never mind they had managed to get ahead of him. It was a pain, though he couldn't concern himself with the Touareg now, he would worry about that later. First, he needed to cross the border into Algeria as soon as possible

All the side streets were of hard packed sand, the signage appeared to be non-existent, but he kept zigzagging left and right through the often-narrow streets keeping the sun behind him to ensure he kept moving in a north westerly direction. Eventually almost as if by accident and with much relief he cleared the North-West outskirts of Arlit. He had been so angry at the sight of the Touareg and having to concentrate so hard on his thirty-minute transverse of Arlit he had little time for the previous anxieties.

Suddenly Kinikanwo and the Discovery were at the north-west edge of Arlit town where a signpost to Arlit Airport marked the end of the tarmacked road. Instead it was now hard packed sand worn solid by the heavy transport crossing the Sahara. To differentiate the road from the surrounding desert there was a central divide of continuous piled sand, marked by upright petrol drums, they were painted white, with a dirty orange ring making up the central third ring.

A pick up raced down the other carriageway trailing a plume of dust in its wake, he could see in his rear-view mirror a similar plume from the rear of the Discovery but for all the trucks in the truck parks of Arlit the hard-packed sand road ahead was empty of any transport.

The road was rutted by the heavy loads it carried, Kinikanwo found that at anything much above sixty kilometres an hour, the Discovery felt uncomfortable. He realised slower was safer as he couldn't risk causing damage to his only means of exiting the country safely.

He took another slurp of water from one of the bottles he had thrown onto the passenger seat. Kinikanwo realised he had been running on adrenaline and hadn't eaten since the previous night. Common sense and his bladder told him he needed to stop shortly. He had to balance this against the need to get well clear of any possible chase. It was all a race against time and he could only hope no-one would find Damilola before he and the Discovery crossed the border into Algeria.

Glancing at his watch Kinikanwo realised it was nearly two in the afternoon, he could see Arlit Airport with its desert runway on the right and the salt pans to his left. From his earlier research he knew he had just over two hundred kilometres to the border, another four hours at his present speed.

He thought about it and decided he wasn't going to make the border with Algeria before nightfall and there being no other traffic or dust plumes in sight he pulled off the road onto the desert. This gave him the chance to plan the next move, consume some rations and ease his painful bladder.

***

Oscar and his Scottish partner saw the dusty black Range Rover Discovery passing them where they stood negotiating with the Manager of the Society of National Nigerien Transport. It was Oscar's sixth sense which made him look up and catch sight of and point out the rear of the vehicle as it fishtailed round the next right-hand bend.

Mac flowed Oscar's pointing right arm and nodded his head in acknowledgement as he spoke to the Transport Manager. The manager was a Palestine refugee who had been involved in heavy transport for many years, working all over Africa. His latest job had been advertised in a trade magazine the previous year, it had given him the opportunity of moving his young family out of Gaza and to the relative safety of Agadez.

He now worked for the Government of Niger and the National Gendarmerie to ensure the safety of trucks moving through Arlit to the border with Algeria. The Palestinian Manager didn't know for sure but thought the rebellious Touaregs were uninterested in threatening the truck route but by showing intent they were causing the Government in Niamey as much embarrassment as possible.

As they had turned the corner of the N25 to pass the last truck of the convoy which was entering the truck compound. The Manager had left talking to an incoming truck driver and raced out in front of the Touareg urging them to stop. Oscar who was driving, had pulled over and lowered the driver's side window of the car.

'Hi guys, my name is Omar, I'm Manager of the National Transport Association and I would like to help you if I can.'

Mac leaned across and looked at the light-coloured man dressed in smartly pressed short-sleeved white shirt, dark-blue trousers and black dusty safety boots. Smiling he asked.

'Why's that?'

'What can you do for us?'

'Look my job, in cooperation with the local Gendarmerie, is to see everything reaches the border safely.'

'By now everyone in Niger knows you're making this trip, if you got kidnapped it would be a big embarrassment locally and to the National Government.'

Oscar interjected.

'We aren't anything special just shifting this veteran car home.'

'Don't you believe it, you're headlines in News Now and all over the Nigerian television stations.'

Mac looked at Oscar and laughed.

'Well bugger me.'

'My fault for painting our names on the doors.'

Oscar shrugged and laughed at Mac.

'Well it seemed like a good idea at the time.'

'I know, it looks good as well.'

Replied Oscar who turned to the Palestinian.

'How do we get out of here safely then?'

'That's easy I've had an idea to get you and the Touareg securely across the border if you two are up for it.'

'There is a lot of pressure from the local Governor to make sure you get into Algeria without any problems, so I've come up with a plan.'

Mac was impatient to get on and growled somewhat grumpily at the offer of help.

'What's that then?'

'I'll put you and the Touareg into a high-sided empty north bound truck.'

'You'll be able to sit up front.'

'The driver will take you right through the Niger border post and up to I n Guezzam the first stop in Algeria.'

The Transport Manager also gave the Touaregs occupants room for thought.

'Otherwise the local Gendarmerie isn't going to let you out of here without some sort of escort and that could take a while.'

The pair of them glanced at each other and in unison nodded agreement to the Transport Manager's suggestion.

The truck depot must have been ready for them because as soon as they agreed to the Transport Manager's idea, the latter waved his arm in the direction of some parked-up trucks. Immediately one started up and a small wizened man with a heavily wrinkled face and toothless grin drove up alongside the Touareg in a very dusty high sided truck. It had once in a previous life been painted white. It looked bedraggled, its livery was rust streaked and it looked as if it was hardly fit for purpose.

Mac though nodded his head in approval as he listened to the idling Ford engine its seven-point three turbo diesel burbling happily under the rusty white bonnet.

'Doesn't look up too much, sounds alright though.'

He nodded to Oscar, the Transport Manager and the little Arab driver.

'Okay let's do it.'

The little driver taking Mac's nod and okay for assent in their adventure, grinning happily, leapt down from his cab and rushed round to the rear of the trailer. He quickly lowered the high rear door which dropped vertically offering up a long ramp. He stretched out both arms to indicate the truck and trailer were ready.

Oscar took the driver's seat of the Touareg, not wanting to risk his partner on the ascent to the trailer of the truck. He manoeuvred the Touareg, so it was lined up ready to drive into the gaping space.

The truck driver waved a dirty, oil-stained, negative-indicating forefinger at the Englishman indicating he should wait. The little man in his dirty brown grubby oversized boiler suit, that once had a company logo on the ripped right chest pocket, raced up the ramp and one at a time pulled down two long rectangular well-worn baulks of wood into position on the ramp.

He indicated with his hands for Oscar to drive the Touareg up to the edge of the ramps, Oscar carefully drove the vehicle into position. The little Arab driver positioned the planks in line with the front wheels of the Touareg. Then satisfied he raced up the ramp into the trailer, turned around and indicated with both his hands for Oscar to come forward slowly.

At first the Touareg's front wheels didn't want to get up on the end of the ten-centimetre square supports. Oscar realised he would have to use a bit more power. With judicious use of the clutch and accelerator he got the front wheels up onto the planks. With the help of the truck driver's signals, he managed to keep the Touareg straight and the rear wheels bumped up as well.

Now in position the truck driver stood to one side and holding onto a piece of rope trailing from the left side end of the trailer he leant out well clear of the approaching vehicle. He then gesticulated wildly, to exhort Oscar to accelerate up the ramp. Oscar needed no second hint, briefly he floored the accelerator and the Touareg without any second urging, leapt into the rear of the truck, Oscar had to brake sharply but there they were safely ensconced and well hidden.

He had some difficulty exiting the Touareg because the car was so close alongside the tall walls of the truck. The sun was beating down through the open top of the trailer and by the time he had manoeuvred himself out of the body of the car it was already heating up.

By the time Oscar dropped down onto the sandy floor of the compound he found the planks were already back on board and underneath the Touareg. The little driver was waiting to close the rear and urging the two of them into the cab of his truck. It was grubby like its driver and Mac had to throw a lot of rubbish out before he considered the grimy passenger bench fit to sit on.

The Transport Manager shouted up at them.

'If you hadn't realised already, Ali your driver is dumb, nobody tends to bother him because he can't answer their questions and round here people are used to him.'

'He transports most of the local goods up into the mountain villages, everyone thinks he has no fear because he takes this truck into the direst of places but he's a brilliant engineer and no one should trouble you while you're on his truck.'

He stood up on the wheel arch reached through the open passenger window and shook their hands as they sat sweltering in the forty-degree heat of the truck's cab.

The pair of Britishers thanked him gratefully before the Transport Manager slapped the nearside door of the cab and jumped down.

Oscar took that moment to speak to Mac.

'That Discovery just went past.'

Mac grinned

'Doesn't matter does it, they're going to lose us now anyway.'

The grinning truck driver having secured the rear of his trailer returned to the cab and slammed his driver's door shut. He looked over at the other two occupants, grinned, nodded and put the well maintained engine into gear and carefully eased the truck out of the compound and set its nose north west towards the border with Algeria.

***

At that moment at the Hotel Tidene in Agadez the only member of staff on the Hotel Reception was greeted by the uniformed officer from the National Police Force and his companion. The awkward member of the Gendarmerie National was scowling over the Police Officer's shoulder.

After a polite greeting the Police Officer questioned the receptionist while the Gendarmerie picked at his fingernails listening carefully.

'Where's the Rally car gone?'

'Sir I don't know.'

'Why not, you can't really miss it?'

'It wasn't here when I came on duty sir.'

The receptionist was becoming rattled by the Police Officer's questions. His nervousness wasn't helped by the ferocious stare of the Gendarme.

'When was that?'

'Eight, eight o'clock this morning.'

'Well are they still booked into the hotel?'

'I don't know.'

'Bloody well look, will you?'

Rasped the Gendarme ferociously.

The Police Officer glanced behind him at his companion and shook his head to indicate he would manage the situation, while the panicking receptionist scrabbled to find the answer to the question.

After what seemed an age but was in fact a minute or so, the receptionist finally got his act together.

'They've gone sir.'

'They checked out before seven this morning, I know that because my night colleague did it and he finishes at seven.'

The Gendarme took over from his colleague at this point.

'You have two Nigerians staying here, driving a black Land Rover Discovery?'

'Oh yes sir, they're still booked in, I know because the keys are still out.'

He pointed to the empty hook for room 103, hoping he was right but not knowing of any other reason for the keys not being there.

'Well, where are they?'

'I don't know sir, they extended their booking for another night.'

The Gendarme snarled at the Receptionist.

'I didn't ask that, I asked where they've gone, there's no sign of their vehicle.'

The receptionist perked up he knew something he thought might be helpful.

'I think I can help you their sir.'

'What!'

The loudness of the Gendarmes replies scared the receptionist, but he ploughed on regardless, wishing one of his colleagues, or the Manager would appear to help him out. The latter hearing the furore just outside his office had no intention of getting involved.

'On my way to work this morning I saw their car in the city and there were only one of the two guests in the car.'

'Where's the other one and where's the car?'

'I don't know sir but there is a no disturb sign on the door.'

The Police Officer stepped in at this point and spoke to his colleague.

'They haven't gone, and we'll just let the Border Post at Assamakka know to stop the two in the Rally Car before they cross into Algeria unless you want to let them go.'

The Gendarme thought about it for a moment and snorted.

'Leave them, it's that arrogant Nigerian in the Land Rover Discovery I want.'

'We'll come back this evening.'

The Police Officer told the Receptionist as the Officials turned and departed the hotel.

Chapter 30

Crossing the Border

Finishing his impromptu ablutions, Kinikanwo returned to the desert road on its generally north of west direction towards where it crossed the border north of Assamakka. The 212 kilometres took nearly four hours to complete his speed much restricted by the state of the hard-packed sand road on which he was driving.

It was nearly five thirty in the evening, although late in the year, the temperature was still approaching forty degrees. The sun was about to disappear over the horizon ahead of him, its low winter trajectory threatening to give him a headache even with his sunglasses in place.

Assamakka came upon him suddenly, many of its buildings partially buried to dissipate the desert heat. Approaching the village, he could see a pick-up truck ahead overloaded with newly made bricks. The buildings on either side of the road looked strange their rooftops just about poking their way above ground. The local semi-nomadic Touaregs partially underground properties their old fashioned, effective answer to air conditioning.

There looked to be people from all over Africa sat on the ground or walking about on the side of hard packed sand road around the village. Kinikanwo assumed they must be economic migrants trying to make their way to the shores of Europe. They had been told when entering Niger about this, apparently the truck drivers would carry the immigrants to the border with Algeria but no further. The penalties imposed by the Algerians for helping these migrants were quite severe. Niger's attitude seemed to be to allow the free rapid movement of the emigres through their country, reckoning their fast passage would have little effect on its own stability and security.

Kinikanwo knew this part of the journey was going to the hard part. He couldn't go through the Border Posts as he wasn't meant to be there. He had no idea if Damilola's body had been discovered at the Hotel and the alarm raised, plus he didn't know whether a watch been put out for him and the Discovery anyway.

Kinikanwo didn't want the Nigerien authorities to know he had entered Algeria either, he wasn't sure that once Damilola was discovered and the hue and cry commenced the Algerians wouldn't just dump him back in Niger for their authorities to arrest him.

He had a vague plan, to wait for darkness close to Assamaka, and follow the desert north, bypassing both Border Posts as he went.

On the road map the desert west of Assamaka looked the best bet. He hoped there would be the lights of the trucks on the road north, for him to parallel as he was crossing the desert close to the border.

In the middle of the Assamakka there was a hairpin bend, here the sand highway turned from its south-south-westerly heading one hundred and forty-five degrees to a north easterly one. Not sure whether to make the turn his mind was made up for him when dark clad figures leapt out of the near darkness and tried to jump in and onto the Discovery as he slowed for the hairpin.

Fortunately, the central locking was in play which prevented him being boarded by migrants. Without thinking he accelerated and carried straight on and out the other western side of the village making it impossible to board the Discovery. Once about a kilometre clear of the few houses on that side of the village he turned the Discovery in the right direction, stopped and waited. While the darkness closed in he took the opportunity to eat something and get a drink of water.

***

Approaching Assamakka the high sided white truck with its dumb driver, passengers and Touareg cargo watched the sun disappear ahead of them. Ali put his thumbs up and indicated they should lock the door of the cab as he exaggeratedly did the same with his own cab door.

He switched on his lights, not only the headlights but five large spotlights across the top of the cab of the truck. These lit up the sand highway almost better than daylight, elongated shadows highlighted any obstructions and the buildings as they approached the village. Ali changed down, they all clung on as he swept the truck viciously around the hundred and forty-five-degree turn.

Oscar could see a huge grin on Ali's face as he did his best to accelerate away. Neither could understand why their driver was silently laughing until Mac spotted the dark clad people trying to rush the truck. Oscar got it first and nudged his Scottish partner. 'Illegal immigrants, they're trying to board the truck, I reckon Ali thinks it's funny because they've no chance of climbing over the high sides of his trailer.'

Very quickly the Niger Border Post was upon them, Ali tooted the deep horn of the truck twice, slowed to a crawl and they were waved through by a sole border guard.

***

Out to the west in the desert, Kinikanwo seeing the lights of the Touareg's truck started moving slowly forward in what he hoped was the right direction. He was only making about ten kilometres per hour, without lights and felt silhouetted briefly by the lights of Ali's truck as it made the hairpin turn to the east of the Discovery.

As it raced away to the North West it helped him correct his direction of travel and as long as it was in sight he was able to make progress to the north with few problems.

The desert appeared to be completely flat around him although the Discovery's engine note would change slightly as it moved up and down the small inclines. He was helped by the clear skies and the light shed by the millions of stars. Remembering his army Officer training he worked out the direction of the Pole star from the position of the Plough and tried to keep the dim star in front of the vehicle as he crawled to the north.

His progress was halted when suddenly the front of the Discovery dipped sharply and unexpectedly. He braked immediately and reversed rapidly avoiding possible disaster. Fetching a torch from the glove compartment and tucking the Steyr into his waistband, he went around the front of the car to investigate. It turned out to be a little but short drop into a dry wadi something that could have been a major problem if he had continued.

Turning about to go back to the car he was shocked to hear humans talking quietly, the voices appeared to be all around him and then he realised what it was.

Like him there were people trying to cross the border into Algeria undetected, the starlight showed them as dark shadows walking slowly north, all of them appeared to be carrying something.

As his eyes adjusted to the darkness he turned right round. There were incredible numbers of them out here in the desert. When he turned back to the car he found four young men trying to steal the Discovery even though he had never been more than a few metres away. They were unlucky he still had the keys as well as most importantly his equaliser, otherwise they might have overwhelmed him.

Kinikanwo pulled the Steyr M −A1 from the right pocket of his shorts and placed the business end of the guns barrel on the head of the boy in the driver's seat.

'Out.'

The miscreant extracted himself carefully from the front driver's seat and went down on his knees in the desert as Kinikanwo kept the muzzle of his gun pressed tightly into the boys left ear.

'Right the rest of you out and join your pal before I put a bullet through his skull.'

Kinikanwo lined the four youths up outside his vehicle.

'Tell me why I shouldn't kill the lot of you?'

Three of them pleaded for mercy but the one who had been trying to hot wire the Discovery had more spunk and spoke up.

'So what, we've nothing to lose.'

Kinikanwo was beginning to have the semblance of an idea and thought he might be able to use these young men to his advantage.

'Alright I'm not going to shoot you, but we could help each other.'

'Where are you from?'

The braver lad stuck out his chest and piped up acting as the foursome's spokesman.

'Lagos, Nigeria.'

'Alright I'll drive the car and one of you can run in front with the torch, the other three can travel in the vehicle.'

'We'll need a drink.'

'Every runner does fifteen minutes and after the first hour you'll each get a bottle of water.'

'Then when I'm certain we've crossed the border, I'll feed you all.'

There was a nodding of heads as all agreed to his suggestion.

'Right on your feet and gather round.'

He got them organised, pointing out to each of them the Pole star and telling them to always run towards that. He thought they had about ten kilometres to the border and another twenty to I n Guezzam about three to four hours maximum.

They set off with the first boy trotting along at about eight kilometres per hour, the torch being his only guide as the rest of them followed closely behind in the Discovery.

To distract them Kinikanwo made each of the boys, who could not have been much over sixteen years of age tell him about how they had made their way to the Algerian border.

It turned out to be a tale of good and bad luck. They all lived in Lagos's port town Apapa and had got on the wrong side of their local gang. This meant they couldn't go to school and their parents needed them to work so they had done a runner and wanted to go to England.

They had made their way northwards on the back of the large trucks, sometimes with the permission of the driver by helping him load or unload and other times not, often incurring a driver's displeasure. It had taken them two weeks so far, they had little money and few effects although they did say they always tried to keep clean. Kinikanwo asked about dental hygiene and almost in unison the three in the Discovery at that time produced toothbrushes out of their shirt pockets.

After an hour and a half Kinikanwo stopped and fed them all from his emergency rations, they had run well and according to the odometer they had made sixteen kilometres since Assamakka. He thought he could see the loom of lights from the first civilisation on the Algerian side of the border, I n Guezzam.

***

Ali had done the thirty-five kilometres into I n Guezzam from Assamakka in only forty minutes. The two ex-pats were surprised to see the incongruous sight of a boulevard with street lighting and kerbs at the entrance to the Algerian Border Town. Ali didn't give them time to think he stopped amongst a lot of other trucks dropped out of his cab and had the rear open within moments and before the Brits even had time to descend from the cab.

This time Mac helped Ali drag the boards into place, Oscar had the Touareg reversed down the ramp within moments and they were ready to go.

Ali indicated with his hands that they should wait, then mimed refuelling and pointed them in the direction of a filling station before miming that they should drive as far away from the border as quickly as possible.

The two of them hugged the fantastic little driver as a gesture of thanks and did as he suggested after giving him most of their remaining Rally Car photographs.

Refuelling was easy and cheap, they found they could even pay with Mac's credit card. By seven in the evening they were following the lights of a northbound truck on Algerian National Route 1.

Mac was looking at the map to check where they were and informed Oscar.

'This is the northern section of the Trans Saharan Highway; the road should be tarmacked from now on.'

'Good as long as this truck ahead keeps going I reckon we'll be fine.'

He yawned covering his mouth with his left hand and continued.

'I'll let you know when I'm knackered, and we'll just pull off into the desert but as long as that driver ahead keeps illuminating everything with his big floods I'm eager we keep on moving.'

'Fine, seems good to me the further from the border we are the safer I'll feel.'

***

Shortly after the stop to feed the four boys, the first lights of I n Guezzam became visible about seven kilometres to the north. Thanks to his preparation Kinikanwo was aware of the refuelling station to the north of the town and got the latest runner to angle their approach so they would pass close to the West of the settlement.

By ten in the evening they were approaching the highway to the north of the town, the three boys in the car were pleading with him to take them on through Algeria, and he was on the point of agreeing with them.

While they had been crawling across the desert Kinikanwo had concluded that a car full of people was less likely to be recognised by the authorities as the one sought by the police in Niger.

He was still very concerned that if he got stopped and picked up by the Algerian authorities they might just ship him back to Niger and their debatable justice.

Nearly back to the highway north of I n Guezzam he needed one thing to be right before he could take the boys with him.

At the next change of runner, he made sure they could pass muster if they were stopped by the authorities.

'Have you all got passports?'

'They were eager to prove in the affirmative, all of them waving their Nigerian documents so he could see they were being truthful.

'Right I'll take you north, this is how it's going to work.'

At that the two boys swapping over as runners outside began dancing around and they all started screaming with joy.

Once they had calmed down he explained what they needed to do once they reached the Highway.

'We have to go back into the town to refuel at the garage on its northern edge.'

'To the cashier and anyone else it will look like we have come from the north and I want to keep it that way.'

'You haven't finished with running in front because when we leave the town we are going south and then circle it by going back into the desert to confuse the authorities.'

They refuelled the Discovery and the plan worked perfectly, Kinikanwo was even able to cut the circuit of the town short by turning down a side street and coming back into the desert to the west of I n Guezzam.

By midnight they were headed north on the Trans Saharan Highway with a Discovery full of Nigerians. Unknown to either party there was less than sixty kilometres between the Discovery and the Touareg.

The tarmacked road was at times overrun with drifting sand, unlike the Touareg which was following a truck with big lights, the Discovery kept running into problems when sand crossing the highway loomed out of the dark and Kinikanwo had to almost stop as they negotiated and bumped over the obstacle. After about ten kilometres Kinikanwo could hardly keep his eyes open, it had been a long and fraught day since Damilola had come out of their bathroom in the Hotel Tidene firing the Steyr at him.

Exhausted and without warning he pulled off the highway and got one of the Nigerian boys to go ahead with the torch eventually parking in the desert about half a kilometre from the road.

Chapter 31

Tuesday 10th Through Algeria

Oscar who had been driving at an auspicious distance behind the large truck they were following up the Trans Sahara Highway was tired and hungry. Except for the odd snack while driving, they hardly seemed to have eaten all day. A couple of chocolate bars back at the petrol station had given him a caffeine kick and kept him going for a while.

It was just after eight in the evening and they had done about one hundred and fifty kilometres since Ali had unloaded the Touareg back in I n Guezzam.

'What do you think Mac, a bit of off-road parking, eat and get some kip.'

'I'm with you on that.'

Oscar pulled off to the right side of the road and carefully found a completely flat piece of desert to park on. They got out some rations used their survival stove for only the second time, had something hot to eat and drink before putting their seats back and getting some sleep.

Mac deliberately set his watch alarm for five in the morning, they had discussed possible banditry by local Touareg's and Al

Quaeda, so not wanting to be stationary and visible at the same time they were determined to be back on the road by dawn, at around six in the morning.

Sure enough after a decent night's sleep in the relative comfort of the Touareg, Mac's watch alarm woke them both at five.

He himself was pleased when he woke, the throbbing at the back of his head seemed to have disappeared.

'Might be able to drive today the headache seems to have gone.'

Mac sat up and put the car seat upright he felt all round his head, stretched and slowly moved his head from side to side.

'Yeah I'm right.'

Oscar who was still lying down in his sleeping bag, looked up.

'You sure?'

'Yeah definitely.'

Oscar sat up, rubbed his eyes and stretched in the darkness.

'Alright I'll do the first hour just to make sure, then you can give it a go.'

'No heroics though, if you feel at all wobbly stop and I'll take over.'

'Of course, come on you are beginning to sound like my Mum.'

They both laughed and looked out through the windscreen at the multitude of stars in the cloudless sky, it was quite cool, Mac pulled his sleeping bag over his shoulders to keep warm.

There was a slight pinkness in the eastern sky, notice of the approaching sunrise. While they waited for the imminent dawn

Oscar made some tea on the portable stove and they ate some oat cakes for breakfast.

By six it was light enough to see clearly, although sunrise was still twenty minutes away. Oscar drove them the half kilometre back onto the Trans Saharan Highway, where he pointed the bonnet of the Touareg northwards.

They calculated that the next major point of civilisation, Fort Laperine or as the Touaregs called it Tamanrasset was about two hundred and sixty kilometres ahead.

According to Oscar's previous research this stretch was the most dangerous part of the journey, Al Quaeda had recently killed civilians and taken hostages in this area. Except for changing drivers, they had already resolved not to stop except in the most extreme circumstances.

Once they reached the Tamanrasset they should be safe, it now being the centre of the Algerian and Central African nations fight against the North African branch of the Al Quaeda terrorists.

It appeared the highway must be quite secure though, there was a continual flow of the huge overloaded trucks southward bound for the border with Niger. For some unknown reason they only occasionally caught and passed northbound traffic.

***

Kinikanwo slept soundly, he had little conscience about Damilola, so was untroubled, although the stress of the previous day had meant he was exhausted from his travails.

He was curled up on the driver's seat and locked into the Discovery with the four Nigerian youths, his hand in his right-hand pocket, curled around the Steyr M-A1, in case of incident. He woke as it was getting light to find the Discovery surrounded by about a dozen black Africans. Apparently, they had come silently out of the desert to use the car as a shelter from the cold night breeze.

Cautiously he took a swig of water and started up the engine, the noise woke those in the Discovery and those outside. Not wishing to get mixed up with anymore illegal immigrants, he carefully drove away and back to the highway and like the Touareg ahead of them, turned north about half an hour before those in the Touareg got on the road and thus cutting the intervening distance to now only twenty-five kilometres.

The young men in the car with him, had come round and were helping themselves to his fast vanishing stocks of bottled water. Kinikanwo wasn't bothered for the moment. Everything now was about getting away from the border area, reaching one of the northern Algerian cities before finding a safe way of returning home.

***

About half past seven the endless desert horizon began to change, the first inkling of brown hills appeared ahead of them. At first Mac thought it was a mirage, the sun was well up and the desert temperatures were already in their mid-thirties.

'Oscar, I thought we were crossing the Sahara not the Himalaya's that surely is a mirage ahead of us.'

289

Oscar laughed.

'No Mac they're real, we're going up and through them, the next civilisation Tamanrasset is somewhere in that lot.'

'One thing though Oscar we must have lost the Chief's Discovery no way they could have followed us across the border like that.'

'Maybe, but Mac they don't have to keep us in sight, there is only this one road out of here.'

Shortly after this conversation the road began to rise, and the horizon ahead was filled with many brown and grey peaks, the paved road was better here and eventually there was a sign indicating an upcoming junction with an incoming road from their right. This had to be the first indicated junction since they left I n Guezzam.

They rounded a sweeping left-hand bed, a steep brown cliff towering above them on their left. Just as the incoming road on their right came in sight so did a road-block. The road was obstructed at the junction by several Algerian army vehicles. Some of the uniformed men were pointing serious looking weapons at them.

Oscar braked hard and they were both thrown forward against their seat harnesses. By the time they had slowed to a crawl they were alongside a halt sign in four languages placed on the central white line of the highway.

Oscar drove the Touareg forward cautiously, they approached the road block with some trepidation. Mac placed his hands where they could be seen, on the dashboard in front of him.

A uniformed, armed soldier of the Algerian forces stepped out from behind what looked like and armoured personnel carrier and indicated with his free left hand that they should come up to him and stop.

When they reached the armed man, his Sergeant's stripes now prominently visible he indicated to Mac that he should lower his window. Casually pointing the gun away from them but obviously alert and with the support of at least three other armed soldiers.

'Papiers Monsieur.'

Mac thinking, he understood the soldier but not wanting to cause any misunderstanding replied.

'Non parlez vous Francais, English please?'

The sergeant shouted something behind him in French and one of the soldiers lowered his rifle and double-timed it to the Touareg.

'Please sir can we see your papers and ask why you are in an old Dakar Rally Car.'

Mac smiled and passed the soldier their visas and passports and explained what they were doing with the car. The soldier passed this information on to the Sergeant who had taken the documents and was checking their visas.

For a moment he looked grim faced as he fumbled his way through the different bits of paper. Then he grinned and shook Mac's hand enthusiastically through the open window of the Touareg.

He said something to his translator who stiffened to attention then spoke again in English to Mac.

'My Sergeant recognises the car he was part of the army support teams when they came through Algeria nine years ago.'

'He thanks you for saving such an icon.'

The Sergeant waved for them to follow, he led them through a slalom of military vehicles and out the other side where they could see a queue of waiting southbound trucks.

At the Sergeants signal they pulled up alongside a soldier sitting at a collapsible table who was checking documents and stamping them. The Sergeant marched up to the table shoved an unfortunate truck driver out of their way and got their visas and passports stamped without anyone else examining them. When he returned the documentation to Mac he stood back and saluted and indicated they should wait.

Meanwhile the Discovery was fast cutting the distance between them.

At the road block selfies were being taken by the enthusiastic sergeant and his colleagues and it was another fifteen minutes before the Rally Car and its occupants were ushered on their way by the beaming Sergeant and one of his colleagues.

Mac commented as they drove past the southbound queue.

'That was lucky, fancy him being involved with the rally back then.'

'Lucky for us I was dreading some awkward questions about no Niger exit stamp or an Algeria entry one either.'

They were quickly into Fort Laperine/Tamanrasset where they stopped briefly to change drivers and continued their mainly northerly passage. For a few kilometres the road went west around Tamanrasset Airport. The highway was accompanied now by a fresh water pipeline and there was more evidence of civilisation with a herd of domesticated black and white goats being looked after by a Touareg boy. The young lad in his grubby white Thobe waved enthusiastically at them as they flew past.

The N1 was intersected by the N55A, a highway which disappeared south west into the Sahara. Just after the turning was a petrol station and a café which the pair welcomed, not having eaten properly for about thirty hours.

On entry to the white sand blasted building the French influence was immediately apparent, they could smell freshly baked bread before they saw the Brioche's sitting on the wooden counter. This sight made both their mouth's water and for an hour they did their best to consume a decent meal. It was warm in the windowless café sitting under a large rusty white fan which was slicing through and dispersing the hot air from the small dining area.

The meal finished Oscar went and fetched the road atlas into the café. They worked out and planned the rest of the trip. They were now in a relatively safe part of the world and thought they could plan without risk of danger. After looking through all his information Oscar came to certain conclusions and explained them to his partner.

'Right we decided we would get the ferry to Almeria in Spain from either Ghazaouet or Oran.'

Mac agreed with that statement with a nod of his head.

'The next ferry is at fourteen hundred tomorrow from Ghazaouet and that is about a shade under two thousand kilometres from here.'

'What's the alternative?'

'Friday at midnight from Oran plus there's all the daily ones from Algiers but they take a couple of days across the Med as you know.'

Mac thought about all the alternatives and grinned.

'Well then let's have a bit of fun, test out the car and ourselves and go for the two o'clock ferry at Ghazaouet tomorrow.'

'I'm impatient to get home.'

'Fair enough, two-hour stints and we'll see where we are at midnight, then we can make a decision.

Oscar's voice took on a more serious tone.

'If you feel crap at all in any way, we'll back off and change the plan, alright?'

'Okay, that's fair enough, it's ten now, I'll take over and drive until midday.'

Oscar drained his caffeine-laced, thick, black coffee.'

'You ready then, we had better get on with it.'

Leaving the Café, they had to wait for a sand-covered, black, Land Rover Discovery with Nigerian plates barrelling north at speed to pass before they could cross the highway and return to the Touareg.

It was Oscar who spotted it.

'There's the Chief's car again what the hell is he playing at?'

'Come on Mac I know it's weird, I can't think why he would send anyone to follow us.'

'There's nothing to be gained is there, besides it seemed full of people and there was only a driver yesterday.'

'I don't know Oscar but if we see it again I want to give it a clean pair of heels.'

'Alright I'll agree with you it is strange, let's get out of here and do as we planned we'll just have to be careful if we pass them and at changeovers.'

Oscar partially satisfied his partner was taking his concerns seriously led their way back to the car and they set off again which just for a change hadn't attracted the normal sightseers there being no one around, except those serving in the Café.

***

Kinikanwo was shocked to see the Touareg and its occupants.

'That's a bit of fortune.'

He thought, and concluded it was time to resume communication with the Chiefs in Port Harcourt.

'He might just be able to regain the situation.'

They had also hit the Algerian Army roadblock, it hadn't been as easy for them as the Touareg and its occupants. He had prepared the boys and the five of them had their story right. They said they were all travelling north for work in Algiers. Because they had the car and were obviously not destitute they got through. Having Nigerian, passports meant they didn't need

Algerian visas, the Army Sergeant had instructed the clerk to stamp their passports and let them pass.

The youths were still excited about passing through the army road block without being deported, they were happy with Kinikanwo for taking them north. Their excitement permeated to Kinikanwo who was now thinking he could complete his mission and be able to return home in glory.

Thinking this he pulled the satellite phone from its resting place, instructed the boys to be absolutely quiet and speed dialled his boss.

He was greeted by anger at the other end when he got through, Chief Kudo wasn't very happy at the lack of communication over the last two days.

'Where the hell have you two been?'

'You bloody better have caught up with that poxy rally car otherwise you better not come home.

Kinikanwo who was still driving had the phone jammed between his left ear and shoulder waited patiently for the rant to finish then gave his boss his own made up version of the last couple of days.'

'Don't blame me, I'm ahead of them and I'm having to do this on my own.'

'What do you mean, you're on your own?'

'Damilola cleared off two nights ago and I've had to manage it all myself.'

'I can't bring the Land Rover Discovery back, I've had to smuggle it through the Niger border with Algeria, some Copper wanted to take it off me.'

'I'll have to sell it when we get up to the Mediterranean.'

'Alright, alright but don't lose them.'

Chapter 32

Caught

Just at that moment the Touareg caught and passed them on a narrow bend going like a bat out of hell.

'They've just passed me I'm going to have to go, please tell the Chief at this rate we'll be up to the coast tomorrow night.'

Kinikanwo switched off the satellite phone and put it back in the driver's door pocket.

The one-sided conversation sparked interest in his passengers, the leader of the four offered to share the driving now they were obviously in a chase.

Kinikanwo questioned him.

'How old are you, honestly?'

'Eighteen.'

'Have you got a driving licence?'

The eighteen-year-old thought about his answer and what Kinikanwo was looking for.

'Well no but I can drive, I'm really fast.'

'How's that?'

Deciding he couldn't get into any more trouble and eager to help he admitted.

'I've been stealing cars since I was thirteen, I can drive almost anything.'

The rest of his gang were all nodding their heads in agreement, the smallest one of the boys sitting in the middle of the back seat piped up.

'He's ace, really good, we wouldn't have escaped Apapa without him getting us away from the cops.'

Kinikanwo had heard enough and pushed the Discovery up to one twenty kilometres per hour.

'Right you're on, look out for that thing which flew past us just now.'

All four of the Apapa boys were now wide awake and peering out of the windows trying to spot the flying Touareg ahead of them.

They came around a long right-hand bend and through a cutting in the Hoggar Mountains.

One of the boys pointed out there were occasional flashes of the blue of the Touareg some way ahead of them.

Kinikanwo had the Discovery up to one hundred and thirty now and they were only just managing to keep their prey in sight in the far distance.

The road was very straight with the massive water pipeline on their outside and sheer rock faces occasionally plummeting to the very edge of the highway on their nearside.

Kinikanwo found he had to take few risks overtaking the slower trucks northbound like themselves to keep in touch with the fleeing Touareg. Only once did Kinikanwo have to brake sharply, this to allow an oncoming wagon to go south otherwise their much superior speed took them past these obstacles rapidly.

Kinikanwo wasn't worried about fuel he reckoned the Discovery would go longer than the ex-Rally Car.

He was only concerned about having to hand over to the bright young kid from Lagos and whether he would drive fast and safe enough or kill them all.

Within the hour they had completed the one hundred kilometres to the tiny outpost of In Ekker, previously famed because it was the site for French Nuclear bomb testing. Then things became more difficult as they made their way up into the mountains proper rising up to over a thousand metres above sea level.

For both vehicles this was a time of great frustration, the Touareg would race along then suddenly on a bend there would be one, sometimes two slow-moving overloaded trucks on the mountainous road ahead of them. They would themselves be slowed to a crawl.

For those in the Discovery astern they had long since caught up with their quarry thanks to the dawdling obstructions. They would lose the Touareg for a while because it had got past one of these slow travelling road blocks. Then they would clear the same problem to quickly catch up at the next slow truck crawling up hill.

Once having not seen the Touareg for a while, Kinikanwo rushing round a tight bend, nearly rear-ended the Rally Car as he found it held up once again, after that he tried to give the

Touareg reasonable space. He knew he wouldn't look suspicious because except for the Easterly N55 junction there had been few places where someone might be expected to turn off the highway.

Just after midday, Kinikanwo felt tired, he had been driving without respite for over four hours, the mountain bends and sometimes risky overtaking had exhausted him. He was fortunate because just before the road started its descent out of the mountains they flashed past the Touareg parked up on the side of the road, it was obvious the two occupants were changing positions.

Kinikanwo reacted immediately.

'Quick swap.'

He braked sharply dragging the Discovery to a halt just off to the side of the road. The eighteen-year-old car thief was into the driver's seat and ready to go almost before Kinikanwo had pulled himself through the passenger door.

Even so, before he had even sat down he was shouting to the lad.

'Go, go let's stay ahead of them now we're in front.'

The lad needed no more urging and with a slight spin of the wheels in the off-road gravel, they were back onto the highway long before the Touareg came back into sight.

It was easy to keep an eye on the following car as there were long straight sections on the descent from the high rocky desert back onto the sands of the Sahara.

The kid from Apapa proved to be as skilful as he had suggested, it was he, who after two hours spotted the Touareg in the mirror pulling over for another driver change.

Kinikanwo decided there was no need for them to change drivers and instructed his driver to pull farther ahead. He had been checking his maps and calculating. The next place to refuel was about two hours away and whatever happened they must fill up there, even though he had spare in cans he didn't want to dip into these reserves unless absolutely necessary. He told the boy driving.

'They have to refuel soon, according to the map there is only one place they can do it.'

Kinikanwo planned their stop and instructed the driver to leap out and refuel while handing the nearside kid a wad of Euros to pay for the refill.

Finally, six hours out of Tit, where they had first caught up with their prey, the Discovery pulled over into a refuelling station at the oasis of In Salah. On Kinikanwo's instructions they parked in the empty Service Station alongside the pump furthest from the road. As instructed the driver leapt out to fill up the Discovery while the appointed lad raced off to pay for the fuel and gather whatever refreshments he could find

The idea worked and the Touareg which followed them in parked alongside a pump that accidentally hid them from the occupants of the Discovery.

They were all back in the Discovery well before the Touareg and its occupants were refuelled and ready to leave.

Kinikanwo in the passenger's seat looking at the road atlas spoke to the lads.

'Right we're going to let them go first, then follow, I only need to know which turning they take further on.

***

Oscar paid for their fuel and took the passenger seat, letting Mac take over for his second stint at the wheel. He thought the Scotsman seemed to be alright and appeared unaffected by the concussion of a few days ago. The refuelling station was suddenly busy with trucks, and off roaders and the Discovery didn't register at first on the far side of the pumps.

They partially hidden Discovery became obvious when Oscar went to pay for their fuel. It confirmed his suspicions by not moving even when the kid paying for the Discovery's fuel returned to the car and it didn't depart.

Mac spoke first when Oscar returned to the Touareg gesticulating in the direction of the Discovery.

'I've seen it, you're right they're definitely following us.'

'Yeah I know, let's give them a run for their money, we're fully fuelled and only need to stop once more before Ghazaouet on the coast.'

'Fine, Mac started the engine put the car into gear and they raced off the forecourt and back onto the highway.

Oscar was worried that although they were progressing well and had done nearly six hundred kilometres, they had just over twice that, still to do. A lot of it was going to be in the dark.

Still he reminded himself he would do the first stint when the sun went down, and Mac could work out whether the oncoming lights affected his vision.

***

The chase went on much as before, Kinikanwo had to urge caution a few times as his driver's attitude was to think of the whole thing as a race. He wanted to overtake everything in sight including the Touareg. The three kids in the rear were dozing now, for them there was little to see just the endless rolling desert split by the highway.

Kinikanwo took time to check the maps and his calculations again before asking the driver to pass over the satellite phone. About five he picked it up and this time contacted the Chief.

'I'm up with the Rally Car and it's going like a bat out of hell.'

'That's good, you're doing well.'

'They're probably going for the Ghazaouet ferry at two tomorrow afternoon, can't be anything else unless it's Algiers, there's nothing from there until Friday,'

Kinikanwo asked the Chief.

'What does that mean for me?'

'Well if they come off the Trans Sahara just east of El Menia and go left and straight north on the N107 they aren't going to Algiers.'

'I'll settle for knowing that.'

'Where is Damilola?'

'My sister is not pleased you've lost her daughter.'

Kinikanwo cursed to himself he had almost forgotten about Damilola and her relationship to the Chief

'Sorry about that, one minute she was there, the next she had gone.'

He decided he didn't need any more questioning on that point and made a feeble excuse to disconnect.

'Sorry have to go, I'm driving,'

At this point he switched off the phone.

In some ways Kinikanwo was quite surprised how prepared the old bugger was, having all the routes planned and knowing the times of the ferries like that.

The sun was starting to disappear over the desert horizon to their left and the reflection from the heated sands was helping to create a red banded sky in the west.

Kinikanwo reckoned they would be at El Menia about eight that evening, he also guessed the drivers of the Touareg would change again around six. So far, the two ex-pats had been religious about their changeover times, they were in a hurry, he guessed the Chief must be right about Ghazaouet.

Sure enough on the dot of six the Touareg pulled off the road and Kinikanwo instructed his young driver to keep going.

'Pull over soonest and I'll take over.'

'But I'm fine I can go for ages yet.'

'That's not the point it's going to be dark soon and I need you to watch the rear lights of the Rally car.'

Now the idea was accepted they changed over smartly.

Kinikanwo had other unspoken plans and he set off in pursuit of the Touareg as soon as it passed them.

Just before eight they began to pass to the west of the town and oasis of El Menia, at the north end of the town the A1 turned ninety degrees to the right, it was pitch black and the lights of the Touareg had disappeared briefly.

Kinikanwo nearly missed the turn and almost overshot into the front of southbound, lumbering truck which fortunately had slowed to a walk itself for the hairpin turn. He scraped the Discovery into the bend almost halting in the process. They got around just in time there was only a short distance to the left turn for the N107.

There was no evidence of the Touareg ahead of them but the eagle-eyed passenger next to him spotted the disappearing tail lights heading north up the side road which constituted the N107.

Chapter 33

Wednesday 11th Rush to Ghazaouet

Mac almost overshot the left turn onto the N107 and was delayed in making the manoeuvre. Due to Kinikanwo's own near miss at the earlier corner Mac had time to reverse up and force the Touareg into the left turn and onto the N107 before accelerating away up the branch road.

It was only because of this slight delay in making the turn that Kinikanwo now knew which direction the Touareg had taken. Oscar was looking back, watching for the lights of the following vehicle, it was fortunately easy to spot because they had noted earlier the off-side light of the Discovery was slightly out of kilter and the beam was too high.

Thus he was relieved when he saw the lights of the Discovery race across the junction and make no attempt to follow them, excitedly he spoke to his partner.

'They've missed us put your foot down and let's lose them for good.'

Mac laughed at his pal.

'I know, we do have a rear-view mirror you know.'

Just to reassure his partner he speeded up a fraction more, the full beam headlights lit up the road and surrounds for some way ahead of them.

Even with this apparent good news this was the part of journey that was really concerning the pair, there were warnings about flooded wadi's washing out the roads at this time of year. Mind you they had seen no evidence of rain, although they were approaching the Saharan Atlas Mountains where extreme precipitation was more likely.

They expected their route to be little used, in his researches, Oscar had found advisories warning the road may disappear into the desert in strong winds which could cause problems especially as they were night driving.

When they realised they were going to take this route Oscar's pre-planning was especially useful. He knew they could do the four-hundred-and-fifty-kilometre chunk to Brezina without rushing over the desert roads. If it took all night, they would arrive at the mountains at first light and still be in range of the ferry.

Mac belted along at first until they came to a junction where the N107 melded with the road from Metlili to the east of them. They turned to the west at this point, parts of the road had a thin covering of sand. At times they were slowed to as little as sixty kilometres per hour. Even so they made good progress, there was nothing to overtake, although an eastbound convoy of heavy military vehicles passed by when they were changing drivers around midnight. Its backwash battered them and left a thick dust cloud in its wake.

Just after five in the morning Mac was driving the Touareg along the desert road, there was a light breeze and he was struggling to always see the tarmac ahead of him. At last and a little ahead of schedule he saw the lights of the small town and oasis of Brezina ahead of them, the first sign of civilisation since they had branched off and left the Discovery in their wake.

Oscar was stretched out on the passenger seat, Mac didn't wake him he could tell his colleague was asleep because of the snores emanating from the wide-open mouth.

He drove carefully into and the short distance through the town which marked the boundary between desert and Mountains. The road started to rise bringing with it tight bends and occasional steep drops, at first the headlights of the Touareg produced weird dark shadows from the cliff faces ahead of them.

At six as the rising sun started to lighten the scene, he looked for somewhere to stop and wake Oscar to take over the driving. Conveniently they arrived at Brezina Lake a man-made stretch of water used for Hydro Electric Power and local water supply. They stopped on the bridge, the sun in the east allowing them to see the gap at the end of the lake where the dam had been built.

Oscar walking round the Touareg and stretching out his tired muscles commented on the scene of calm blue water between the sandy, brown, rock faces.

'You think about it, it's the first decent block of water we've seen since the Bonny River over four thousand kilometres ago.'

Mac took pleasure in correcting his colleague.

'You forgot the Niger.'

'Oh yeah, anyway it looks cool, wish we had more time, I'd jump right in.'

'Never mind that, more importantly, you're the navigator, how far to go and can we make the ferry at Ghazaouet?'

Oscar now back in the driver's seat was checking his maps and calculating.

'Should do it, I reckon, we're about on schedule, can't really afford any delays though.'

Putting the maps down Oscar talked through his conclusions.

'We've four hundred and fifty kilometres or thereabouts to go, if we aim for midday we have to average seventy-five klicks an hour.'

'I reckon it gives us time for a brief break to grab a hot drink and some grub somewhere.'

'Changing the subject, how's your head?'

'It's fine though, I'm knackered, can't wait to collapse into a bunk on that ferry.'

'Just think, if we were to make it, you'll only have one more stint to do.'

Oscar set off and started cutting into the remaining kilometres to Ghazaouet with some gusto. Mac stretched out on the passenger seat and immediately nodded off, even though the

Touareg was moving his limp body from side to side as Oscar negotiated them round some of the big mountain bends.

It didn't take them long to reach the road's summit, they were soon cruising downhill. They finally left the N107 and joined the wider and better tarmacked N47 this turned into the N6A. Fortunately the road didn't pass through and only clipped the edges of the small villages' en-route.

Before Oscar completed his stint, the one hundred and eighty kilometres to Bougtob. A small town in the valley between the Saharan Atlas and the Coastal Atlas Mountains. They took the opportunity to do their final refuel in Algeria, it was quite cold here between the mountain ranges and made a refreshing change after all their time working in the Tropics.

After a quick stop where Oscar refuelled the Touareg, Mac found a local bakery and grabbed hold of a couple of freshly baked brioches with which he was able to acquire some local goat's cheese. He ripped the bread open and stuffed some of the cheese between each of the two pieces creating a rudimentary sandwich for their breakfast.

'I know you've fifteen minutes left of your slot but to save time, alright if I take over now?'

'Fine by me.'

Oscar mumbled, mouth stuffed full of the makeshift sandwich. Mac leapt into the driver's seat and still eating set them back on track.

They joined the North West bound side of the N6 on the edge of the town and immediately ran into problems with road works.

This held them up for fifteen minutes. There was a man with a stop/go sign in Arabic who was more interested in trying to light a cigarette in the strong breeze than turning the sign to green. Oscar sighed looking at his wrist watch, all the time recalculating their ETA at Ghazaouet in his head.

At least they were at the at the head of the extensive line of traffic when puffing at his now lit cigarette the stop/go man nodding at them finally turned his sign to go. Mac took the opportunity to accelerate past the half a kilometre of roadworks. He took advantage of the now empty road ahead of them to try and make up some of the lost time.

They whipped through the five kilometres to El Kheither a small mountain town and met another obstruction. On a two hundred and seventy degree left turning hairpin, lined closely with two storey houses, they came upon an overturned truck blocking the whole thoroughfare.

Mac's rapid getaway at the previous road works worked for them, he was able to reverse up enough to left turn into an alleyway, before the next vehicle blocked them in.

It was then up to Oscar who somehow by instinct, rather than navigation managed to guide them through some hardened-sand alleyways and towards the N109 the other side of the obstacle. The streets were narrow and not meant for vehicles, Mac scraped the offside mirror on the white painted wall of one of the houses, so limited was the space. Twice Oscar had to get out and move objects to the roadside to allow them to pass through. The funniest part was the line full of washing he had to release then lash back up as the Touareg couldn't pass under the line.

They returned to the main road and raced along to Marhoum only fifty five kilometres from Bougtob. There they were slowed to a crawl by market day. People, cars, stalls, vans, donkeys' hauling carts and other animals were everywhere. Another time they would have appreciated the colour, smells and variety of different objects on sale.

Not today, Mac had to force the Touareg through the crowds, honking the car's horn continually, joining the cacophony of noise from other frustrated drivers, the animals and crowds in the market.

This time the easily identifiable Rally Car was a hindrance, everyone wanted to see the famous vehicle. They had to be careful not to run anyone down as the crowds surged around them.

It took precious time out of their schedule but finally they escaped the throng and returned to the main highway, meanwhile Oscar was re-calculating.

'Christ we've lost so much time, it's half nine and we've still miles to go yet.'

'We're never going to make it.'

'We're going to bloody well try,'

Mac replied forcefully, cutting up a lumbering truck in the meantime. The road was good he had the Touareg up to one twenty most of the time. Now they could no longer afford any more delays, this was going to be tight alright.

Sixty kilometres and half an hour later at ten o'clock in Ras el Ma they swapped positions both racing round the car to try and save precious seconds. Oscar steered them onto the mountain road which would take them over the Coastal Atlas Mountains to the Mediterranean Sea at Ghazaouet.

On the mountain road to Sebdou the traffic was light, they were able to claw back a few minutes and by ten forty-five they were negotiating the small town. Here the road still rose briefly, further into the mountains and they joined the W46. Oscar knew this part of the journey was going to be difficult, with its hairpins and zig zags on the descent. Shortly after Sebdou they summited at Mount Zahra and swept downwards towards the coast.

As Oscar expected the road was now an almost continuous sweep of hairpin bends, he would accelerate rapidly between each one, brake hard, sweep round the often one hundred and eighty degree turns before accelerating swiftly away from each bend. Mac in the passenger seat hung on for dear life as Oscar used all the roadway even with its precipitous drops on one side or the other. They did well, thanks to the lack of downhill traffic, eventually reaching the valley at Sidi Medjahed. They had done a full sixty kilometres of difficult driving in a straight hour.

Mac could see Oscar was exhausted and even though it wasn't his turn took over for the final assault at quarter to twelve with just over sixty kilometres to the ferry at Ghazaouet. Things were going to be tight anyway, they couldn't afford any more delays if they were to board the boat before it sailed.

Mac ratcheted their speed up as they crossed the valley via the large town of Maghnia and then they were zig zagging upwards again into the coastal hills, progress wasn't fast, there was a lot of slow traffic and it was one o'clock when they finally descended into the ferry port.

Mac drove straight down to the sea, there was a helpful ferry sign in Arabic, French and Spanish directing them to the port, where they easily found the white with orange stripe, twin funnelled Acciona Ferry.

Chapter 34

Kinikanwo

The Touareg having roared off up the N107 just to the north east of El Menia Kinikanwo decided he had done more than enough in difficult circumstances. Now it was time to look after himself and find a way of getting home safely and dealing with any of the repercussions.

The youths from Lagos had been useful up to this point. It had been easier to get through the checkpoint with the car so full. Without their help driving up to this point he wouldn't have been able to keep up with the Touareg. Now they were just dead weight and most likely to impede his future plans.

They were stopped just off-road at the junction, the Touareg had disappeared north. Kinikanwo turned to the lad driving.

'Right pull over I'll take her now.'

The unsuspecting lad who had been driving, took the keys from the ignition and handed them over to Kinikanwo. He got out and walked round the front of the vehicle. Kinikanwo exited the passenger seat, went the other way to the point in front of the Discovery where they crossed paths.

Just as they were about to pass and out of sight of the other three in the rear seat Kinikanwo pulled the Steyr M-A1 Pistol out of his pocket and waved it in the face of the surprised lad stopping him.

'I don't intend there to be any trouble but for my own reasons you and your mates are going to pick up your belongings from the car and get out right here.'

'But.'

'No arguments.'

'Get them out now.'

The youth was thinking bad thoughts. Kinikanwo could see it in the eyes which were lit up by the glare of the headlights. The kid was planning to do something silly.

To give the kid something else to think about, Kinikanwo launched his free left fist into the lad's gut.

He didn't go down but gasped painfully.

'Alright, alright I'll do it.'

Kinikanwo ground the Steyr into the youths left ear to emphasise his point.

'Do it!'

'Now!'

That loud shout, accompanied by the grinding pistol barrel was enough to tip the balance and bring the kid to his senses. He started yelling.

'Get out, get out of the car with our gear.'

The other three lads could only see silhouettes in the glare of the headlights but reacted quickly when they heard the terror in their leader's voice.

Rapidly they piled out of the Discovery with their possessions. The three hovered in the shadows to the rear of the Discovery wondering what they should do next.

Not giving them much time to think Kinikanwo now holding the leader round the neck with his left arm the Steyr still grinding into the lad's ear instructed him.

'Tell them to walk away and back towards the town.'

With his mates close by the lad got a little braver.

'Fuck off you won't shoot, we're going to take the bloody car off you.'

Kinikanwo lifted the gun from the recalcitrant lad's ear and fired it above the heads of the other three kids.

They didn't need to be told twice and stumbled off into the darkness dragging their gear with them. Kinikanwo didn't muck about, being in the ascendancy he kicked the remaining lad hard enough in the backside that he ended up on all fours.

'Stay like that until I've gone, otherwise a bullet will follow the boot.

The lad on all fours turned his head and asked.

'Why are you doing this?'

He was talking to the empty night, Kinikanwo had moved rapidly into the driver's seat of the Discovery quickly starting up the engine and activating the central locking.

318

The young man who was still dumbfounded by the actions of Kinikanwo was left kneeling, frozen in front of the vehicle. Kinikanwo had no qualms about running the lad over if he didn't move, started to shift the car forward. This caused a reaction and the boy crawled quickly out of the way, giving Kinikanwo the opportunity to drive back onto the A1 and head north towards Algiers eight hundred and seventy kilometres away. After about five kilometres he pulled over to the right, with lights on full beam drove carefully into the desert and parked up. He was shattered and needed to get some kip but first he had some telephone calls to make.

He rang the Chief, he needed to report in and get permission for some of his ideas otherwise he wouldn't be able to return home. The Chief answered his mobile, sat in his office at home.

'This had better be good, what have you got for me?'

'It's like you thought, they've taken the western route, must be going for Ghazaouet as you said.'

'Fine that's your job finished.'

'What about me getting home.'

'You sure, you can't bring the car back.'

'No I daren't go back through Niger, we've broken all sorts of laws there.'

'Well sell it, get a decent price with a receipt, you can use some of the money to get home.'

The Chief now had lots to do, cut off the signal, angry at the loss of the Discovery. The Matriarch, his mother was going to give him hell over losing her precious vehicle and it was going to cost him.

Being cut off like that Kinikanwo felt he had been treated like a piece of dirt, instead of ringing his own boss he rang Chisaru's mobile.

He hoped she was at home, it would be rather pleasant to chat to her knowing her father was in the same house.

Chisaru didn't recognise the satellite phone's number and answered cautiously.

'Hallo.'

'It's your favourite lover.'

'I don't know about that, I'm not sure you care about me anymore.'

Chisaru reacted sulkily to the call because he hadn't telephoned her for at least forty-eight hours. At this point in her love life, 24 hours was a long time. Kinikanwo had been gone for over a week which was an absolute age wasn't it.

'I've got good news for you I'm going to be home soon, I can't wait to take all the clothes off your gorgeous body.'

Chisaru giggled and blushed even though he was miles away, she was at home lying on top of her bed dressed in an unflattering pair of pyjamas. Then thinking she would get her revenge for him not being with her she coyly asked.

'Guess where I am?'

'In your bedroom.'

'How did you know?'

'It's quiet at your end of the phone, I guessed.'

Having guessed right Kinikanwo thought he might as well have some fun and unzipped his jeans.

'Have you any clothes on?'

'Yes.'

'Take your top off.'

Chisaru who was now sat up on her bed was already complying with the request but decided to tease the man at the other end of the line.

'Why should I do that?'

'Because I told you to sexy, you're supposed to do what I say.'

Chisaru breathed and had delicious sexy thoughts at his masterful orders she replied huskily.

'Of course, master.'

'Do you have a bra on?'

'No.'

'I want you to pretend this is me doing this to you.'

'Yes.'

'Now using your right hand, I want you to hold your left nipple between your thumb and index finger and squeezing till it just hurts and roll the nipple between your thumb and finger.

Kinikanwo's answer was the heavy breathing and gasps emanating from the phone at his end. He lifted out and stroked his hardening penis.

'Now both at once.'

Chisaru gasped it was painful and exciting her sexual senses. She couldn't believe how erotic this phone sex was and it had only just started.

'Now I want you naked but don't stop teasing your breasts.'

'Oh yes.'

One handed Chisaru quickly dragged off her pyjama bottoms and resumed playing with her nipples which were now throbbing with pleasure thanks to his voice and her attentions.

'I'm lying on my bed without any clothes on.'

'Oh Kinikanwo, I wish you were here.'

'So do I darling, now start playing with yourself, imagine it's me about to enter you and tell me what you're doing.'

Chisaru was close to climax telling Kinikanwo her erotic thoughts while he, who had released his member from the confines of his pants and jeans was masturbating hard.

They both climaxed close together and could hear each other's joy at the other end of the phone.

Chisaru lay on her bed with her hand still between her thighs thrilled with what she had just achieved, she didn't want Kinikanwo to stop talking to her, his sexy voice was making every one of her now sensitive nerves tingle throughout her flushed body.

Kinikanwo wiped himself down, temporarily sated, thanks to the phone sex. He needed to make another telephone call. Only then could he get his head down, he felt exhausted, it had been a long day.

'Thanks darling, got to go, will be home pleasuring your body soon enough.'

Despite Chisaru's protests he cut off the call and dialled his boss's office number. He was wary of the reaction this phone call was going to cause to emanate from the night club in Port Harcourt.

'Hi, it's Kinikanwo sir.'

'What's happening?'

'I've confirmed the Rally Car is going to cross to Europe tomorrow afternoon from Ghazaouet.'

'Good, the Chief has just rung me.'

'What about you, I believe you've lost the Chief's lackey.'

'Yeah in Niger, don't know what happened to her.'

'Fine, will see you next week when we get back.'

'Right sir.'

Kinikanwo broke the call and looked out of the Discovery windows, except for the occasional set of lights on the N1 about a kilometre to the west, the only other source of illumination was the clear, starlit, moonless, night sky.

He double-checked he was still locked in, got himself stretched across the more comfortable rear seats, gripped the Steyr to his chest and even though the interior of the vehicle stank from the unwashed bodies of earlier, immediately fell asleep.

***

He was unlucky, back at the Hotel Tidene in Agadez no one was yet concerned about the do not disturb sign that had been hanging on Damilola's and his room.

Probably nothing would have happened until the afternoon of the following day if it hadn't been for the frustrated Gendarme. He arrived at the Hotel Tidene Reception at eight that evening and started demanding answers of the frightened, male, member of staff on duty.

'Has anyone seen the Land Rover Discovery, or either of the two men in it?'

'I don't know sir.'

'I only came on duty after lunch.'

'Do you mean the two Nigerian gentlemen from Port Harcourt?'

'I certainly do.'

Frustrated the Gendarme leaned forward the palms of both hands placed firmly on the marble Reception counter and demanded loudly and angrily.

'Where are they?'

The hotel manager who had disappeared to his office when he had first seen the approaching Gendarme realised frustratingly that he couldn't hide away any longer. When he heard the angry tones of the Officer he concluded he had better return to the scene of the crisis.

His receptionist had backed away from the counter and was mouth agape slumped against the cream painted wall behind the desk. The Gendarme was leaning across the counter repeating his question forcefully.

'Where are they?'

'What have you done with them?'

The Manager arrived briskly in front of the reception counter, arms spread in a placatory manner.

'Sir, sir, I'm the Manager how can I help you?'

'Those two bloody Nigerians in the Discovery, where are they?'

The Manager waved his pass keys which he unhooked from the chain on his belt and attempted to mollify the irate policeman.

'We don't know but I'm so glad you're here, I've wanted to look and investigate their room and you'll be the ideal witness.'

The Gendarme calmed down and followed the hotel manager as he moved away from reception towards the guest room. The Manager was congratulating himself on defusing the situation and putting some of the responsibility into the hands of the grumpy Gendarme.

On reaching the room he searched for his master key while commenting to his escort.

'You can see the do not disturb sign, my staff tell me it has been there since yesterday morning.'

He inserted the key and looked at the Gendarme, who nodded in assent, at which point the Manager opened the door.

They were greeted by the smell of putrefaction, the buzzing of hundreds of flies which surrounded the body of Damilola lying as she was on the furthest of the twin beds.

The Manager vomited, while the Gendarme pulled the door too, ripped the keys from the indisposed Manager and relocked it.

He turned up the volume of his radio which was secured to his left shoulder and spoke into the mic, demanding immediate assistance from the local constabulary.

Just as Kinikanwo was dropping off to sleep in the Discovery in the desert north of El Menia, Algeria. Nearly two thousand kilometres south of him in Agadez the Gendarme re-entered the murder scene, this time with local police officers whose crime scene this had become. He was able to identify the dead Damilola as one of the two Nigerians who had been staying in the hotel.

Of more interest to him because it now came within his jurisdiction was the hunt for the murder weapon, the Discovery and Kinikanwo.

He made it very clear to the local constabulary that this was now personal and was heard to mutter.

'Your mine, you arrogant Nigerian bastard.'

Chapter 35

The Chief reacts

After confirmation from Kinikanwo that the Touareg was probably bound for Ghazaouet the Chief put his plans into motion.

He first confirmed his next day early morning flight from Port Harcourt to Lagos and his Business Class seat on the Virgin flight to Heathrow. Transferring money to an Algerian bank account, he woke the Manager of a certain shipping agency in Ghazaouet to confirm these monies had been received and verify the Manager knew what the Chief required. They spoke in English, a language of which shipping agent invariably had good command, this being the vernacular of the sea.

'Have you received the money?'

'Hang on, I'd just got into bed, who is this?'

'Your Nigerian contract, you remember?'

'Oh yes sir, you have sent the fee.'

'Certainly, it should be in the bank account you gave me.'

'I'll just check if you don't mind.'

'Of course.'

The agent clad only in a long nightshirt lifted his sleeping naked secretary off his grey, peppery, haired chest and raised his large body off the bed. He stretched and looked back at the young girl lying on his grubby sheets, grinned at the sight of the fresh naked body thinking what he might do with her when he returned.

Padding in his bare brown feet across the cool white- tiled floor, he found his lap top and powered it up. He didn't trust anyone, especially those from south of the Sahara He would only engage in contracts for them when the money was in his bank account.

Sitting alongside a noisy air-conditioner, he entered the passcodes into his account at the Societe Generale SA and was satisfied to see the expected money had been transferred into his bank account.

The Shipping Agent returned to his bedroom, sat down on the side of the bed and picked up the phone with his right hand.

'It's there.'

The Agent reached over to the naked girl and with his left thumb and forefinger started to play with her left nipple, this hardened almost immediately, a little moan escaped from her partially closed lips and his body reacted to the sound.

'You're to phone this mobile number and leave a message keeping me informed of when the Rally Car arrives and if it takes the ferry.'

'Alright yes, it'll be done.'

The Agent was getting more excited as the young girl writhing thanks to his ministrations and was eager to explore her reactions further, he breathed heavily down the phone.

'Got to go, important business to see to.'

'The Chief was left with a disconnected line while the Agent pulled off his night shirt in preparation of ravishing the nubile young woman who was now awake and waiting for his full attention.'

Shaking his head at the Agents sudden departure the Chief next telephoned a land line in Almeria.

He instantly recognised the voice and accent of one of his distant nephews. Duncan was, with another cousin Obo, staying and working illegally in that corner of south east Spain.

'We think it should be on the ferry from Ghazaouet late tomorrow night.'

'Yes sir.'

'Are you ready?'

'Yes sir, we'll be ready, we'll buy the new Android phone as you requested.'

'It must be the right one, so I can lock onto it as well.'

'It's the latest example like you said but it costs five hundred Euro's.'

'That's alright you'll need to be at the Post Office first thing with your passport.'

'I'm transferring you two thousand Euros now.'

The Chief still logged into his computer, transferred the money from his Swiss Bank Account via Western Union with a few strokes of his computer keys.

'Right take your passport to the Correos on Almanzor, there is two thousand Euros there waiting for you to collect in the morning.'

The Chief ensured Duncan had pen and paper ready before reading out the pass code he would need to collect the cash

'Just to recap, you'll collect the money from the Post Office in the morning, pick up the new phone and text me its number. When the Rally Car turns up on the ferry you're to follow it, while keeping me informed by text.'

'Yes sir.'

'Have you got something to attach the mobile phone to their vehicle?'

'Not yet.'

'Make sure you do, we'll speak about midnight tomorrow.'

'I'll ring your mobile then.'

'Yes sir.'

At that and satisfied he had done everything he could in Almeria the Chief briefly thought about what he had to do next.

The Chief thought it was regrettable, he should really inform Chief Kudo who was going to be full of awkward questions.

Through the dining room and across the hallway in her bedroom Chisaru was having her sexual conversation with Kinikanwo up north in the Sahara Desert. The walls of her bedroom were covered in posters of local and international pop idols, pride of place going to Slim Burna a local idol from Rivers state. She was having to cover her face with a pillow to quieten her moans as with Kinikanwo's help she drove herself to an orgasm. Chisaru didn't hear her father pass by the bedroom door on his way out although the noise of the front door closing did impinge onto her consciousness. She was just luxuriating in the end of her conversation with her lover, lying naked with legs open, when with only a brief knock her mother brusquely entered the room.

'Where's your father gone?'

'He's not said..........'

Seeing Chisaru naked trying to drag a sheet over her naked body her mother's eyes widened.

'What are you doing girl?'

For a moment Chisaru didn't know how to reply then dropping the sheet covering her ripe breasts she confidently answered.

'I'm masturbating.'

Her mother gasped, clapping her right hand to her mouth with the shock.

'Come on mother I bet you did it before you were married to father.'

Not knowing how to answer, mother face screwed up in anger screamed in disgust at her daughter.

'You're a whore.'

Chisaru was taken aback and physically upset by her mother's reaction, the shock caused her to burst into tears and she sobbed hardly realising what she was saying.

'You can't call me that, I love him.'

It took her mother a moment to realise what her daughter had said, she reacted by walking over to the bed and slapping Chisaru across the face.

'You've slept with someone you dirty bitch.'

She screamed, grabbed her daughter's shoulders, shook her and yelled in her face.

'Who was it?'

With her mother so angry and screaming at her, Chisaru was overwhelmed by her parent's reaction and whimpered in reply.

'Kinikanwo.'

'I love him.'

Her mother already aware of the man's reputation took pity on her daughter, let her go, took a pace back and shook her head.

'You young girls, you've got no idea.'

'See a good-looking guy and you open your legs for him as soon as he looks at you.'

'Mother!'

'All I can say is, I hope you aren't pregnant?'

'I don't know.'

'Your father has to know, you're grounded.'

'Noooooooooooooooo.'

The girl started wailing again, everything didn't seem such fun anymore and her lover wasn't there to rescue her.

Then her mother made it even worse.

'You're to stay in your room until your father decides what's going to happen.'

'Also give me your phone, I don't want you communicating either with that, that, paedophile.'

Grabbing Chisaru's mobile her mother stormed out of her daughter's bedroom slamming the door behind her, leaving Chisaru curled up on her bed sucking her thumb and sobbing her heart out.

***

About the time his wife was departing their daughter's bedroom, the Chief had completed the short distance to the nightclub of his partner. He had called ahead and was expected.

Chief Kudo greeted the Chief effusively clapping him on the shoulders enthusiastically.

'Can I get you a drink?'

The Chief waved his hand in acknowledgement, while the Night Club Owner picked up the phone and ordered for both while looking over at the Chief.

'A bottle of Black Label and two glasses.'

The Chief nodded in agreement and sat down in one of the black leather lounge chairs.

'Have you news?'

The Chief pulled his mobile out, silenced the phone before returning it to his trouser pocket.

A scantily dressed waitress arrived carrying a metal tray with a bottle of Black Label and two cut-glass whisky glasses containing fresh ice.

Chief Kudo poured the whisky and handed the Chief a glass before taking his seat in the Office Chair behind his desk and frowned at the Chief asking icily.

'Well.'

'The Chief disconcerted by Chief Kudo's stance, glared back across the room before starting.

'The Touareg will arrive in the western Algerian port of Ghazaouet about lunchtime tomorrow, here I expect them to catch the ferry to Almeria in South east Spain.'

'I will be told if they board the ferry, they will also be followed if and when they arrive in Almeria.'

'Who by?'

'A couple of Nigerian ex-pats who live there and are from the Rivers State.'

'I've also arranged for them to put a bug onto the vehicle if they get an opportunity.'

'Where do we come in, we're a bit far from the action?'

'I'm on the Arik Air to Lagos at seven thirty in the morning and then the Virgin flight to London.'

'I'll go straight over to Paris to take over the chase.'

Chief Kudo was furious, the Chief had acted without consultation and without their knowledge.

'Didn't you think to ask me?'

'I only knew myself an hour ago.'

'I'm coming with you.'

The Chief Kudo got busy on his laptop and managed to scrape himself onto the London Flight from Lagos although it was one of the few Economy seats left, there being nothing in Business Class. He didn't have any luck with the only morning flight out of Port Harcourt.

'I'm booked on the Heathrow flight but can't get on the Arik Air to Lagos in the morning.'

The Chief smiled to himself and pulled his mobile from his pocket.

Switching it back on he could see a missed call from his wife, ignoring this he dialled a mobile from his voluminous list of saved numbers.

It was quickly answered and the female on the other end of the line greeted him effusively.

'Darling where have you been, I've missed you.'

The lady concerned was an occasional fling of the Chief's, more importantly she was head of Arik Airs ground staff at Port Harcourt and would do anything for her occasional lover.

'Lera I need a favour?'

'I'm on the seven thirty tomorrow morning and I need another seat for a colleague.'

'Only if you come around later.'

'I can't.'

'You must if you want the seat.'

The Chief realised there was no way out of the dilemma and after all it was rather tempting.

'I'll be with you shortly but only for an hour, I've not packed yet.'

'Two.'

'Split the difference.'

'Well alright but only because I have to go to work at four in the morning.'

The Chief ended the call.

'I've got you a seat but it's going to cost me.'

Chief Kudo laughed.

'Sounds like an enjoyable interlude.'

'Hopefully, I'll see you at the airport at five thirty tomorrow morning.'

The Chief left in a hurry dialling his wife's mobile as he departed.

When she answered he didn't give her a chance to interrupt.

'I'll be with you in about two hours. I have to go London in the morning, pack me the small case for a few days, put the laptop in its case with a charger and organise a car for five in the morning to the airport.'

'Okay.'

Before she had a chance to speak further about their daughter Chisaru, he had cut the connection without even asking about why she had phoned earlier.

It was midnight before the Chief was able to get home and clamber into his own bed, he was exhausted thanks to the ministrations of his lover. He set his alarm for four and went straight to sleep.

His wife on the other side of the bed, pretended to be asleep, she could smell the other woman on his body the strong perfume the erstwhile lover used offended her sensibilities. She wouldn't complain though, he was otherwise a good husband and loyal to her and the girls.

Chapter 36

Chief's Chase, Kinikanwo moves

Four hours later the alarm on the bedside table started to sound its shrill call, it wasn't till his wife shoved him impatiently, the Chief became aware of the noise. He was deeply asleep, it took him a few moments to realise where he was and what was happening. Finally, he switched off the alarm and clambered out of bed before he could drop-off again.

His wife rolled over and tried to go back to sleep as the Chief headed for the shower, shortly after dressed in a summer weight grey suit and highly polished black loafers he was almost ready to go. He just had to collect his passport and a wad of mixed sterling and Euro notes from the office safe.

There was a toot outside as the taxi announced its arrival, he grabbed his small pre-packed suitcase from the hallway while carrying his laptop in its briefcase over his shoulder.

His partner was already waiting at The Arik Air desk when the Chief arrived at Port Harcourt Airport, Chief Kudo wasn't pleased and grumbled.

'The girl says she's no ticket for me.'

The Chief was tired and grumpy and not happy with his petulant partner.

'Don't be impatient, just wait a moment, it will be sorted out I promise you.'

Just at that moment the Chief's lover stepped out of her Office at the back of the Arik Air Desk, they could see a young female clerk gesticulating to which the lady frowned. The clerk pointed in the direction of the Chief and his partner, this brought out a beaming smile from his beau and an indication they should approach.

She said to the Chief.

'Tell your friend to give my clerk three thousand Naira and she'll bump someone off the flight.'

The Chief Kudo was about to argue but the Chief nudged him sharply and his partner reached for his wallet.

'Credit Card?'

The Chief laughed.

'Cash you fool, it's for the girl and it's cheap because you don't have to pay my friend.'

His lady friend nodded in approval as the money was handed over. It quickly disappeared into the clerk's brown handbag below the counter. She got busy on her computer and looked querying at the screen while rubbing the dimple on her cute chin.

'Passport.'

She looked at it and photocopied the main page before handing the document back to Chief Kudo. Her fingers rattled rapidly over the keyboard once her decision had been made. Something made a noise alongside her, reaching down below the counter she picked up and passed over a boarding card. 'You need to disappear through security, someone is going to be very unhappy as I've had to bump them even though they already have a nominated seat.'

The two of them quickly checked in, passing an older, overweight, male Nigerian who couldn't understand why one of the check-in clerks was denying he had a seat on the flight. The clerk seeing the two of them pass into security used the tannoy and called Mr. Oboko to her desk. She told the poor man, who had just been arguing at Check-in there had been an overbooking and he wouldn't now be able to fly until the lunchtime flight.

***

Just as the two Chiefs were boarding their flight at Port Harcourt the rising sun's rays were waking Kinikanwo in the Sahara Desert north east of El Menia and the Touareg with its occupants was creating long westerly shadows as it entered the Atlas Mountains.

Kinikanwo stretched out on the rear seat of the Discovery, hadn't slept properly, he had tossed and turned, his normally calm countenance worried by the possibility of being attacked by local tribesmen. About five in the morning exhaustion had overtaken him, only for the brightness of the dawn sun blazing into his upturned face to wake him around seven.

He sat up and looked around him the only sign of movement was a dust cloud from some moving vehicle to the west and some vultures lazily circling something to the north of the car. He rummaged around the car and could only find a single bottle of water and little to eat apart from a packet of crisps. Consuming both he stretched, moved into the driver's seat, fired up the Discovery and bumped his way across the desert to the N1 before heading north.

The road wasn't busy and in just over an hour he was passing through the small desert town of Hassi Fehal. The highway then became busier and was split by a central reservation lined with palm trees. All the signs were in Arabic and most of the yellow buildings were single storey. The only service station came early on the other side of the road. There was a large gap in the central reservation and this was turned into a roundabout by the simple method of placing a single painted red, white and red petrol drum in the centre of the gap.

Kinikanwo drove the Discovery into the service station topped up, bought half a dozen bottles of water before finding a local café next door. Here he was able to fill up his near empty stomach with mutton curry and rice.

***

By the Kinikanwo left the small town northbound once again, the Arik Air flight had landed at Murtala Muhammed airport in Lagos and the two Chiefs were rushing to check in onto the

Heathrow-bound, London flight. They were only able to make the flight because they were merely carrying hand baggage. Even then they were almost last through the boarding gate, where they split up as the Chief turned left for the comforts of Business Class.

After the lack of sleep from the night before he took the opportunity after take-off to get his head down. Chief Kudo struggled to cope, he was stuck in the middle seat of three on the port side of the aircraft, being frequently kicked in the back by an excited eight-year girl old behind him.

Chapter 37

European Chase

It was a simple task for Mac and Oscar to buy their ferry tickets from the Ticket Office next to the dock. They were able to include a top-quality double cabin and looked forward to getting some much-needed sleep.

The Vronskiy a thirty-seven-year-old, Dutch-built, Cypriot-registered, ex- Sealink ferry, on its third name looked like a beacon of hope to the Touareg's occupants when they drove onto the Ghazaouet dockside.

By one thirty in the afternoon, they were through the immigration and customs and being directed to their parking space on board the ferry. They had made it with only half an hour to spare but now were just about to depart Africa.

Parked up they relaxed for a moment in the dusty interior of the Touareg and looked at each other smiling. Mac in the driver's seat made the first move reaching across to shake hands with his partner.

'Done it pal, we made it.'

Oscar grinned back patting the dashboard.

'Wow it's amazing, what a bloody adventure, five thousand kilometres and the car didn't miss a beat.'

Mac laughed and opened the car door.

'Let's go and try this luxury cabin for size, I need to wash off this grime and then try the bed mattress out.'

'Couldn't agree more.'

Oscar followed his partners lead as grabbing their bags they wandered off the vehicle deck in search of their cabin.

While Mac got first use of the cabin's bathroom, Oscar took the opportunity to make a call on his mobile while he still had a signal.

His contact at a number in Paris answered on the second ring.

'Monsieur Oscar, where are you?'

'You haven't reached Paris already, have you?'

'Bonjour Pierre no but we're about to leave Algeria.'

Pierre, Oscar's contact in France had been investigating the possible value of the Touareg to a collector in Europe.

'Oh, that's a real shame you'll have no chance of catching the big game.'

'Big game?'

'Ouis Francais versus the Germans tomorrow night and I've got the chance at two more tickets.'

'Shame you'll not make Marseilles until tomorrow lunchtime so you'll not be able to make the game.'

'But Pierre we'll be in Almeria at midnight.'

'Why where are you?'

Pierre had no knowledge of the Ghazaouet to Almeria ferry and was quite surprised.

Oscar who had all the facts at his fingertips, already knew the driving times and distances from Almeria to the French Capital.

'Don't know if we could do it but it's about sixteen hours give or take Pierre.'

'That's alright Oscar I'll keep in touch, if you can make the Stade de France I'll have a VIP parking space and the tickets ready for you.'

'I'll see what Mac says, I'm sure he'll want to try, he's a football nut.'

'Anyway, thanks very much but what about the car.'

'You'll be fine, I could sell it to half a dozen people in Paris alone, I think we'll need to have an auction.'

Mac wandered into the cabin only wearing a white towel around his waist and drying his hair with another. He looked at Oscar with a look of query.

'Pierre I've got to go, maybe see you at the match.'

Oscar cut off the call.

'Do you want to see the French play the Germans in the Stade de France?'

'Aye that'd be brilliant.'

Oscar shook his head.

'What.'

'It's tomorrow night.'

Mac rubbed his chin with the fingers of his right hand and thought about the offer.

'I'd like to see the footie, but I'm knackered, it's a bloody long way isn't it?'

'Yeah about eighteen hundred kilometres.'

'Alright then you get your shower and let's see how much sleep we get on this rust bucket.'

'We can make a decision when we get to Spain.'

Mac dropped both his towels onto the floor and clambered into the top bunk pulled a sheet over his naked body and dropped off to sleep immediately. It didn't take long for Oscar to get clean and he like his companion was soon dead to the world.

It was nearly two pm and the ferry crew were singling up the ropes ready to depart. Down on the waterfront a representative from a local shipping agency had watched the Rally Car driving onto the ferry and now after walking the short distance back to his office on the Avenue Achouhada was preparing to make a telephone call to the Chief's mobile.

Not unexpectedly the answering machine chimed in and the agent left a message as he had been instructed to do.

'It is two pm the Vronskiy ferry is leaving the port with the car and its two drivers on board.'

'It should be in Almeria about midnight.'

Satisfied he had done what he was being paid for, the Shipping Agent wandered back to the waterfront and watched the ferry depart.

***

Two hours later the Second Mate on the Vronskiy was handing over the bridge watch to the Chief Officer. He pointed out the contrails of a northbound jet in the sky above them.

On board the Airbus A330-300, the Virgin Atlantic flight 652 was just about on time nearly two and half hours from Heathrow.

In Business Class the Chief was fast asleep, his companion was still very uncomfortable and cursing his luck at being stuck in probably the last available seat. At least the small child in the seat behind had at last been restrained after Chief Kudo complained loudly and bitterly to a red suited stewardess.

Three hours later they were flying over the River Thames past the Houses of Parliament, they dropped down gently onto Heathrow's two seven right runway It was now five in the evening on the 14th November 2015 and outside the low dark cloudy skies were partly illuminated by the lights of the city.

The Chief wanted them on the Eurostar to Paris that evening so was quite frustrated when his colleague took nearly twenty minutes to depart the plane. He had been close to the rear of the aircraft and was himself angry with the time it had taken the sluggish queue of passengers to exit the fuselage.

Immigration took a while as it is a busy time in Terminal 2, with many African flights landing all together. Although both Chiefs were regular visitors to London, it didn't prevent immigration questioning them closely about their reason for visiting.

As they left Immigration the Chief urged his colleague to move faster.

'Come on we've got to shift, otherwise we'll not make the Eurostar at St Pancras.'

'Why have we to get on a certain train?'

'It's not that, the last train of the night leaves at a minute past eight.'

Chief Kudo looked at his watch and speeded up, adopting a fast walk.

'Hell, we'll never make it.'

'We can but try, we can't hang about.'

They just managed to board the Heathrow Express to Paddington at three minutes to seven. Both slumped into their seats panting from their exertions.

Twenty-seven minutes later they were standing at the forward door awaiting the slowing train's arrival into the Paddington terminus.

As soon as the doors opened they jogged down the platform and five minutes later the Chief leapt onto the Circle Line Underground train just as it was about to leave from the eastbound platform. Chief Kudo was struggling to keep up and was still ten metres from the train's doorway when the driver attempted to close the train's doors.

The Chief realising his colleague wasn't going to make it stood in the way of the closing doors preventing them shutting. They reopened and the driver after once again announcing that the doors were about to close, started to shut them again. This pause gave Chief Kudo just enough time to stagger exhausted onto the carriage where he collapsed into an empty seat.

Thirteen minutes and five stations later, both still breathing heavily and sweating profusely after their previous exertions. They had again to stand up, ready and waiting to dash up out of the depths of the Underground and into St Pancras main line station.

They were fortunate, there was no queue at the Eurostar Ticket Office, and managed to buy tickets on the last Paris train of the day. After quickly passing through the security and immigration checks they were in time to subside into their seat on board their carriage as the train pulled smoothly out of St Pancras. The Chief finally got the opportunity to check his text and phone messages, there was confirmation of the readiness of Duncan and Obo in Almeria and more importantly one from the Shipping Agent in Ghazaouet verifying the departure on the Almeria ferry with the Touareg and its occupants on board.

***

At the same time Kinikanwo who had a hard day on the N1 to Algiers drove into and through the city. He found himself on the Boulevard de l'Aln, the dual carriageway alongside the docks and then the beach further north. Although it was eight in the evening the Boulevard was well lit and crowds of people were perambulating along the beach pathways.

He was exhausted and pulled into a blue-fronted non-descript hostelry just off the front. It had a sign in Arabic, French and English declaring vacancies and looked decent enough for Kinikanwo's few needs.

Sure enough he was able to book a room for a couple of days and within the hour he had parked up, showered and was eating a meal in the hotel dining room.

Chapter 38

Almeria and Paris

Once they had recovered from their exertions, the two Chiefs settled back into their First-Class seats as the Eurostar rushed through the damp, cold, darkened Kent countryside to its rendezvous with the Channel Tunnel and eventually its emergence onto the Continent.

The Chief pulled out his I Pad and got to work. He hired a Mercedes C Class, for a week, from the Avis outlet on the Rue Maubeuge close to the Gare du Nord.

That concluded he looked for a hotel with parking and settled on a Mercure within walking distance of the station and free parking. There were only rooms vacant for that night, he booked two and advised the hotel of their expected late arrival.

***

Oscar woke first when he heard the tannoy call for drivers to get ready to go to their vehicles. They were twenty minutes out of Almeria and it was just after half ten that evening.

He woke Mac and they both had a quick shower and got dressed before making their way down to the Touareg. It was attracting a lot of attention from other drivers on the upper vehicle deck.

It wasn't long before they were following other vehicles down and out of the stern of the Vronskiy, Mac was driving. Oscar looked back at the rust-streaked, ferry which was already preparing for its next trip. An impatient queue of cars and trucks waited on the dockside.

In the garish bright lights of the port the ferry looked all of her thirty-seven years age and not at all like the smart Channel ferry she began as in 1978. Yet to him and Mac only eleven hours ago she appeared as a safe haven after the rigours of North Africa.

Mac joined the queue for the customs and immigration shed. Naturally they were pulled over for inspection. It wasn't about what they might be carrying but all about the Touareg. There was a rush of mobile phones to record the event and questions to answer about their ownership of the vehicle.

The two of them didn't mind, this would be their last immigration check as they were British Citizens and back in the EU, even so the delays meant it was nearly one in the morning before they cleared the port.

They were now fully awake, ravenous and determined to fill up with food at the first opportunity. While Oscar directed Mac to the west of the city to gain the entrance to the A-7, he checked the map.

'We have to go west and then do a big curve back on ourselves to get on the A-7 to go north.'

'Sounds complicated just keep directing, I'll just go where you send me.'

It wasn't as awkward as it looked, after following the mountain-hugging one hundred and eighty degree turn behind others who had just left the port, they found themselves above and driving round the west and north side of the City of Almeria. They could see from the unlit motorway out over the city lights and into the Mediterranean where the Vronskiy was just starting its journey south, on its return trip to Algeria.

At the north-eastern side of the city they found a lit-up underpass, where they left the motorway making their way under it and onto the A-92. There was little traffic on the dual carriageway and Mac opened up the willing car, they were soon cruising up around one thirty kilometres per hour.

Oscar looked at the one twenty speed sign just after the junction and laughed at Mac.

'Looks like you've made your mind up and we're going for Paris.'

'I'm just bloody hungry and eager to find some sort of service station, I need to fill up my empty stomach.'

'There's one in about half an hour at the Abla junction.'

'That'll do, we'll work out whether we go for it or not while we eat.'

Neither of them noticed the silver-grey Opel Astra following them, if they had wondered about the following pair of lights, it would have been hard to distinguish the shadowing vehicle, there being no lighting on the motorway.

Duncan found it easy to keep the rear lights of the Rally Car in sight, the only other traffic were trucks from the Ghazaouet ferry, these had departed before the Touareg due to its popularity with the Spanish Officials. Both cars were passing the slower vehicles with ease.

They were a bit surprised in the Astra, when forty minutes later the car ahead indicated to turn off at Abla, they soon realised the Touareg was making its way to the Calle Los Barrios service station.

Parking in the shadows, of the darkest corner, of the partially lit car park, they sat back to wait as the two occupants of the Touareg made their way into the well-lit service station buildings.

This was what Duncan and Obo had been waiting for. Duncan grabbed the new mobile phone and some tape and they keeping to the shadows as far as possible found themselves crouched down on the nearside of the Touareg in a matter of seconds. They used the car's body to hide them from anyone peering out of the service station buildings. The only risk of being spotted was if another vehicle entered the car park.

At first, they couldn't work out where to secure the mobile until Obo put his head under the car just forward of the rear tyre and decided he could secure it above the rear axle.

He switched the phone on and put it onto the ledge, where he wrapped it tightly in place with the sticky tape they had purchased earlier in the day.

The two Britishers entered the service station with ideas of a proper meal but their hopes were soon dashed, they had to make do with pre-packed food from the shop. This was the only part of the nearly empty service station available in the early hours of the morning.

A small, grey-bearded, uninterested, local man in red and yellow uniform served them continually yawning with gaping mouth. They both found themselves gulping when the shop assistant breathed out his heavily garlic-tainted breath.

They laughed between themselves and Mac as was his wont paid for their edibles with his credit card.

Oscar had his maps ready and open on a table and was recalculating their Paris ETA when Mac impatiently interrupted. Are we going for Paris today?'

'Well its seventeen fifty kilometres from here on really good roads at say two fifty every two hours its thirteen hours which would be just after three this afternoon.'

'Okay then shall we eat here or on the road?'

'On the road, let's get underway and see what sort of progress we make.'

'Fine we'll top up the tanks as we leave and make the best use of these near-empty roads.'

They departed the buildings and made their way to refuel, Mac did this while Oscar who was going to drive the first two hours took the opportunity to eat some of their just bought refreshments.

***

Meanwhile Duncan who was sat in the rear of the Astra powered up his mobile and looked at the locator map to check he was receiving a signal from the parcel above the nearside, rear-axle of the Touareg.

He found the locator worked and could see the pulse on the map which showed the nearby location of the Touareg he pointed this out to his colleague.

'Look Obo it works okay.'

Obo turned around from the driver's seat and looked at the mobile's screen.

'Do we have to keep up with them for this to show up like this?'

'No, they and us, just have to be in range of a mobile phone mast for the signal to show their location.

The Touareg started to move out of the service station and away from the petrol pumps where it had just refuelled.

Duncan realised what was happening, nudged his partner.

'Quick we'd better go, they're off.'

Obo started up while Duncan reached over plugged a charger lead into the cigarette lighter with a mobile phone attached and stretched out onto the rear seats while Obo set the Astra off in pursuit.

***

By two in the morning of what was now Friday the thirteenth of November 2015, the Touareg and its occupants were making good progress towards Madrid, hoping to push through the Spanish Capital before the morning rush. They were both well rested after their sleep on the Vronskiy and determined to push on.

***

For the two in the Astra following behind, they hadn't been so lucky, having both been at work the previous day. They had only the benefit of the siesta the previous afternoon. They had tried to work out the best way to cope if the present situation occurred and the drivers of the Touareg decided to get under way immediately after leaving the ferry.

Obo had volunteered to drive the night hours and for that reason Duncan was stretched out on the rear seat doing his best to get some sleep.

They were soon speeding along behind but out of sight of the Touareg with Obo having to push the Astra to keep up.

Four hours later at six in the morning both cars were north of Madrid and The Touareg was pulling off the E5 at the Repsol services at San Agustin de Guadalix. Obo followed them into the service station he was congratulating himself on keeping up with the Touareg throughout the night.

There had been one moment of panic when the pursued vehicle suddenly braked and pulled over onto the side of the road and Obo suddenly realised he had caught up and was passing the Touareg. It was four in the morning and Mac and Oscar, unknown to Obo were changing drivers'.

There was nowhere to stop without alerting those in the pursued car, Obo had slowed down and pulled off at the next junction, where he had sat on the bridge overlooking the motorway until the Touareg had passed underneath. This was where the attached phone gave the pursuers an advantage. Obo could see the Touareg hadn't diverted anywhere.

He then seriously broke the speed limit catching up and getting within range of the Touareg which had now gone out of sight ahead of him. It took ten minutes of pushing the Astra hard before he caught up with what he thought were the rear lights of the Touareg which was only confirmed when it was lit up by the lights of an oncoming truck.

Obo shouted at his colleague to wake up as he pulled alongside a pump on the service station's forecourt. Duncan sat up in the rear of the Astra and looked around him.

'What's up?'

'We need fuel, go and pay while I fill up.'

Duncan stumbled out of the rear of the car in the direction of the kiosk while Obo started refuelling. They needn't have hurried because after refuelling, the Touareg pulled into the car park, where they followed and because the two men from the Touareg were going for refreshment the Africans copied them. They found the pursued, ordering a meal and decided they would take the opportunity to do the same. It was while they were eating the Chief awake early in Paris called Duncan's mobile.

He was surprised by the unexpected warble in his right trouser pocket, then he couldn't at first dig it out of his pocket to answer the instrument, when he did he received a barrage of questions.

'Are you still on them?'

'Where are you?'

'What's happening?'

Before answering, Duncan cautiously, although well away from the table where the occupants of the Touareg sat, covered up the phone with his free left hand and turned away so he couldn't be heard or seen by others in the busy cafeteria.

'It's alright we're past Madrid, everything's under control.'

'Thank God for that.'

'Have you attached the mobile?'

'Yes we have.'

'They've only stopped the once since Almeria and they're really shifting, I don't know if we'll be able to keep them in sight much longer.'

'Why not?'

'We might arouse they're suspicions if we're always behind them.'

'What are you driving?'

'A silver-grey Astra.'

'They'll not notice you, those things are ten a penny and anyway if they get away you'll be able to locate them with the phone.'

'It's six in the morning there's hardly anyone about and yet everyone is attracted to that car.'

Duncan was looking across the car park, to where the Touareg even though it was covered in dust and sand from its rough trip across the Sahara, was still surrounded by a dozen admirers.

'Right keep on their tail and from this end we'll monitor their progress.'

'You have to stay with them in case they divert to somewhere else, however unlikely that seems.'

'Alright sir.'

'Good luck.'

The Chief broke off his call rang Chief Kudo in his hotel room. It took over five rings before his sleepy voice answered.

'Yes?'

'We need to get on the road, the stuff is on its way north.'

'I'll see you in the hotel restaurant for breakfast in thirty minutes.'

After a brief protest about the hour of the morning and lack of sleep, Chief Kudo gave in to the Chief's suggestion.

By seven in the morning both Chiefs were eating breakfast and just north of Madrid the two cars were back on the road north. All their occupants fully refreshed after the break and petrol tanks refilled.

There was another change of driver at nine o'clock in the Touareg. This time with both awake, Duncan in the Astra was able to drive straight past the stopped Touareg, while Obo watched the mobile phone locator to make sure it followed on. They were leading when they reached the Bay of Biscay in North eastern Spain. They slowed to make sure the Touareg's driver had the same idea of routing as them and sure enough it raced past as they bypassed San Sebastian and by half eleven they were across the border and into France close to Biriatou as they skirted the northern edge of the Pyrenees.

Meanwhile the two Chief's had left the hotel at nine after a leisurely breakfast, checked with the occupants of the chasing Astra and were now convinced the ex-pats were making for the French Capital.

They picked up their hire car from hotel car park and made their way out of Paris in a south-westerly direction, towards the oncoming vehicles.

Chapter 39

Kinikanwo sells the Discovery

While the Touareg and its pursuers were crossing the Spanish/French border near Biriatou, Kinikanwo was at Algiers Houari Boumediene International airport.

After supper on the previous night at the Hotel, he gave some thought on how to sell the Discovery. He knew no-one he could trust or even approach in Algiers. With little choice he decided to approach the Hotel's Concierge, who for the right price should be able to arrange most things

Kinikanwo approached the sallow-faced, clean-shaven Arab in his royal blue with gold insignia uniform. The concierge was stood behind a one and a half metre tall wooden pedestal, a closed red notebook, small hand bell and white telephone atop its pale, well-polished, wooden surface.

The Concierge already knew, due to a signal from the Reception Clerk, he would need to use English. In a slightly French-accented voice he greeted Kinikanwo warmly.

'Good evening sir, how may I help you?'

'I'm wondering if you knew anywhere I may sell my car as I won't be taking it home with me.'

'Well that depends on a number of things sir.'

'What do I need?'

'Proof of ownership and condition of the car.'

With a flourish Kinikanwo produced the documents for the car with the Chief's authorisation.

'It's a black, Land Rover Discovery 3, three-litre diesel less than three years old.'

'I've come up from Nigeria, so it's covered in dust otherwise it's in good condition and low mileage.'

'Ah cleaning of the car isn't a problem, it can be done immediately if my staff can be properly paid.'

Kinikanwo was aware he would have to use some of the Chief's money to smooth things along. He pulled out a folded wad of mixed denomination Euro notes and peeled off a hundred in twenties.

'Will this be adequate to compensate you and your staff?'

The notes disappeared with alacrity into the Concierges waistcoat pocket. He rang the small bell which tinkled out across the Reception Area of the Hotel.

'Keys please sir.'

Two young men in their blue hotel uniform jackets, blue trousers and incongruously their tanned bare feet gripping onto thin flip flops, raced to the Concierges Dais.

The Concierge spoke to the bell boys and quietly handed over the keys to the taller of the two as quick as they had come they were gone out of the front entrance of the Hotel to set about their task.

'God willing, the vehicle will be spotless within the hour.'
Reaching to a hidden shelf in the back of his Dais the
Concierge pulled out an I Pad and tapped in a request.
'I have a distant Uncle who might be very interested, I of course
will need some sort of recompense for calling him out and
selling your vehicle so promptly.'
'Say five percent as an agent's fee.'
Kinikanwo loved a good haggle and smiled at the Concierge, he
knew the Discovery was worth around eight thousand Euros
back home in Nigeria and was hoping for at least half of that.
Still the Concierges commission would help him get back into
practice, adopting a solemn face he countered.
'One percent.'
'Ah but sir I have the contact and you'll be robbed if you take it
to a garage.'
By this time the Concierge was wringing his hands, back
hunched and with a thoughtful expression. Suddenly he smiled
and straightened bringing himself to attention and smiling once
again.
'Four percent.'
Kinikanwo laughed at the idea.
'Let's stop mucking about we both know, you'll get something
off your contact that's even if he is your Uncle.'
'One and a half percent.'
The Concierge acted as if upset at the suggestion but realised
Kinikanwo wasn't as dumb as he first thought and came back
with his next offer.

'Two per cent.'

'Agreed but only if you get me over five thousand Euros plus and a flight back home.'

The Concierge picked up his I Pad and entered some figures into the calculator before reaching across to the Nigerian to shake hands.'

'Done how soon do you want to leave?'

Kinikanwo shook hands and didn't take a moment to think about how soon he wanted to leave.

'Tomorrow.'

'That might be difficult there are no direct flights to Nigeria and it depends whether you have permission to land in Europe or not.'

'Why's that?'

'The quickest way is to fly to Rome and back down to Lagos but if you don't have a visa for the European Union you won't be able to transit through.'

'I don't, so what's the answer then?'

'Royal Afrique du Nord.'

'Flight to Casablanca tomorrow afternoon and then onto Lagos just after midnight, arriving at five fifteen Saturday morning.'

'Thanks, it all depends on the car, if it's above five thousand Euros it stays here otherwise I'll ship it.'

Kinikanwo bluffed, feeling he had shown too much of his hand to the Concierge already and trying to grab back some advantage.

'But we have an agreement.'

'We do but only if you and your Uncle achieve my price.'

Kinikanwo left the Concierge to negotiate and sat down in the hotel reception within sight of the Concierges Desk.

He had less than an hour to wait, before a large fat Arab arrived. He wore a dark-grey, grubby suit and incongruously a stained Paisley scarf around his neck He kept dabbing the sweat from the rolls of fat encompassing his face with a large red handkerchief as he rolled his unfit body across to the Concierges desk. He stopped and leaned against the dais, breathing heavily from the exertions of moving from his vehicle to the Hotel's reception area.

Having recovered he took a couple of deep breaths and lifted a red Fez from his balding pate before speaking to the Concierge in rapid French which was too quick and accented for Kinikanwo to follow.

It seemed from their gestures that the possible buyer was upset at being rushed away from his evening meal and the Concierge appeared to be apologising while the buyer continued with his rant.

Suddenly he stopped his complaint turned, with the change of direction the previous attitude totally changed, he beamed quizzically at Kinikanwo before saying in the soft tones of the English Shires.

'I believe you have a Land Rover Discovery 3 series you wish to unload.'

Kinikanwo greeted this sudden change with surprise and caution limiting himself in his reply.

'Yes.'

The car Dealer extended an immaculately coiffured right hand for Kinikanwo to shake. Kinikanwo accepted the offered appendage and carefully shook the proffered appendage. Taking in the Algerian it was obvious he wasn't someone who figuratively was likely to dirty his hands

'I am Ali from Algiers Prestige Motors and will undoubtedly make you a generous offer for your esteemed vehicle. He waved his hand indicating the Concierge.

'This creature will no doubt want to charge you a percentage of the sale for finding me, ignore him and give him a hundred Euros although I have no doubt you would have found and come to my premises tomorrow morning.'

He paused to catch his breath while the Concierge looked crestfallen as Kinikanwo pulled a hundred Euro note from his wallet and handed it over.

The Dealer looked back at the Concierge.

'Coffee I think.'

The concierge nodded his head as Kinikanwo followed the waddling Dealer over to a pair of blue lounge chairs where the latter collapsed into one and indicated with his right hand that Kinikanwo should take the other.

While they waited for coffee Ali started pulling wads of notes from the different pockets in his suit jacket. He had Algerian Dinars, Euro's, US Dollars and even Nigerian Naira.

Kinikanwo's eyes lit up when he spied his home currency, it wasn't meant to be exported but he would take it because he was going home.

'I see you have Naira which can't be much use to you as it isn't tradeable outside my country.

'If you were to be reasonable about the deal, I could perhaps relieve you of most of the Naira.'

The Dealer nodded.

'As you say but let us agree on a currency in which we can deal and then argue over conversion rates afterwards.'

'I'll give you three thousand Euro's in whichever currency you want to trade.'

Kinikanwo laughed, at least he now knew the low point and it wasn't as bad as he expected.

'Not very generous and I'm not giving you some old banger, this is a classic in excellent condition with little mileage.'

'Seven thousand five hundred and my air ticket home.'

'It's not a Rolls Royce you know, I have my profit to consider.'

'Three thousand eight hundred and your ticket home.'

They paused while a waiter rushed over with their coffee, when he had finished serving their espresso's Kinikanwo taking his time thoughtfully sipped at his brew before coming back with his next offer. He really felt he needed the equivalent of five thousand Euro's to satisfy the Chief and was thinking how to achieve his target.

'First let's agree that the air ticket will be included whatever we decide.'

The Dealer nodded in agreement and waited for Kinikanwo to make his next offer.

'Six thousand five hundred.'

The Dealer wrung his hands together glanced down at his coffee and complained.

'You're trying to beggar me and my business, I have five daughters to marry off.'

'Alright my last and final offer four thousand five hundred Euros but only if you take most of it in this worthless Naira.'

Kinikanwo was enjoying himself and sat back relaxed wondering how willing the Dealer's daughters might be. Still if they were as fat as him they might not be very tempting.

'Six thousand.'

'No, no, much as I respect you have a right to the best price, it is you who wants to sell, I don't have to buy, no matter how tempting the vehicle.'

'Ah but I don't have to sell, it is only because I don't want all the hassle of finding a shipping agent and arranging to send it home where it will be worth eight thousand Euros easily.'

The Dealer pulled the big red handkerchief out and wiped his brow to give himself more time to think.

'The Nigerian must be a good poker player he didn't appear to have any tells.'

'This wasn't going to be as easy as the Concierge, 'the son of a whore,' had led him to believe' he might have to pay a decent price after all.'

'Five thousand and that has to be it, I'm not a charity.'

Kinikanwo was pleased he had made his price and it looked like he would be able to squeeze it a touch higher.

'Five seven any less and I'll ship it, it won't be worth it otherwise.'

The Dealer knew he could be stuck, if he only knew what the bastard was really after, he was determined to buy the Discovery, he already knew who he could sell it onto.

'Especially for you and much against my better judgement seeing as you are beggaring me, five thousand five hundred Euros.'

Kinikanwo reached across the coffee table to shake the Dealer's hand.

'Done.'

It was only then as the Dealer counted out Euro's and Naira that they realised neither of them knew the exchange rates.

The Dealer waved across the Concierge.

'What's the Euro to Naira exchange rate this morning?

The Concierge pulled out his I Pad and after a few moments leaned over and showed both that mornings figures.

They did some calculations and agreed the split of Naira and Euro's which would be paid out when the car was handed over at midday the following day.

The concierge was in attendance and borrowed Kinikanwo's passport to book him on Royal Afrique du Nord to Lagos via Casablanca.

Kinikanwo rose from his chair and went to shake hands, he had to wait a moment for the Dealer to struggle out of his chair and once the hands were shaken Kinikanwo confirmed their arrangements.

'I'll meet you at Algiers Airport at midday with the Land Rover Discovery and you'll bring my money and airline tickets.'

'Correct!'

The Dealer smiled across at his erstwhile foe and smiled through his wobbly jowls.

'I'll be there, we can hand everything over in the car park.'

Kinikanwo recognising his vulnerability, had other thoughts.

'I don't think so it ought to be in the departure area close to the Royal Afrique du Nord check-in.

The Dealer admired Kinikanwo for his caution but regretted the lack of opportunity to mug the Nigerian and relinquish him of the Discovery without payment.

'That's good then until tomorrow midday.'

By the time the negotiations were concluded and Kinikanwo was making his way to his Algiers hotel room, the passengers on the Vronskiy, just south of Almeria were being woken in readiness for its arrival. The two Chiefs were de-training at the Gare du Nord.

Chapter 40

To Paris - Friday 13th November 2015

At eleven thirty in the morning the Touareg now on the N-320 was passing to the East of Bordeaux and transferring to the A-10 for the run into Paris. Even though they had been swapping places every couple of hours, the two ex-pats were both shattered from the continuing journey. This had only been broken up by the ferry ride and for the last three days they appeared to have been battling the clock.

The two Nigerians, in the silver Astra, were in close attendance, three cars to the rear. The driver Duncan and his partner were similarly exhausted but for them relief was at hand. Obo was conversing on his mobile with the Chief who was with Chief Kudo in their hire car converging on Bordeaux from the north.

'Yes sir, we've just joined the A10 to the north of the city.'

'We aren't far off you, we're just crossing a river called the Dore.'

'Hang on a minute Obo.'

The Chief who had a road atlas open in his lap screamed.

'Take that next junction.'

Chief Kudo indicated to pull right from the middle lane of three into the inside lane. He had some difficulty, three large trucks, nose to tail were blocking his exit. He slowed to let them pass and incurred the wrath of the following black Citroen C4. The irate driver flashed his car lights and honked its horn until Chief Kudo was able to pull in behind the third of the trucks. He was only just in time as they were pulling alongside the final exit sign.

The Chief who hadn't appreciated the difficulty in moving over, impatiently banged the dash with his right hand and pointed with his left, which still had hold of the mobile to the white sign overhanging the nearside lane.

'That's it the N-41, Ambes.'

'Got it.'

The hire car swept off the N10 and made its way down onto a convoluted set of twists and turns. This led them to a roundabout and onto the slip road marked with a blue sign for Paris.

They made their way onto the entry slip, which for a hundred or so metres was alongside but at one hundred and eighty degrees to the northbound carriageway.

The Chief resumed his conversation with the Astra.

'We'll be northbound shortly.'

'Where are you?'

'Coming up on a bridge.'

'I see it, I see it.

Yelled Chief Kudo as the Touareg flashed by in the opposite direction in the outside of the three lanes of the northbound A10.

'We've seen the Touareg and will be up with you shortly.'

'We'll take over then.'

Chief Kudo pushed the rental car hard and both could feel the camber as they swept through the one-hundred-and-eighty-degree hairpin turn, up the slip road and onto the northbound A10.

Within moments he had the vehicle into the outer lane as they re-crossed the bridge over the rain-swollen River Dore.

The Chief got back on the phone to Obo.

'When are they likely to refuel?'

'Probably when they next change drivers at one o'clock.'

'How come?'

'They change drivers every two hours and so do we.'

'Can we leave it to you now, we're shattered?'

The Chief thought about it for a moment but decided against allowing that to happen yet.

'No wait for the next changeover.'

'Yes sir, alright.'

Chapter 41

Friday afternoon Algiers Airport

Kinikanwo had breakfasted leisurely at his hotel, before at half eleven checking out and driving the Discovery the thirty minutes out to Houari Boumediene, the Algiers International Airport.

He parked the Discovery in the short stay for Terminal 1 and made his way into Departures which was a maelstrom of noise and colour. The departure board showed the reason, with thirty flights due out before his. Their destinations varied, all over North Africa, the Middle East and Europe including many local airports in Algeria.

The dress was mixed, with smart business suits, Parisian Haute Couture, Sheiks in their Arab robes, and harassed parents trying not to lose their adventurous offspring.

For a moment he was overwhelmed but soon paid attention when tapped on his right shoulder by the Dealer, who despite his size, had managed to sidle up alongside Kinikanwo unnoticed.

'The car here?'

'Yeah in the short stay.'

'Shall we go then?'

Kinikanwo was hesitant, he didn't trust the Dealer and was reluctant to leave the safety of the crowds in the Departure Lounge.

'I think I'll stay here, you can have a look, it's in the short stay and you can't miss it.'

The Dealer grumbled, he didn't blame the Nigerian but although the idea of a mugging had crossed his mind. The security and closed-circuit cameras were a bit too plentiful to risk anything like that at the airport nowadays.

The Dealer raised his eyebrows and nodded his head towards the car parking exit. One of his acolytes, in jeans and grey T shirt, positioned ready for such an eventuality sidled out to check the state of the Discovery.

Kinikanwo wanting to keep control of the situation, turned a full circle and tried to identify any other watchers, he soon realised it was hopeless but decided to take some sort of control.

'You have the money?'

'In my bag.'

The Dealer opened his black shoulder bag and showed Kinikanwo the money within. It looked right, but they weren't in a position to count the money out in such a public place, Kinikanwo had a solution already in place.

'Follow me.'

He led the Dealer across the airport concourse to the disabled toilet which was vacant.

'Inside.'

The Dealer hesitated a moment and looked back at the entrance to the Departures Area, there was no sign of his man. 'No thanks, we'll wait until I know the car is in place and you aren't about to rob me.'

'Alright that's fair enough.'

The crowds of people milled around them as they waited for the Dealer to receive the signal from his minder.

Moments later he appeared in the doorway at the other side of the hall and looked around trying to spot the Dealer in the crowded concourse.

Realising the squat Dealer was difficult to spot in the crowds, Kinikanwo raised himself to his full height and waved his right hand. He was spotted almost immediately. The minder gave them a thumb's up and Kinikanwo looked at the Dealer.

'Alright now can we do the deal?'

The Dealer checked all around them before agreeing with a nod of his head and following Kinikanwo into the still vacant disabled facility.

As soon as they got inside Kinikanwo locked the door.

'Money!'

The Dealer handed over the shoulder bag, Kinikanwo rested it on the hand wash basin and rummaged through the wads of money inside doing a quick check. He didn't want to hang around but needed to make sure the Algerian wasn't trying to fleece him.

He looked up nodding, the Dealer was stood with his back against the white Formica cubicle door pointing a snub-nosed revolver at Kinikanwo's middle.

'Now just a minute.'

'No there is no time you will listen to me and we will have no problems.'

The Dealer pulled a Royal Afrique du Nord air ticket from his back pocket with his free left hand.

'You will put the keys and papers for the car into the bag and we will swap it for your ticket home.'

The Dealer smiled.

'I would rather you leave Algeria but if you want to make a complaint and not do as I say you'll never leave this room.'

He paused and licked his lips before grinning and whispering.

'Alive.'

Kinikanwo hesitated momentarily, his brain racing, he tried to think of a way out of this situation but all he could think of was the gun in the Dealers unwavering right hand. His brain recorded it was probably a brown handled Smith and Wesson Bodyguard whose .38 could do him a lot of damage.

The Dealer saw the hesitation, he didn't want to give his victim time to think and wanted to keep full control of the situation, he snapped out loudly.

'Do it!'

'Now!'

Cautiously Kinikanwo pulled the cars papers and spare keys out of his own holdall and put them into the shoulder bag. He pulled the other keys from his pocket and they followed the spare set into the bag.

'Now what?'

'Slowly and carefully hand me my bag, no sudden moves, we don't need to alert anyone, I would hate to have to use this on you.'

The Dealer briefly looked down at the bag and waved the revolver at his victim.

Kinikanwo had been waiting for this slight moment of inattention, he reacted instantaneously when the Dealer took that momentary glance at the bag.

The Dealer had no likelihood of winning at this point, his opponent had years of military training behind him, he was young and fast. The adrenaline pumping through his body enhanced the speed of his reactions. Kinikanwo threw the shoulder bag in the Dealer's face and dived for the grey tiled floor of the small room. He based his moves on the assumption that the Dealer had rarely fired the gun, any recoil if the revolver was fired, was likely to send the bullet upwards.

Kinikanwo was right the Dealer reacted by pulling the trigger of the revolver. The .38 bullet hit the top of the mirror above the hand wash basin, shattering it and sending shards of glass outwards from the wall.

Kinikanwo swept the dealers legs from under him and his opponent collapsed onto the tiled floor. The fat Dealer was gasping for breath and lay flat on his broad back. Kinikanwo who had only just avoided the fat man landing on and incapacitating him, leapt up and immediately jumped onto his assailant's fat belly with his knees driving all the air from the man's lungs. With Kinikanwo astride the belly of the Dealer it was easy to twist the Smith and Wesson out of his limp right hand. All this took a fraction of a second and before the Dealer could react Kinikanwo was angrily gouging out his left eye with the barrel of the gun.

'You, you, useless bastard of an Arab whore.'

The Dealer was squealing in pain, gasping for breath and using both hands to try and drag the gun-holding hand away from his face. Kinikanwo was fuming, much stronger and had the advantage of being atop the luckless Dealer.

He did however seem to relent for a moment, lifting himself off his opponent with the gun still pointing at the poor unfortunate below him.

Not much had gone right the last few days, this was the final straw, some crappy car shark, thought he could take Kinikanwo for a ride.

All his frustrations came to the fore, without any thought for the consequences of what he was doing, he shot the dealer through the left eye killing him instantly.

The second crack of the gun was quite loud, there seemed to be no external reaction so Kinikanwo set about clearing any evidence of his presence from the scene. He wiped down everything he might have touched, including the revolver which he dropped into the toilet. He transferred everything from the shoulder bag back into his holdall and looked around him to make sure he was clear.

Carefully he eased the bathroom door open and scanned the airport concourse, there were no interested people or police waiting for him. The Dealer's acolyte still hadn't moved from his position by the outer door and was looking uninterestedly in the direction of the disabled toilet. The noise of the gun firing must have been overshadowed by the clamour of the people in the crowded concourse.

Stooping so he couldn't be seen by the minder he opened the door to the minimum necessary and squeezed his way out of the bathroom. With the help of a car key Kinikanwo managed to jam the lock sign over to red, the toilet now appeared to be engaged.

After that he checked-in, made his way through Security to the Departure Lounge as quickly as possible, hoping to leave on his flight before the Dealer's body was discovered.

He was lucky, the Minder was cautious, after waiting twenty minutes he broke into the toilet. His reaction on seeing the dead Car Dealer was to flee the scene. He was able to re-lock the door and quickly depart before the police took an interest. The airport cleaner employed to clean the toilet never looked inside and used the apparently 'engaged' sign as an excuse to give that one a miss and grab a crafty smoke instead.

Royal Afrique du Nord Flight number AT561 to Casablanca rose into the clear sky above Algiers, with Kinikanwo safely aboard on his way home.

Chapter 42

Paris

At about the same time, sitting in the passenger seat of the Touareg, Oscar was on his mobile phone to their French contact in Paris. Pierre was in his office in the centre of the Seventh Arrondissement, on the Boulevard Saint Germain by the south bank of the Seine

'Pierre, Oscar here, looks like we're going to make it.'

'Where do we need to go when we get to the Stade de France?'

'Bravo Oscar, where are you now?'

'Well north of Bordeaux and no problems with traffic.'

'No way you are going to make it my friend.'

'Even if you get inside the Peripherique without any problems, you've to come right across the City.'

'I can still get rid of the match tickets.'

'Mac from the driver's seat shook his head vigorously.'

'No way I'm missing the match after all this, tell that Frog bastard we're coming whatever.'

Pierre hearing laughed over the phone.

'You tell that big Jock lump, I know my father does he know his?'

'But alright I've a space for you in priority VIP parking and if you don't make it the tickets will be at the main entrance in Mac's name.'

'Security won't be able to miss you in that machine, it will make for easy identification and I'll warn them to expect you.'

'Thanks Pierre, see you tonight.'

'Allez France.'

Oscar finished the call and asked Mac.

'How are we doing?'

'Going great, just coming up to where this road merges with the A-68.'

They had been able to push hard up the A-10 and as Mac thought they were at the point where the A-10 merged into the A-68 at Fresnes south of the city. They were less than twenty-five kilometres from the Stade De France, but time was getting on.

Their biggest problem was the rush hour traffic which was filtering its way out of the city. It had been alright up until then, the major part of the traffic had been flowing the other way, now as they joined the Peripherique and made their way round the east side of Paris, they were struggling to cope with the slow crawl of the City traffic.

The Chief and his companion were crawling along with their target only four cars ahead of them but importantly in the same lane.

By seven in the evening their proposed meeting time with Pierre at the Stade de France, the Touareg was still struggling in the north bound traffic on the Peripherique.

Oscar called their Parisian contact.

'Ah Pierre you were right about this bloody Peripherique, we're making slow progress.'

'That's alright, you'll get here, when you do.'

'Everything is in place, the Gendarmerie are looking forward to seeing the Touareg, your tickets are as I said ready and waiting.'

'I'm going up to the box now, you might not be here yet, it doesn't mean I have to miss out on the free Champagne.'

For the Chief following the brightly painted Touareg, it was easy to follow, and they were now sitting two cars to the rear.

He was wondering where they were going to end up and if there would be an opportunity to retrieve the diamonds quickly.

Neither he nor Chief Kudo had talked much since they had slotted in behind the Touareg north of Bordeaux.

The Football match had extended the Paris rush hour with thousands of French and German fans converging on the Stade De France. Now the traffic ahead of the Touareg and their pursuers was starting to ease as the football supporters filled the stadium and it got closer to kick off.

The Touareg was able to gather speed and the pair of them could see the floodlights of the stadium as they turned north off the Peripherique onto the Autoroute du Nord the N-1. As per their instructions they drove past the stadium before turning right and into the entrance for the VIP parking.

The security guard sitting in his box waved at them with his copy of L'Equipe and came out of his box with an envelope. Mac lowered his driver's door window and the guard said something to him in French.

Mac shook his head.

'Non parlez Francais.'

The Frenchman shrugged and pointed out to where the only space was left in the car park. He indicated by waving his arms and pointing exaggeratedly that they would have to drive around the north side of the stadium to a point halfway down the east side of the arena car park.

Oscar leaned across to the open window and thanked the guard.

'Merci Monsieur'

'Bon.'

The Guard lifted the single metal pole, so they could enter the car park, with the driver's window open they could both hear the roar of the football crowd as they drove between all the other parked cars, to their allotted space.

Oscar rubbed his stomach.

'Made it.'

'Don't know about the football but I should think there'll be some decent grub.'

'I'm ravenous.'

They left the car to make their way into the stadium, Oscar opened the envelope they had received off the security guard, and this held their tickets as promised. They had been expected.

Oscar led Mac to the VIP entrance where after passing through security a smartly dressed female concierge inspected their tickets before directing them up towards the Colonnades restaurant. They were warmly greeted by their host in the restaurant overlooking the pitch. The match had just got underway and the whole thing was quite civilised after the traumas of North Africa, even the noise of the crowd was lessened by the double-glazed windows.

If they had turned and looked behind them as they entered the stadium entrance, they would have seen a sallow faced young man of Middle Eastern origin, wearing a bulky coat, being refused entry by the security guards.

***

The Chiefs' were surprised and bewildered when they saw the Touareg take the off ramp from the Autoroute du Nord flyover and drive down below onto the N-1. They could see the well-lit car park and floodlights of the stadium as they followed the Touareg onto the lower road. There was no traffic and they were right behind their objective and had to ease off to allow the ex-pats to pull further ahead of them as they couldn't afford them to become suspicious.

It was fortunate they pulled back otherwise they would have been right on top of the Touareg when it slowed to a stop, before turning abruptly right, into the stadium car park.

The Chief wanted to stop at the side of the road, to watch the progress of the Touareg into the stadium car park but they had to move on, when a police car pulled up alongside and the Gendarme in the driver's seat waved at them to get going.

It took them nearly thirty minutes to find a parking space some way from the Stade de France, the crowds of football fans had taken up every available opening close to the stadium.

The Chiefs had come prepared for the cooler evening in Paris. The Chief himself in a black gabardine coat and Chief Kudo wearing a long green Barbour. They soon warmed up as they made their way briskly south towards the lights of the stadium. Shortly after leaving the rented car they heard the crump of an explosion but didn't recognise it for what it was. Chief Kudo had an idea.

'Fireworks do you think?'

The Chief looked at his watch.

'No it can't be, the match will have kicked off about fifteen minutes ago.

They continued their rush towards the stadium but the closer they came, the more obvious it was, there was some sort of emergency.

They heard many sirens and could see the reflection of flashing blue lights intermittingly lighting up the shadows of the five and six storey buildings, lining either side of the Rue Gabriel Peri, down which they were both walking.

When they came out of the enclosed streets, the road ahead was blocked by several police cars their blue lights flashing. The vehicles were surrounded by armed gendarmes facing outwards. Although some of them were glancing nervously back towards the football stadium.

The Chiefs realised the floodlights were still on and above the noisy sirens they could nevertheless hear the noise of the crowd.

Although the road was closed towards the stadium, the red pedestrian bridge across the Canal de St Denis was unblocked. The Chief apprehensively but keeping control of himself cautiously led his compatriot unhurriedly across the front of the nervous French Constabulary and made their way up the stairs and onto the pedestrian bridge.

They were just in time to hear a second explosion, more distinct because of their elevated position but its location was hidden by the bulk of the Stade de France, where it was obvious from the roar of the crowd that the football match was still taking place. Suddenly the sirens close to the stadium stopped, almost simultaneously, although there were still plenty of blue flashing lights illuminating the exterior of the Stade de France and the buildings lining the avenues alongside.

Even from their higher perch, it was at first difficult to spot the Touareg amongst the hundreds of vehicles surrounding the stadium. They were lucky because to their left almost hidden by the sides of the stadium two gendarmes could be seen taping off that area of the car park. Just inside the taped off area was the colourful Touareg, now easily identifiable once they knew where to look.

They might have been lucky to spot their objective but there was going to be no way of getting close to the scene.

Resignedly they made to return to the hire-car.

They were too late, having come to the attention of the French Police who were now very agitated by the situation and taking no risks.

They turned to descend from the pedestrian bridge and were confronted by a pair of National policemen, their Sig Pro 22 service pistols held in their fully extended right arms. Both the policemen shouted loudly and nervously.

'Allongez-vous sur le sol.'

'Neither of the Chiefs knew enough French to understand what was said but they had seen enough movies to realise what was needed and promptly dropped to the ground with their hands behind their backs.

They were quickly handcuffed, locked in a cage in the back of a police Renault Traffic van, which straightaway rushed off through the streets of Paris, blue lights flashing and siren blaring.

***

Just after Mac and Oscar had entered the stadium a suicide bomber who failed to gain entry to the Stade de France had attracted the attention of the private security team. One of the squad approached the renegade as he made his way through the car park. In panic the terrorist set off his bomb, this killed the approaching member of security as well as the suicide bomber. The detonation not only caused the implosion of the bomb vest which eviscerated the bomber himself, but the ball bearings contained within also exploded outwards at great force. Besides killing the approaching member of the private security team, the others travelled at great speed until their force was either expended in the night air or they met something solid. Depending on how close and how strong the object was decided which ball bearing either forced a passage through onto the next more solid body or expended its energy on the original.

One of these ball bearings finely clipped the wing mirror of a highly polished light blue, nearly new Citroen C5 of one of the executive guests. Its progress was hardly halted by the minor collision but the meeting of the two metals, the inert wing mirror and the solid ball bearing was enough to divert and reshape the dynamic object. Instead of being an almost round shape it was now misshapen with part of its round sphere now jagged and extremely sharp.

The misshapen ball bearing now on its diverted course collided with the rear, right, side of the blue Touareg. It still had enough dynamic force to cause damage and it struck the carbon fibre bodywork just below the VW decal. The now finely sharpened edge of the inanimate object was able to penetrate the normally solid structure. After passing through the side of the car with the last of its energy it penetrated the base of a spare green plastic can, still half-full of unused fuel, the ball bearing, energy expended, dropped to the bottom of the fuel can.

Immediately the volatile liquid started to weep out into the interior of the car, like all liquids it oozed its way to the lowest point, some of the fuel dripping onto the tarmac below the Touareg.

Shortly after the explosion, two French Gendarme's fixed security tape around the location of the first detonation and the body of the suicide bomber. They were now taping off a larger area of interest, including the part of the car park which included the Touareg.

It was unlikely they would have noticed but they failed to spot the small hole in the offside rear or the reek of leaking fuel from the partially-full, spare fuel can in the rear of the car.

Chapter 43

That Night

By ten that evening the Chief and his partner Chief Kudo were fed up, a little scared and concerned about their situation. They had been locked up in the rear of the French-National-Police, cellular, Renault Traffic since their arrest. There was obviously a crisis in progress, the police radio had been going non-stop throughout their imprisonment. At first after their arrest the van had rushed off round a couple of corners then stopped as if their driver didn't know what to do with them.

They had tried banging once but the rear doors had opened the driver had waved his Sig Sauer with his right hand, said something in unintelligible, rapid French and then put his left forefinger to his lips indicating silence.

Chief Kudo had started to say something until the policeman hissed at him, pointed the gun in their direction and vigorously tapped his left forefinger against his lips again.

The Chief fiercely looked at his partner and nodded in agreement, Chief Kudo realising the hopelessness of their position reluctantly nodded his head as well.

The Police driver grimaced slammed the rear doors and locked them again.

The Chief risking the wrath of the policeman whispered to Chief Kudo.

'What do you think?'

'What's happening?'

'Don't know but it's like he's nowhere to take us.'

Chief Kudo was closer to the truth than he realised, they had just left the area of the Stade De France where the two Nigerians had been arrested when the police radio went crazy with shootings on the rue Bichat. The driver had been told to stop and wait as St Denis, the nearest police station was on full alert and couldn't take them in.

The police driver was in a quandary his city appeared to be under siege and he had two prisoners. He couldn't and didn't want to interrupt the extremely busy radio net to ask where to go so he was stuck waiting impatiently for instructions. He hoped someone would remember him and his prisoners

***

Further south in North West Africa, the General in charge of the ten thousand UN peacekeepers in Mali was in an emergency meeting with his advisers. Mali a republic to the west of Niger was at constant threat from Al Quaeda and its acolytes. A previous insurrection had only recently been put down by French forces, France being the previous colonial power. Hence the need for the UN peacekeeping force.

The Danish Major General made the decision while the unfolding situation in Paris was turning into a major crisis. He was reminded of recent unexplained air attacks on civilian airliners and wished to avoid the risk in this time of heightened tensions.

His communications people were already telling him of increased rebel traffic, he was concerned they might be tempted to attempt an attack on a civilian aircraft in his area. After a brief consultation with his senior team, he decided to raise the alert status of his forces and close the air space over the country until the crisis in Paris was resolved and they could see what effect if any it would have in Mali.

***

In Paris the siege at the Bataclan night club was underway, all the other attacks of the night had taken place. The International football match between France and Germany had finished with a two-nil victory to the French. It was at that point that the French National Police took charge of the Stade de France and the spectators began to realise something was amiss. The pitch was used as a safe haven until the spectators could be released securely and with least risk.

It was only now, the two ex-pats, up in their executive box realised Paris was under siege and how close they were to the action. The lounge televisions had all now been re-tuned to the local news channels.

Mac looked at the unfolding crisis in horror.

'Now I'm beginning to wish we hadn't rushed.'

'Yeah but at least we got here safely, it looks like this is as safe a place as any now.'

Their shocked French host kept them informed of what the commentators were saying on the different French news channels. It was quite horrifying, there was some news footage of the carnage on the rue de la Fontaine-au-Roi and talk of at least three suicide bombings close to the stadium. They realised they had heard the three crumps of the explosions but had put it down to fireworks, both looked with concern at each other.

It was midnight before the French Police released them from their executive box. There had been a careful and methodical approach to the evacuation and as they had been seen to be in the least danger they were amongst the last to be allowed to leave. Only certain VIP's like the German Foreign Minister had been rushed away earlier.

It was only when they tried to exit the way they had arrived, they were told to leave from another exit, the two colleagues realised they might have a problem accessing the Touareg.

They got close enough to see it taped off by the crime tape, but a line of French police prevented them getting any closer. Pierre re-assured them.

'I can see the Touareg, not to worry you'll get it back.'

'My car is outside the tape and there is nothing you can do, I'll take you to your hotel and we can see what's happening tomorrow morning.'

Oscar looked at Mac.

'It must have been close to the time we arrived.'

'Yeah doesn't bear thinking about.'

Resigned to leaving the Touareg, Oscar sighed.

'Thanks Pierre let's make for the hotel.'

Thirty minutes later they were dropped off at their hotel out by the Charles De Gaulle airport.

Somewhat dishevelled, tired after more than twenty-four hours with little sleep, they were glad to approach the Reception Desk. The receptionist took little notice of them even though they were without luggage. He processed them rapidly, being more concerned with the chaotic scenes being played out on the television, overlooking the Reception lobby.

***

In Casablanca it was just after midnight Moroccan time, one in the morning in Paris. Flight AT555 a Boeing 737 of Royal Afrique du Nord was racing south west, down the asphalt left runway of the airfield at Mohammed V. Its pilots hadn't yet received the notification of the Mali airspace closure.

The denial of airspace over Mali, was due to start at midnight their time. A miscommunication of the cessation of flights to the Moroccan authorities meant a delay in communicating to their airports. The tower in Casablanca was only just receiving the news as the 737 wheeled away to the south east bound for Lagos.

Once airborne the Royal Afrique du Nord plane had been handed over to Moroccan Air Traffic Control who told the pilot of the closure. He helped the crew with their re-routing east to crossover into Niger's air space rather than the more direct route over its westerly neighbours closed air space.

The aircrew of the Royal Afrique du Nord 737 took it all in their stride, they had plenty of fuel and would only be about thirty minutes late into Lagos on the new routing. Taking on the guidance from the Moroccan Air Traffic Control they crossed over into Algerian air space slightly north of their normal course. Halfway down the starboard side of the aircraft Kinikanwo set himself to get a few hours of sleep in the economy section of the air liner. He had been lucky the plane was only partially full, and no one had been allocated either of the other two seats in his section. He took the opportunity to lie down curling his body across the three seats.

Two hours later still in Algerian air space the plane approached Niger's northern border. The air crew were preparing to contact Niger Air Traffic Control in the Capital, Niamey. They didn't foresee any problems overflying Niger instead of its more westerly neighbour even though their flight plan had to be changed after take-off.

Three hours into the flight Kinikanwo woke from his intermittent slumbers, he hadn't slept too well, a seat belt buckle had annoyingly caused him some discomfort sticking into the left side of his chest. He sat up, re-positioned himself into the window seat refastened his seat belt and out of curiosity slid up his window blind.

What greeted him was the horrifying site of flames rushing out of the starboard side engine of the Boeing 737. Fascinated for a moment at the unexpected sight he stared at the flames hustling back towards him. The speed of the plane, causing an inferno like trail onto the fuselage alongside him.

Up front in the cockpit, the highly-trained, experienced pilot and his young co-pilot were handling the sudden emergency as best they could. The pilot had taken over manual control of the aircraft and was descending as rapidly as possible.

'Where's the nearest emergency strip.'

The co-pilot replied instantly having briefed himself when the route had changed.

'Agadez.'

'Okay read me the check list.'

The Co Pilot started to read out the emergency instructions, he had little need, the pilot was reacting almost before he could get the words out. Years of annual rating checks and simulator training made the Pilot's reactions to the crisis almost automatic.

Within moments he had cut off the fuel to the burning starboard engine and extinguished the fire with the inbuilt fire extinguisher. This quick action meant the fire was extinguished rapidly and the pilot set course for Agadez about two hundred and fifty kilometres to the south east.

The Co-Pilot got on the radio.

'Mayday, Mayday.'

'Niamey Control, Niamey Control this is Royal Afrique du Nord, Delta Zulu.'

There was a rapid response to the emergency call.

'This is Niamey control go ahead Delta Zulu.'

'We have an engine flame out on the starboard engine and are descending, request permission for emergency landing Agadez.'

'You have permission, wait one while I alert Agadez.'

While all this was going on Kinikanwo had watched mesmerised as the fire was extinguished almost as rapidly as it started. He looked around him, no one else appeared aware of what was happening. He knew they were descending because his ears were popping.

They were descending fast while crossing over the Air Mountains. The pilot had everything under control now, he had re-trimmed the plane to allow for the loss of the fuel weight on the starboard side and had the plane gently descending towards Agadez.

Back in Niamey, Air Traffic Control swung into action and airport authorities in Agadez were dragged out of bed and emergency procedures implemented, both sections of the Niger police were notified.

Even though this only took minutes the pilot and his co-pilot were getting concerned about the lack of communication. The senior man was just about to call Niamey again when they came back to the 737.

'Delta Zulu this is Niamey control.'

'Go ahead Niamey control.'

'Delta Zulu switch frequencies to 118.1 for Agadez tower.'

'Good luck Delta Zulu.'

'Thanks.'

The co-pilot responded and switched frequencies.

'Agadez Tower, Agadez Tower this is Delta Zulu.'

Minutes before the Agadez tower controller, a forty-year-old half French, half Nigerien, dressed in brown-striped white pyjamas, had been asleep in his bungalow alongside the airport when he had been woken by Niamey and told to get moving pronto.

The controller yawned, still pulling on a shirt, reached over to his mic as he rushed into the control tower and replied.

Delta Zulu this is Agadez Tower come in.

Agadez Tower this is Delta Zulu declaring an emergency.

For the controller emergency standbys weren't rare but real ones were unusual, realising there was an immediate emergency he lit up his radars and switched on the runway lights.

The lights of Mano Dayak airport in Agadez greeted the stricken Royal Afrique du Nord Boeing 737's crew. The local fire brigade had been summoned and representatives of the National Police and National Guard were in position.

'Okay Delta Zulu we are ready and waiting, you should be able to see the runway ahead of you.'

'Thanks, Agadez tower, now we just need to land this thing.'

The controller lifted his binoculars and looked to the west where he could see the ever-expanding lights of the aeroplane as it approached the airport.

The co-pilot spotted the runway immediately it was lit, right ahead of them and just to the south east of the town which was the only other area of light visible.

The Air Traffic Controller left the pilot's alone and only checked to see they were following the guide path onto the only runway. In the cockpit of the aircraft the pilot followed the well-practised emergency landing procedures as his colleague read them out. With warning alarms ringing in the cockpit around them the pilot thumped the plane onto the runway.

All the while he was compensating for the port engine bias, which was trying to drag the aircraft in that direction. Completing the landing he braked the aircraft to a shuddering stop and told his crew to put the emergency procedures into operation. The port side slides thumped down onto the tarmac and the aircraft crew urged the passengers onto them, within minutes the aircraft was clear, and the pilots had shut off everything possible, before jumping onto the forward chute themselves.

The relieved passengers and crew were urged away from the aircraft by a mixture of local police and the local fire brigade who were already unfurling hoses in case of the engine fire regaining ground. Once everyone was clear they were led across the tarmac to the small airport terminal.

When Kinikanwo had seen the burning starboard engine, he had grabbed his holdall with its few possessions from under his seat and clambered his way across to the other side of the fuselage and found himself a spare seat there.

When the emergency procedures had been shouted through the aircraft's tannoy by a near panicking stewardess in French and English. He had copied the passengers around him and adopted the brace position and prayed to every god he could think of.

Like the other passengers he had little idea where they had landed and was quick to make the amidships emergency door and launch himself down the emergency chute. He was mightily relieved to jump off the chute and feel terra firma under his feet. While some of the passengers were crying and hugging each other with relief at their safe landing. Kinikanwo couldn't stop giggling, he was so happy it was all over and he was safe.

It was only when he was a part of the crocodile of rescued passengers making their way to the small row of buildings that he saw the unlit terminal sign. It read out Agadez and he realised he might have jumped out of the frying pan and literally into the fire.

Thinking quickly, he tried to burrow himself into the middle of the largest group of the passengers walking towards the terminal. He hurriedly fumbled his passport out of his holdall and stuffed it down the front of his trousers. Desperately he tried to remember if he had any other identifying documents on him, realising it was unlikely the authorities would have a passenger list, he resolved to claim his passport had been left on board in the emergency evacuation and resolved to use a friend's name from Okrika when asked by the Niger authorities.

Kinikanwo knew he was in major trouble, he could only hope to buff his way out of the situation. He stiffened up his body and tried to put on an air of confidence as he joined the queue of passengers giving their names to a member of the local police force, who was sitting at a desk writing down each identity. Each passenger either showed identifying documents or spoke their name to the Gendarme.

Kinikanwo was more confident now, after all they were only taking names not necessarily checking paperwork. He reached the desk at the front of the queue and gave his pseudonym when the uniformed policeman asked his name in French. Relieved that it had been so easy Kinikanwo relaxed and strolled casually around the terminal and approached a window to look back at the stricken aircraft. He was confident they would only be stuck here a few hours until Royal Afrique du Nord flew in a replacement aircraft. It might be boring and uncomfortable but with his previous experience of this god forsaken place he suspected they wouldn't be allowed to leave the airport terminal.

Placing his hands on the full-length glass window he watched interestedly the figures walking around the darkened plane. It was lit up only by the fire engines and an airport truck. He wondered how the broken plane would be fixed, stuck as it was in Agadez. He could see few facilities around the darkened facility it was going to be awkward for someone he thought.

Suddenly his reverie and feeling of unconcern was rudely interrupted when a strong hand gripped his right shoulder and forced him to turn around.

The first thing he saw was a pistol then he looked up into the grinning face of the National Guardsman he had riled on his previous visit a few days before.

'You are now my responsibility and will be answering questions about the death of your colleague.'

At that his face full of despair, Kinikanwo was handcuffed by two accompanying Officers and marched away and thrown in an overcrowded rat-infested cell with no furniture, a concrete floor and a filthy stinking hole in the corner for a toilet.

Chapter 44

Conflagration

By five in the morning, the Police National were back in control of Paris and the Bataclan siege was over. The City of Paris, France and the rest of the world were in shock at the terrorist killings of so many innocent civilians.

The areas around the Stade de France were being patrolled by armed members of the National Police dressed in their blue riot gear. Their faces were covered with bandanas and they were holding their Heckler and Koch MP5's across their chests. They patrolled in pairs, walking round the outside of the security taped areas so as to not contaminate the explosion sites of the suicide bombers.

The Touareg became a point of interest as each patrol walked past on their patrols, soon other members of the police waiting for orders, began to congregate in that corner of the crime scene, outside the tape speculating as to why a Paris Dakar Rally Car of such vintage was parked outside the Stade de France.

For those awaiting orders during the long night hours the Touareg was a welcome distraction from the events of the night, all of them were tired and some were speculating about whether they could be more useful elsewhere chasing the perpetrators of the massacres in their city.

A couple of them lit up cigarettes and continued to wonder about the car and the attack on their countrymen. There was a lot of anger combined with confusion about why Paris and France had been picked on again.

None of those present were aware of the leaking diesel fuel from the Touareg, the paving around them was shadowed by the other parked cars around the Rally Car. The smell of the fuel which should have indicated a problem was quickly dispersed by a strong south-westerly gale.

A burst of French came over the individual radios, one of the policemen smoking a cigarette answered the call for his presence at some other point round the stadium. He discarded his still lit cigarette onto the paving around him and with his left boot attempted to stamp it out.

The cigarette butt was blown under the security tape and he gave up trying to extinguish it. Calling to the rest of his waiting troop, they trotted off towards the south end of the stadium.

Unfortunately, the cigarette, partially flattened by the policeman's boot, was still alight. A fresh gust of wind fanned the stub and moved it end over end towards the pool of diesel now surrounding the paving at the rear of the Touareg.

A freshly fanned cigarette burns at a temperature of over eight hundred degrees centigrade, while the auto ignition temperature of the diesel spilling from the Touareg is only two hundred and ten degrees centigrade, if the lit cigarette and the diesel met there was likely to be a conflagration.

For a moment or two an eddy of wind picked up the partially burnt cigarette and blew it into the lee of the rear tire of the silver, German registered Porsche Carrera next to the Touareg. The cigarette gradually burned down, occasionally tugged at by wind eddies and with the bulk of the other car between it and the pooled diesel.

The continued burning of the cigarette stub was the undoing of the developing situation. It became light enough, for one of these light eddies to lift it out of the lee of the Michelin R8 tyre and deposit it into a particularly strong gust of wind. The cigarette, thanks to the fanning breeze was now burning at over eight hundred degrees when it was blown briskly into the diesel fuel spillage, there was no chance of it being drowned by the fuel even though it was cooled by the low ground temperatures. The glowing end of the cigarette ignited the vapours in the air above the diesel.

Within moments, the fuel itself ignited, suddenly there was a flash as a streak of flame burst into the Touareg itself. The car was soon ablaze and threatening the other vehicles around it.

The authorities reacted quickly, so many people were alert and in the area. The burst of flame was quickly spotted by an armed police patrol who rushed towards the conflagration MP5's at the ready. Within minutes and due to the Touareg being at the end of a row it was being attended to by the local Paris Fire Brigade.

The Bombiers a military force were not put off by being surrounded by armed police.

It was too late for the Touareg to be saved, the exothermic chemical reaction of the burning fuel with the carbon fibre caused the chemical bonds to break. The creation of carbon dioxide, which with oxygen from the surrounding air caused the carbon fibre bodywork to burn fiercely. Within minutes the fuel tank had ignited and there was a flash and loud explosion as it blew up scattering particles and belongings into the car park and over the surrounding cars.

Fortunately, none of the emergency services were injured, the conflagration occurring so rapidly.

The empty water tank melted almost instantly encasing the diamonds in a plastic chrysalis.

Forensic examination of the area at a later date quickly gave the authorities the answer to why the Touareg had been destroyed.

Chapter 45

Chief Kudo's ire and Diamonds

About midnight someone decided they needed the cellular van and remembered the patient Gendarme with his two prisoners. After all that had gone on he was directed to his first intended stop St Denis where he was able to relieve himself of his two Nigerians.

By 0900 on Saturday 14th the Chief and Chief Kudo were still in custody, awaiting questioning as to why they were for an unexplained reason in the vicinity of the first explosions. It would take two days, a high-powered French Lawyer and the assistance of the Nigerian Ambassador before they were released and deported as undesirable aliens. They were never to find out what happened to the diamonds because the French authorities not believing their stories withdrew their visas.

On Monday the 16th they were escorted to Charles de Gaulle and seated in economy on Air France flight 104 to Lagos. The Airbus A330-200 took off on time and they landed back in Lagos on time just before seven thirty in the evening.

By this time Chief Kudo wasn't speaking to his partner, he was very angry, having lost a lot of money, been locked up in French police cells and now having his access to the major cities of Europe withdrawn by the loss of his visa.

Although they were sitting next to each other in the aircraft, the Chief's attempts to communicate with his compatriot were completely rebuffed.

Being stuck for seven hours in the close confines of an aircraft next to the cause of all his problems didn't help Chief Kudo's mood either and on landing at Lagos he was quick to make a call on his mobile.

Being the conduit for many criminal enterprises in Port Harcourt Chief Kudo had several illegal contacts in Lagos and it was to one of these he made the phone call to a violent gang boss in Lagos's port Apapa. Not bothering with the preliminaries, he launched straight into his request.

'Nelson, Chief Kudo I need something done immediately.'

'Alright Chief depends, if I can, I will.'

'I want someone picking up and taken somewhere safe where he can die a slow, painful death.'

Nelson wasn't fazed, in fact he was quite pleased that for a change Chief Kudo would owe him.

'Where are you?'

'I'm at the airport but my quarry will be booking into a hotel shortly.'

'Just find out which one and meet us outside departures.'

'That's easy it will be the Marriott out by the airport I can see him getting the courtesy bus.'

'That's good we'll be with you shortly.'

Forty-five minutes later a black mini bus stopped outside Departures and Nelson in the front passenger seat waved to Chief Kudo to get into the side door which slid open.

Besides the two of them, there were two large Nigerians casually dressed in black T shirts and trousers both the driver and the one in the rear with Chief Kudo looked menacing and neither spoke.

Nelson turned in his seat looked back and spoke to Chief Kudo.

'Who are we looking for?'

Chief Kudo explained his problem and his need to avenge the disasters that had occurred over the last few weeks.

There was no talk of payment, that was understood, Chief Kudo would owe Nelson until the latter wanted some form of restitution either financially or a personal favour. In the end, it was all very easy when they reached the Marriott airport hotel.

The Chief had only just completed checking in, Chief Kudo was able to point out his quarry and Nelson's two aides acted immediately.

The Chief was deep in his own unhappy thoughts, as he waited for the lift. Although he had lost the diamonds the sale of the Touareg and Kudo's original payment meant he wasn't out of pocket. The loss of his visa was going to impinge on his lifestyle and he was a little concerned about Chief Kudo's reaction.

The lift doors opened, he waited for a couple to leave before entering himself, nodding to them as they passed. He went to enter the elevator when his elbows were painfully gripped by two black clothed men who suddenly appeared alongside him.

He gasped and went to shout for help when a voice whispered in his left ear.

'Don't say a word otherwise I'll cut your head off.'

Briefly a six inch bade was put to his throat.

'Nod if you agree.'

The Chief nodded, he was terrified, his heart raced and even though in an air-conditioned lobby he broke out into a hot sweat.

His two escorts still painfully gripping his elbows turned the Chief round and marched him out of the hotel and into the side door of the minibus. His escorts followed him in because by this time Nelson was in the driver's seat Chief Kudo alongside him, the latter not wanting to get his hands dirty in achieving the Chief's demise.

Once the Chief realised who was the cause of his kidnap he started to whine.

'You can't do this.'

Chief Kudo said to Nelson.

'Are we going to have to put up with this whinging?'

Nelson nodded and one of his men tapped the Chief behind his right ear with a truncheon concussing the man who rolled to the floor where the two men used his body as a footstall.

It was about an hour before the Chief came around, he was in a brightly lit, large white room. The first thing he noticed as he forced his eyelids open was the spattered blood on the walls. Looking down at the green tiled floor where the drains were streaked with blood and he could see attached to a black cast-iron tap a yellow hose with a spray jet nozzle. He quickly realised his wrists were bound together and the rope was looped over a hook which was hanging from a metal rail which ran the length of the room above him.

Holding the spray jet was one of Nelson's colleagues dressed in a full-length yellow polyurethane apron with matching wellington boots, seeing movement from the Chief he opened the nozzle and sprayed his face with lukewarm water.

The Chief gasped as some of the water flooded into his open mouth, he realised he could only just hold himself upright by standing on his toes and his position was extremely painful. Nelson spoke from behind him.

'It appears you have caused my friend Chief Kudo unnecessary harm and because of that you are about to die quite painfully and slowly.'

'We are in an enclosed part of the Apapa abattoir and being late at night there is no one except a bribed security guard to interfere with your death.'

'It will be slow and painful as requested.'

The Chief fainted but soon came around when as promised the man in the yellow suit taking his time with a well-honed machete began to hack the Chief into tiny pieces. At first the slices were thin but as he got into his work they became larger, The Chief screaming for a long time was discarded into the waste bins meant for the local pig farms.

Chapter 46

The Diamonds

For Mac and Oscar, the loss of the Touareg was disappointing, they had lost little except some Naira enjoyed a great experience becoming lifelong friends. The spares from the Touareg which had been shipped would provide some compensation.

After questioning and commiserations from the Parisian Gendarmes they were allowed to leave on the Monday morning. About the same time the remains of the Touareg were being loaded onto a low loader for transport to a forensic garage.

They said goodbye at the Gare du Nord where Mac was catching the express to Charles de Gaulle where he hoped to get a flight to Scotland. Oscar was catching the Eurostar to St Pancras from where he would switch to Euston and return to his parents in the North West of England for the remainder of his sabbatical.

It was two weeks later, Oscar who was preparing to return to Nigeria to continue his contract when he received a telephone call from the Foreign Office.

After confirming Oscar's identity, the Consular Official got down to business.

'Sir, the French police in Paris have asked us to contact you about the remains of your car which their forensic teams have finished with.'

'Yeah that's alright they can dump it, I don't suppose there's much worthwhile left. '

'Well apparently sir you would be wrong, a rucksack which can be identified as yours has apparently survived except for some external charring.'

The Consular Official continued.

'They have concluded that although the leak from your fuel can was caused by a ball bearing from the terrorist bomb the explosion of your vehicle was caused by a discarded cigarette butt.'

Oscar remembered the rucksack held a lot of his trip paperwork including the vehicle's insurance papers.

'Do you think the destruction of the vehicle could be classed as an accident then?'

'That's not for me to say sir but I think it is a possibility.'

'I'll have to go back to Paris, won't I?'

'Yes sir, when do you think you can go?'

'Tomorrow.'

'That's fine sir, you are to report to St Denis Police Station, I'll tell them to expect you.'

'If I can be of any further help please don't hesitate to call me at this number.'

The Official gave Oscar a number he could ring and ended the call.

Oscar went straight on the net and checked flights from Manchester Airport the following day. He found he could get an Easyjet flight out at seven and one back at seventeen fifteen.

It was expensive by the time he had booked the flights and a space for baggage in case there was more than the rucksack to bring back. While he was on the net he also booked car-parking using his mother's car which he hoped he could borrow the following day.

Oscar tried telephoning Mac but there was no answer, he left a message explaining the situation.

The following day at ten in the morning, Oscar as instructed, presented himself at St Denis Police Station. An Officer who spoke good English made a phone call and Oscar was asked to wait.

After about ten minutes a door into the interior opened and two Officers came into the waiting area dragging two large plastic bags.

This is all that could be recovered from your car sir, can you sign my paper to say you've received the two bags.

Oscar signed for the bags dumbfounded and was left in the Reception area not quite knowing what to do. He persuaded the

Reception Desk Officer to call him a taxi and dragged the bags outside to the waiting cab.

Only an hour after he had left Charles de Gaulle he was back there with the two plastic bags on a luggage trolley and eight hours to wait for his plane. Oscar wasn't going to waste this time, after enquiring he found a shop selling luggage in Terminal East. Appropriately the store was named Rolling Luggage and Oscar bought the biggest suitcase they had in the shop.

He found a café where he could sit outside and empty the plastic bags into the suitcase. There was wasn't much that was worth taking on the flight with him, most of the weight in the bags was due to the tools from their toolbox which Oscar discarded.

There was Oscar's slightly scorched rucksack as promised, eagerly he looked inside and sure enough the paperwork and clothing were untouched. Mac's rucksack was badly burnt inside and out and so was discarded. There was nothing much else except for a large piece of green melted plastic which had something in it because it rattled when he shook the item.

Sipping his coffee, he felt silly he had bought a large suitcase and only had his rucksack and this weird piece of melted green plastic to put in it. Knowing he still had a long wait for his flight he ordered up his lunch and started writing out a claim on his I Pad for the loss of the Touareg and impatiently waited for his flight.

After a long day, Oscar returned to his parents, dumped his new suitcase in his parent's garage and went straight to bed. The following day after emptying his rucksack he sauntered out to the garage to investigate the strange piece of green plastic, He was curious he still couldn't work out what it was and tried telephoning Mac again.

This time there was an answer. Oscar told Mac about the previous day's trip and what little he had recovered then he told Mac about his strange find.

'What was large green and plastic?'

'A Leprechaun?'

'No you Jock idiot in the car.'

'Hang on a minute let me think.'

Mac pictured in his mind what was in the car, the two spare fuel cans were blue he thought for a moment he didn't get it because except when they had turned over and it dripped out they hadn't used the water tank at all. It was Oscar complaining about the dripping when they turned over that reminded him.

He shouted down the phone to Oscar.

'The water tank, the bloody water tank we never had need of the sodding thing.'

'Well it has melted down to about a quarter of its size and it rattles, what was in it that could make a noise like that?'

'Nothing there wasn't anything only plastic and the plastic baffles.'

'I'll ring you back I'm going to hack it open and see what's inside.'

'Fair enough.'

Oscar rang off and tried to work out what of his father's tools he could use, the Stanley knife didn't work, he found the hacksaw to be the best implement to use.

It took over thirty minutes before he came across a sealed package, he ripped off the gaffer tape holding shut the metal tobacco box containing the hard objects inside.

At first, he couldn't work out what he had found and then it came to him especially them being followed through Africa. He rang Mac.

'Well what was it some pebbles?'

'No, you aren't going to believe it.'

'Well come on then out with it.'

'Diamonds.'

Acknowledgements

Thanks to Chris Herbert in beautiful Rosevears, Tasmania, who through his own traumatic times has read, and re-read my various drafts of this novel. His advice and encouragement have moved me on through times of brain block.

Thank you, Maureen, for just being there and quietly reminding me to carry on, you're a great final draft proof reader.

Thanks to Formby Writers for your fortnightly enthusiasm, especially my Irish friend.

Grateful acknowledgement to Gabrielle Rollinson for reading the first draft and for her terrific enthusiasm when teaching us aspiring authors.

I must apologise to Volkswagen and the Rivers State Tribes of south eastern Nigeria for any liberties I might have taken.

Author

Thank you for reading Sahara Diamonds this is my second novel. The first set in Australia 'Nullarbor Chase,' spans the breadth of Australia.

For 15 years I was a Deck Officer in the Merchant Navy and spent 27 years working for HM Prison Service.

I am retired, have been married to Maureen since Australia Day 1974 and we have a grown up son, Richard.

I live in Southport in NW England, am a cricket umpire, a member of Southport U3A and a season ticket holder at Turf Moor

36381116R00246

Printed in Great Britain
by Amazon